CULL

CULL

Tanvir Bush

Unbound

Unbound
6th Floor Mutual House, 70 Conduit Street, London W1S 2GF
www.unbound.com

© Tanvir Bush, 2019

Text design by Ellipsis, Glasgow

A CIP record for this book is available from the British Library

ISBN 978-1-78352-592-8 (paperback)
ISBN 978-1-78352-594-2 (ebook)

Printed in Great Britain by CPI Group (UK)

Special thanks to Susan Erb, Ruth Hartley, Polly Loxton and Green Park Dentist for their support of this book

For Maggie, Tim and Grace, my partners in crime

The Dog's Prologue

Chris has a few free minutes while his human, Alex, is talking on her phone. He is off his lead and therefore allowed to sniff *dog-proper* and he does. It is a much-needed relief from the work of guiding; all those straight lines and non-sniffable kerb stops. It's wonderfully stinky here too. They are close enough to the river to smell the mud and duck poo and just at the edge of the new Grassybanks building development with its harsher aromas of tar and fresh cement, diesel and spiced wooden planks. His nose is joyful in the shimmer of stink, but as he mooches *sniff sniff sniffing* to the nearby culvert, he hears a scuffling, squeaking noise coming from the grate.

Chris lowers his snout and scents rotting leaf mould, cigarette butts and the less subtle smells of shitty water and rat piss. The rats are freaking out about something . . . something floating in the sewer beneath the pavement. He can sense their excitement; their eager little bellies growling with anticipation. They are holding a sort of 'rat forum' or what Chris's human Alex would call 'a mischief of rats'. She prides herself on her knowledge of the weirder names of animal groups. Chris's favourite is a 'nuisance of cats'. He shakes his head to focus and lowers his nose again.

The rats are getting more obstreperous. They only ever get this excited over food or flooding. Chris hasn't smelt rain for several days so he is guessing it's the former.

He whimpers down to the rats but they are too agitated to respond. Rats and dogs can speak to each other, although not as humans do. Animals use sound and stink but mostly life fuzz, the electricity that holds all component atoms together. It is a kind of vibration, more than anything else.

'What is it?' Chris, insistent, asks the rats.

'Scrumptious plenty of! More food, more sex, more babies, more rats! Scrumptious plenty!'

Chris is happy for them but he is a dog and so there is also a part of him anxious to know what food exactly and if he can get his chops around it too. He sniffs and the rats tear through plastic, unleashing the distinct ammonia-putrid pong of rotting meat. Yet there is another underlying stink too, which Chris inhales into his wonderful nose. Immediately his hackles rise and his ears flatten.

'What the hell . . . ?' he whines. Under the thick waves of rot is a shuddering ribbon of chemicals. 'What am I smelling in that? Unripe red smell . . . splintering smell . . . not earth . . .'

He knows rats have even better stench scenters than dogs. Surely they can smell it.

'It smells like . . . like the vet's!' It has the spiral high notes of the stuff they put in him when he was made 'less'. Chris is horrified. He hates going anywhere near the vet's.

The rats sneer. 'It's still meat not that long dead,' they sing. 'It bleeds so tasty still. The medicine's not Warfarin, so rats it cannot kill!'

'What's—?'

Chris's human, Alex, has finished talking on her mobile phone and strides towards him on her long legs. Chris and Alex are very close although they can't communicate as easily as Chris does with other animals. Humans have mostly forgotten the art of vibration, but Alex does her best.

She uses air, vocal folds, her larynx and her pharynx and spurts sound waves. It's a slow process. 'What is it, Chris?' she asks. Then, 'Yuk, what's that smell?'

Chris tries to explain. Alex hears him whine and feels him back away from the culvert and into her knees. He is a handsome dog, a mash-up of golden retriever and black Labrador, sporting a glossy black coat with gold highlights around his muzzle and over his eyes, and a white star on his chest. The thick ruff around his neck gives him a slightly lion-like look but in truth he prefers Alex to deal with the scary stuff.

'Something nasty in the gutter, darling dog? OK, leave it.' She reaches out and rubs his head. Her fingers are strong and gentle. It comforts Chris although he can still smell the poisoned meat and hear the cries of delight from the rats.

Alex puts Chris's harness over his head and picks up the handle with its yellow sign reading, 'Please don't distract me – I'm a working guide dog.' 'Forward!' she commands and Chris sighs and steps up. He likes his work, and the pay, an exceptional kibble, is good. After a moment, his tail flares up high and he begins singing to himself as he trots along. The rotten meat floats away on its raft of rapacious rats but there is nothing to be done about that.

*

TRANSCRIPTION: LOWDOWN RADIO
THE DAY PROGRAMME

The government has today responded to the *Malick Report into the Care and Supervision of Elderly Deaf/Disabled and Vulnerable People*. The report – which highlighted key issues arising directly from the current cuts to the independent living allowances, social care provision, home care, nursing and home adaptations – recommended immediate action at every level, citing appalling care standards and shameful negligence. Baroness Malick said earlier today that she was saddened and shocked by the report's findings, especially in the light of recent claims by the government that the cost-cutting measures would not impact on the most vulnerable.

BARONESS MALICK: 'It is apparent to me that there is a cataclysmic failure on the part of the government to respond to the needs of the most vulnerable in our communities. Austerity cannot be a byword for abuse.'

In the light of this damning report, the government intends to implement the Care and Protect Act drawn up by the Tory minister John Thorpe-Sinclair. The Act is intended to ease the burden on home carers and social workers. The Care and Protect Act will ensure that all vulnerable groups, including elderly or severely disabled, will be offered places in high-care facilities with excellent twenty-four-hour nursing and medical support.

The government intends to reach out in the first instance to those people trapped in their homes by impairment or illness.

THORPE-SINCLAIR: 'The key aim of our response is to do the right thing by the elderly and vulnerable in our communities while also to ease the burden on the hard-working British taxpayer who has, up to this point, had to cover the costs of home adaptations and social care to all and sundry.'

The first relocations of volunteers to the new residential homes will begin in the next month. Already thousands have been signed up in the hope that this will ensure better care of elderly or severely disabled relatives. This will, at the same time, cut costs previously being spent on inadequate home care, too-short nursing visits and home adaptations. This will also allow those previously locked into caring for their relatives to return to the work environment, putting once economically unviable families back on their feet.

CLEARANCE

The Extraction of Mrs Tunny

Inside it is still an ambulance, but with the new paint job it looks more like a shortened grey bus, with 'TOSA Community Transport Ltd' emblazoned in bright orange along its sides. It is currently parked up at the Willowside Estate; badly parked, its back wheels sticking out over the white lines as if abandoned in a fit of pique. The May afternoon is grey and murky, and Andre, the new trainee driver, can smell the sweet dung of overfull bins at the bottom of the stairwell. He is trailing up the stairs after his paramedic colleague Mosh, feeling sour inside, pissed off, muttering to himself. *It was just a bit of banter. Fuck knows why Mosh has got the hump.*

'Yo bruv,' he calls up at his colleague. 'If it was something I said, you gotta get over it, man. I was joshing. I just don't see what the big-ass deal is, right?'

He stops talking when he realises Mosh has stopped moving. Standing above him on the stairs, his bearlike girth blocking the light, Mosh turns slowly until he is towering over Andre, looking down from the landing above.

'Andre,' says Mosh a little too quietly. 'When you look at me what do you see?'

'Err . . . I see, you know . . . I see . . . a big man.'

'A big *black* man.'

'Well, obviously, yeah bruv, a big black man so . . . ?'

'And you?'

'Me?'

'What are you?'

'Umm . . .'

'You, Andre, are a small, spotty white boy from East Cambright.'

'Hey . . .'

'And so, Andre, as regards our last conversation, and in a nutshell, I am your supervisor. In no situation, even when having a bit of a laugh, am I your "nigger". I am not anyone's "nigger", and if you ever use that word around me, or any black person again, in my hearing, I will have you up on a disciplinary charge. You get me, "bruv"?'

'Yeah, OK, OK . . . calm it down. No need to get vex.' Andre tries to make a 'tchaa' sound like his favourite comedian, *who is black, incidentally*, thinks Andre sulkily, but Mosh has already turned around and is climbing slowly to the second balcony. *He's fuckin' up himself*, Andre whines inside his own head. *Thinks he's posh and that, just 'cos he went to unifuckingversity. Well, I am University of Life, man. And I call you nigger if I want to.* But of course he won't.

'You sure she's a wheeler?' Andre asks Mosh at the top of the stairs. 'I don't want to have to go back down for the stretcher.'

Mosh consults his clipboard again.

'Mrs Dorcas Grace Tunny: severe dementia, paranoia, partial hearing loss, macular degeneration, osteoporosis, but she's not bed-bound. Her husband says she has her own wheelchair.'

'It's just, after this morning, bruv . . .'

4

Mosh looks at Andre, eyebrow raised, and Andre blinks.

'I just mean . . . well . . . I still don't understand why we were supposed to extract that kid . . . he looked perfectly sound to me . . . OK, maybe a bit spazzy, but he wasn't buggin' or nothing . . .'

Mosh wishes Andre would stop quizzing him on things he should have already picked up in the training.

'I have told you several times, Andre. When the client isn't able to communicate coherently, or know exactly what is in their best interests, then we are reliant on the request coming from the relative, the person paying the bills.'

'But the kid was all like, "Waaa, I don't want to go!" It was nasty.'

'The kid was epileptic and refusing treatment, Andre. His dad was scared he would fit and hurt himself but the dad couldn't get time off work to look after him. He didn't qualify for the Chronic Carer Component so no nurse, and with no other family to help, the dad needed a break.' Mosh chews his lip, remembering the relief on the man's face when they had finally got his son into the back of the ambulance. He can't imagine growing so tired of his own kid. He is a new dad and at any given moment can smell the creamy goat-milk smell of his baby daughter, Serena.

'What you smiling at?' Andre is querulous. His face wrinkles in places it shouldn't on a twenty-year-old. In that moment Mosh can see the fifty-year-old Andre and it's not a particularly pretty sight.

'It's a beautiful world, Andre. That is why I am smiling.'

Andre looks down at the stained concrete underfoot. There is a puddle of something nasty and a cigarette butt to step over. He opens his mouth and shuts it again. He can't afford to put

Mosh's back up too much. He's a W4B, a Work-For-Benefits recruit. He cannot lose this placement. He follows Mosh along the balcony, swallowing down his irritation.

'Here we are,' says Mosh, and rings a bell.

The men stand side by side, heads slightly lowered, doing the foot-to-foot shuffle of people waiting for a response to a doorbell. The door is a scuffed light blue with the number 46a hanging precariously from a couple of nails next to the letter box. Someone has sprayed 'Crazy Crip Bitch' in red across the lower half of the door. It has been partially washed off, taking some of the blue paint off, too, but it is still readable.

'Aw, come on,' breathes Mosh and plonks his finger on the button again.

Briiiiing!

The sound shakes the dirty concrete under their feet.

'If they didn't hear that they must be dead already,' says Andre.

Mosh rolls his wide shoulders, head still down, listening.

'I hear something.'

They wait.

They listen.

A plane drones high in the greasy grey sky overhead. It is muggy, and Mosh can feel sweat bubbling up from his crevices and dripping down his back into the crack of his arse. *Jeez, I haven't time for this*, he thinks, homesick for his little family, and squats down, knees cracking, so that his mouth lines up with the letter box. He prises up the metal lid to peer inside and gets a light waft of stale piss laced with a ghastly apple room freshener, but his view is blocked by the stiff plastic fringe on the inside.

'Mr Tunny!' he hollers. 'Are you in there?'

'Go away!' The voice is thin and warbling. 'I know what you are up to!'

A woman's voice, thinks Mosh and calls, 'Mrs Tunny?'

Andre's eyebrows go up. 'Is she on her own? Where's the fucking husband?'

Mosh ignores him.

'Mrs Tunny? Can you hear us? Your husband has asked us to come by to help you.'

'You shit fucks!' the woman screams. And then she is laughing. 'Shitfuckshitfuckshit!'

'Good morning.'

Mosh and Andre look around to find a tiny old man in a button-down shirt, waistcoat and linen trousers. His face is coffee-coloured and his scrawny beard is yellow with nicotine but his eyes are bright, green as seaweed behind his glasses.

'Mr Tunny?'

'That's me. Apologies for not being here. You are earlier than I thought you would be. You said end of the afternoon, and so I just nipped out to the shop.' He squeezes between them, key in hand. 'You might want to let me go in alone first. She is probably a bit unsettled now.'

Mosh and Andre look at each other, unsure, and Mr Tunny's eyes sparkle as he watches them. 'Just five minutes, lads. Remember it was me that called you, after all.'

'Yeah, after twenty-five complaints from your neighbour, old man,' mutters Andre under his breath.

Mosh ignores Andre and nods, stepping back to let Mr Tunny open up. The little man opens the door just a crack, steps in and quickly closes the door behind him.

The demented laughter and *shitfuckshits* peter out and instead there comes a low moaning sound. They can hear Mr Tunny soothing his wife, and although they cannot make out what he is saying, it seems to do the trick. Gradually the moans and wails fade further into the flat and then die away altogether.

Mosh and Andre sigh and wait. The radio crackles on Mosh's shoulder. 'Five five oh, report.'

'Awaiting extraction. Will advise when clear. Out.'

A door a little further along the balcony opens and a bedraggled young Asian woman with a pushchair emerges.

'Awright darling,' says Andre all bantam-rooster-breasted, but his smile flickers off as she keeps her head firmly turned away from the men, locks up and pushes her squalling infant towards the stairs.

'Lezzer,' says Andre to her back. 'God, this place is depressing.' He stretches. 'Should we go in, do you think? It's been five minutes.'

'Something's up,' says Mosh, and as he says it Andre senses it too.

Mosh shoulders the door but it remains shut. He bangs, huge fist heavy against the blue door.

'Mr Tunny! Open up!'

'Why do the old fucks have to make it so difficult?' Andre bellyaches. 'We're doing them a bloody favour.'

Mosh is about to speak into the radio when the door is wrenched wide open. The little bearded man with the twinkling eyes stands blinking up at them.

'She had a little accident. I was just changing her dress.' He is perfectly composed, unsurprised by the two men's wary glaring. 'She is ready now.'

Andre rolls his eyes at Mosh but says nothing.

'You aren't going to cause us any trouble now, are you, Mr Tunny?' Mosh asks.

'Oh, very funny!' The old man chortles, and Mosh relaxes. He is a good old boy. Of course he is. Mosh is too tired for this, that's all.

'Let's do it then,' says Andre, pushing past the old man.

'Wait, wait!' Mr Tunny tries to hold Andre back. 'You'll scare her!'

'No he won't.' Mosh's long arm reaches over the little man and firmly grabs Andre's lapel. He yanks Andre backwards, growling, 'Get your arse back here now.'

Choking, Andre staggers back a step. Relieved, the old man nods at Mosh. 'Best to let me go first. I did give her one of her sedatives but it may not have started working yet.'

Mosh lets the old man lead on into the flat. Andre pauses for a moment, his face twisted with rage. *That's fucking abuse, that is*, he thinks. Any other time in his life he would just walk off and fuck the job. But he can't. Lose this, lose everything. Next step down is the street. He takes a deep breath and steps in after the two men.

The hallway is very dark, and Mosh blinks as his eyes adjust, nostrils flaring from the stronger whiff of urine amplified by artificial apple. It's not that bad, really, and anyway, one gets used to these things pretty quickly. *We all finish up pissing our knickers in the end*, thinks Mosh.

'Aww rank!' he hears Andre whimper behind him, flapping his hands at his face.

Where did they get this kid? thinks Mosh. *He's a disaster.*

The room at the other end of the hallway is full of light. No curtains, of course. Why would there be? Even Mosh has taken the street-facing curtains down in his house. The Believe in Better campaigners patrol between 7 a.m. and 5 p.m., and it's too risky now they have the little one. When Mosh is on nights and needs to sleep during the day, he either uses an eye-mask or, if Jenny needs the bedroom, he heads into the dark of the hall cupboard and sleeps on a pile of cushions.

The Tunnys' flat is, to Mosh's surprise, sparsely furnished and very, very tidy. He is also relieved. He has noticed the way Andre looks around the houses of the old folks they are clearing and it makes him uncomfortable. Andre looks as if he is making shopping lists in his head. Again, Mosh wonders about Andre's previous placement. There has been a recent spate of robberies from some of the very houses they have extracted old folk from.

Mr Tunny leads Mosh through into the bright living room where Mrs Tunny is sitting in her wheelchair at a polished dark-wood table. She is a lot larger than her tiny husband; perhaps twice as wide, although it is hard to see how tall, given she is squeezed into the chair and covered in a large red and green travelling blanket. She is almost totally bald and her face is very round, her cheeks bulge and her chin – her chins – hang softly in layers from her jaw. Her eyes are astoundingly beautiful, wide and long-lashed with barely a crow's foot. Thin, arched brows add to her ingénue film-star stare. Mosh is captivated.

'Good afternoon, Mrs Tunny.'

She blinks at him with those Bambi eyes. 'Clayton? That you, honey? Have you finished your homework?'

'It's not Clayton, Dorcas,' says Mr Tunny, gently. 'Drink your milk.'

Mrs Tunny raises a plastic cup with a straw to her lips and sucks, eyes wide as a child's looking at the men.

'Dorrie, these are the men I told you about. They are going to take you for a ride.'

'Yes, Mrs Tunny. My name's Mosh. It is a pleasure to be your taxi ride today.'

Mrs Tunny smiles shyly and shakes her head, and a little milk squirts from the side of her mouth. Mr Tunny gently reaches out to wipe her chin with a spotless white hanky. 'I'm going for a ride with these shitfucks?' she whispers.

'Yes, my love. You are going to have a little ride, and I'll be there when you get to the next place.'

Mrs Tunny's eyes seem to get wider still. 'Will there be dancing?'

'Yes, darling,' says Mr Tunny, squeezing her hand. 'I am sure there will be dancing.'

'I bet you were a great dancer?' says Mosh as he checks her bag of medication.

Mrs Tunny pulls the straw from her mouth and nods. 'I love dancing.' Her expression changes, as if she has been shouted at. 'No, no! Wait, we need to look after the baby! We can't go any-where . . .' And then her panic evaporates and she blinks like a doll. 'Fucking dancing,' she says dreamily.

Mr Tunny kisses her cheek. 'No babies here, Dorrie. It's going to be fun. You'll see. Now finish up all your milk.'

He turns to Mosh as his wife pops the straw back into her mouth and sucks. 'She'll be fine,' he says, his green eyes still twinkling. 'Do you need . . . ?'

'Ah yes, Mr Tunny, just a few last questions and a signature, and then that is that.' Mosh reaches for his clipboard again and turns a couple of pages. 'Most of this you have already been through with your GP, so it's just . . . this one. If you could check all the information is correct and you understand the veto on visits during the settling-in period?'

'Yes, yes,' says Mr Tunny, but he barely glances at the clipboard. He is more concerned with his wife.

'All the milk now, Dorcas. That's it. Now let me take it.' He slips the empty beaker from her grasp and tucks her into the chair. 'Make sure you are nice and comfortable under that rug. You must be feeling sleepy already?'

Mrs Tunny yawns widely, showing a delicate pink tongue and haphazard teeth. 'But dancing?'

'When you wake up, darling.'

Mrs Tunny's eyes shut and she begins to breathe deeply.

'Good one,' says Andre. 'Out like a light, these oldies.'

'Any other relatives we should inform?' Mosh turns back to Mr Tunny, a little concerned. He feels for some reason that the old guy is a bit too calm, too 'together'.

'No, our son, Clayton, died some years ago. It was . . . is just us.'

'OK then.'

Mr Tunny signs the papers. Mosh countersigns and hands the clipboard to Andre to witness, and then it is just a case of wheeling the old woman down to the ambulance. Mr Tunny kisses his sleeping wife goodbye and steps back to let Mosh spin the chair in a gentle arc to face the front door.

'Don't worry, Mr Tunny. We'll take good care of her. The

nurses at Grassybanks are the best in England. She will be treated like a queen.'

There is a small lip in the front doorway. Mosh tips the wheelchair a little to get the front wheels over and the chair bumps down on the other side but Dorcas sleeps on. Andre strides off without a backward glance and Mosh pushes Dorcas gently along the concrete terrace towards the stone steps, feeling the little dapper man watching him from the doorway. *It must be heartbreaking for him*, he thinks, praying that Andre will keep his mouth shut. Dorcas is heavy and the descent is going to be a tricky one.

'Don't worry, Mr Tunny,' he calls back over his shoulder as he catches up with Andre at the top of the stairwell. 'She'll be perfectly safe with us.'

Mosh can't see but Mr Tunny's eyes are no longer twinkling. The green has darkened, all light fled. 'It is done,' he says and closes the door.

Both Mosh and Andre are dripping with sweat by the time they get to the ground floor. Mosh has taken the lower end of the chair and therefore most of the weight but Andre still managed to bitch and moan at every step. Finally, they are down and a tepid breeze kisses Mosh's ears; he pauses, catching his breath before clambering into the front of the ambulance to lower the hydraulic lift. He is so glad that this is going to be the last extraction before the weekend. In a couple of hours he will be holding Serena in his arms, her small, warm body in the crook of his elbow, her scrunched little face blinking up at him.

Mosh picks his phone out of his pocket to text his wife, and so doesn't see that Mrs Tunny, in her sleep, has reached out and grabbed at Andre's jacket as he is trying to load her into the back of the vehicle.

'Leggo!' Andre hisses into her face but the woman is deeply asleep and her fist clenches tighter around his collar. A thin stream of milky drool catches the light as it falls from her lips.

'Get off, you old bag,' says Andre again and tries to twist her hand but the old woman has a grip of iron. Sneaking a quick look to make sure no one is watching, Andre grabs two of the woman's fingers and pulls them back and back until he hears them crack and her grip relaxes completely. She twists a little in her chair but does not wake, and Andre bends the fingers back into the right shape and stuffs her entire arm under the travel rug. He feels strange, almost as if he has missed a step, is tripping over, a falling, light-headed feeling. He isn't sure if it is bad or not. He just hopes no one will notice until the old girl wakes up and then maybe they will think she did it to herself.

Upstairs in his flat Mr Tunny turns the lights off and watches the grey sky darken slowly to blue-black. He has a bottle of Jim Beam rye whiskey, a pipe and the tobacco he had been out buying in front of him. He hasn't smoked the pipe inside in ten years – not since Dorcas started to get ill. The smoke upset her. Now he can smoke as much as he likes. He can do anything he likes. He could go to the pub. He could play cards with Johnson and Maverick. He could go to the café on Turton Street and listen to some jazz at the Cricketers' Arms. His pipe lies unlit on the polished wood table next to the bottles of his wife's Librium. The milk he gave her before she was taken had enough in it to kill an ox. She won't wake up in Grassybanks, thank God! No one was taking his wife off to that terrible place. He still has enough of the Librium for himself when the time comes. He isn't sure if the time is now. He sips the whiskey and retreats into his memory, dancing 'with you, Dorcas, my love, with the most beautiful woman in the whole wide world'.

Blind Woman's Buff

A gobbet of lemony dawn light hits the far wall and slides slowly down the flock wallpaper. Feeling its buttery glide on her eyelid, Alex has an urge to get up and draw the hotel curtains, but she is still, happily, trapped beneath the Poet.

'Ah . . . *kochanie* . . . you are so . . . so . . . so . . .'

The Poet's large head moves up and down above her, blocking out the light momentarily, leaving a trail of garlic-infused morning breath like mist. Alex rocks her hips and bites into his shoulder to stifle a little yawn. It has been a wonderful night, and although Alex is now mostly sober and, after several hours of hectic sex – potentially more cystitis than sensation – she doesn't want it to stop. The priapic Poet is passionate, imaginative and adept and, more than that, enthralled by the same ecstatic surprise as she at this fortuitous communion.

Their initial shy clumsiness had caused a clunking of foreheads so extreme that the Poet had sprung backwards with concern, still half in his trousers, and fallen off the end of the bed. This had resulted in them both getting delicious hysterical wheezing giggles like wicked children. Although what they did later, Alex's introduction of the game 'Blind Women in the Buff', for instance, and the inventive use of the room service fruit basket, was definitely for adults.

But they are both tiring and only human after all. Wriggling around beneath him, Alex manages to release a leg, snaking it up and across his sweaty back; then *hup*, she thrusts up, twists and flips him over. Before he can remonstrate, she sits astride him, and leans in to nibble his earlobe.

'I cannot get enough of you,' he says. His hands twist in her long, dark hair as she slides down, pausing to suck his nipples and lick the soft, furry skin around his belly button. She moves lower still and, after a long inhaled exclamation in Polish, the Poet explodes sour and salt down her throat, his hips pumping uncontrollably, his face contorted.

And it's over. The Poet smiles sweetly at her, closes his eyes and almost immediately begins to snore softly. Alex lies for a while, the sweat on her body cooling, thinking she might allow sleep to tug her under too. But Alex has work to get to and, more importantly, she has Chris. She has to get up.

Sighing, she swings her legs off the bed and stretches, plucking a stray pubic hair from her lip. In the corner, Chris, her guide dog, takes his cue, sliding out from his makeshift camp under the desk at the other end of the suite and shaking himself. Alex raises an apologetic hand in his direction and rolls her shoulders. In the gloomy room she is encased in shifting spiderwebs of soft shadow, her damaged retinas objecting to the laws of physics. The room is briefly distorted, squeezed and released as if breathing. Slowly, as her optic nerves grapple with her brain, she is able to make out the glint of empty bottles and glasses littering the table, along with the remains of the room service the Poet had ordered. How delicious that congealed muck had been at midnight.

Remembering what they had done with some of that food makes Alex turn pink. She really needs a shower.

The Poet mutters something in his sleep, and Alex kneels up on the bed, carefully so as not to disturb him. Now able to take her time, she scans him from head to foot, something she couldn't do while he was awake. Although she has a smorgasbord of retinal malfunctions, she does retain a clearer keyhole of central vision just over her nose. She sweeps the world with this, like now, taking in slivers of the Poet at a time and slotting them together like a jigsaw. In his sleep he looks younger. His shaggy dark brown hair is greying at the temples. Alex leans closer in, peering intently as if he is a sculpture. He is lean and pale, muscles and veins of marble dusted with black body hair. He has a large, slightly beaky nose and thick brows, his mouth is a little wide and now slack, the lips parted over excellent, and unlikely to be original, teeth. There is stubble on his handsome dimpled chin. The Poet is a very good-looking man.

Alex had met the Poet two days before, on that Friday afternoon, squeezed up together on the commuter-crush train from London. The carriage was so full, Chris hadn't been able to guide Alex to a free seat and, as the train lurched forward from the platform, she had, literally, fallen into the Poet's lap. He had laughed, called her a 'little *ptaszek*', 'little bird', which was kind, she thinks, considering she is more obviously ostrich than greenfinch. She had felt the strength of his arm around her waist, caught the flash of those teeth and fallen deep into the dark blue eyes. Squashed together so tightly that they had almost synchronised heartbeats, she had asked him about the book he was making notes in and discovered he was a poet. In fact, he had just released his sixth volume in Polish and English. By the time the train drew into Cambright station, she had been invited to accompany him to his book signing at Waterford Booksellers. Alex happily tagged along, gulping down the free wine, noticing that he had a lot of attractive female fans. Two of them cried during a poem he had read called 'Bleeding Jack', apparently written after his father's death from cancer. Another woman, long red hair flowing down her back like Millais's Ophelia, got a little hysterical in the Q and A session after his reading, talking so fast in a mixture of Polish and English that the Poet had held up a hand and said, gently, '*Uspokój się,* calm down.'

Alex had felt a little heady from the poetry herself. It seemed to pluck at her spine. He twined words into sticky ropes that caught her up, held her above the world for a moment. *Shit, he is good,* she had thought, a little panicked, and wondered what the hell she was doing there. She couldn't compete. Her hair needed washing, for God's sake, and she could smell the day's sweat on her clothes. *I must look terrible.*

Yet afterwards the Poet sought Alex out, shouldering his way past the redhead and the other lovely ladies to where she was standing by the celebrity cookbooks. He had been euphoric, high on the night. People kept coming over to ask him to sign copies of the book and yet he was oblivious to the fluttering lashes and trembling voices.

'Tonight I want to concentrate on my new friends,' he had said, one arm about Alex's shoulders, one hand ruffling Chris's silky ears . . . and he had. They had bought a takeaway that first night, decent wine and a bottle of Polish vodka, drifting slowly back to Alex's flat, talking about literature, about the power of words and the power of silence. Occasionally, as they meandered through the city streets, the Poet would pause, leaning across

Alex to discuss these things with Chris, who would wag his pennant of a tail and roll his eyes up in adoration. *I do believe you too have been seduced, old buddy,* Alex had thought, grinning.

'The flat . . .' Alex never called it 'her' flat for some reason. 'It's a disgraceful mess and no one in the estate has curtains, of course.'

'That's nothing,' the Poet had replied. 'I once shared a squat in Łódź with a community of postmodern conceptual artists. Now that was a shithole. Literally. When the toilet backed up and exploded, they filmed it and then projected it onto the walls of the Izrael Poznański Palace.'

At the flat, Alex and the Poet stayed up all night, sitting on the sofa, while Chris, content and full of kibble, dozed in his dog bed. They had talked of childhood, loneliness and adventure and why they were how they were. He was sharp and funny and Alex found herself laughing, out loud, from deep in her belly. She couldn't remember the last time that had happened. In fact, Alex could not remember a time she had been so open with any man. She almost feared the feeling and when – in the rusty light of dawn – he checked his watch and said he had to get back to his hotel as he was chairing a lecture series at the university that weekend, Alex had felt a wash of relief. He seemed almost unreal, this beautiful, clever man on the sofa. Alex could feel her expertly crafted emotional armour beginning to split open under the pressure of his presence.

'But you will come to the hotel later?' He had stood in the doorway, insisting, and when she had hesitated, he had leaned in and kissed her, leaving her with both the liquid heat of lust and a hot prickle of tears.

She had spent the rest of the day thinking about him, pulling clothes out of drawers, trying to recall where she had last stashed a pair of pretty knickers, a bra with all its underwiring in order. She washed her hair, put it up, let it down again, found mascara and even lipstick, put it on, washed it off and put it on again. Chris watched her, unsure of the state of play. They had been together a long time but this version of Alex was new to him. He cocked his head, fascinated.

At the hotel, Alex had been worried that she wouldn't be able to make the Poet out in the low light of the lobby, but he had been waiting right at the entrance.

'Thank God you came,' he said and his hands were cupping her face, his eyes dark indigo, blazing, a little bloodshot. 'I can't damn well concentrate on anything else!'

He took her up to his hotel room, where Alex's anxiety about what clothes to wear quickly became irrelevant as within minutes they were all on the floor.

Now as she watches him sleep, she feels a surge of something akin to hope and wonders for a moment about staying around for breakfast. She and Chris could show him the city. Maybe take him punting along the Backs. So the article she's writing for the local paper would be late . . . so she might lose the job . . . but it might all be worth it for once.

Alex is about to lie back down again when the Poet's mobile phone rings with an unpleasantly loud faux bell. The Poet groggily raises his head.

'Shall I get it?' asks Alex. She is closest.

'No, no . . .' He rubs his face and reaches through the condom wrappers to his phone.

'Ahh, *serduszko* . . . darling? Is everything all right?'

He is alert now. Muscles tense, casting shadows along his back, as he swings his legs off the bed, turning away from Alex. He speaks quietly, cupping the mouthpiece.

'What a wonderful surprise, my love! When? No . . . not at all . . . I can't wait.'

Alex, without a word, gets up, groping through her shadows to find the drawcord for the curtains. Pale light floods into the room, filling her eyes with glitter. The tiny sparkles fade, along with some of the spiderwebs, leaving her keyhole of sight sharper. The Poet puts a hand up, shading his eyes as he says, 'See you soon,' and makes kissing noises into the phone before he hangs up.

'That sounded like a wife?' Alex hates the shrill tone in her voice.

The Poet is using the glare of the sunlight to evade her eyes, although Alex herself is unsure why she should feel angry. In all the time they were together she never asked him if he was in a relationship. Probably didn't want to know.

'Yes,' he says. 'She was on a research trip in Prague but left early. Flew into Stansted a couple of hours ago. She was going to surprise me.' Now it is his turn to survey the room.

'Shit,' he says, looking at the carnage.

Alex has found her jeans and bra but is still missing her knickers.

'That's nice for you.' *Keep it light*, she is thinking. *Get it over.*

'Yes.' His voice is flat but then he twitches, looks across. 'She said she was in a taxi and passing through somewhere like . . . Allingtington? How far away from here is that?'

22

He is asking Alex how long he has to clean up.

'Oh, don't worry. It's about twenty miles from the city centre. Do you want some help with the—?'

'No, no!' He is too quick, the words like small shoves to her chest. He is looking at her as if she is the problem, which of course she is.

Clumsily Alex pulls up her jeans, finding her knickers in a wodge down one leg. She kicks them out onto the floor, stooping to pick them up and stuff them in her pocket. She has her T-shirt on backwards and is getting that panicky feeling, that sober and sad feeling. The Poet's body is shut to her now. She wouldn't even risk a last kiss. He stands and begins clearing up the mess on the table with short violent movements that make his reddened, swollen prick swing wildly from side to side. His buttocks are white as milk. They almost glow.

'I can't let her find me like this,' he is muttering. 'Not after last time.' He seems to have forgotten Alex is still in the room.

A bottle falls to the floor near her foot but makes hardly a sound on the thick carpet, rolling into the void of her peripheral vision. Chris, sensing the tension, lopes to Alex's side and waits while she picks up her handbag.

'Right then . . .' Alex clears her throat and realises with a kind of dim horror she isn't actually sure of his surname. *Gunter . . . ?* She has a signed copy of his book in her handbag, but without her magnification glasses she wouldn't be able to read the cover.

'Err . . . well, thanks for a great night.'

'Yeah, yeah . . . you were great . . . it was a great . . . oh hell! I am sorry. I guess I've got time for a shower . . .' He is battling with the dirty sheet and doesn't look over but raises a hand. 'Oh wait . . . you will need some money.'

'What?'

'I mean . . . well . . . I just remember you saying . . . for transport or something? You said times were hard.' He trails off, sheepish, looking around for his wallet.

Alex can't speak: her throat has closed up and she feels angry heat rise up her neck. She picks up Chris's lead and harness from the back of the chair next to the bed and, together, they make a rush for the door. Outside in the carpeted hotel corridor she pauses. She had lied about Allington or 'Allingtington', as he had called it. At this time on a Sunday morning the woman on the phone would get here in the next five minutes. Water pipes tinkle and a far-off loo flushes. Alex backs up and plucks the knickers from her pocket, looping them over the door handle of Room 23.

No one likes to be treated like a whore . . . even if they act like one.

The lobby is quiet and the receptionist has ducked out of sight, so Chris and Alex leave without raising any eyebrows. She is just a dishevelled, fuming, sour-smelling guest with her guide dog. Outside the sun is clambering slowly up into the sky, and the morning is full of birdsong. It's going to be another scorching day, but for the moment a cool dawn mist hangs over the city. Chris lifts his muzzle, dragging in the smell of mould and tarmac, mown grass and old chip fat.

He pulls Alex along the side of the pavement to steal a quick sniff, and she doesn't correct him; after all he's had a very disturbed night and no breakfast. Instead, she unharnesses him briefly so he can pee, then hooks him back in.

'Come on, love. Home!' Chris flicks his ear but obediently

turns down around the back of the hotel, heading through the city centre. It is a relief for Alex, walking at this time on a Sunday morning. No cyclists, tourists, yobs, commuters or workmen. Half the city is swathed in scaffolding and usually the noise of smashing hammers, drills and traffic turns her head inside out, but now she can hear her feet slapping the pavement and the tinkle of Chris's collar. A crackling plastic bag flees past in the gutter. A dove charoos. *A piteousness of doves* flits through Alex's mind.

They round the corner into the large piazza outside the shopping centre. Above them hangs the mammoth government 'Shop a Scrounger!' poster taking up over three storeys of the car-park wall. Instinctively Alex winces away from it, ducking her head into her shoulders and almost tripping over the large crack in the patio stone in the very middle of the square. Three years ago an eighteen-year-old called Laura Shandy had rolled her wheelchair off the roof of the car park and landed right here, cracking the stone flags and smashing herself to oblivion.

There has been a lot of that lately. A fellow journalist in Birmingham had only been half-joking when he'd told Alex they had to keep an eye on the skyline driving into work in case of falling bodies. He had said they were averaging about three crip jumpers a day. 'One way to solve the welfare bill,' he had laughed. Alex hadn't thought it funny, but then he had never met her face-to-face, eye-to-eye, so to speak. He didn't know he was talking to a crip.

The crack is the only memorial to Laura. Some of her classmates had laid flowers here the day of her funeral, and the council had had them arrested for defacing public property.

An uprush of wind wags the corner of the poster into Alex's tunnel of sight. There is something malevolent about those posters. The garish blood-red background frames a greasy-haired fat bloke in a wheelchair, grinning lasciviously, his lap flooded with £20 notes. '75 per cent of people claiming Incapable Benefit are perfectly fit for work!' yells the poster in big black lettering that even Alex can read. 'If you suspect your neighbour is a scrounger, let us know and we will name and shame!'

Underneath, there is a telephone number for the switchboard of the *Daily Spun* newspaper followed by: 'Vigilance brings rewards! Shop a scrounger today and you may take home £100 cash!' The flap of red makes Alex nervous. During the day people hang out around here, under the poster, absorbing the red energy of the thing, and usually it is the place where she will have something flicked or thrown at her – a lit cigarette, a plastic bottle and, once, a shoe. The shoe she had picked up and walked swiftly off with, Chris gamely jogging beside her. Someone with a pubescent kid's creaky voice had yelled, 'Oi! Crip bitch, give my shoe back!' and Alex had hefted the trainer into the traffic, half-hoping the little twat would run after it. She has no idea if he did or not.

Chris whines softly. His nose bumps into her hand. He is right. Alex is tired and getting depressed. She already misses her Poet fiercely, stupidly. What was wrong with her? *Toughen the fuck up!* she swears at herself. She steps up, past the community centre where the queue for the food bank is already forming, down the steps behind one of the colleges, and in a couple of minutes they stagger out from the narrow back streets and into the wide green space that is Lion Green. All the creaking and rumbling of the city becomes muffled as they head to the centre of the grassy green. The mist is lifting, the grass is dewy and sweet-smelling beneath their feet. Alex scans around, using her tunnel of clear vision, and is assured they are alone in the midst of the green. Both she and Chris exhale. *Whew.*

The word 'deadline' dings rudely in the part of Alex's brain that controls her inner financial adviser. Chris's head comes up too, although his 'ding' is 'breakfast!'

'Come on then,' Alex says, but Chris is already pulling her home.

The flat Alex lives in is a single-bed, corner flat in a large housing block. It is not a bad place, really, just always cold. It's on the ground floor, facing north, and not a single shard of sunlight has ever found its way into the interior. Stepping in from the bright light outside is like stepping into a cave, both in its dimness and its sudden chill. It also smells of wet cement no matter how many incense sticks or scented candles she burns. The empty takeaway containers piled up in the recycling bin make her stomach lurch. *He was here just yesterday,* she thinks. *Oh God, I wish . . . I wish . . . Ah, shit! How could I have been such an idiot?*

Chris couldn't give a toss about the single pong of cement or old food packets. His sense of smell is so powerful he can scent both inside and outside at the same time. He can smell the individual items in the supermarket down the street, each person walking past. Chris sees in smell. His world is a vivid technostink of wonderful and extraordinary stenches, of which many are edible and those that aren't should be tasted just in case.

He waits patiently as Alex scrabbles for her keys in the bottom of her handbag, drops them, tries the wrong one, swears, finds the right one and finally opens the front door. Inside and free from his harness, Chris shakes and dashes off to find his stuffed toy sheep, Myrtle. Alex slopes in after him, pulling at the crotch of her jeans where they have chafed on already raw skin. She doesn't turn the lights on, though the room is always, even in daylight, so dark she has to walk with one hand along the wall. It's not just that she can't really afford the electricity any more, but also this way she can't be watched. Across the road Mr Green will be sitting at his open living-room window with binoculars at the ready and his hands down his pyjamas. He isn't being 'lewd' or committing a public offence if he is in his own living room, apparently, or so the police have told the neighbours several times now.

Not having curtains is a serious downer for everyone around here. No curtains any more, of course, not even net ones for anyone at street level, since the Chancellor of the Exchequer's 'It's Curtains for Skivers!' speech roused the mob of Believe in Better campaigners into early-morning window-smashing sessions. Alex has a spare mattress she uses in the windowless bathroom when she needs to catch a nap during the day.

Right now, though, there isn't time for a kip. Stomach growling, Alex heads straight to the fridge. Two lemons, a nuclear-accident-resistant tub of margarine, half an onion and something grey in a Tupperware dish. She licks her chapped lips and instead picks up the empty bottle of vodka from the recycling box on the floor. A shake proves there is at least a mouthful left, so she taps in some water, swirls it around and chugs it, the sharp clean hit making her gums go cold.

Being tall, Alex finds the kitchen a little cramped. She man-oeuvres around Chris to organise his breakfast kibble. At the heft of the food sack he becomes very focused, his large golden-brown eyes watching every move. He is part black Labrador. That part thinks almost only of food.

'Sit!'

He sits.

'Wait!'

He waits.

'OK!'

The food is already half gone. It's as if he inhales the stuff.

Alex shuffles off to shower. It's nearly 7.30 a.m. The article she is writing on the newly opened extension at Grassybanks Residential Home is due at 12 p.m. for the Monday edition of the *Cambright Sun*. 'Grassybanks: The New Face of Care in Britain?'

Andre's Conversion

'The Believe in Better Conference has over fifty volunteers,' says the skinny woman at the table. 'So, if you need any help finding your way around, just look for the people with the yellow-and-black rosettes.' She pats her own, which is so large it hangs from her chest like a dartboard.

Andre's mum smiles but without showing her cigarette-stained teeth. She has dressed 'nice' in a skirt and cardigan combination that Andre hasn't seen since the Queen's Diamond Jubilee street-party celebration, a blue-and-gold shiny acrylic number. Every time Andre touches her he gets a static shock. It is her birthday and Andre and his brother had made the mistake of asking her what she wanted. 'I want you both to come with me to my Believe in Better Conference,' she had said. And she had meant it. Grudgingly the boys had agreed, wary of Mum's new hobby. Politics? Who'd have thought it. She had never voted in her life.

'We'll come to keep you company, Mum,' Ralph had said, 'but no way are we gonna end up going on their stupid rallies or volunteering for their street patrols, OK?'

And so here they are. The huge conference hall is stuffy, all brown nylon carpets and orange window blinds. Yellow-and-black 'Believe in Better' banners are draped along the walls and hang from the ceiling along with hundreds of rosettes laid out like bunches of exotic jungle flowers. The clash of colours is giving Andre a headache and he can feel a whine building in his throat. The carpets muffle the sound of their feet as they move along and into the crowd of people circling the exhibits and stalls while they wait for the key speakers to arrive. All the posters seem to be promoting British manufacturing, farming and fishing. Andre hates any kind of fish unless it is coated in batter and comes with chips.

He has refused to wear a suit, even if it is Ma's birthday. Instead he is in his Jay-P-Did baggy jeans, white T-shirt and Hinterland boots. Ralph, however, is wearing one of his work suits. The shiny blue suit isn't a great fit any more, not since Ralph gave up football on Saturdays, and the shirt buttons look like they are about to pop at any moment. 'You look like a knob,' says Andre.

His brother says nothing but punches him hard in the arm.

'Owwww! That fucking hurt!' hisses Andre.

'Don't you show me up, you toerags,' says their mother. 'Why can't you bloody act your age?'

Andre hadn't wanted to come. He isn't really interested in politics and he's been flat out with work for the first time in his life *thanks to fucking Mosh*, but once his old mum gets all in a tizzy about something there's no stopping her. And she was well grateful when Andre and Ralph finally agreed to come along. She almost shed a tear.

'I promise you it makes sense,' she told them. 'And it's about time you got off your arses and did something for your country. I wish they would bring back National Service. Teach you two a thing or two about respect.'

Andre is hoping for totty. If he is going to have to sit through an hour or two of speeches he needs a decent pair of tits to focus on, at the very least. Looking around the crowded hall, he can see plenty of women, but most look as old or older than his ma. *Bunch of hags.* He begins to wonder about sneaking out for a break when his mum grabs at his arm.

'Over there! It's Mr Pooleigh!' (She pronounces it 'Poo-lay' as if it has an acute accent over the 'e'.)

A tall, bony man in a striped suit and a flaming yellow-and-black tie is walking down the concourse. Around the man are a flock, an entourage, of absolutely stunning women, about ten of them. To Andre they look like catwalk models. He hears Ralph whistle under his breath. 'Fuck me,' he says. 'Prime beef.'

'Mr Pooleigh is the BIB leader, boys,' says his ma over the sound of the blood pounding in their ears.

One of the incredible-looking chicks turns her fabulous cheekbone as she sashays past and winks at them.

'Where do we join up?' asks Ralph.

Sitting in the auditorium later, Andre has to admit that the speeches are pretty chuffing good too. It's all stuff that makes sense to him, and the speakers are off the hook, cool. He had been anxious when the first one had started by bringing up a load of graphs and stuff on the huge screen behind her. *I don't need to be fuckin' skooled*, he had thought, but she had been a bit pretty, a nice firm arse considering her age and stuff. And she had talked about immigration, one of the things that usually gets Mum all vexed. Only now Andre can see, what with the graphs and the charts, that it really is a serious situation. The lady speaker makes it real clear. *Real clear.* In fact, Andre feels a bit panicked by what she is saying. *Surely something should be done about it? Why isn't anything being done about it?*

Another man called Pratt gets up onto the stage to review the welfare situation. Andre thinks it'll be boring, but the guy starts right in with the jokes. 'What's the difference between an amputee and a freak? . . . Political correctness!'

He is fucking funny, like a comedian, and gets everyone yelling out all together, 'Benefits for the needy and not beds for the lazy!' Andre likes that. He tries to keep it in his head so he can use it when Mosh is getting het up over something or other. *Fucking Mosh. Such a pussy. Always banging on about the injustice of the system and stuff.* The funny man also shows a couple of videos about people on welfare, and it brings it home to Andre just how many crips are abusing the system. He had no idea things had got so out of control. *Another thing to learn Mosh about.* There's this one video showing a man who claims to have some nasty-ass disease taking part in a half-marathon. 'He says he is in remission!' says the voice-over. 'His "remission" is costing the good British taxpayer over £50 a day!'

There is a compilation of the top twenty 'Biggest, Baddest Benefit Cheats'. The fucking cheek of these people is mind-blowing. Each one worse than the next, and the audience starts catcalling, then whooping and then actually yelling at the screen. The welfare-talk guy on the stage finishes with, 'What's the hardest part about cooking vegetables in a microwave? Getting the wheel-chair in the door!' and gets a standing ovation, and Andre feels shamed for ever having been on welfare at all.

It all gets a bit hectic then and there's loads of banter from the audience, and then a real comedian gets on stage, some old bloke called Bobby Britain, and he brings the house down with his impression of a Romanian whore trying to negotiate a price with a man from Bangladesh. Andre laughs so much he almost pisses himself.

There's a coffee break, and Andre and Ralph get to stretch their legs and their necks, searching for the posse of beautiful long-legged lovelies while their mother heads outside for a smoke. Andre thinks he sees the girls over by the main entrance but when they get there, pushing through the excited crowd, there is only the old hag on the reception table.

'All right, boys? Very good of you to support your mum.' She smiles at Ralph in a way that makes Andre grin.

'She's up for it,' he hisses to his brother and ducks away from another dead-arm-punch and then it's time to settle down again for the last speech of the day.

Mr Pooleigh ('Poo-LAY') leaps up onto the stage and the audience goes wild. He could be a rock star. Andre can't help but notice his mother's rapt expression. She is clapping her hands so hard they're going pink.

Mr Pooleigh handles himself like the major star, millionaire and ex-radio shock jock that he is. He blows kisses at his entourage, all now arranged like a kind of harem along the front row, and then leaps up to the mike stand with a, 'Hello Cambright! Hello Eastern Angleside! Hello Southern England! Hello England! And hello to the world! We Believe in Better!' It takes a while for the conference delegates to calm themselves and quieten down, and when they do, Pooleigh launches into his speech with gusto.

It kind of covers the same ground as what the other peeps have said, thinks Andre, but when Pooleigh says the stuff it makes even more sense. *He is bangin' and them chicks can't get enough of him, even tho' he isn't tonk, like well-built or even that good-looking.*

34

He's a bit old and his hair is greasy and his nose sticks out, like, well far.

'I'm not against immigration,' Pooleigh is purring. 'Far from it. Migrants have qualities we all admire. Looking for a better life. They want to get on. I like that. We admire that. So I'm speaking here as much for the settled ethnic minorities as for those who have been here forever. Half a million new arrivals a year! It's just not sustainable. Anyone who looks at it honestly knows it's not sustainable. We Believe in Better! We are the people who talk about it honestly. Directly. It's a serious problem and we are taking it seriously!'

As he goes on, Andre finds himself nodding and clapping and thinking, *Yeah, yeah, this dude is righteous. I get him.*

'So, who are we?' Mr Pooleigh grabs the portable mike and jumps down from the stage. One of the lush chicks jumps up and kisses him on the mouth. *Sick!* thinks Andre. Pooleigh grins, kisses her hand and waves her back into her seat before moving along the rows of adoring supporters.

'Who is the typical BIB voter?' he asks. 'I'll tell you something about the typical BIB voter – the typical BIB voter doesn't exist.' He pats a man on the back, shakes another's hand. 'When I look at the supporters that are coming to our meetings, that are here at this conference, I see a range of British society from all parts of the spectrum.' Mr Pooleigh kisses yet another woman's hand and heads back onto the stage. He points at the crowd. 'Workers, employers, self-employed. Big businessmen, corner-shop owners. Well off, comfortably off, struggling. Young as well as old. Not ideologues. Some left, some right, mostly in the middle. Some activists, some haven't voted for twenty years. One thing we have in common: we are fed up to the back teeth with the cardboard cut-out careerists in Westminster. The spot-the-difference politicians. Desperate to fight the middle ground, but can't even find it. Focus groupies. The triangulators. The dog whistlers. The politicians who daren't say what they really mean.'

Yeah! Andre and Ralph are on their feet, cheering with the others even if they are not entirely sure what Pooleigh has been banging on about. It is the energy in the whole building. The whole thing is a rush and there is Pooleigh smiling down at them from the stage.

'We are the people who Believe in Better! Who Believe in Britain! And we must fight on, because when we know we are right, when we truly believe something, we must act! We must say it out loud. That's why BIB is the most independent-minded body of men and women who have ever come together in the name of British politics. We must take the fight onto the streets, into the homes, into the minds of all the people that can make Britain Great again!'

Pooleigh has climaxed, and the crowd roar until they are spent. Andre feels fired up, itchy, energised. He wants to 'do something' but he isn't sure what.

'Hey,' says Ralph. 'That's Brian Mate from my old five-a-side team. I heard he landed an ace job with your TOSA lot. Be nice and maybe he'll get you a pay rise.'

Andre looks over and sees a fat blond man wearing a large yellow-and-black rosette standing by one of the exits with several other young men. The men look hot and bothered, faces flushed. Brian looks up, sees them and waves.

'Err Mum—' Ralph begins.

'Oh, don't worry about me, boys. I'm just glad you came along. You go on and join your mates,' Andre's mum says. 'No doubt you'll want to go to the pub. I'll see you back home. I am going to queue for Mr Pooleigh's autograph.'

Andre and Ralph join Brian, who slaps them on their backs and calls them 'Bruvs'.

'What did you think?' Brian asks.

'Yeah, the conference was jokes, man. Hectic.' Andre nods but he isn't sure how he feels now it is all over.

'Then why you looking so flat?' Ralph nudges him.

'I just want to . . . you know . . . do something,' says Andre feeling lame.

Brian looks at him sideways. 'Yeah, after the meetings we all feel like letting off steam, don't we, boys?'

The other blokes around Brian laugh and one of them makes a fist and punches it into his other hand, palm flat. The noise of knuckles hitting flesh is strangely exciting to Andre.

'Fancy getting a pint or two across? Maybe we should take some of the BIB issues to the street, get a bit "face-to-face" with some of the people bringing our country down.' Brian winks at Andre. 'We'll start with a couple of pints and then see what the boys come up with.'

THE DAILY SPUN
The People Speak: Don Poppet on Tuesdays
Eleven children and never worked a day in her life!
Dole Scum Queen gets her just desserts!

In an overdue U-turn, the government has crumbled under public pressure! It will, at long last, agree the bill proposing 'voluntary' sterilisation for any long-term unemployed parent caught cheating the benefit system. No longer can parasites like Ms Kelly be allowed to parade their tribe of half-neglected, feral children around while living the life of Riley off the back of the hard-working taxpayer.

After the first episode of the documentary series *Scumbag Street* was aired in last month's prime-time slot, our outrage rocketed. We demanded that our government take action immediately to prevent such disgusting 'in-yer-face' (to quote Ms Kelly) stealing from the system. Finally, a result! The Minister for Women and Equality, Amelia Baker, agreed the outrageous filching of resources from the British people must stop. She told us of her decision to look into voluntary sterilisation for long-term dole-scrounging parents. There was more good news from our mate, John Thorpe-Sinclair, Minister for Work and Pensions. He is capping benefits on families claiming for over five children! We, the people, think that's a right and proper response to the current situation.

Ms Kelly said in her 'defence' that being a mum was a full-time job and she hadn't had a day off since having her first sprog at age 14. She said she had looked for work but was told she lacked the right skills. However, when I visited her mini mansion with its five bedrooms, all paid for by guess who, the children were at home alone and she was in the pub across the road!

Today she is moaning that her house was ransacked and the windows broken by the Believe in Better campaigners and her children scared witless. Well, Ms Kelly, we say to you: Get a job, you lazy scum. Maybe your children need a good scare to teach them that no one gets the life of Riley for free!

A Rumour of Promotion

From where he is standing, Mosh can see Andre and the mechanic laughing, over by the parked private ambulances. It has been six weeks since the incident with the Tunnys, and Mosh has been growing more and more uncomfortable every day. They were not fired, not even reprimanded, in spite of the fact that Mrs Tunny's fingers were broken and she was already deep into a fatal coma by the time they got her to Grassybanks. Mosh goes over and over it all in his head. The husband killing his own wife right there, in front of them. How desperate does a man have to be? The poisoned milk squirting from her mouth. *It is done.* It all keeps him awake at night . . . that and Serena's colic.

It isn't so much the death. Mosh is wearily used to death. In the last couple of years so many of the ambulance call-outs he has done as an NHS paramedic have been to the dead or dying. A new ruling had been brought in to the welfare programme called 'extreme sanctions'. A majority of those people facing the sanctions had some form of mental health or learning disability. All it took was filling in a form incorrectly; speaking in the wrong tone of voice to a Job Central staff member; not getting to an interview within three minutes of your set time; or not being able to prove you were applying for at least fifty jobs a week.

'Extreme sanctions' meant all benefits were stopped. All. This information was sent to you, depending on whether you had an address, in a simple brown envelope stating the sanction but not the cause. Some people couldn't read, couldn't believe, or just didn't realise what they had done. Some might try to call someone to ask how they were to eat, to pay rent, to pay for electricity, for water – but Job Central was not allowed to respond to any person who had been sanctioned. Catch 22. The most unlucky, the ones that Mosh and the ambulance crew were called to, usually because of the smell offending a neighbour, would already have starved, died from hypothermia or killed themselves. Mosh had stopped counting the number of body parts he had collected from train tracks over his last year in the job.

Of course, Mosh had been appalled. He had even asked a mate of his who worked in one of the re-employment teams at Job Central to help him find out why this kept happening. But it simply turned out that 'due to the current recession' Job Central had a target to sanction at least ten people a week, and the mental health cases were the easiest fodder. 'Completely off the record, mate, but it's either them or me,' his mate had said.

Mosh then decided to move from hospital paramedic to this job with TOSA Community Transport Ltd, the now privatised medical extraction unit. He had felt that moving vulnerable people to a safe and caring environment was going to be a hell of a lot better than finding rotting corpses in bedsits three times a week. But perhaps he had made a mistake, and anyway, now there was another layer to the grimness. Andre. Mosh knew without a doubt Andre had broken Mrs Tunny's fingers.

He raises his mug of sweet tea and watches Andre from behind the steam. Andre is telling a joke. He is making faces and doing a funny walk. The mechanic is braying with laughter. Andre's confidence has grown with his cruelty. Mosh can see that he is mimicking one of the old men they had to clear earlier in the week. The man, very senile but still strong, had broken free from Andre and run away from the ambulance. He hadn't gone far, though, as his pyjama bottoms had slid down around his knees. Andre had run up and tackled him. The old man had fallen clumsily and hurt himself so badly he could barely stand.

'Swollen Balls!' Andre had named him. He gave nicknames to almost all the clients they picked up. That was one of the kinder ones. Exasperated by Andre's refusal to listen to his remonstrations, Mosh had gone upstairs to the freshly carpeted administration suite to speak to the newly promoted TOSA community transport administrator, Brian Mate. He had noticed the man's Believe in Better tie pin, his knock-off designer suit, his overpowering and offensive cologne. Another relative youngster, white and jowly.

'Are you ratting on a colleague?' Mr Mate had asked from behind his large desk. He hadn't offered Mosh a seat.

Ratting? What kind of word was that? Mosh had thought, incensed. 'Our clients are vulnerable and often elderly. Surely it's important . . . ?'

Mate had stopped him, holding up a hand. 'Mr Jameson, are you implying these clients are more important than any other? Honestly, Mr Jameson, these clients, and yes, especially the geriatrics, are practically husks of their former selves. Human husks. It is hardly likely they are even aware of what is happening to them, is it?'

Mosh was dumbstruck. He had felt as if the air had become rancid and he didn't want to breathe it in.

'I'm only joshing with you,' the man had said, seeming to wince a little, as if Mosh's reaction had hurt him. 'I'll have a word with young Andre, but I am sure it's just a bit of over-enthusiasm. From what I see, he's a very capable staff member.'

Mosh doesn't know if anything was ever said. It doesn't seem like it, and if anything, Andre is getting worse.

And something else is troubling Mosh. Andre has applied for a job at Grassybanks, and there is a rumour that he has been shortlisted.

'For the assistant supervisor position,' Gill in HR had said to Mosh on her tea break.

Sweet Jesus, Mosh had nearly choked on his doughnut. 'Andre hasn't got any experience! And he's a fucking psycho.'

Gill had peered at Mosh over the top of her glasses. He noticed the dark circles under her eyes. She looked exhausted. 'He has "connections", apparently. Some Believe in Better bigwig put his name forward . . . anyway, I think "psycho" was one of the key requirements,' she said. 'All that lot from TOSA seem to believe a sociopathic trait is vital for medical administration these days.'

Mosh isn't sure if she was joking.

Job Central: Alex Asks for Help and Is Punished

From the crossing point at the bottom of the bridge you can gaze left along the glittering punt-strewn river towards the colleges, ancient and modern, or turn to your right to Peter's Green with its tennis courts, green playing fields and towering horse chestnut trees. Unless circumstances dictate otherwise, there is no need to look over the bridge to where Job Central is conveniently shielded by a high bank topped with fences and thick bushes. This is a good thing, as Job Central is one of the ugliest buildings in the city.

It's a formidable five-storey rectangular building with small windows. There is a sullen greyness to its exterior, and the elaborate frontage – a series of ramps and sharp concrete steps – is confusing and, for the less mobile, potentially dangerous. As Chris guides Alex carefully into the building her sight dims; her addled rod and cone cells, unable to process light properly, cannot cope with a sudden change from sun to shade. Back come the teasing, shifting shadows through which she can just make out another cat's cradle of ropes criss-crossing the lobby and a couple of small signs she can't read. Chris can't read either, and although there are several people in the various queues watching Alex, no one says a word. She can make out people's outlines but not faces, and scans around until she happens upon what she presumes, by the crackling radio and stance, is a bored security guard.

'Which queue, mate?' she asks.

She waits for a response. After a couple of moments she realises he is pointing.

'Err . . .' She also points, at Chris in his guide-dog harness. 'I'm visually impaired. Pointing is not going to work. You need to use your voice or actually guide me.'

'Yeah?' His voice is slow and suspicious. 'Well, you don't look visually impaired . . . and you saw me.'

'And you don't look learning impaired,' says Alex. 'But how would we know?'

'No need to take that attitude,' he grunts sullenly, yanking her elbow and pulling. She refrains from saying that he also reeks of something ghastly that he probably believes passes as aftershave. Only a man with a job already would be wearing aftershave in here. He hovers while Alex's handbag is screened for weapons and then shunts her along into the main hall.

'Thanks,' she says, breathing shallowly. 'The dog will take it from here.'

As this is an age of reason and enlightenment, Job Central's main hall has been redesigned to encourage and excite the jobless. A large blue-and-orange banner proclaims 'Technical Outcomes for Social Advancement (TOSA) welcomes you to your new career!' Gone are the wipe-down linoleum floors, the booths with the stab-proof glass and the prison-visiting-room decor. Now the hall is rampant with fuzzy orange; the carpets, the lighting and even the Vivaldi being softly excreted from invisible speakers give off a buzzy, greeny-yellow kind of effervescence. Alex heard a rumour the colour has been tested on monkeys, but isn't sure why or what the outcome was. There is a slight acrid smell too. It reminds her of the powdery mould on lemons left too long in the fruit bowl.

The hall is circled by semi-partitioned booths, all quite open-plan, so you can listen to your neighbour being told that their Child Benefit is being axed, or that their CV won't get them into marketing unless they would consider an actual stall in an actual market. And even then they would probably need a maths qualification.

The thick carpet absorbs sound as small groups of people cluster around the electronic exhibition boards advertising jobs and courses. On every desk and table and in racks hanging from every space along the walls are endless leaflets all showing happy, helpful, smiling Job Central staff and radiant, relieved, excited job applicants.

Chris guides Alex to their usual seat. On the seat to her left a young woman is sobbing quietly into her hands. Ignoring her, another woman chews gum, snapping it loudly and waggling a deadly heeled shoe from one foot. A pram is parked between them with a quietly mewling baby. Several men in long green parkas trail the smell of onions and old beer as they circle the seats, as if playing musical chairs.

Alex is early for her appointment and could sit over in the cordoned-off crip area if she wanted. It has better lighting, blue seats and more space. She goes nowhere near it, however, because the 'blue corner' is currently the haunt of Joanna Honey.

Joanna is there now. Alex glances over, peering down her keyhole of clear sight and can make out Joanna's skinny, sway-backed shadow flitting from empty seat to empty seat. Any closer and they would be able to hear her muttering to herself, crying, asking for her mother.

Actually, it was Joanna's poor old mum who stuck her there in the first place. She does so every morning, on the dot of 8 a.m. If the situation wasn't so fucking tragic, it would be a laugh line on social media sites. 'Look how Mrs Honey solved her social care problem! #systempranklol' or something similarly perky.

But in reality it is just more dark shit. Joanna Honey is in her late forties and has severe mental health issues, epilepsy and a tendency to scream and then vomit when she gets anxious. Under the new welfare reforms she has been assessed as 'fit for work' and her Disability Benefit axed. As a consequence of Joanna's new status, her mother's Carer's Allowance has been withdrawn, which means her mother, after forty-seven years of caring full time for Joanna, has had to find paid work, which she has done, part-time for a local cleaning company. Only there is no money for a carer for Joanna, and anyway, Joanna is supposed to be 'actively seeking employment'. It doesn't seem to matter to anyone that Joanna has the mental age of a seven-year-old and is terrified of being out of her bedroom. No one cares.

So, what does the feisty Mrs Honey do? She makes the very sensible decision to drop Joanna off at Job Central every day, and let them look after her.

Alex knows all this because she had been sitting in that very crip area waiting for an interview when Mrs Honey had first brought Joanna in.

'You can't leave her here!' The staff had jumped up and down, wringing their hands, calling for backup.

'You said she should be actively looking for work.' Mrs Honey had waved the brown envelope like a freakin' lottery ticket, her eyes flashing. 'So here she is, "actively looking for work". She is your responsibility now.' At this point Joanna had begun screaming.

'I have to go,' said Mrs Honey over the din, handing a bag of adult nappies and wet wipes to the trembling Job Central liaison manager. 'I'll be back at lunchtime.' And she had scarpered just before Joanna had begun throwing up – and, oh hell, can Joanna project her vomit! It was the most elegant revenge Alex had ever seen.

Only it isn't funny any more. Every morning Joanna's mother drops her off on her way to work. Distraught Joanna is left alone, rocking back and forth on a plastic chair, clutching a little bag with her plastic bottle of apple juice and a couple of flapjacks. After a few minutes she stops keening, and the staff relax and move back to their desks. Only Joanna is stick-thin now and in a constant state of terror and misery.

Her mother isn't faring any better. When Alex first saw Mrs Honey waving that envelope she was magnificent, a tower of passion and righteous fury. Now she is an exhausted shuffler. A head-bowed, back-bowed shuffler. After five hours on her hands and knees cleaning toilets in the university colleges, Mrs Honey picks up her gibbering daughter, who now needs double the care and reassurance, and there is still not enough money to feed them both properly.

Alex had written an article about it, but her editor had axed it at the last minute to go with a story about a local paedophile getting beaten up.

Today Alex has a new motivation and empowerment officer. She is small and plump with a pink face and looks rather sweet, although clearly anxious. She reminds Alex of a white mouse released into its first laboratory maze.

'Good morning. My name's Lucy,' she says and leans over the desk to proffer a hand. 'How are—' Before she completes that sentence she freezes. Already, in her first twenty seconds, she realises she has committed two grave mistakes. One, she has offered to shake Alex's hand. Two, and worse even than that, she has almost asked the client how they are. No, no, no! This is entirely outside of TOSA protocol when dealing with crips. NEVER make physical contact, and NEVER ask them how they are! Apparently this implies interest in the health of the crip client, which could lead to what they call 'negative empathic stereotyping'. Crips by definition have health problems. TOSA does not believe in allowing anyone to dwell on this aspect of the client. Including the client. Positivity is key for the work-shy.

Lucy is still frozen.

'Hi, Lucy. Nice to meet you.' Alex, amused, pretends she hasn't noticed Lucy's extended hand and sits. Lucy glances over her shoulder in case her faux pas has been noticed by her supervisor. It hasn't. She is lucky. She plonks back into her seat and picks up Alex's file.

'Alexandra? Alex? Yes, well, what can I do for you today? According to our records you have a placement already. It says here you saw my colleague Ismail three months ago?'

Ismail, the previous incumbent, had been a delightful and ineffective man who laughed an awful lot and shook his head in a weary 'haven't we seen it all now' kind of way. He had organised Alex her current part-time placement at the local newspaper.

For this, TOSA had received a large wad of cash from the government. If Alex stays in the job for over six months they will get another large payout.

'Is there a problem?' Lucy is rummaging through Alex's file.

'The thing is, Lucy, it is a part-time placement.' Alex leans in, talking low, as if Lucy is a good friend at a bar. 'I am, therefore, still not actually in paid employment. Having previously had actual paid work, I feel I could do a great deal better.'

'Is there a problem?'

Lucy's supervisor has crept up behind her like Nosferatu, only with a clipboard. He doesn't introduce himself but leans over Lucy and picks up Alex's file.

'I am sorry,' Alex says, although she isn't. She is irritated. 'You are reading my file, so you obviously know who I am, but you? You are . . . ?'

He is wearing gold-rimmed spectacles purely so he can glare at people over the top of them. He does so now at Alex.

'My name is Mr Timms, and I am Lucy's supervisor. I see your file is marked with a silver star. That is excellent. We have already been able to place you in work.'

Alex sighs. 'Mr Timms. Lucy. I am in "a placement", i.e. a temporary part-time experience. I did this kind of thing in my sixth form at school. As people who actually work in an employment office, you must be aware that a placement is not a job. It does not actually pay.'

Mr Timms is looking at Alex's CV. She has a lot of qualifications, and this seems to annoy him.

'It says here you had a job with TV Voyager, embedded with the troops in Iraq? In spite of your err . . . ?' He waves vaguely at Alex's face. His tone is suspicious.

She doesn't respond.

'And Channel Fourteen Films . . . goodness, all very glamorous.'

'Not really,' she mumbles, although it had been.

'And now a much sought-after placement with the *Cambright Sun*.'

'Yes, all this I know already,' she says. His eyes flicker up over his glasses again. It's like being poked with a stick.

'Are we going to be having trouble with you, Alex?'

'It's Ms Lyon actually, Mr Timms. I am Alex to my friends. And one of the main problems with the placement is that, because it is part-time, the *Cambright Sun* is not in any way obligated to help me with assistive technology. I really can't use the office computers easily, and so am having to work additional hours, using printers and magnification, from home. So not only is it NOT an actual paid job, but I'm spending additional personal money that I do not have, to stay in the placement. It doesn't make any sense.' Alex's voice is getting a little squeaky. It's not a good sign. Chris rests his muzzle supportively on her knee.

'Have you applied for the Work Learner's Access?'

'That only applies for people under twenty-five,' she says, glaring, *as you well know.*

'The TOSA Empowerment Fund?'

'That is £25 a month. And if I am on that I will no longer be eligible for my Single-Room Supplement.'

'Yes, but every little helps. I don't think rejecting help in your situation is sensible, is it?'

Alex's heart skitters slightly. She knows from bitter experience that rejecting anything TOSA may offer, no matter how ridiculous, will end up in sanctions against other entitlements. She may now have to fill in several more intrusive and upsetting forms and probably go through yet another so-called 'medical' in order to receive £25 a month, which she can't afford to have, because she will then lose her £30 Single-Room Supplement. She rubs Chris's ears, which are cool and silky-smooth. She concentrates on them for a moment.

Mr Timms leans closer over Lucy. Alex doesn't like the way his hand is on Lucy's shoulder. *A wee bit too close to the top of her breast*, she thinks. She can smell his stale-tea breath.

'As you are so well connected in the industry, then perhaps you feel you would like to leave our programme and utilise your own contacts?' His eyes up close are pale blue with a pinky hint of conjunctivitis. He has her file. He knows she cannot go back to her previous workplace. No TV crew is going to take on a blind journalist. He takes pleasure in watching her squirm.

Interesting how some people get off on their little bit of power, thinks Alex. *They may never have met you, know nothing about you, but they will always resort to the Chinese burn, to the pinch, the scratch, the kick in the goolies. I am meeting so many of them these days.*

'I would advise you to stay in your current position, and we will send out the forms for the TOSA Empowerment Fund. I will also then need you to sign a consent form for our medical team to call on you, as and when they have a free booking in their schedule.'

Alex is trapped. She tries once more, ignoring Mr Timms and imploring little Lucy.

'Lucy, could you just check if there are any jobs going in PR or communications . . . perhaps even some teaching I can—'

Timms cuts in. 'Ismail went over that with you. You do not

have teaching qualifications and with your—' here he pauses '—*condition* and the current benefits you are on, I am afraid it would not be in your interests to take on any more hours. You would lose your Housing Entitlement.'

'I know,' Alex says, thinking about wrenching his pen from his hand and ramming it through his pink-rimmed eyes and deep into his brain. She can almost hear the crunching *squelch*. Then again, she realises she can also get to his brain by getting up his nose.

She breathes out and leans back.

'Whatever you think.' Alex smiles widely, expansively, like they are all great friends. 'Mr Timms, I am sure Lucy will learn so much from you. You really know the system, and I just know you will do what is best for me. Thank you so much.'

It is he who flinches now, pretending he hasn't heard Lucy's nervous snort of laughter. He removes his hand from her warm, round and now quivering shoulder. 'Well then. Right. I need you to sign this form.' He plucks some paper from his clipboard.

Alex looks at it. The font is tiny and the page, to her, is a shuddery blur.

'Do you have it in large print?' She is still smiling as if she is in love.

Timms sighs as if Alex has asked him to loan her a month's rent.

'I will have to order a special provision form and pull a large-print permit. In the meantime Lucy will read it to you.'

'I would prefer to—'

Lucy is prodded. 'By signing this form, the client agrees to the terms and conditions,' she begins to drone, and Alex switches off, already knowing it by rote. *I am not going to sign it anyway,* she thinks. It would mean she had signed to having: 1. had a pleasant experience; 2. been treated with respect and competence; and 3. had her current questions on work and benefits answered to her satisfaction.

Mr Timms slides away and Lucy mumbles on; after all, the time-slot allocation is ten minutes and she still has three to fill.

'So, if you could just sign here.' Lucy is holding out a pen and pointing a finger at the form.

'Oh Lucy, thanks.' Alex gets up and pulls the form from under her hand. 'As I said, I never sign anything that I haven't read through myself, as you can of course understand, but I will pop it in the post later today.'

'I don't think we do "post" any more.' Lucy has become pinker. 'Everything has to go through the central computer system. Although it has crashed today . . .'

'Well then, I will scan it and email it.'

'But the form won't have been officially approved. You will be sanctioned—'

As the form has already disappeared into Alex's handbag and she is already standing and moving backwards, Lucy has little choice.

'Thank you for your assistance.'

Startled, but without the steadying hand of her supervisor, Lucy can only shake her head with worry and reiterate that if Alex doesn't send the form in, she won't be able to activate the TOSA Empowerment Fund and could potentially be penalised.

Alex nods, although in her head she is packing a bag and heading to a far-distant country to raise chickens. *Fuck TOSA*.

Introducing The Good Doctor Binding

The Good Doctor Binding is getting a small headache right between the eyes. He puts a thumb on the spot and rubs hard, blinks and squints down at the thick wad of paper on his lap. He is a doctor, for God's sake, not a bloody economist. It is hardly his fault if the projections are off by a few thousand pounds.

The thrumming of the aeroplane all around him is comforting, and in his little well of overhead light, The Good Doctor is beginning to think about shutting his eyes and dozing off for a couple of hours. There is another file to wade through but that would mean getting up and reaching into the overhead locker for his briefcase, and he is tired. He has done three countries in two weeks and is looking forward to having a shit in his own toilet, a glug of his own twelve-year-old malt and a catch-up of his favourite soap opera (a secret obsession that only his very close family will ever know about).

The rest of the cabin is in almost total darkness apart from the flickering movie screens and the occasional reading light. Every few minutes there is a rustle as one of the cabin crew moves deftly down the aisle to attend a passenger. Doctor Binding glances down again at the papers and, noticing a rogue apostrophe, draws a little black circle around it, tutting. 'The *physician's* duty to protect the wider society', in this context. One physician . . . not plural.

A swish of cabin crew again, only this time it stops. He looks up to see a form hanging over him, a female steward tall and stern but with some of her hair leaking out of her once immaculate chignon.

'Excuse me, Dr Binding. I am terribly sorry to disturb you but . . .'

'Yes?' The Good Doctor tries to keep the irritation out of his voice.

'Only we have a . . . situation with one of the passengers.'

Doctor Binding nods without asking another question and gets up. He is The Good Doctor, after all. He stumbles a little, lurching, as his legs remember what to do after five hours in his seat. The steward is fast; her nylon tights rasp as she whisks up to the galley curtains and pulls them apart to let him pass.

It is bright in the galley and the stainless-steel and chrome surfaces glint. On the other side of the tinkling drinks trolley sits a middle-aged man in a T-shirt and jeans. He looks up as the doctor appears and some of the panic in his eyes dissipates. Doctor Binding has that effect on people as, although he is a trim man of medium height, he exudes an air of quiet strength and confidence. He has a handsome, intelligent face, rather piercing light blue eyes and a strong jaw, which he emphasises with a well-groomed, distinguished greying moustache, unfashionable but effective.

As the steward introduces him to the man, Doctor Binding is already assessing the patient. The man looks to be in his forties, Caucasian, not in pain but presenting with a severe facial droop on his left side.

'Don't worry,' he says gently to the man. 'It doesn't look like a stroke to me.'

At this, and delivered by such a man as The Good Doctor, both the patient and the gathered stewards visibly relax.

The doctor smiles, asks the man to raise his arms, then to grimace, wink, raise an eyebrow. He asks a few more questions – *has he had a recent virus, yes; any dizziness or discomfort, no* – and gives a probable diagnosis of a form of facial palsy, possibly Bell's palsy. He recommends seeing the GP back home for a full check-up and a course of steroids. 'But I don't think we need to divert the plane,' he says and all around him are happy grins, half grins from the man, of course, and sighs of relief.

Back in his seat and now wide awake, The Good Doctor Binding is once again staring at the papers on his lap.

'Ah excuse me . . . Doctor?'

He looks up to find the same stern stewardess, now looking a little less tight-lipped.

'Is he all right?'

'Oh yes, sir. We just wanted to thank you very much from all the crew. The captain has said I may offer you some of his personal stash of malt whisky. It's a fifteen-year-old Glenfiddich. May I get you a glass or two?'

'That's very kind,' says The Good Doctor Binding. 'I would be most grateful.

An Invisible Committee

'Could you wear one of these, please, sir?'

The Good Doctor Binding has not yet been home to read his post or kiss his wife. He still has post-flight flatulence and that tight little headache between his eyes, but he doesn't complain. He is being paid more than even he feels comfortable with for this particular jaunt, and so he will suck in his gut and stick on the yellow hard hat and follow the young man through the building site and over the muddy ground to the single Portakabin in the middle of the mess of concrete and scaffolding.

'Up there, sir,' says the young man, pointing to the steps of the cabin. 'They're waiting for you.'

'Thanks,' says The Good Doctor, hefting his briefcase and clambering up.

There are six men and one woman inside the Portakabin already, all seated around a large plastic trestle table and still with their jackets and coats on, although the cabin is warm and smells of glue and coffee. They turn, words clamped behind tight lips, and stare at him as he enters. He doffs his hard hat, impressed by the turnout.

'At last, Dr Binding!' A bald, wide-cheeked man in a blue

bow tie comes forward, arms outstretched. The Good Doctor shakes his hand.

'Afternoon, John,' he says. 'Apologies for being a little late. I had a minor medical emergency to deal with on the flight and just needed to ensure the patient was offloaded safely.'

'Not to worry, not to worry.' The Right Honourable John Thorpe-Sinclair MP wipes his shiny pate with a large blue hanky. 'Let me introduce you to the others. An unnecessary formality in some ways as none of you are "really here".' He uses his pudgy fingers to apostrophise the air. 'And this meeting is not actually happening.'

The Good Doctor Binding recognises many of the figures around the table already. The tall string bean of a fellow is Professor Erwin Bore, Chair of Botany at the South-West Agricultural College Research Centre.

The silver-haired woman in the Chanel suit is Dr Maxine de Crinis, Infectious Diseases Unit, London Institute.

The oafish Julian Hallywooden, an ophthalmologist and brain-stem specialist, is new to him. The man's eyeballs bulge slightly and The Good Doctor guesses Graves' disease. Oddly appropriate for an ophthalmologist.

The baby-faced man in black is his colleague, Professor Fred Pansy: Psychiatry, Royal Manchester Hospital. *He smiles and winks too often*, thinks The Good Doctor. He finds the man a mite sinister. Then there is his close friend, the handsome and warm Warren Hyde, Professor of Law at Ruskin.

'And of course, you know Monsieur Henri Rennes from TOSA,' says John, concluding the introductions.

The Good Doctor shakes hands; some are hot and slightly sticky, others cool and soft. One, Julian Hallywooden's, is a competitive squeeze and grind. The Good Doctor suppresses a wince. The Monsieur with the thick black hair and manicured fingernails gives him a knowing nod.

'Right, all present and correct. Please take a seat and let's begin this extraordinary meeting of the . . . well, what shall we call ourselves?' says Thorpe-Sinclair, as the men and woman settle into their plastic seats.

'Do we need a name at all?' asks Maxine.

'I think it helps us with focus. I had jotted one down earlier . . . hold on. Yes, here.' The minister pulls a scrap of paper from his waistcoat. 'How about the UK Co-operative for Hospitals and Nursing Homes, or UKCHNH?'

'Does that cover my rehabilitation centre?' asks Pansy with a wink and a smile.

'Yes, of course.'

'I like it.'

'Just for the moment, then.'

And that is that. The bundle of eminents are 'officially' named. As there will be no records of this meeting, no minutes, no texts, no invoices for expenses, no imprints of lipstick on coffee cups or muddy smears from Italian loafers, it matters little to them what they are called. But the Rt Hon. MP is right. It does help with focus . . . and focus they do.

As a specialist in liver disease and alcohol-related cancer, The Good Doctor Binding has treated hundreds of men and women and even, traumatically, children as young as eleven. For the past three years he has been working on the dilemma of providing medical care to chronic alcoholics, many of whom have become homeless, in part due to their addiction. Things have escalated for the 'chronics' with the welfare cuts. There has been a spout, a gush, a torrent, now, of people falling into impossible debt, being evicted and made homeless. The new lot of street people are different from the human detritus of the past thirty years. Now the newly evicted are couples and families with different needs requiring different responses from the beleaguered government and councils. The old guard of rotting-livered hobos were finding their patches invaded by hungry, confused people who needed – demanded – greater attention. The Good Doctor Binding had been tasked with separating the old guard of repeat-offender alcoholic homeless and 'solving their particular problems'. He, in collaboration with Fred Pansy, had started by setting up the first experimental 'therapy' unit at the Royal Manchester Hospital. They had called it 'Homeless Action!'.

'And these are the results of my research,' he says proudly, and lays down the folder with 'CDD' written in black on the cover. 'The "CDD" on this file cover stands for "Clearance, Disinfection and Disposal", which will soon become clear. The local trials have been successful, and we are ready to move forward, to widen coverage. In short, we can escalate, and quickly.' There is a pause as the copies of the file are circulated, shuffled and pages turned.

John Thorpe-Sinclair clears his throat. 'I am sure I don't have to remind you all that these files do not leave this room . . . there is a shredding machine in the corner.'

Does The Good Doctor truly understand the consequences of his actions? He had purported to be morally outraged when TOSA and the Department for Work and Pensions conspired to 'delay' medicals for the new and repeat Chronic Condition Benefit applicants. 'I am morally outraged,' he had blustered, and yet . . .

And yet he had understood the basic economic argument. The argument ran thus: the European Union quoted thirteen weeks as being a fair time between application and medical assessment for the Chronic Condition Benefit. During the time they were waiting to be medically assessed, applicants, or 'malingerers' as John Thorpe-Sinclair called them, would be on the lowest level of Job Strivers' Benefit. If the medical went in the applicant's favour, they could end up receiving nearly triple the Job Strivers' Benefit by being moved into the Chronic Condition Benefit category, and this was very costly. Too costly.

TOSA has already, and quite deliberately, developed an almost incoherent tick-box system of which Monsieur Rennes, its CEO, is very proud – insisting it ensures that over 70 per cent of applicants fail at the first hurdle: the form-filling. The form is indeed a masterpiece of waspish misinformation, running to at least fifty pages of questions ranging from such banalities as 'Can you lift a cup?' and 'Can you wash yourself?' to 'Given the choice to work, even from your own bed, would you do so?' As many people could lift a cup occasionally and wash themselves a little and would love to work, even if their illness or disability caused them to be unable, they would tick 'yes'. A 'yes', even just one, on any part of the monstrous form would guarantee an immediate FAIL. And yet, still some people were managing to find a way through the red tape and wangle themselves onto the higher amount of benefit. And worse even than that, almost 90 per cent of the FAILs went to their doctors and appealed, and in court TOSA decisions were usually ruled as 'unfair' and overturned.

Appeals cost. Chronic Condition Benefit costs. These useless, economically unviable scroungers cost.

John Thorpe-Sinclair and Henri Rennes had put to a panel – very similar to this one – that they could save money and minimise the irritating issue of appeals by extending the time between application and assessment indefinitely, say eleven months or twelve, by which time the applicant would either die – depending on the severity of their condition or disability – or be forced to find other sources of income. No one, especially someone with extra care needs, could really survive on the basic Job Strivers' Benefit . . . especially with children, not in the long term.

This 'extension' between application and medical had been approved and had indeed saved hundreds of thousands of pounds already. Malingerers died naturally, or by suicide, by the dozen, and many more just disappeared out of the system entirely. Thorpe-Sinclair was extremely proud of himself, but it wasn't enough. Not by a long shot. And so they had approached The Good Doctor.

The Good Doctor had searched his soul. He had taken the Hippocratic Oath and felt he had a firm grasp of medical ethics. What Thorpe-Sinclair and Rennes were suggesting meant that many people with genuine medical needs would potentially die before receiving the benefit they were entitled to. On the other hand, The Good Doctor had seen hundreds of his patients commit virtual suicide by refusing to take his advice or the advice of any health professional. Time after time, the same patient would stagger in to his surgery, a little more yellow, still smoking, still obese, still moaning about how the medication made them queasy when in reality it was the ghastly diet and the litres of cheap vodka they were guzzling. He found their deliberate ignorance interesting but exhausting and perhaps, he thought, Rennes and the idiot Thorpe-Sinclair had a point. It couldn't hurt, anyway. Not really. These people were unlikely to be much missed.

'The CDD initiative seems to me to be both kind and practical,' says The Good Doctor Binding to the faces around the table. And the faces blink and nod. 'Ward B in Grassybanks Residential Home is already welcoming new clients, and we open Ward C this summer.'

Switch Gets Fed, and Alex Gets Suspicious

The underpass connects several main roads by a series of concrete tunnels beneath the main Newtonmarket Road roundabout. The tunnels converge on a central hexagon, open to the sky, and at the centre of this is a raised flowerbed and an enormous street light. More raised beds with thick bushes line its edges and there has been an attempt to make it slightly less of an eyesore, with tiled murals in the tunnels and several benches nailed down for weary commuters to sit on and eat their lunch. Up above, traffic booms in endless thundering circles, round and round, but down below – in an interesting quirk of acoustics – it is relatively quiet. Alex uses the underpass several times a day, and it can be a little disorienting as each tunnel entrance looks exactly the same as the others, but comes out at a different road junction. She is reliant on Chris remembering which is which . . . although, strangely, they often end up on the park side and not the town side. Wicked dog.

Today, Chris has frozen right in the middle and is not moving.

'What is it, boy?' asks Alex, scanning around with her tunnel of sight for movement or blurry shapes. She can't see anyone else down here. Opposite them something in the bushes makes a small whining noise. Chris's tail had flattened but now it is up and waving. He makes a low growl in the back of his throat; warning, and yet calling. *Another dog*, thinks Alex. And she is right.

'What's wrong with you?' Chris is asking, because although he knows the other dog, her scent is somehow wrong. She usually carries the scents of road tar, alcohol, cigarette smoke and vomit on her coat – none of which are her smells but those of her feeder, Phil. Her own deeper smell is an orangey brown, warm and sunny with iron blue running through it. She is a very loyal dog, but fierce. But today the orange is greyer, and the iron blue of her is thin and faded. She smells like half of the dog she was. Chris barks for her to come out of the bushes and feels Alex jump.

'Shit . . . Chris!'

'I don't want to be seen,' says the other dog. 'Oh, but I am hungry, hungry, hungry. Afeared. I quake.'

Chris, being a dog, must bare his teeth at weakness. It is essential because weak is close to mad and must be dominated or it will bite. He draws his lips back and flattens his tail again. 'Come out!' he demands.

And she does, fast, slinking from underneath the bushes and running across their path, pausing for a single moment to show deference to Chris and then dashing over to the far side of the hexagon, tail tucked beneath her legs, ears and muzzle flat almost to the ground. She cowers and whines. 'So sad, so hungry, so empty.'

'Switch? Is that you?' Alex has recognised the German shepherd bitch. 'Oh my God, you poor old girl!'

She signals Chris into a down and stay, laying his lead across his back, then moves slowly over to the shivering dog. She knows that Switch belongs to Phil, one of the homeless men who use the underpass to drink, brawl and sleep in. Alex likes Phil. He is a good-natured drunk with a quick wit and he loves his dog. Alex likes Switch too, but is wary of her. Switch has always seemed a gregarious, sweet-natured beast. She played with Chris with no trouble, but life on the street is tough, and the dogs are often protection as well as companionship. Phil and Switch are a good team, and Alex has never seen Switch looking scrawny or dirty, but now, as she gets closer, she can see the dog is filthy and her ribs are obvious through her ragged coat.

'Switch?' she says in a low voice and kneels close to the dog, extending her hand with one of Chris's disgusting fishy treats. It doesn't take long before Switch has taken the bait, and Alex is able to catch hold of the string around her neck. Switch is still shivering as Alex gently moves her hands over the dog's legs, back, head and abdomen. She can feel no breaks, finds no blood, but the dog is malnourished and terrified. *How could Phil leave you like this?* she thinks, but Alex knows that Phil would never have left Switch like this. Something is very wrong here.

It isn't hard to get Switch to follow them, although by the time they are back at Alex's flat there are almost no treats left. Alex wonders if Switch will come inside, but the dog doesn't hesitate, following on Chris's tail. She heads straight to Chris's water bowl and drinks and drinks until it is almost empty.

'Don't make yourself sick, Switch,' says Alex. She looks over at Chris who is sitting very upright, holding his sheep toy, Myrtle, in his gob and watching Switch quite calmly. *OK then. Two dogs.*

She thinks *What the hell happened to Phil?*

Homeless Action!

The night shelter, more commonly known as The Station, is wreathed in scaffolding like the rest of the city. It used to be a huge old church and still hulks over the main West Road as if about to slam a Bible down upon the city in evangelical pique. The land and buildings are owned by the Church and a group of wealthy trustees who, for over thirty years, have been providing a sanctuary for the homeless of Cambright. Last time Alex visited she was following up a story about a group of trafficked Romanian men who had been conned into believing they would be part of a work team and had instead ended up abandoned and passport-less, living in the graveyard behind Turton Street. That had been over four years ago, and of course by now those men would have been rounded up and sent to the offshore holding rigs. Cheaper than trying to repatriate them. They had been better off in the graveyard.

Back then, The Station had offered the Romanians and the other assorted transient folk an evening meal and a spare bed when one became free. Then, they had room for thirty people and three dogs based on the level of the emergency. There was also access to legal help, advice and information services, and various useful workshops, mostly based around self-esteem and

CV writing. There was a regular GP/care assistant (and vet), and access to clean needles, condoms and more.

That was back then. Four years is a long time in politics.

No longer would that have been an option for the Romanians, or for any other immigrants, illegal or otherwise. 'Foreigners' were no longer allowed access to charity. This was made very clear by the ban on any published leaflet or general information offered in any language other than English. *If you cannot read it, write it or speak it, then you shouldn't be here.* And so say all of us, quoth, in effect, the Lord Chancellor. The Believe in Better campaigners now made regular sweeps of all the shelter- and food-based charities for this seditious literature, or for anyone with a foreign accent mooching around looking like they were freeloading. Men, women and children 'hanging around' food banks and emergency shelters who couldn't respond appropriately to the question 'Where are you from?' were usually roughed up a little and then handed over to the new private H5 police force with their exceptionally silly sci-fi uniforms. The H5 police force had made a request that the campaigners listen carefully to the accents before embarking on these so-called 'shakedowns'. Every week they were having to apologise to the Welsh.

'Even leaving migrants out of the picture, the housing situation is hopeless,' says Glenda, the on-duty manager. It is three days since Alex and Chris took in Switch and now they are all looking for more answers at The Station. Glenda is giving Alex the tour, accompanying it with a stream of facts from the front line. 'Most of the country's council accommodation tenants are in rent arrears, and the eviction rate is running at over five hundred a week in Cambright alone. Ironically, many of the desperate find occasional work as bailiffs. There is money to be made in repossession.'

Alex gleans from Glenda that in response to the current situation, The Station has expanded to engulf the little park that had stood to its left. No more an avenue of trees and a children's play area. Now there are cheaply built four-storey stacks. Each stack has sixteen one-bedroom, single-bathroom, airless and unheated 'sections' on each floor. There is no kitchen as all meals must be taken in the main hall. Every stack is rammed full of families recently evicted following the last welfare slashes to Housing Benefit. The far-left stack is for single parents under twenty-five. Any woman with only one child is required to share. There is a waiting list for every bed, and more often now than ever the beds are released in the single-parent block by sickness or prison sentence.

'We are trying to get a laundry block built,' says Glenda. 'I can hardly bear to watch the young mothers trying to cope with just juggling nappies. You know, they can only stay in their rooms during the day if the baby is under six months. Otherwise they have to vacate at 9 a.m. and can only get back in mid-afternoon.'

'Seems terribly harsh,' says Alex.

'It's the contract. We are an emergency shelter but not a permanent place to stay. They must keep moving, looking. It is absolutely heartbreaking.'

The sun is blasting down, crisping up the dusty litter, as Alex, Chris and Switch trot along beside Glenda through the walkway between the stacks.

'What about the old homeless guard? Phil and the rest of that gang?'

'Most of them aren't around any more. Haven't been for a while. Phil, though . . . I can't remember when I last saw him here . . .'

Glenda is short and tough, her skin blue with tattoos and glinting with piercings. Her eyes are tawny-lion-coloured. Alex cannot tell her age, and has never asked. She guesses forty-odd.

'I am pretty sure Phil was one of the recruits,' says Glenda.

'Recruits?' *Seems a funny word to use*, thinks Alex.

'I must say, I am really surprised he left Switch behind. He was totally doolally about her.' Glenda pauses to rub Switch's ears and slide a hand down her muzzle. 'Poor old thing. I've never seen her looking so skinny. Phil always took such good care of her.'

They are heading over to the main building. It's nearly lunch-time and the queues are forming, fanning out across the concrete pathway relatively calmly, heads down, concentrating on not making eye contact. A young woman in a cami top and shorts clambers on to the back of her boyfriend but there isn't much laughter. 'Geroff me,' he says and shakes her off.

A toddler grabs Chris's tail. He turns to the boy, smelling confusion and an endless weary hunger. Switch growls a question, which the kid misunderstands as a warning. The little boy starts crying.

'What's with the fucking dogs, Glennie?' asks the toddler's mother, flushed, but not with heat. Red blossoms of booze-related rosacea on her cheeks, her nose, her chest. In the woman's hand is a can of what smells to Chris like old apples and the detergent used in the public toilets.

'No booze in the main hall, Shirley.' Glenda points at the can.

'You know the drill. This way, Alex. We'll go in around the back and I'll get some water for the dogs.'

'Maybe he didn't mean to leave her . . . or she got separated from him.' Alex is pondering on Switch while Glenda pops on the kettle and pours water into a large plastic tray for the dogs. They are squeezed into the little office behind reception, which smells strangely of sharpened pencils – a nice woody, metallic combination.

'I don't know for sure.' Glenda is twisting one of several nose rings. 'I think he was with a bunch of the old guys who were taken for the specialist rest and recuperation project in Manchester.'

'What? Manchester?'

'Yeah . . . I know it's a bit weird but it kind of makes sense. In just the last eighteen months we've lost a third of our funding and been completely inundated with newly evicted families – I mean whole bloody families – mothers with two or three kids, parents with new babies. It's bloody nuts, and of course anyone with children is priority. And it is so fucking hot! People are turning up with dehydration, babies foaming at the mouth. We just aren't able to give the old guard the care they need, and this new scheme is supposed to take the weight off us. Hang on, I'll call Donnie. He knows all about it.'

She picks up the phone and dials, and in moments a slight, grey-haired man in black trousers and short-sleeved black shirt appears at the reception desk and calls into the office.

'Hey Glenda. What's up?'

Rev. Donnie. He has the pale, slightly greasy look of a man who does a lot of night shifts, and he brings with him the waft of endless saucepans of cheap mincemeat. With mugs of tea, Donnie, Glenda and Alex hunker down on stools around the small office table. It is Donnie who tells Alex about Homeless Action!.

'They used to just run simple national awareness-raising campaigns,' he says. 'Been around for . . . well . . . certainly over five years. I knew one of the original volunteers. When I last spoke to him, eighteen months ago, he told me they had secured a really big grant. The money was for both Homeless Action! and their sister charity, St Mark's Hospice, a palliative care unit set up by a doctor called . . . um . . . Binding, I think. I didn't hear any more from him until we got half a ton of Homeless Action! flyers and a request to hand them out to our clients. Glenda, do we have any left?'

Glenda nods and steps carefully over the two sprawling dogs to open the filing cabinet.

Donnie continues, 'They were recruiting for volunteers for a new treatment centre and seemed especially interested in long-term addicts, long-term homeless with mental health problems, you know, chronic homeless, derelicts, the old guard as you call them, like Phil.'

A new treatment centre? Alex is surprised. 'I don't remember hearing anything about it at the *Cambright Sun*.'

Donnie shrugs noncommittally as Glenda returns and slaps down a leaflet.

Alex squints at it through her heavy magnifying specs. There is almost no information on it – a couple of phone numbers, a strapline 'Help us to help you!' and lots of dull photos of clean single rooms and smiling men and women sitting in what looks like a sunny refectory.

'They came down to collect recruits several times.' Donnie taps the flyer. 'We never really knew when but we are always so busy here it was hard to keep tabs.'

'The address is the St Mark's Hospice in Manchester,' says Alex. 'Why would local homeless allow themselves to be taken all that way on such a vague promise?'

'There was a rumour . . .' Glenda is stroking Switch's head and won't meet Alex's eyes, 'that there was to be some remuneration.'

'They were bribing them? Did you tell anyone?'

Glenda raises her leonine eyes and stares directly into Alex's brown ones. 'Who would we tell, Alex? Who cares?'

'I am surprised Phil went,' says Donnie into the tense silence. 'He really wasn't keen, especially as he wasn't able to take Switch.'

'How many of them were selected?' asks Alex. 'Who went?'

'They picked up a group last month but I couldn't tell you exactly who. Phil and his pals haven't been coming here much lately. There just isn't the space for them any more and so, to be frank, Homeless Action! may be able to help more than we can. Also, it does mean we can concentrate on the new lot. And speaking of . . . I best get back to the hall.'

There is a crowd forming at reception now, and first in line is a man with his arm around a woman who is sobbing her eyes out, her arms a griddled mass of fresh scars. They look like they should be in a hospital emergency room, not at a shelter.

'Err, I'll leave you to it,' says Alex, watching Glenda begin to process the latest group of desperate people.

'Oh, hang on . . . before you go.' Glenda has an odd, hopeful expression on her face. 'Switch?'

Switch looks up at the sound of her name, her tail wagging.

'Could Switch stay with me here, do you think? I mean, she is such a gorgeous girl, and it might be nice for some of the younger clients. Phil used to encourage the kids to play with her.'

Switch wags her tail harder and whimpers softly. She can hear the sweet tone in Glenda's request.

'And you know, when Phil gets back she'll be here.'

'Of course!' Alex is hugely relieved. She had been thinking her next stop would have to be the Dog Rescue Centre, and that wasn't always a good place for a dog like Switch to end up.

Chris nudges Switch and growls a goodbye. 'Nice human choice,' he says. 'Smells less mouldy than your last one.'

Alex Looks for Snakes to Poke

At the flat, Alex calls both the numbers on the leaflet and leaves short messages at the electronic peep when no one answers. She types 'Homeless Action!' into the search engine and scans down through the results. New housing initiatives on the west coast, insurance companies, anti-anxiety self-help groups . . . but no private medical project that she can see. She wonders if the staff at The Station had heard it right. She tries a different angle, trawling through the government web pages, scrolling down, up, sideways, but no Homeless Action!

She stretches and clenches and unclenches her sweaty feet, wishing she could afford a fan. Chris snores loudly, whimpers softly, asleep in his dog bed in the corner. Alex watches him for a while. His muzzle is getting greyer, and he has two more long white whiskers. For a moment Alex feels The Fear. The Possible Loss of Chris. The feeling drives her quickly into the kitchen towards the fridge, and while she is reaching for the cheap vodka and an ice cube, she has an idea.

Back at the computer she types in 'TOSA', 'St Mark's Hospice' and 'Homeless Action!', and there it is.

'TOSA are pleased to announce that the Social Initiative Grant, in collaboration with government departments and local authorities, has been awarded to St Mark's Hospice and their Homeless Action! initiative, implemented as part of the wider Care and Protect Act.'

And that is all it says. When she clicks on Homeless Action! she is just redirected to the full text version of the Care and Protect Act. There is no other information about the project, no leads to any one person behind it and, in fact, no real information on what it actually is.

Strange.

She looks up the detail on the Care and Protect Act. Once again, up comes a link to the TOSA website, but no more information on Homeless Action!

'Curiouser and curiouser,' says Alex.

She picks up the phone.

'You have reached the TOSA head offices. Please dial the extension of the person you require, or wait and an operator will be with you as soon as possible.'

Bloody Vivaldi again, thinks Alex as tinny hold muzak floats wearily up into the handset. She waits.

Eventually there is a click and, 'Hello. My name is Jill. How may I help you?'

'Hi Jill. Would you be able to put me through to someone who knows about the Homeless Action! group?'

'I am sorry?'

'The Homeless Action . . . ?'

'Do you know what department that group would be under? I am not aware of having seen it listed here.'

Alex can hear something defensive in the woman's tone. 'It is an initiative you, TOSA, are running with the government,' she says, exasperated. 'It has something to do with the implementation of the Care and Protect Act.'

'Oh, my apologies, but anything to do with that is being handled through our Manchester offices. I can give you a number. Do you have a pen?'

She rattles off a number and Alex just manages to jot it down.

Alex dials Manchester and again gets an earful of electronic Vivaldi, but this time broken up with a voice repeating, 'We are sorry, but all our agents are busy at the moment. Please call back at another time.' After three attempts she hangs up.

She looks up John Thorpe-Sinclair MP, the minister who introduced the Care and Protect Act, dials a number and eventually speaks to a cold, clipped voice that alleges to be that of his secretary.

'I was hoping to speak to the Minister about the Homeless Action! initiative,' says Alex.

'If you send an email enquiry, he will get back to you when he returns from his holiday next week.'

'Is there anyone else I could talk to?'

'Have you tried calling the offices of TOSA Central?'

'Yes—'

'Well, I am sure you have all the information you require, then. Good day.'

The line is cut. Alex sits back, sips her drink from the cracked mug and thinks *stonewall*. The pips go on the radio, signalling the six o'clock news. Drought tops the bill, accompanied by hosepipe bans across the country, record temperatures, crops failing, war in dark places, bankers' bonuses getting bigger. Same old, same old. And don't forget yet another Cabinet reshuffle.

The Right Hon. Stella Binding MP has become the new Secretary for Health and Social Care.

Alex taps 'Stella Binding' into the search engine, then waits. The photo that pops up is of a very attractive middle-aged woman wearing a cleverly subtle suit that cleaves to her in all the right places without being gratuitous. Her hair is twisted up in a bun and her earrings are pearl, make-up minimal. In the picture she has been caught by the photographer as she is getting out of the back of a limo. Behind her, still in the shadow of the car, is a man. Alex pushes up the magnification. And then quickly pushes it up again. Her heart twists as the darkly handsome face of the Poet stares back at her.

Hastily, she scans the article. Stella Binding and her husband, the writer and poet, Gunter Gorski.

Wow, thinks Alex. *Gunter is it, you toad? You cheated on Stella Binding?* She can't quite catch her breath for the memory of his hands on her body and the messy dismissal in the morning. *Her fault? His fault?*

Her eyes flit briefly over the article beneath the photo. It covers Stella's stellar career, her love of horse riding, skiing and philanthropy and the fact she is a committed Tory to the bone. There was a previous unsuccessful marriage to another MP, but no children. A miscarriage is hinted at. Her father is the eminent Dr Barnabas Binding, OBE. She is ambitious and intelligent, and the prime minister expects great things from her.

Dr Binding. Dr Binding? Now where has Alex heard that name before? Or has she seen it? 'Think, damn you!' she hisses to herself. Chris wakes and yawns widely, and, seeing Alex sitting squinting at the magnified print on the computer screen, plods over and puts his head on her knee. *Didn't Reverend Donnie say something about a Binding being behind St Mark's Hospice? Could it be the same man?*

Her inbox dings. It is another email from Gerald, editor of the *Cambright Sun*. 'Where is my copy, Alex? By 8 p.m. or else.'

Fuck. She trudges to the fridge for another bolt of vodka and does her homework, the promised article.

WHY WORK WORKS
A Cambright mum has turned her life around after being told by her daughter that she was 'a lazy pig and fit for nothing'

Jade Dunn, 35, a mum from Bales Hay Street, Cambright, has turned her life around following a fight with her daughter Kylie. Ms Dunn, who had previously been living off benefits for over ten years, had told social workers, doctors and the Benefit Agency that she had been suffering from depression and anxiety and was not able to work. Her daughter Kylie, now 15, had a different point of view. She told her mum that it was time to 'change her life around', and that she was 'ashamed' of her mother, who she accused of being a 'lazy pig and fit for nothing'.

'I knew I had to take myself in hand,' said Ms Dunn. 'I couldn't let Kylie down.'

Ms Dunn started by volunteering with a local charity, and after six months she applied for, and got, the assistant manager placement she had dreamed of. Now she is working full-time and loving every moment.

'I would never have got off my couch if Kylie hadn't shouted at me that day,' Ms Dunn told the *Cambright Sun*. 'I am so grateful to have my life back. Work definitely works!'

Alex feels nauseous as she finishes the article and slams it over to Gerald's inbox. In fact, Ms Dunn was still struggling with depression and anxiety, further complicated by exhaustion and what looked like the beginnings of a Parkinsonian shake. Having spent a couple of hours with her in the miserable dark second-hand shop she was now managing, Alex had a suspicion that the woman wouldn't make it through another six months. She had stood in the back room, tearful, shivering like a beaten dog, telling Alex what a wonderful thing it had been to be screamed at by her daughter. 'You sure you want me to say she called you "a lazy pig"?' Alex had asked.

'Yes, yes!' Ms Dunn had bitten her already frayed lips. 'I was. I was a lazy pig. Kylie was right. And look at me now! Work definitely works!'

Alex sighs, feeling like a complete bitch. It was a mean article and badly written to boot, but these articles were her contracted requirements. She has been commissioned to write ten of these ridiculous pieces for the paper as, to quote the brief given to Gerald by the *Cambright Sun*'s owners: 'a counterbalance to the negative portrayal of the current welfare changes'. It wasn't journalism, as far as Alex was concerned, but if it got Gerald and Job Central off her back and allowed her to carry on investigating Homeless Action! and Phil's vanishing act, then she would compromise. There were only three more to do anyway: the disabled war veteran, now Paralympian and sports coach; the ex-junkie who was now a veterinary nurse ('off the record, great access to product,' she had nodded to Alex); and the ex-con who was now a parole officer with the H5 Police Group plc.

Alex glugs more cheap vodka. She had decided, looking at the remnants of change in her purse, that she wanted to drink more than eat this evening, but now her stomach hurts and she feels a bit foolish. She'll have a bad hangover in the morning, and she is supposed to be covering the opening of the flower festival at St Bartholomew's Church. Funds are being raised for the opening of the new Grassybanks extension. Another ward, apparently . . . as if the place wasn't monstrous enough. Alex had gone to the exhibition of the proposed extension at the Town Hall the previous year. It had been impressive: blueprints, billboards and a intricate model Grassybanks of the Future under glass, surrounded by trees with the river curving past.

She wonders what else had been in the running for that bit of land by the river and her fingers clip and trip over the keyboard. There had been three other proposals: a library and café, a skateboard park and a crematorium had all been put to the council, but the Grassybanks extension had won outright. No surprises there.

But wait. Again, she ups the magnification on her screen. *That's odd.* The scanned proposal of the underground crematorium has not got a formal rejection stamp on it like the others. *A mistake?* She sits back for a minute, brain fizzing, and then leans in and clicks on the Grassybanks proposal again. She can't be sure without printing both of the blueprints out, but it looks like Grassybanks has incorporated the crematorium into the east wing of its car park. They haven't called it crematorium although it is in the same place and the dimensions are all the same. They have listed it as an 'Underground Extension'.

Oh well, maybe it's for storage . . . ?

She goes to the St Bartholomew's Church community page to check the times for the opening ceremony and sees that the doctor in charge of overseeing the new Grassybanks extension will be there answering questions. She blinks and her mouth drops open.

His name: Dr Barnabas Binding.

A Bouquet for Dr Binding

As it transpires, it is Dr Binding who sees Alex first. He is being harangued by the mayor's consort, a vile woman called Clarissa, who has fastened onto him like a tick. She is waving a bouquet of lilies in his face, and he is trying not to sneeze, although his eyes are beginning to water. Knowing his tendency to choke up around pollen, he is loaded up with antihistamine, but he still breathes shallowly and mentally crosses his fingers that he will make it through his speech. Why on earth did he agree to a flower show, for heaven's sake?

A bearded roadie is checking the podium acoustics. 'One-two, one-two,' he breathes into the mike, and feedback screeches, causing the entire church hall to flinch. At that moment Binding catches sight of a tall, attractive woman with long, dark, frizzy hair pulled back into a high ponytail that swings almost insolently down between her shoulder blades. She seems to tower over the mass of geriatric flower-pushers milling about the echoing hall, her broad shoulders and voluptuous bosom encased in a tight white shirt. *Amazonian*, thinks Dr Binding. The crowd breaks for her, and it is only then that Binding spots the guide dog. *Interesting, she doesn't look blind*, he thinks, shuffling through the possible retinal malfunctions he knows about.

Clarissa is whining about this year's drought causing havoc with her *Pelargonium nubilum*. Her sour face is ripped through with anguish. The woman seems to Binding to be in a constant state of crisis and fury. If it isn't the flowers or the weather, it is the economy, the scroungers and the layabouts who seem to ruin her city. She rarely pauses for breath and is completely uninterested in anyone else.

'. . . as I was saying, Doctor, the ground is just so hard now that my husband nearly did his back in . . .'

Over her shoulder, Binding sees the tall woman stoop to ask one of the stallholders a question. The stallholder, an elderly man with enormous lupins, looks directly up at Binding and points. The woman asks again, this time making an obvious sweeping gesture over her eyes, and the man, realising his mistake, speaks into her ear, then grudgingly offers her an arm. She refuses. She turns her face towards the doctor and says a word to her dog, and they move directly forward in The Good Doctor's direction.

'Excuse me,' she says as she closes on the tense back of the still querulous Clarissa, 'I am looking for a Dr Barnabas Binding?'

'You have found him, my dear,' says the doctor and, reaching past Clarissa, takes her proffered hand. For a moment he almost kisses it, then catches himself, feeling foolish. She is quite the most attractive flower in the building, though.

'Dr Binding is very busy, I am afraid, young lady.' Clarissa, sensing The Good Doctor's change of focus, doesn't want to let go. 'He is about to open the flower show.'

'It's all right, Clarissa,' Binding soothes. 'How can I help you . . . Miss . . . ?'

'Alex. Alexandra Lyon. I am a reporter with the local newspaper, the *Cambright Sun*.'

A journalist. Dr Binding's lips and sphincter tighten. Of course, there will be journalists, he tells himself. It is part of the process. It's all manageable, all fine. She will be here for the flower festival and the ward extension.

'You will be here about the flower festival and the ward extension,' he tells her. 'It's a very exciting day. I am not actually organising any of this, of course. I just felt duty bound to come and personally thank the wonderful fundraisers.'

'That's good of you, Dr Binding. I am sure you are a very busy man, what with working with St Mark's Hospice and now taking on Grassybanks. It is a huge project, I gather? Another ward being built, and I heard a rumour there was an underground extension . . .'

How on earth did she hear about that? The Good Doctor is cross but doesn't show it.

'We are all very proud of Grassybanks,' he says. 'An absolutely state-of-the-art rehabilitation and high-care residence. Have you had a chance to look around? I will be leading a tour after this for the Mayor's Committee, if you would like to join us?'

The woman is almost the same height as him. Her eyes are dark brown, so dark one can barely make out the pupils. Long lashes. She doesn't seem to blink very much. He also notices that her eyes are slightly bloodshot, the skin beneath a little too dark and yes, her hand trembles ever so slightly. *Ahh*, he thinks. *Likely one of my alcoholic flock. What a shame.*

'Dr Binding . . . it is a bit of a long shot, but with your connection to the St Mark's Hospice in Manchester and so forth . . . well, I was just wondering if you had heard of the Homeless Action! initiative. Some kind of therapeutic experiment for transients?'

And there it is. Binding's forehead goes cold, and his ears get hot.

'I beg your pardon?' He is trying to think of what to say.

'It's just a friend of ours, a homeless man called Phil, was apparently selected by them for specialised treatment in Manchester, and now he can't be found anywhere. I tried calling the Manchester link number that had been left but I couldn't get through.'

'Dr Binding!' Clarissa is back, and for once Binding is pleased to see her. 'Dr Binding, you are being called, I'm afraid.' She has grabbed his elbow and is actually pulling him towards the stage. Binding takes Alex's hand again, a short, hard shake this time.

'It was lovely meeting you, my dear, and good luck with your research and finding your friend . . . Phil, did you say his name was? I am sure he'll turn up. And do take a tour of Grassybanks. I am sure you will get a great deal from it.'

Alex watches him as he is shuffled like a card back into the pack of city councillors and church committee members on the stage. Alex, in spite of her degenerating eyesight, can still see the colour red. In fact, it is almost the only colour she can still see clearly, and so she did not fail to notice The Good Doctor's ears light up like beacons when she had mentioned Homeless Action! He knows something, that's for sure.

She and Chris stand through the next half an hour of speeches and presentations, lost in thought. A homeless man, a new but secret therapy and a doctor, an expert on alcohol-related disease and a partner of TOSA . . . what were all the connections? Her pocket is vibrating, and she reaches in for her phone. It's Glenda from The Station.

'Hold on, Glenda, I can't hear you. I'll just go outside and call you straight back.'

Outside in the graveyard, Alex pauses and unharnesses Chris before dialling.

'What's up, Glenda?'

'It's Phil.'

'Phil? He's back?'

'No. No . . . err . . . apparently he is dead.'

Alex Joins the Dots

The *Cambright Sun* offices are up a twisty flight of stairs littered with boxes of paper, trailing electronic kit and other detritus that somehow Chris has to steer Alex around. On the second floor the office is more than a little cramped. Desks rammed up against desks; whiteboards, flip charts and storyboards flapping down from every partition. All the staff hot-desk, and only the editor has his own office. This makes life difficult for Alex, with her visual impairment that requires large-print text and magnification software. Every time she stumbles in she has to find an empty desk and redo the settings on the monitor. Today she is in luck. Half the team are out and the rest have parked themselves by open windows in search of some respite from the heat.

She gets a muted 'Hey Alex!' from her friend Terry as he squeezes past with another stack of slippery posters. 'Fancy a drink, later?'

'Yeah, that would be good.' Alex has known Terry for years. Back in the eighties he had been a roadie working with one of the bands Alex had been sleeping her way through. Later, disillusioned by the rise of 'instant-pop TV', he had retrained in IT. Now he works as a technician for the *Cambright Sun*, and it had been Terry who had suggested the newspaper to Alex as a possible job placement. She tries not to hold it against him.

Chris loves Terry and his tail helicopters in adoration. This is because Terry is not only a deeply gentle soul, but also because he has nowhere to hang out his washing apart from in the kitchen where he fries or reheats all his food. He never lets the clothes dry properly, so even ironed and folded they still stink of mushrooms and old onions. And he doesn't wash as often as most, but does change his pants every day, which Chris feels is a shame as he has a particular warm 'den' smell that Chris is very fond of.

'Can't talk now, boy,' says Terry, disappearing through another door, 'but we'll hook up later.'

It is very hot up on the office floor. All the windows are open and there are several desk fans churning up the warm air. Chris's tail wilts, and Alex's hair becomes sticky and frizzy. She sweeps it up off her neck and twists it, lodging a pencil through the knot to make it stay put.

'Ooh, get you. Very elegant.' Dino from Fashion is at the desk by the window. Alex can't make him out against the light, but she knows he will be wearing a white linen suit and a cravat. The heat won't worry him. Dino doesn't seem to have sweat glands. 'Haven't seen you for a while, Killer.' 'Killer' is Alex's nickname in the office. Dino had found a piece about her in an ancient copy of *Ms Sassy*. There had been a photo of Alex in camouflage: 'one of the youngest journalists to be embedded with the troops'. The article had gone on to big up her 'killer instinct'.

'Been working from home,' Alex mumbles with a pen between her lips, tapping at the keyboard. 'Dino, do you know if Gerald is coming in this morning?'

'Talk of the devil,' says Dino, and Alex looks up as the door across the office opens. Gerald is short, wiry and walks very fast. Once he is in his office there will be no chance to grab him, so Alex literally stands up and flings herself in his path, managing to fall over a pile of recycling paper.

'Morning, Gerald.'

'Good morning, Alex. Always nice to have women at my feet. Do you need a hand?'

'No . . . sorry.' Alex gets up carefully and realises her hair has come down and is frizzing out like Medusa's. Chris is by her side looking a little anxious, and she can hear Dino giggling.

'I am guessing you want to talk to me?'

'Gerald. I think I've got a real story.'

'Really?' Gerald's eyes narrow. He had agreed to take Alex on, in spite of her miserable situation with the blindness and all, because of her glittering past. He hasn't seen much of the glitter as yet.

Alex leans in. 'Can I talk to you in your office?'

Gerald hesitates. There are three other journalists at their desks listening, and he is not a man who likes to be dictated to.

'Well, I am pretty busy . . .'

'Gerald. People in Cambright are disappearing!'

Gerald's office is air-conditioned and the windows have blinds blocking out the sun. The air is like a drink of cool water.

'Um . . . Can I say hello to Chris?' asks Gerald.

'Sure,' says Alex. She is fully aware Gerald's one weakness is a very British, all-consuming love of dogs. Trying not to feel mercenary, Alex lets Chris out of his harness and watches as

Gerald, now jacketless, rolls around the floor with an ecstatic hound.

They are playing tussle with a rather expensive-looking sofa pillow when Gerald asks, out of breath but happy, 'So spit it out. What story?'

'May I use your whiteboard?' asks Alex. *Not the flip chart.* She needs to be able to wipe off what she is about to write.

She writes 'Homeless Action!' then 'St Mark's Hospice'. She writes 'Grassybanks' then 'TOSA', and then she connects them all with a line that leads to a name, 'Dr Barnabas Binding'. Gerald is no longer on the floor with Chris. He is standing straight up and staring at the board. Before he can speak, Alex explains about Switch and Phil and The Station. She says she knows that Homeless Action! are affiliated to TOSA, and she has a hunch they are collecting homeless men and women and 'experimenting' on them 'and then maybe . . . well, they die'.

Gerald scowls and shakes his head, hands out in disbelief. 'Are you insane? You said "people" were going missing. I count one. A tramp. Really, Alex? A homeless man goes missing and you decide government conspiracy?'

'Not missing any more. I had a phone call from the warden at The Station. She told me that Phil had died. They had received his death certificate from the treatment centre in Manchester. All official. On Homeless Action! and TOSA headed paper.'

'So what's the big issue?'

'It said on his death certificate he had tragically died before treatment for appendicitis. But Glenda told me that Phil didn't *have* an appendix. She had been with him three years ago when he had it out at Allenbrook Hospital.'

'That's all? An administration screw-up.'

'Well yes, sure maybe, but that is one hell of an error, Gerald. It says on the TOSA website that they are upgrading Grassybanks. It is going to be overseen by, guess who, Dr Barnabas Binding.'

'Let me get this right.' Gerald is walking in a slow circle around Alex. It is unsettling. Chris watches with his ears cocked, head on one side. He likes Gerald, but the man is circling Alex as if he is stalking her. If Chris has to rip his throat out, he will. He would do that for Alex. Alex is his love.

'You think that this Homeless Action! are picking up stray homeless people and then . . . killing them? For what possible reason?'

'I know it sounds absurd, but I just have a hunch. Something about the setup isn't right. They pick up street people with no family ties. None of the men and women listed by The Station have been heard of since, but because they had no family, no links with anyone in the community, no one has made a fuss. We found out about Phil only because Glenda at The Station made a few calls—'

'And Grassybanks?' Gerald cuts across her.

'It's too big.'

Gerald blinks.

'It's just too big.' She shrugs. 'It isn't a hospital, and it isn't a residential centre. It's both, or maybe it's something else. Why the underground extension – *that no one is talking about*? And Dr Binding is tied into the Manchester project somehow . . . he is definitely dodgy. I can smell it. I can't understand why no one seems to know anything about the new setup.'

Gerald stops pacing and sits heavily on his sofa. 'Alex, you know how this sounds. There is no way I can approve an investigation into Grassybanks. Even if I believed it was a story that has legs, it isn't a *Cambright Sun* story. Have you been to the police?'

Alex shakes her head. She turns and wipes down the board. Empty. White. They both stare at it.

'The H5 police are not going to be interested in a homeless man going missing, or in a residential home. They would take some notes, and after I walked out of the door they'd bin them. It has to be journalism. It has to be investigated by the people.'

'Running for office, are we? Jesus, Alex.' Gerald is mulling it over. 'You know TOSA is one of the big boys. You shake their trees and something heavy may fall out on your head.'

'But . . . ?'

'But I may let you do some snooping. However, you will need to make a compromise.'

'Oh no, not those fucking articles.'

'Yes. Those fucking articles, Alex. You promise me that you will finish the sanctioned pieces on "Why Work Works" as requested by the Ministry and Job Central, and I will let you do a little gumshoe around Grassybanks.'

Alex puts her hands on her hips and sighs. 'It is so unfair. Like making the starving man bake the cakes for the party.'

'Go bake,' says Gerald. And he gives Chris one more cuddle.

Back at her desk, Alex does a search on Dr Binding again. He is kosher from birth in 1949 to the OBE of two years previously.

'Hey, Killer?' Dino sways over from the water cooler. 'Gerald says you're covering the "Why Work Works" articles? The "crip reports"?' His laugh is a little forced, but then his white pants are a little tight. 'You ever heard of Kitty Fox?'

Alex shakes her head, eyes still on the list of Binding's awards.

'Well, you should check her out, my dear. She is such a heroine, and she even works locally. Here.' He flips a piece of bright paper under Alex's nose, a flyer.

'Ladies' Defective Agency . . .' Alex reads the big black print. 'Is this a joke?'

'Oh no, I don't think so. Kitty Fox . . . come on, you must remember? She was *the* glamour model of the eighties and now a wheelchair crip-turned-porn-entrepreneur.'

That gets Alex's attention.

'What?'

'Yup. As I said. She, my dear, is a real hero!'

DISINFECTION

Mrs Honey Gets a New Cleaning Job

Mrs Honey is trying not to look shocked. She and her four companions, Jojo, Piet, Kelvin and Letitia, arrived as part of the cleaning team for the ward extension at Grassybanks, but instead of being led to the appropriate room and left to get on with their jobs, they have been strip-searched, their cleaning gear confiscated and replaced with Grassybanks' own. Now they are in an office being given a lecture in cleaning standards and secrecy. There are also several forms for them to sign.

'You are kidding, right?' asks Jojo. He has been cleaning for the Shine Bright Cleaning Company for over thirty years. His question isn't directed at the arrogant young man by the whiteboard, but at his boss and friend, Kelvin, who is sitting next to him, looking anxious and embarrassed.

Jojo is asking about the form they are being asked to sign that states that they will be prosecuted to the full extent of the law if any of them mention their work at Grassybanks to another person. Ever.

'Look,' Kelvin shrugs miserably. "It's just a form, Jojo. I mean, it isn't like you are going to want to talk about the cleaning here . . . it is just that they have procedures. If we don't sign, we don't get the cleaning contract.'

'Procedures . . . *eish*.' Jojo whistles through his crooked teeth. 'What about earlier? We gonna have to show our bollocks every time we come in here?'

'The strip-search is mandatory for all staff.' The man-boy over by the whiteboard in his oversized blazer and tie is rocking his chair back and forth, grinning and looking at Letitia in a way that makes Mrs Honey feel cold inside. Mrs Honey has a feeling about the young white man, a bad feeling. Here they are in their ugly blue overalls, mops in hand, ready to do what they do every day, and yet she feels more than a little frightened. Grassybanks is not the sunny place on the brochure. Why else would there be all the secrecy? She purses her lips and looks at the tray full of cleaning products at her feet. The bottles are colour-coded: red, blue, yellow, white. On each, someone has written the product name in black marker pen: bleach, toilet cleaner, wood polish, disinfectant. What was wrong with the stuff they had brought with them? Part of her hopes Jojo and the others will refuse to sign the forms, and they will all just leave and find other work elsewhere. The other part of her knows that she must be here at Grassybanks. It is the only way.

'What you got that is so secret anyway?' Jojo is belligerent, but Mrs Honey knows he too feels uneasy.

'We got crappy, shitty, sick people is what we got, and a hell of a lot of cleaning to do,' says the spotty white man. 'We need to ensure their privacy, not ours. It's all about client confidentiality.'

There is something in his manner, the way he talks about the people he should be looking after, that makes Mrs Honey want to scream. She clenches her fists, looks down, tries to relax her aching shoulders. She thinks of Joanna. For the first time she is now able to afford a carer, and so her daughter is at home, safe and quiet, as opposed to being tortured at Job Central. Mrs Honey must work, and she must work here. *For you, sweetheart*, she thinks.

The young man stands. 'Look, if you don't want the work, that's fine. You know the situation. You walk out of the door and there will be a hundred other cleaning companies lined up to do the work.'

They all shift in their seats. It is true. Kelvin looks at Jojo and shrugs apologetically. Jojo, the old Jamaican, looks at Piet the Pole, who glances at Mrs Honey and over to Letitia, the youngest and shyest little thing in the room.

'I have to work,' Letitia whispers. 'My dad's sick again.'

And so they sign.

On the way out of the door, the spotty man waits for the men to leave before moving to block Letitia's exit.

'Excuse me,' whispers little Letitia. She keeps her head down, stares at the floor.

'You know you are fine,' the man rasps, standing so close to Letitia that Mrs Honey, waiting behind, can see the hairs rise on the back of the girl's neck. He swaggers, pushing her backwards into Mrs Honey. 'You know, if there is anything you need, any questions at all, you come straight to me. Yeah? You copy? Just ask for Andre.'

Andre, is it? thinks Mrs Honey. A name to remember and avoid. She smooths down her blue pinafore and shoulders past, knocking Andre roughly out of Letitia's way.

'Come on, Lettie,' she says. 'You work with me on this shift.'

She can feel Andre's eyes on her back as they leave. 'What a nasty piece of work,' she says to the other cleaners as they set off down the shining corridors.

'No one let Letitia out of their sight,' Jojo says, and the others nod.

Dr Binding Does a Ward Round

Ward A

The Good Doctor's hands are dry and warm, healer's hands. He can take a temperature through them, feel a pulse, reassure a person just by placing those long fingers on a cheek or forehead. The nursing staff, technicians and even the cleaning staff love him. He has the energetic geniality and thoughtfulness of a man who knows how important everyone, every cog in the wheel, is to the good running of the system. He cares about them all.

The cleaners:

'Good morning, Jojo. You look like you had a good weekend? Did you get to your salsa lesson this time?'

'Thank you, Doctor, yes, Doctor.'

The nurses:

'Nurse Dyer, I trust you got some much needed rest? You've been working terribly hard these last few weeks. You must look after yourself.'

'Yes, Doctor, thank you, Doctor.'

And the patients love him too. He doesn't sugar-coat anything. His bedside manner is assured, competent and efficient but he really looks, really sees, really feels for each and every person he treats.

'Good morning, Ginni. And how are you feeling this morning? Your colour is much better and your temperature is almost normal. A couple more days in bed and you'll be up and at 'em again.'

'Yes, Doctor, thank you, Doctor.'

'I see you haven't eaten your jelly. Now come, come. Jelly is the wobbly bedrock of British hospital cuisine. Surely you can't resist?'

'Oh, Doctor!' Polite laughter all round.

With Grassybanks, The Good Doctor is only required to visit twice a week, although as Ward B and soon-to-be Ward C are his own personal projects, he is in most days. He always meets first with the nursing staff, clinical officers and any additional staff to discuss the patients and how they have spent the night or day. He answers questions and cracks a few jokes, and then he and his entourage will head off to the wards. In Ward A he meets patients, reassures them, reviews medication, listens to the clinicians and nurses and makes decisions on future rehabilitation.

'Pauline here can go up to 160 milligrams of the sertraline and reduce her zopiclone to 7.5 and only three nights a week. Hey Pauline, can you look at me, my dear? There, that's right, good girl. How about trying a swim today? I bought you the most colourful swimming cap, so you won't need to get your hair wet. See, no excuses, eh?'

'No, Doctor. Thank you, Doctor.'

'Morning, Dominic. I had a word with the engineer, and he promises to look at your wheelchair today and get that wheel to stop squeaking. Then you can go and spy on the girls without getting caught again.' There is more polite laughter. 'How's Dominic's bowel movement? Oh, good. Great, Dominic. Good boy. If you keep that up for a couple of days we can review your carbohydrate intake. Nurse, could you make a note to get the nutritionist in for a chat?'

'Yes, Doctor. Thanks, Doctor.'

In Ward B there is less chat.

Ward B

Here is The Good Doctor in Ward B. The lights are dim and the patients are all still in their beds, unresponsive lumps that breathe beneath thin blankets. The blankets are especially thin in Ward B.

Dr Binding has a pale blue stethoscope, a gift from a niece. He applies it to the concave chest of the unconscious wretch on the bed. The lub-dub of the heart is slow but steady.

Blast! thinks The Good Doctor. He had expected the man to be 'end stage' by now.

'What do you think, Doctor?' asks Nurse Dyer behind him.

'I think, unfortunately for this fellow, we may have another week to go. He has a strong heart.'

Nurse Dyer sighs. He can tell she is thinking about beds.

'Continue the Librium and the cold baths. We can't move any faster but there may be another sedative that has better results. How did—' he consults his notes '—patients 78 and 79 go?'

'Both slipped away without a fuss exactly on cue, Doctor. We have them bagged for the Resomator. They will be the first to go through. The team are really quite excited.'

'Good to hear. I want to be there when they are processed, Nurse. Please let the chemist know.'

'Yes, Doctor.'

'Have we any new recruits?'

'Yes, six, Doctor, all on the women's side. Three indigent, three single-elderlies.'

'Right, well, you know what to do. Set them up. I'll keep two of them as control, and the others we will kick off with the revised Formula.'

'Are you sure, Doctor? The Formula is known to have certain side effects . . .'

'I am aware, Nurse Dyer. However, it had side effects at 120 milligrams. The revised version is set at only 80 but seems to have the same overall effect without the fitting. Maintain the Librium.'

Nurse Dyer nods approval without losing the frown that tips the corners of her mouth down deep wrinkles and into her jowls. Those frown lines make her look like a ventriloquist's dummy.

God, she is a hag, thinks the doctor, moving to the sink to wash his hands. A damn good nurse, though. If he were on his way out, he would want Nurse Dyer administering the medication. *Though perhaps not in Ward B*, he smiles to himself.

He is in a hurry now. Monsieur Rennes and a couple of other team players are meeting to discuss the new wing. He wishes he could boast about the work he is already doing in Ward B. His experiment has been extremely effective, and the results fascinating. In years to come it will be apparent what a crusader he is, but in the current climate he knows he will just have to batten down the hatches and keep schtum.

'Next patient, please, Nurse.'

Alex Follows the Flyer

Alex puts the flyer Dino gave her under the CCTV and blows it up to four times magnification.

On pale yellow paper in spidery lettering is a logo: a naked woman, head thrown back in ecstasy, sitting astride a phone handset. Underneath is written in big bold letters:

THE LADIES' DEFECTIVE AGENCY
SPECIALISED VOICE WORK FOR WOMEN
EXCELLENT RATES, FLEXIBLE HOURS
CONTACT KITTY TO ARRANGE AN AUDITION

'What the hell is this?' Alex is more irritated than bemused. She wants to crack on with the investigation of Homeless Action! and creepy old Binding. 'Why Work Works' and bloody Kitty Get-your-tits-out Fox is just an annoying diversion. Sighing, she taps the number into her phone.

'Well heeellooo,' breathes a voice. 'You have reached the offices of the Ladies' Defective Agency. How may I help?'

'Yeah. Right. Umm . . . may I speak to Kitty Fox?'

'Hold the line, please.' Click, more clicks, and then: 'Hello,

Kitty here.' It is certainly not a voice that Alex is expecting. It is deep, mature and pleasant.

'Ah, hi, Kitty. I know this is going to sound odd, but I was handed your flyer by a work colleague. Dino? You may know him?'

'Is this Alexandra?'

Alex is astonished. 'How did you know?'

'The *Cambright Sun* number has come up on my digital readout. I happen to know that an Alexandra Lyon has interviewed a couple of other disabled entrepreneurs in the area, and I put two and two together. I am right, aren't I? I heard your voice on the radio and thought you had the kind of talent we are looking for. I was hoping you might give us a call.'

'That is kind of you, but I wasn't actually looking for work. I mean, it would be great, but I am actually investigating—'

'I need to ask you a couple of questions,' Kitty interrupts her.

'OK, but—'

'Are you over eighteen?'

'Yes, but as I—'

'Are you currently or have you, or any family member, ever been employed by or volunteered for any of the following: the police force, local or national government, TOSA, H5, or a similar agency?'

'No.'

'Do you have any current convictions?'

Not current, thinks Alex. 'No.'

'OK, good. Now, are you mobile? I know you are visually impaired.'

'I travel by dog,' says Alex.

'An interesting way to get around, I imagine. Have a think on it, and if you want to come for the audition, make your way to Market Square and wait by the clock. You will be collected at 2 p.m. I really look forward to meeting you.'

'Err . . . audition . . . ?'

There is an empty humming. The phone call has ended.

Alex gets to the stone clock early. The sunlight hurts her eyes and her head aches. Distorted blobs of oily colour dance across her vision. She perches on the stone steps under the clock and watches a bored seagull pluck chips out of the top of a rubbish bin. Chris tips his muzzle to the sun and his whiskers quiver with delight. Town smells are so fascinating. He could follow them for hours, if he weren't working.

'Alexandra?'

Alex turns. Chris stands up, stepping on Alex's foot. He sniffs but doesn't lean forward. He doesn't recognise the human either.

'I'm Jules.' The person – Alex really cannot tell the gender – is tall and elegant. Alex can make out a large quiff of blonde hair, the glint of John Lennon glasses and a large leather jacket. 'Sorry, can't shake your hand.'

Alex is confused. Jules leans down. 'I haven't any arms. But please feel free to grab a sleeve.' Jules has a light tenor voice, a little too musical for a man.

Disconcerted and a little embarrassed, Alex does. The leather is warm and rough and sturdy.

'Don't worry. You won't pull my jacket off. You OK for me to lead?'

They make their way through the crowded market easily. Jules is quick, sure-footed and no one seems to notice that her sleeves hang loose and empty. Alex hangs on and lets her lead, Chris trotting, ears and tail up, beside them.

They are quickly free of the crowd and moving down along the river. Past the weir and now alongside the canal where it is less pretty and more industrial. Not many strollers. Even the swans stay uptown. Jules lopes along, humming tunelessly under her breath.

'Is it far?' asks Alex. She is unsure about making small talk. She is intrigued, but her head is still pounding.

'Nope. Just a few minutes.'

They move away from the banks and into what looks like a long line of huge derelict warehouses. Torn plastic flaps from rusty scaffolding, and broken breeze blocks and bricks litter the floor. Chris baulks a little as they head further into the darkened far end.

'Forward,' says Alex, but Chris stands still, his tail drooping. He isn't trained to take Alex into places like this.

'Oh sorry,' says Jules. 'Sorry, dog. I should have said. It looks a mess, but that is really just to stop people snooping. We do our best not to advertise the premises for reasons that will become obvious. It's not so bad inside and gets much better on the next floor.'

There is a massive lift with a clanking metal door that rolls upwards when Jules knocks a lever with her knee.

'Jesus, you could get a tank in here,' says Alex.

Jules blinks. 'Hadn't thought of a tank. Not a bad idea. Could you pull the door handle down? It's on the right about halfway up.'

The lift grinds up and rocks to a stop. Alex, still holding on, pulls on the handle and the metal door rolls up to reveal an entirely different setting. The same huge warehouse space as below, but bright and white and humming with activity. Rows of small booths line a wide walkway, giving an almost end-of-the-pier feeling to the sunny room. Each booth is brightly painted in sweet pastels, and gorgeous lush plants flow from pots and hanging baskets, from windowsills and ceiling. Alex can make out walls hung with art – photographic, abstract or classical, she can't be sure from this distance. As Alex's eyes adjust, in so far as they can, to the change in light, Jules gently tugs her over to a reception desk manned by a young woman in headphones. All around there is the muted sound of phones and low chatter.

Telesales. Alex's heart sinks. 'I hate telesales.'

Jules nods at her kindly. 'OK. You are to see Kitty. I think she will be about ten minutes. I hope you do hang around. It's not all about the sex,' she says with a wink and turns on her heel. 'I'll organise us some tea,' she calls over her shoulder.

Alex is left staring blankly at the receptionist. 'What did she mean, "It's not all about the sex?"'

The receptionist glances up from tapping her keyboard. 'Hi, I'm Laverne. I'll just be a minute,' she says to the air next to Alex. *Her eyes*, thinks Alex. *There is something up with her eyes.* The receptionist is blind. *Oh*, thinks Alex. *Oh* and *oh.*

Scanning, peering around the space. Yes. Everyone in her tunnel of sight is female *and . . . and . . . and . . .* they all have, well, something . . . other. There are women in wheelchairs, lots of women in wheelchairs, in fact, as well as on buggies, with crutches, with hearing aids, with scars and with worse. There are little women and twisted women, half women and whole women, there are old, middle-aged and young women.

'The Ladies' Defective Agency?' muses Alex. *Very bloody funny.*

'You can sit and listen in while you are waiting,' says the receptionist, proffering a headset. 'We aren't shy. Chairs to your right. Volume and channel change on the earpiece. You can feel it.'

'Thanks,' says Alex. 'Find a seat,' she says to Chris, and he happily pulls her over to a soft red sofa. Alex sits, dumps her handbag and pulls on the device.

Alex and Kitty

'Filth. Extraordinary filth.'

'Thank you.'

'No really . . . I am completely shocked. I mean, I am not a prude by any means but this . . . ?' Alex is in Kitty Fox's office, her cheeks still burning.

'Phone sex.' Kitty is smiling from behind her desk. 'And of course we do games and voice-overs too. Anything audio and smutty, really.'

Kitty Fox, it turns out, is indeed the Kitty Fox glamour model of the 1980s. She is not a glamour model any more. No, she gave that up after being diagnosed with a tumour on her back and having much of her spine cut away and repinned. It was harder to get those Page 3 photo shoots in a wheelchair.

'They used me up and chucked me out like a tissue. I was sorry for myself for about, oh, an afternoon, and then I thought sod it. I may not be able to spread my legs any more but I know how this shit works. Porn-audio-ography. Made a bloody mint.'

Kitty is sitting in the most high-tech wheelchair Alex has ever seen.

'Nice, isn't it? I've got a lot of dough in research, and I get to experiment with the product. Lucky me.' She presses a button and the chair unfolds, straightening her up to a standing position. 'See, now it's a robotic walker.'

She, or rather, the ex-wheelchair, hums, whirrs and takes a couple of steps. 'It can go up stairs, apparently, but I haven't road-tested it yet.' Another button and the wheelchair folds itself and Kitty back to a seated position. 'I own or have shares in almost every phone-sex line in southern Europe, though this one is a bit different. I've been running this gaff for the last five years – it's my favourite. Wish I'd thought of it sooner, you know, employing disabled women. They are much more imaginative on the whole than the smack dollies we usually get.'

Alex is still trying to collect herself. 'This is incredible!'

Kitty smiles. She is still artfully glamorous: perfect teeth, chiselled cheekbones, arched brows over turquoise eyes with barely a crow's foot. She sports a magnificent bosom too and is wearing a low-cut black T-shirt to prove it. Again, barely a wrinkle in sight, which is impressive considering she must be pushing sixty-five.

'Now you, Alex. You are working part time as a journalist, right? We could really do with a girl like you on board, especially right now.'

'What do you mean? As a journalist or as a . . . umm . . . what do you call them?'

'Voice-over artist, and yes, you would be top-notch totty voice, I can tell. But equally, I am sure we could eventually make use of your investigative skills and your contacts.'

'I would actually like to write a piece on you, Kitty,' says Alex, finally broaching the subject. She has read up on Kitty and knows that she very rarely gives interviews.

Kitty waves her hand, dismissively. 'Oh yes . . . a "Why Work Works" special? I have read the local rag, you know.'

Alex winces, embarrassed, and drags her fingers through her hair, catching a couple of knots. She yanks. 'It's not my best work . . .'

'Lame, Ms Lyon, totally lame. You are a good journalist. I was impressed with your documentary on the Nestling Corporation scandal. You won an award for that, didn't you?'

Alex blinks. 'That was a long time ago, I'm surprised you remember,' she says. She is flattered. 'And yes, I was awarded the Flame Keeper's Award for Social Responsibility in Documentary.'

'What happened to the Nestling Corporation?'

'Well . . . err . . . they were pretty much untouchable. They promised to clean up the ground water and compensate the families but . . .'

'Didn't you chase them?'

Alex is confused about where this conversation is going. 'I chased for a year and was then given a posting as foreign correspondent in Iraq?'

'Ahh, you moved on?'

Alex stays quiet. She moves her chair a little closer so she can get a better view of Kitty Fox. Kitty stares back, neither smiling nor frowning, just waiting. Alex can't figure out what the woman wants from her.

'Do you want to ask *me* a question?' Alex asks finally.

'Not yet,' says Kitty.

'OK . . . well, will you let me write a piece about you?'

'Not for that Work Works trash but . . .' Kitty holds up a long, carefully manicured finger. 'I might let you be the journalist who interviews me for *Parade* magazine and even the *Chuffington Post*.'

Alex nods, trying not to look too excited. She can't believe her luck. 'On what condition?'

'Ah yes, conditions.' Kitty grins, and her face is like a naughty child's. 'There are conditions. Look, tell you what, I'll ask Jules to show you the setup and studio, and then perhaps we could chat again before you leave? Why don't you do a trial recording? It's cash in hand, up front, and forty pounds an hour. You sign nothing. You are beholden to no one.'

Alex, who has exactly 68p in her wallet and nothing for the electricity meter, takes less than a second to decide.

'Go on then,' she says. 'Let's see what this is all about.'

Jules smiles beatifically when Alex emerges to say she wants to have a go. 'Good-oh. Let's get you set up with the best of the best. Kitty's second-in-command, Helen, voice coach to the stars, is going to take you through your paces. Studio three. Right this way.'

She guides Alex and Chris through the maze of individual booths where women of all shapes, sizes and abilities are muttering and groaning in feigned ecstasy. Chris's ears flicker back and forth. The larger studios are towards the back of the first floor. Each one is blacked out and muffled with soundproofing insulation. In Studio 3, Alex is left alone briefly. She stands under a spotlight in front of a large mike that hangs down from the ceiling. A technician has handed her a script printed off in twenty-six point size. It is an utterly depraved monologue written in the voice of an uptight businesswoman who finds herself being screwed silly in the loo of a Boeing 747 by the first officer. It is graphic and crudely written and . . .

'And pure fiction,' says a liquorice-voiced person who has come quietly whirring in behind Alex in another state-of-the-art wheelchair. She has a glossy chestnut bob, a sharp little face, red lipstick and the most delicious voice.

'I'm Helen,' says the woman. 'I've been working with Kitty for over twenty years and she believes you have "something".' Here she makes apostrophes in the air with one hand, the other remaining still, curled claw-like in her lap. 'I am the person to find out if this is true. Now tell me, darling, I hear you have had some previous experience?'

Alex takes a moment to remember that Helen isn't referring to the script. 'I have done some TV and radio, yeah. Nothing quite like this, though.'

'Oh, I'm sure you will be a sensation, darling. Let's do a read-through and see how it all goes.'

Alex looks down at the script. In large print it looks like it's shouting gratuitous smut. She swallows.

'Come on, darling. It's just words.' Helen spins the chair right in front of Alex and conducts with her slender hand. 'One, two, three, action!'

Alex jumps straight in and is doing fine until the first officer has her pinned up against the sink with her knees up to her ears.

'I feel his tongue licking its way down the crack of my arse and I shiver. That tongue. Long and strong and wet and hot. He pulls apart my pert arse cheeks and I feel the hot flickering near my arsehole. I cannot help but groan out loud . . .'

Alex pauses, trying not to giggle. 'That's disgusting!'

'For you, maybe,' says Helen, deadpan. She coughs and pauses to inhale something from a tube connected to a small canister attached to her chair.

'Don't worry,' she says, seeing Alex's raised eyebrow. 'It's just oxygen, sadly. Got an annoying case of muscular dystrophy.'

'I'm sorry,' Alex is trying to think of what to say.

'No, darling. We don't do "sorry" here, not any more. We do work, yes?'

'Yes,' nods Alex, trying not to look too obviously relieved.

'OK, so the groan?' demands Helen.

'Err . . .'

'You have a few options. I would go for a short, low groaning pant. How about this?' She takes another hit from the canister and then a deep breath and groans, and the groan is exceptional when it comes. Alex can immediately hear why she is top of her profession. Chris, who up to this point has been lying silently, politely, is shocked enough to leap to his feet and howl.

'Wow!' says Alex.

'Yes. The trick, darling,' Helen winks, 'is all in the pelvic floor. At least I still have some of those muscles intact. Do your exercises every day.'

Alex goes back to having her arsehole licked in a toilet, and after a couple of hours' work it is recorded and in the bag. Helen is pleased with her.

'It's just that final orgasm that needs to extend out over a few more seconds.' She places her hand on the flies of Alex's jeans. 'There . . . show me again.'

Alex takes a deep breath and manages to keep the orgasm going over the twenty-second mark.

'Excellent, darling. You have nice vibration. Keep practising and there will be a lot more work for you.' She pats Alex's lower belly. 'A natural. Let your vulva do the talking!'

It isn't Jules who comes to guide her back to reception but another woman, a smiling black woman with glasses whom Alex is shocked to find she recognises.

'Mrs Honey? Mrs Honey, is that you?'

'Yes, dear. It's Alexandra, isn't it? How nice to see you again after all this time.'

It had been Mrs Honey who Alex had interviewed when Joanna Honey had been passed 'fit for work' by TOSA. Alex had tried her level best to push the story, but in the end Gerald had axed it and run with the paedophile headline instead. Alex had been mortified, but Mrs Honey had patted her arm, told her, told *her*, not to worry.

Back then, Mrs Honey had been in her work overalls, exhausted, shoulders slumping, her hair unkempt and spotted with grey, and she had stunk of pine floor disinfectant. Today she is in jeans and a long, bright white T-shirt with a flower across the front. The clenched, stressed brow is gone, and her hair is knotted back into an elegant braid.

'You look great,' says Alex, and really means it. 'How are you?' *What are YOU doing here?* she desperately wants to ask. *Surely not voice-over work too?* She can't help but imagine what Mrs Honey can do with her pelvic floor.

'I am well, thank you, Alexandra,' says Mrs Honey. 'Making enough money now, doing two jobs, to keep the wolf from the door at last.'

'That's great.' Alex presumes Mrs Honey is still doing the occasional cleaning job as well as working here. 'And Joanna?'

'Home and with a full-time carer.'

'That's wonderful.' Alex is amazed.

'That's Kitty Fox for you,' says Mrs Honey. 'I couldn't have done it without her and the LDA. I've been working here for the last few weeks and it's been life-changing. Come on, you'll need to sign for your money.'

Chris is already getting to grips with the territory and is following his nose back to reception. Laverne smiles when she hears his collar tinkle. 'You might want to meet Albert,' she says to Alex. 'He's back here sleeping.'

Squeezing behind the reception desk, Alex unharnesses Chris so he can meet Laverne's dog, an ancient black Labrador with seen-it-all eyes and white whiskers. The dogs do a short, stiff-legged, smell-arse dance around each other and then Albert lies down again.

'He's nearly eleven,' says Laverne. 'He retires next April.'

Alex's heart goes out to Laverne. 'Jesus,' she whispers.

'Yeah,' says Laverne. 'It is actually physically impossible to even think about it. I am lucky, though. I can keep him, even with a new dog. My husband and kids will walk him when I'm at work. He won't have to go away from us.'

'That is the best way,' says Alex. In her own heart she knows that when it is Chris's time to leave the earth she will die too. She can't imagine the separation being bearable, even with a new dog. Or rather, she refuses to imagine it. And she doesn't mind, really. She has had a good life on the whole. What's the song? 'Why stagger on when the one you love has gone?'

She is paid £100 for two-and-a-half hours' work, cash in hand. Laverne says that Kitty has asked to see Alex again soon.

'Sounds good,' says Alex, eyeing the cash in her wallet.

'There is plenty more work,' says Laverne, smiling. 'Helen says you have a wonderful talent.'

'Pelvic floor,' says Alex. 'Apparently, it's all about the vulva.'

'Hell yeah,' says Laverne.

Alex Goes Back for More

Over the next few weeks Alex makes a good deal of filthy lucre by talking dirty into a microphone. She works a couple of days a week at the *Cambright Sun* still, but her focus has shifted, and in the late afternoon, when she and Chris trot off to the canal and the Ladies' Defective Agency, she feels something she hasn't felt for a very long time. Anticipation. And not in a bad way, but in a *I can't wait to get there* kind of a way. It is absolutely not about the work itself, although she is damn good at it. Reading truly gratuitous porn for hours at a time gradually inures her to embarrassment. She is no longer coy about weeing on the head of a complete stranger in the sauna at the gym or being part of a gang bang at a rock star's house in California. She no longer winces when describing nipple clamps or shudders when being fisted by a lesbian dominatrix. The stuff is not atrociously written, and there is never any specifically female debasement, no rape, not a lot of non-consensual sadism. No, the scripts she can take or leave, but it is the company itself, the ladies of the LDA, she finds endearing. It is Laverne and Jules, Helen and Kitty, and the myriad other odd bods that Alex has found a connection with. Just yesterday she had been in the clubroom – and, yes, of course the LDA would have a staff clubroom beautifully laid out, fully accessible with subsidised drinks and snacks and a lowered bar for wheelchair users. The deaf bartender had shown her how to sign for gin and tonic, how to say thank you and, most importantly, 'It's your round.' Although one is *not* permitted to booze before work, afterwards most people spend a while unwinding before heading home to the challenges of everyday life.

And often they are difficult challenges to face: unpleasant or complicated or both. Like Alex, many of the staff at the LDA work two jobs or care for disabled or vulnerable relatives when not on shift. Between the Believe in Better campaigners and the various shop-a-scrounger media campaigns, being a high-visibility crip, especially in a wheelchair or on a mobility scooter, is asking for trouble. Most of the ladies have to wear rain hats and keep cling film wrapped around their shoulders to protect them from spittle. It could come from anyone, neighbours to schoolchildren, but it comes. And most buses no longer stop, and trains no longer bother with special seating for crips. How does the advert go? '*If you can't fit, you can't sit.*'

At the LDA the women can use computers, a bank of which line the back of the clubroom. They can do their online shopping and have it delivered to the door, but they all still have to negotiate the other stuff: the GP, pharmacy, hospital, dentists, schools, and so forth.

Helen and Kitty do what they can to help. Every staff member is given several pocket-sized canisters of pepper spray and expected to carry them at all times. Additionally, staff are expected to text when en route to work. If people don't check in at around their usual arrival time, Jules and one or two of the other security team will head out to see if there are any problems.

This rule has been doubly enforced since a gang of teenagers set on Dawn about six months ago. They had collected a pile of rocks, waited at the entrance to the warehouse and jumped her before she had a chance to get into the building. Dawn, who, before her encounter with a drunk driver, had been a professional tennis coach, had enough rage and focus to catch a couple of the rocks and throw them back. But with only one working arm and minimal swing from her wheelchair, she had rather got the worst of it, ending up in hospital having her scalp stitched up.

The H5 police said they had given the kids a warning, but, really, a woman with such a conspicuous disability shouldn't be out by herself in the evening. In their opinion, Dawn had brought it on herself. Dawn had said, 'Fuck you very much,' and asked Kitty for a double shift to make up her loss of earnings. Dawn was what Jules called 'hardcore'.

Even so, the security team are on the alert. Six months on and Jules and a couple of others are pretty sure they have seen the same kids lurking around again.

And one night it happens, just as Alex is coming off her shift. She and Chris are mooching, yawning, down the dimly lit corridor towards the reception desk when Alex hears Jules shouting from the lift. Alex has never heard Jules raise her voice before and it makes her afraid. Then there is an almighty dinging as the fire alarm goes off.

Alex, clutching her ears, waits with Laverne, Albert and Chris, conscious of her limited sight and the darkness outside, while others rush forward. Katrina, another of the security staff, runs halfway back down the corridor shouting for Laverne to call an ambulance.

'Get an ambulance. Tell them it's burns, really bad burns!'

Alex can hear that Katrina is trying to keep calm but her voice breaks and she has to stifle a gag. Chris and Albert sit, ears pricked, eyes glowing. They look different, not gentle, somehow more wolf-like in the darkness of the hallway. Alex wonders if they can smell the seared skin in the lift already. In another couple of minutes so can she.

How unlucky can a woman be? Dawn has once again been set on just outside the warehouse. Luckily, instead of plastic around her shoulders, she left the house that day wearing an old leather jacket with the collar turned up. So when the kids leap out at her, spraying her with lighter fluid and setting fire to her, it is the jacket that gets most of the grilling. She is able to push herself into the lift where the smoke sets off the fire alarm and . . . good thinking, Dawn, the sprinklers!

A week later and they can all still smell the charred leather in the lift. Dawn won't be able to use her left hand for a while but, 'That's fine,' she says. She can't use it anyway. It's the dud one. Her eyebrows and eyelashes are gone, and she can't get the smell of burning hair out of her nostrils, but her face is only a little sore and the tip of an ear is an extravagance she can do without.

'What is she, fucking Rambo?' asks Alex. They have closed the offices for the weekend and she, Kitty, Jules and Helen are drinking martinis in the clubroom.

'Dawn is the toughest woman I have ever known,' says Jules, spitting out her straw. 'I should know.'

She should, too. Jules worked for twenty years as a screw in a notorious women's prison in Manchester. She has seen pretty much all there is to see about people. Alex almost gets up the temerity to ask her how she lost her arms, but is relieved when Helen speaks up. She doesn't know if she wants to hear.

Helen says, 'Is it true that the police are refusing to do anything more about the attack? Is that right?'

'Dawn says the kids were hooded, and although she is pretty sure she knows who they are, she doesn't think she could identify them. It happened pretty fast.'

Alex sits up. 'I thought she said they were from the Mandela Estate here on the corner? She said one of the kids called the other one "Danny". That's enough to start an investigation, surely?'

'She said she *thinks* they did,' says Jules. 'But the police say they can't even begin to go door to door on the estate without more proof. Apparently, the estate is nearly ninety per cent Believe in Better campaigners. I think the cops are scared.'

'For fuck's sake,' says Kitty.

'That's awful,' says Alex. She swigs her martini. It's delicious. She almost gets the cocktail stick stuck up her nose. 'Isn't there anything that can be done?'

'You could write about it,' says Helen. She is on her third martini too, but her brown eyes are bright and clear as marbles.

'They won't print it at the *Cambright Sun*.' Alex bites her lip. 'They refuse to publish any more crip-attack stories. My editor says it uses up too much of his copy. I tried sneaking in a piece on the suicide rate last week, a follow-up from a story we ran on that poor kid, Laura Shandy, the one who took a dive off the car park. I got an official warning.'

The mention of Laura Shandy causes Helen to spit her drink back into her glass. Alex glances up and is shocked to see Helen

124

has turned a pale greenish colour. Was it the drink? She is about to ask when Jules butts in.

'Official warning for doing your job? That sucks,' says Jules and dips her head to get at her cocktail.

Kitty has been thoughtful for a while. Her hand rests briefly on Helen's shoulder. 'We just can't let this happen,' she says quietly.

'What's that, Kit?' Jules emerges from her martini.

'Once Only rule?' asks Helen.

'Once Only rule,' says Kitty.

'What's the Once Only rule?' asks Alex.

Jules giggles and then snorts, almost topples and pulls herself back upright. 'Fuck me once, don't get to fuck me twice. Let's just say those kids won't be setting fire to anyone else any more.'

'You are joking, right?' Alex smiles but then peers around the group. Helen's eyes blaze. Kitty looks at the ceiling. Jules dips back into her drink. Alex's smile fades.

'What are you going to do? You sound as if you're planning . . . well . . . violence.'

Jules hiccups. 'Fire with fire.'

'No way!' Alex looks at Helen. 'Violence doesn't solve anything!'

'I disagree.' says Helen forcefully. 'Birth is violent. Surgery is violent. Love is violent.'

'And it might fucking cure those scabrous fucking kids of the need to set fire to anyone,' says Jules and, standing up, she raises her chin to the ceiling and shouts, 'Boudicca!'

'Boudicca!' echoes Helen.

'I will not have you spouting that Boudicca rubbish in here,' snaps Kitty. 'One sniff of a Boudicca lunatic in our ranks and the next thing you know we will be raided, shut down.'

'What on earth are you talking about?' says Alex, but no one tells her.

Tina, the barkeeper, changes the CD on the music system, and the honeyed tones of D'Angelo flow into Alex's bones. Chris, at her feet, sighs, delighted. Another round of glistening glasses are brought over to the table. There is a slightly uneasy silence. Alex feels she should change the subject.

'Have you heard of the "Brown Envelope Syndrome"?' she asks.

'Eh?' Jules squints across at Alex, confused. 'Is it catching?'

Alex tries not to slur but this recent new information has upset her so much she feels impelled to discuss it. 'It was entered into the International Classification of Diseases three days ago. "*Brown Envelope Syndrome; an extreme anxiety created by waiting for, or appearance of, brown envelopes from a welfare agency resulting in depression, hypermania, disassociation and often leading to intensification of existing mental and physical health issues, and on occasion to suicidal thoughts and actions.*"' Alex has the quote by heart.

'Dear God!' Kitty drains her glass and signals Tina to mix some more cocktails.

'I am currently suffering from it,' says Alex, thinking of a letter next to her computer that she hasn't yet dared to open. She presumes she has been sanctioned again.

'So am I and most of the women in here,' says Helen. 'In fact, they sanctioned Tilly in accounts last week for not attending her work assessment, even though she was in hospital having dialysis. Her brown envelope stated that they have cut her Basic Benefit, which means she will lose her rent and her husband loses his Caring Support Allowance. Thank goodness for you, Kitty. Without her work here she'd be homeless.'

'Yeah, right. Thank goodness for me.' Kitty's voice is bitter. Alex looks at her. 'What is it?'

'What is it? Jesus, ladies. I can't single-handedly support the entire British nation of needy crips. I already overemploy, you know, and I get more applications for work every day. We could easily afford to cut at least thirty people from the staff. This is a business, not a bloody charity.' She drums her fingers angrily on the arm of her chair.

'We are not entirely helpless,' says Helen quietly.

'Yes, you bloody are,' says Kitty calmly. 'Singly, on your own, on *my* own, we are. They are right to crush us one by one. A tick at a time.'

'Tick tock.' Helen smiles slightly as D'Angelo kicks in with 'Brown Sugar'.

'Tick tock,' sings Jules. 'Tick tock till the bomb goes off! Alone we fall, together we appal! Aw, feck. I need a slash.' She stands up and wobbles slightly. She is in a white T-shirt and Alex, feeling light-headed, thinks she can see the ghostly arms that are not there.

'You need help?' asks Helen.

'Nope. Just hand me my looper please.' Only it comes out as 'pooper leese'.

Helen nudges Alex, and Alex feels around for Jules's device, a long stick with a hook on the end. She is sitting on it. 'Got it!' She stands, realising she too has jelly knees, and pops the handle into Jules's mouth.

'Ta,' says Jules, dropping it.

'Hang on,' says Alex. 'I'll get it.' She stoops down and promptly falls over.

'Lightweights.' Kitty raises her hand. 'Another round please, Tina!'

'Darling, I think we might need peanuts,' says Helen.

Several hours later, after sleeping off some of the alcohol, Alex drags herself out of her bed and staggers over to the computer. Chris chases something in his sleep but doesn't wake. Alex can't relax. What was it her friends had been talking about? The Celtic rebel queen Boudicca or . . . something else? She types and searches, her eyes riddled with retinal light flashes. Past the pages on the Iceni Queen she finds something that raises her heartbeat and eyelids a little. An article from a national newspaper written nearly six months previously.

THE MENTOR
'Boudicca': Revolutionary campaigners
or just last gaps from the margins?
by Gemma Greengrass, Policy Editor

The recent spate of blood-red graffiti appearing on hundreds of government buildings this month is the work of a previously unknown group who call themselves 'Boudicca'. Little is known about the group's ethos or intention; they were initially believed to be merely student pranksters or some kind of viral marketing stunt. However, this week a letter was sent to our newspaper with the following statement:

'We are BOUDICCA.

We are the people that you want to silence. You have

condemned us, abused us, threatened us, and now you are hoping we will die out, but we will not.

We are BOUDICCA and we know your game, and we will take action.

By condemning us you condemn yourselves.'

In a reaction to the letter, an H5 police spokesperson denied that the threats should be taken seriously. 'It is not clear exactly who this group wish to take action against or for. Are they making a stand for immigration, for animal rights, for vegetarians? It is clearly a load of hokum. The police will arrest anyone performing further acts of vandalism, and we intend to track down the letter writer forthwith.'

Alex spends another few minutes searching but finds nothing else and her hangover is threatening to make her vomit. She lurches back to bed and the soothing noise of Chris's whistling snores.

Alex Takes the
Grassybanks Tour

'No dogs on the tour.'

'He is a guide dog. Legally—'

'Not here. Not "legally" any more, as you well know, Ms . . . What did you say your name was again? You should have called ahead to make arrangements.'

The nurse is so starched and shiny that light bounces off her like mirrored glass. Alex squints to try to make out the frosty features and can feel that nasty itchy feeling she gets when confronted by people who obviously enjoy the little power they have over others. She swallows, makes an effort, and is pleased to hear her own voice all calm and reasonable.

'I did call. As you can see, I am on the list as "journalist for *Cambright Sun*, plus dog". The woman I spoke to said it was fine. And surely you have many disabled people here as clients with assistance dogs?'

'Of course not. They do not need their dogs here.' The nurse's voice changes pitch slightly. She is now loud enough for the whole room to enjoy the abasement of the blind woman. 'If you want to make a complaint, you can fill out the form and we will ensure it gets directly to the manager's desk. However,' she continues in an aside, sotto voce, to her audience, 'as it was Mr Skinner the manager who has approved the current state of play as regards . . . livestock, I don't think you will get very far.'

Now both Alex's fists are clenched and Chris's tail has flatlined. Alex is aware that the legislation around working dogs has been eviscerated. All service-dog owners received letters months ago explaining that new health and safety laws now prohibited them from all restaurants, cafés and public eating areas (to include schools, universities and work-based cafeterias) unless approved by management. This also means that hospitals and nursing homes are no longer obliged to accept assistance dogs.

There is a small crowd of people, mostly children, behind Alex, also waiting for the tour. They are quiet, embarrassed, undecided who to side with or where to sidle to.

'You can leave the dog outside.'

'Really?' asks Alex. 'Where exactly am I supposed to leave him? In a parking bay? And how then am I to get back in here to do the tour?'

The nurse is as cold as formaldehyde. 'If you haven't made the proper preparations, you are wasting everyone's time.'

'Oh, I hope you don't mind me butting in here, but you could come with us!' A woman taps Alex's shoulder and she turns to glimpse a serene face, pink cardigan, a rotund apple figure and a mass of cropped dark curls. 'I couldn't help overhearing. Gosh, isn't—' the pretty black woman pauses to lean in and read the nurse's name badge '—Nurse Dyer having a busy day, children. Maybe we can help her, perhaps even cheer her up a little?'

The nurse makes a shocked, gagging noise and the buzzing contingent of young children in the tour queue politely cover their mouths to giggle. Alex can hear the puffs of sweet laughter and falls deeply in love with her new friend.

'Now, a quick introduction. I am Jenny Jameson, form teacher for Class Twelve of Bishop's Middle School.' She sticks a finger out and taps Nurse Dyer's clipboard. 'Right there, Jameson plus fifteen.'

She turns back to Alex. 'You could come around with us, if that works? My sister is visually impaired, so I kind of know how this works. I would be very happy to loan you my elbow.'

Alex nods, both grateful and moved. It has been a very long time since anyone stood up for her in public. The nurse makes a rather unpleasant sound through her nose.

'The dog will still not—'

'Oh yes, this lovely beastie!' Jenny cuts across the starched-faced nurse, squats down and rubs Chris's ears. 'Your dog could wait with Mr Parnell in the school van. He loves dogs. He has about five rescue mutts himself. Priya?' She turns to a skinny Asian kid with hair braided so tight she is almost unable to shut her eyes. 'Would you nip out to the van and ask Mr Parnell to come in for a moment?'

And so it goes. Alex finds herself in the middle of a wide-eyed crocodile of nine-year-old children, gripping fast to the warm, soft elbow of Jenny Jameson. They start with juice and biscuits in a large airy room full of brightly coloured sofas and beanbags, boxes of toys and shelves of books, simple cooking facilities and lots of tasteful abstract art hanging from the walls. An enormous mirror set into the far wall scatters sunlight around the room.

'This is the family visiting room,' says starched Nurse Dyer. Even she seems a little less rigid in here and hands around a pail of sugar-free sweets with an almost human smile. 'We just need to go through some housekeeping rules, and then my colleague will show you around.'

There are the usual dreary notes about fire escapes, keeping together, toilets, and then everyone is asked to hand over their mobile phones.

'I'm sorry?' This from another journalist, a bald, slender man from the *Health Visitors' Gazette*. 'I can't let you have it. I use my phone for taking notes and pictures.'

'Oh, no pictures!' Nurse Dyer looks furious again. *It'll be a bad old age. Those frown lines are going nowhere*, thinks Alex.

'No, no!' Dyer wags a finger. 'Didn't you read the information on the form? The privacy of our clients is absolutely paramount. If it was thought that we were allowing you to wander through with cameras willy-nilly, I doubt management would allow us to continue with the tour programme.'

'But then how . . . ?' the man begins, but the nurse is frosted glass again. She silently tears off the top pages of her clipboard, folds them into her pocket and hands the clipboard and clean notepaper to the young man. He takes it gingerly.

'And the pen.'

He takes that too.

'It is what is called "writing". I am sure Mrs Jameson can help you out. She is a teacher after all, and such a conscientious citizen.' She manages to make the 'citizen' into a spitball.

Alex squeezes Jenny's elbow and can feel her twitch with suppressed laughter.

The nurse still has her hand out, and after a mini Mexican standoff the young man hands her his phone. Nurse Dyer drops it into the pail that had held the sweets, along with the other phones she has confiscated.

'You can collect them on your way out,' she says.

'The kids are behaving really well,' says Alex. Several of them had wanted to stay behind to play with Chris, so she has promised they can run about the park with him afterwards. 'A school tour, though? Of a residential home?' Alex is surprised.

'Yes.' Jenny Jameson makes a face and shrugs. 'It is a new initiative from the educational council and TOSA. All the new TOSA-funded centres have invited local schools to tour as part of their citizenship module. We are even being filmed by our school TV channel, although we're not allowed to film any patients, of course, only our own children. All footage is to be reviewed before we leave too. That's all up to her.' She points to the young woman with the leather jacket and HD camera who is currently shooting one of the children picking his nose.

'It's lovely in here,' says Jenny, looking in a different direction. 'I don't know what I was expecting.'

'Yes,' Alex has to agree as she sips her orange barley water out of a bright plastic tumbler. 'I was thinking it would be a little more gothic. I've heard that they have recently taken a further hundred and fifty people into the new extension. I mean . . . well, that's a hell of a lot of people to care for in one institution. I can't see how they manage. And all these people are here voluntarily? I don't get it.'

'My husband is a paramedic. He was with the NHS but recently took a job with TOSA's Community Transport Unit . . .' Jenny Jameson pauses, bites her lip. 'Between you and me, he says there's something a bit odd—'

She is interrupted by the arrival of a lanky man, also in a nurse's uniform. Alex is sure she recognises him from somewhere but can't quite put her finger on it. His name is Robin, and he has been working at Grassybanks for nearly a year, he tells the small crowd. He will be their official tour guide. 'Let's head over to the sports centre.'

The children cheer and gather around their teacher, quacking and clucking like ducklings, so Alex doesn't get a chance to find out what Jenny meant.

They go to the Sports and Rehabilitation Centre where a long swimming pool glitters enticingly. Behind the pool is a well-equipped gym, air-conditioned, extremely clean, and a sprung sports hall marked out for indoor tennis, badminton, football and basketball.

'Wow!' says Alex. 'But it's so quiet.' She turns to Robin. 'How come there's no one around? Not even a lifeguard on poolside.'

'Oh . . .' Robin glances around as if he hadn't noticed before. 'Well, this is lunchtime.'

Alex doesn't think 11 a.m. constitutes lunchtime, but she lets it slide.

Jenny Jameson seems to be able to maintain order almost telepathically. She pauses in her chatter to Alex every now and then to speak directly to the children.

'We are holding hands, Maddie . . . not arm-wrestling.'

'Bradley! The walls are not for licking!'

Alex is keen to quiz Jenny about her husband the paramedic's observations on Grassybanks, but there is no time. They all bang through another set of doors and into yet another bright corridor. Along this one, there are indented seating areas where the children can look through windows into the craft rooms, the games room, the library, the staff offices and the storage areas. There is more traffic here; nurses, care workers and clients can be seen busy and occupied. The clients are teenagers and young adults with

Down's Syndrome and other varieties of learning impairment, which Robin rattles through as if reading a script. *ADHD, autism, Asperger's, cerebral palsy, dyspraxia, hydrocephalus . . .*

The kids are not particularly impressed. 'They look just like people,' the nose-picker, Johnny, points out. 'They look like they're at school.'

Robin seems a little chagrined by the dismissal of the show. 'Well, what about Leo? See? That boy over there, in the wheelchair. He was born without eyes!'

'Ahh!' The children rush to the window again, following Robin's pointing finger.

'Really! That is hardly appropriate!' Jenny is furious, but the kids' response of, 'Miss, Miss, does Leo have a dog?' and, 'Miss, Miss, Leo is making a chair and he doesn't even have any eyes,' calms her slightly.

'Miss, why does Leo and them people have to be in here? They look OK enough for school.'

'Leo and "those" people. That is a good question, Priya. Ask Robin again so everyone can hear.'

Robin, however, is suddenly distracted by the man from the *Health Visitors' Gazette* who has run out of paper on the clipboard.

Chris Leads Mr Parnell
into Trouble

Chris can't get over Mr Parnell's shoes. They are not just shoes as a human would see them, slightly muddy brown work lace-ups. No, to a dog with a nose like Chris's, with over 225 million scent receptors, Parnell's shoes are huge puffy clouds of vibrating stinky information, marked and layered with years and years of data input, like, for instance, the pungent information on all Parnell's adored dogs: two invariably filthy mongrels, a dyspeptic collie and a psycho-pug.

There is also Mrs Parnell, unknowingly exuding scent onto everything. She burns a lot of what she cooks for humans, so the dogs get endless leftovers. Love runs through her like raspberries in a rippled ice cream but something also makes her sad . . . Chris sniffs further . . . her own son who is now, luckily, only a faint scent on the back of Parnell's heel. Chris gets all this from a pair of battered work brogues. Imagine what he would do with the man's slippers.

They are sitting in front of the white school van, and as it is hot, Parnell has left all the doors open wide. The car park has only a whippy half-grown birch for shade and Parnell has parked as close to it as he can get. It provides shade for the wing mirror. The van is ten years old and is itself a paradise of stench. Every child, teacher and driver who has ever set foot in it has left their mark, whether they meant to or not. With his wonderfully scented feet up on the dashboard, Mr Parnell is regaling Chris with tales about his pack, although Chris gets most of it from merely inhaling. Parnell is attempting to show Chris pictures of his dogs on his phone. Chris, of course, just responds to the resonance of Parnell's voice and nods and whimpers enthusiastically at what he guesses to be the right places.

'You're a hell of a smart one, aren't you?' says Parnell as Chris twitches an ear in response to a photo of one mongrel, up to his ears in mud, with the psycho-pug, teeth bared, in the background.

Chris can tell many things about humans. This one is older and solidly built, although bits of him don't work as well any more. Parnell has a plastic hip and the cartilage in his knees is frayed. Chris sees this through combinations of vibration, sound and scent. Just as he can hear the multiple textures in Parnell's voice and smell the man's breakfast on his breath. This is, in dog terms, a 'good man', lovely colours and smells all the way through his body, and a relatively rare find. He makes Chris feel easy, and that makes a dog happy and playful.

'Wanna play?' he asks. Chris is using a technique of 'request' that involves every fibre of his body, from his heart rate to the angle of his tail. Humans get this, but slowly.

Parnell looks down at Chris's posture and cocked ears.

'You wanna play, boy?'

Well, duh, thinks Chris.

Parnell looks around but the car park is empty, apart from their van and the cars of the other people on the tour. The staff car park is out of sight. He grins and reaches into his jacket packet, grimaces, tries a different pocket.

'It's in your glove compartment,' says Chris.

'I think it's in the . . . let's have a look . . . yes! It was in the glove compartment!' Parnell has, in his large hand, a small hard rubber ball. Chris almost faints with excitement.

'Come ON! Ball ball ball ballaballaballaball!'

Parnell swings his legs out of the van, stands and stretches as Chris dances manically in circles around his wonderful stinky shoes.

'I thought you were a trained dog? Sit.'

Chris's arse hits the ground like a sack of cement. He sits still, poised, eyes wide.

'Impressive,' says Parnell. 'Boy, you would be embarrassed by our lot.' He looks around scratching his balding head and spies a wide grassy area over by the back of the building.

'Come!' He takes off at a good pace for a man with dodgy knees, and Chris leaps up to his side. The ball is thrown. The ball is returned. And again. And sadly, after not too long Parnell is out of breath and a little sore from the stooping, and the ball is covered in dog saliva and Chris is panting and his teeth gleam.

'Last one, Chris,' Parnell tuts at himself. 'I'm a bit creaky these days.'

He bends backwards to throw the ball and his knee gives a little. Instead of throwing straight, the ball bounces off and over to the back of the building, disappearing around the far side with Chris full pelt after it.

'Chris!' yells Parnell and hobbles after him.

Ballaballaballaball is almost all that is going through Chris's mind as he rounds the corner faster than a greyhound and almost crashes into a great big pile of white barrels. The little rubber ball has disappeared beneath them, and Chris scratches at the ground, pawing at it as if he could ruck up the concrete and pull the little blighter out.

Parnell has come puffing up behind him. 'What the hell is this?'

'Ball!' says Chris pointing with every part of his body, but the man is completely distracted by the pyramid of barrels.

'Bloody hell, that's an awful lot of chemicals.' He reaches into his pocket and pulls out his glasses. Stepping close to the pile, spectacles perched on the end of his nose, he squints at a label on one of the barrels.

'For goodness sake,' says Chris, exasperated. 'The BALL has been LOST, man!'

'Potassium hydroxide,' reads Parnell. 'Wonder what on earth they want with that?'

The barrels are piled up in front of an enormous shed-like structure with an open front. In the dark within, Chris can hear the sound of several men moving around, shouting instructions to each other.

'Left a bit!'

'Over on your side, Bill.'

'Watch it, you stupid fucker!'

Chris, still frantic for the ball, sees Parnell peering into the dark, hesitating.

'The BALL!' He barks loudly and begins scrabbling for it again.

'Who's there?' An angry voice is followed by a young blond man with an angry face.

'Who the hell are you?' He is talking to Parnell and Chris smells something from him that isn't right. He stops barking and moves to stand next to Parnell. His hackles are raised, and his tail is up and very still.

'It's OK, boy.' Parnell puts a hand on Chris's head, but Chris doesn't relax his guard. The blond man smells 'off' like disease, standing with his legs apart, a piece of metal pipe in his hands.

'Sorry, mate. I am just the driver for the school bus parked over there. My dog lost a ball.' Parnell is unafraid. Why should he be? He can't smell the man.

Another man in a hard hat, short, very fat and very sweaty, comes running out. 'Oi, Andre. The Resomator cages are in the—' He stops short as he notices Parnell. 'Err . . . Andre . . . ?'

'Fuck off back to the bus, old man.' The blond spits at Parnell's feet, and Chris feels the shock come down through Parnell's arm. He cannot help it. A growl works its way up from his stomach to his throat.

'All right, Chris. Let's go, boy,' Mr Parnell taps his leg, aware that the growl could escalate. 'Come on, Chris.'

They walk away, both man and dog wanting to look back but managing not to. Chris still holds the growl in his body, ruff still up. He has already forgotten the ball. He is just protecting Parnell.

Parnell scratches his chin and then Chris's head. 'What a plonker,' he says after a while. His voice is even, but Chris can still feel Parnell's disquiet and confusion. 'Such aggression for what? Wonder what a Resomator is . . .' Parnell muses.

The Mini Adventures of Priya

'We are going into Ward B,' says Robin at the next junction. 'This is where we care for the older folks who need a little more attention. Could you impress on the children the need for quiet?'

They have stopped outside a set of large double doors, and Robin stoops, putting an intricate code into a keypad.

'I seen that on a film. It's a security thing.' The little girl, Priya, points.

'Why do you need to keep these doors locked, Mister Nurse Man?' another child's voice warbles out over the heads.

'The thing is, girls and boys, this is for the safety of the people inside. Many of the clients here have problems with their memories. They might forget where they are, and if we don't keep these doors closed they could get confused and walk out into the road and be hurt.'

'My cat Kipper walked in na' road. He was squashed.'

'Well, yes . . .'

The other children are upset. 'That is so sad. Awww.'

'Yes, yes.' Jenny Jameson calls order before the tears begin. 'Anyone else want to ask anything before we go into the ward?'

'Will the old people be naked?' asks Johnny.

'Do they eat with their mouths?' asks Bradley.

'Do they do wees in their beds?'

'Oh for goodness' sake,' sighs Jenny. 'Where on earth do they get this stuff?'

'May I ask how many people are currently on the ward? What are the costings on this setup?' Alex has a very long list of questions, but most of them she cannot ask in front of the children. *'Is it true you have your own crematorium on site?' for instance.* In her preparation for this visit, Alex has tracked down one of the original scaffolders. He, and most of his colleagues, were laid off two years ago but he swears blind there were plans for one.

'As from yesterday, we have one hundred residents here in the high-care facility. About three-quarters are mostly very elderly, some with mental health issues. The rest are long-term disabled people without care facilities at home.' Alex doesn't get a chance to ask him if providing care in their own homes would be of benefit. Robin refuses to be drawn on anything financial.

'Miss, Miss,' Priya tugs on Alex's arm. She looks worried. 'When you get old will you come here?'

'Goodness, no!' whispers Alex. 'Chris and I are going to live on a tropical island together. I've already booked the plane tickets.'

Priya nods, reassured.

'This way now, and quiet please. We don't want to disturb anyone, do we?' says Robin. 'You might want to let the camera in first and she can film you coming in.'

He has done this before, thinks Alex.

The camerawoman pushes past them with the large black digital Panasonic and tripod on her shoulder. She winks at Jenny.

'Give us a min.'

The children are hushed and excited.

'My mum says the people here are empty in their heads,' says a little girl.

'Actually, that is not the least bit true, Pippa.' Jenny is irritated. 'Children, what did we learn in class this morning? People can get sick and . . . come on . . .'

'Sick and confused when they are old,' chorus the children.

'And then?'

'And then they need to be cared for by others.'

'That's right. Just like you and me need to be cared for when we get sick.'

'I feel sick,' says a pale girl at the back.

'OK, I think you can go through now.' Robin waves them forward.

'Children, remember to be quiet and respectful. That includes you, Bradley.'

Jenny Jameson must be a good sister. Without having to be asked, she audio-describes to Alex as they go. The ward is very long and wide, almost a barn, although the temperature is warm and the lighting subdued and carefully designed for tired eyes and weary brains. The central aisle is wide enough for several people to walk abreast, and the tour group – Jenny, Alex, the children and the two other journalists – slowly follow Robin, keeping within the yellow lines painted on the floor that mark out the central walkway.

The huge ward is lined with large beds screened from each other by attractive plastic partitions. Next to each bed is a comfortable chair, portable commode and contemporary sleek storage cupboard. There is also a desk inset with a mirror that can double-up as a dressing table. The desks are all laden with vases of beautiful flowers, baskets of fruit and bright cards.

'I get the impression it is like a warehouse,' says Alex. 'I see a really big room with beds down the lengths of each wall. Who are in the beds? What facilities? Any nurses?'

'Hold on,' Jenny says, turning to the child that is pulling at her trouser leg. 'What is the matter, Lily?'

'I still feel sick.'

'OK, dear.' Jenny puts her hand over the pale child's forehead. 'This one's a puker,' she whispers to Alex. 'Now Lily . . . how bad do you feel? Do you want to go back outside now, or can you wait while we visit the lovely people in here?'

Lily thinks about it. 'I can wait.'

'Good girl, but let me know if you change your mind.' Jenny turns back to Alex. 'I'd say there are over fifty beds in here. Large beds with all the bells and whistles.'

'Bells and whistles?'

'Let's try and get closer. Yeah, bells and whistles. Can you make out that they have movable sections, head rests, foot elevation and inbuilt TVs and radios? I think they are all top of the range. My grandmother wanted one of these in her final years. She spent hours going through hospital catalogues for the perfect bed. Keep close, children!' She lowers her bright teacher's voice. 'There are five nurses' stations, I think.'

'Is that a nurse for every ten patients?' the *Health Visitors' Gazette* journalist asks Robin.

'Ten *clients*. We double that at night,' says Robin. 'And we have backup staff on call twenty-four hours a day for every ward.'

'That's incredible,' says Jenny.

'And wages?' Alex now. 'I hear that most of the care staff are on zero hours contracts?'

Robin doesn't seem to hear her. 'Would you like to meet a couple of the clients?' he asks Jenny.

'If you are sure they won't mind the children?'

Robin smiles and opens his palms, a gesture used by liars everywhere.

'Mrs Gosling loves children, don't you, Edna?'

They all move left and crowd around the high bed of Mrs Gosling. She is so tiny, pale and white in the massive bed she does indeed resemble a baby bird.

'Hello dears,' she says in a clear and surprisingly strong voice. 'Isn't it wonderful? It is almost like having my own room.'

'You look old, but you don't look sick.' Johnny sounds as if he is complaining, but Edna laughs even as Jenny apologises. The children's questions keep coming, and Alex takes a closer look at the desk. Fruit, flowers, a card. She is about to pick it up when Robin hisses in her ear. 'Please don't touch any of the clients' private possessions.'

Alex pulls back her hand, slowly. There is something she just can't quite put her finger on, and it isn't the card.

The man from the *Health Visitors' Gazette* manages to ask a few questions of the next client they are allowed to visit on the other side of the barn-like ward. Alex doesn't catch his name. 'Yes, this is a mixed ward, but the women are on the one side and we're on the other. At our age that is quite a distance, and we can't possibly get up to any shenanigans!' This old man seems weaker than Edna. He is lying back on his pillows and breathing oxygen through a thin nasal tube. He seems remarkably upbeat, all things considering.

'I was brought here a couple of days ago. I had a fall, and the paramedics thought I would be safer in here than left at home.

And I'm very glad, too. The food's excellent, and the nurses pretty.' He winks at Robin.

'Robin is blushing,' whispers Jenny to Alex.

'Well, I think that is enough now, everyone.' Robin is moving the tour group backwards towards the door. The long, darker recesses of the ward will remain unexplored. 'I don't think we should disturb these lovely folk any more. They need their rest.'

'Looking around,' Jenny says to Alex, 'it does look as if most of the rest of the clients are sleeping already.'

Very soft music, the same Vivaldi from TOSA and Job Central, is being played through speakers set high up on the walls. Jenny points and then apologises to Alex. 'Heavens! There are cameras everywhere.'

'Yes,' says Robin brightly, back on the script. 'We have twenty-four hour surveillance of all the wards. It is for our clients' safety, following on from the abuse scandals of the last few years in other establishments. That would never happen here. Anyone treating our clients badly would be caught on film, remanded and prosecuted.'

And he will say no more but presses them all to move. 'Come on, now, quiet as mice, please . . . more biscuits and juice back in the family room!'

At the mention of biscuits and juice Lily vomits horribly at his feet, and for the next several minutes there is minor mayhem as Jenny and Robin rush about organising clean-ups and exit strategies and the camerawoman stands aside laughing, and the *Health Visitors' Gazette* man stalks off, disgusted.

They have only been back in the family room for a few minutes when Jenny gasps and grabs Alex. 'I'm missing one!'

'What?'

An alarm is sounding down the hall, a high-pitched cheeping.
'Priya! We are missing Priya.'
And indeed they are.

It happened that Priya had also been interested in the cards.
While the tour group was moving away from the old man's
bedside, she had plucked up the glittery card to look and
accidentally knocked an apple off the top of the fruit bowl.
Horrified, she had watched it roll off down under the plastic
partition and into the next unit. Being a good kid, she had
crawled off after it, just at the same time that Lily began throwing
her guts up.

'I dropped an apple!' she had called over her shoulder, but no
one had heard her.

'There was another man in the next bed too,' she says to Alex
and Jenny as they cross the car park back to the school bus. 'But
he was fast asleep and didn't even notice the apple coming into
his section, or me, neither. Or at least he was kind of asleep but
his eyes were still open a bit an' he looked horrible. So skinny
and like a skellington.'

Priya had frantically searched around the space for the apple
and breathed a huge sigh of relief when she had seen its shiny
red skin glowing down on the floor next to the leg of the sleeping
man's bed. She reached for it and two things had become apparent
to her almost simultaneously. One, the apple was hard, hollow
and made of plastic, and two, the man's gnarly-toed foot had
slipped from under the sheets and was hanging slightly off the
side of the bed. The man's ankle was tied to the bedpost by a
long leather cord.

Before she had time to think about this, she realised the rest of the tour group were heading out of the double doors at the top of the ward. The doors were shutting. She had been left behind. Still clutching the apple, she had been about to run after them all when she heard the old man in the next bed laughing.

'It was weird 'cos he sounded like he was getting up,' says Priya, wrinkling her nose at Jenny.

Instinctively, she had crouched back down behind the partition. She didn't know why, but she felt frightened. Through a gap in the plastic she watched as the first man pulled the tube out of his nostrils and swung his legs off the side of the bed.

'He was wearing his shoes in bed,' Priya says wide eyed. 'And when he called out his voice was different.' Priya doesn't remember exactly what the man had called out to the woman across the hall, but it was something that made the woman laugh.

And then the alarm had sounded and he had leapt right back into the bed, and been stuffing the tubing up his nose when a nurse had come running straight to where Priya was crouching and dragged her out by her forearm, and Priya had screamed and dropped the apple.

Now Priya is sitting on the front seat in the bus next to Jenny, and Alex is standing in the doorway with Chris on his lead, wagging his feathery tail.

'Am I in trouble?' the little girl asks.

'Oh no, not at all,' says Jenny giving her a hug. 'You were only chasing an apple.'

'But it was a *plastic* apple,' says Priya. 'An' the nurse was really cross. She kept asking me what I had looked at, over an' over.'

'Well, I am just glad you are safe and back with us, Priya,' says Alex and squeezes the girl's knee. 'You had quite a fright.'

Alex leans over and gives Jenny a piece of paper. 'It's got all my contact details on it. Would you call me later? I have some things I want to discuss.'

'An' I took a picture on my phone!' Priya's hand is held out. 'Of the skellington man tied to the bed.'

Jenny and Alex become very still. Slowly, Jenny reaches for the phone.

'Err . . . you had your phone?'

'Oh, yeah. Daddy says I must always keep it with me in my inside pocket. Nurse Dyer never asked me for it, honest.'

Jenny is looking at the picture on the phone. 'Alex, you're a journalist, aren't you?'

'Yes.'

'I think you will want to have a copy of this.'

Binding's Bad Temper

The Good Doctor Binding is in an extremely bad temper. He doesn't exchange pleasantries with Gina, the Colombian maid, as he comes through the door of his daughter's home, merely hands her his coat. 'Where's the meeting?' he barks.

'They are gathering upstairs in the living room, Dr Binding.'

'Right. Need a quick drink first.' He strides off in the direction of the library. 'Tell Stella I'm here, would you, Gina?'

The maid does her usual little duck and nod and dashes off. The Good Doctor is rarely riled but when he is, it is best to steer clear.

In the library and still snarling, Binding throws his briefcase on the central desk and heads to the sideboard to pour himself a very large malt.

'Hello, Daddy.' Stella wafts in on a cloud of expensive perfume. 'You are early . . .' She takes one look at her father and her serene smile flattens. 'Jesus, what is it?'

'That paltry little prick Pansy!' Binding swirls the malt around his gums, drinks and refills his glass.

OK, this is not new, and Stella's shoulders drop from her ears. 'Ah, Professor Pansy. What has he done now, Dad?'

'The "P Formula". He says he has got the whole procedure down to just six days. Six days, Stella? How is it possible?'

'Are you sure he isn't exaggerating? Come on, Daddy . . . it's Fred Pansy, after all. He'll say anything to rile you.'

'Stella, I saw the paperwork. In fact . . .' He strides over to his briefcase and pulls out a file of paper and glossy photographs, which he lays out on the desktop.

Stella is so angry she can barely squeak. She takes a deep breath. 'Daddy. You absolutely cannot be carrying around any of this material. I thought you understood the sensitivity of this project.'

'Yes, yes.' Binding flaps his hands at his daughter. 'I will shred it all as soon as I have had another look through.'

'Now, Daddy. Shred it now!' Stella grabs a metal wastepaper basket from under the desk.

'Stella.' The father in his voice is enough. Stella falters. The basket is dropped to the floor.

'I just don't understand how he is doing it.' Binding circles the desk, peering down at the scribbled figures. 'Pansy says he is processing nearly a hundred people a week. He says he has taken even the fittest and reduced them to ash in the six-day time slot. I just can't believe it. The whole point is to ensure that the cause of death is "natural". You can't do that in six days. He must be cheating somehow. We are still taking nearly fourteen days per patient. We can't compete.'

Stella comes closer to the table and looks down her nose at the papers and the photos of emaciated bodies.

'Look, Daddy, I can't be witness to any of this. It is not officially sanctioned yet. And anyway, you originally costed for three weeks per patient. Two weeks means you are not just hitting your targets but surpassing them.'

'Yes, Stella, but if Pansy is truly clocking six days and a turn-around of ninety-three per week then he will be the man they call on when they roll out the CDD to the wider population. I will lose the contract! And it is *my* bloody project in the first place.'

'Hang on, Daddy. If he is getting through ninety-three a week, how is he disposing of them? He doesn't have a Resomator too, does he?'

'No. No, he doesn't, thank goodness. He is still having to pay off the local crematoriums.' *And, as here, any extra body parts are probably just dumped into local sewer systems*, Binding thinks but does not add out loud. 'But you are right. That is costly, and it will slow him down. Apparently, he also had a couple of his first batch escape. He had to send "people" to track down and dispose of them. More foolish waste. I imagine he will lose points for that too.' He glances at his daughter. She shrugs, heads to the sideboard and fixes herself a vodka and tonic.

'Daddy, I would be very surprised if you lost the contract to Pansy. After all, in the end it is down to Henri Rennes and myself. Have you forgotten to what heights your daughter has risen?' She laughs and Binding relaxes.

'You are right, my dear. But I would still like to know what he is using to get that six-day result.'

'Well, we can go through all this after the meeting, Daddy. I really need you to be on best behaviour for these UN dignitaries. Mummy has brought in an Ethiopian chef just for the ambassador.'

'Oh hell. Gloria knows *injera* gives me terrible flatulence.'

'And you promise you will come right back here and shred this stuff, Dad? I won't have it on the property overnight.'

'Yes, yes.'

He is thinking again, circling. Stella tips back her lovely neck and finishes the vodka in her glass. 'I'm heading up, Daddy. Please don't be long. Mummy is getting frantic about the coffee ceremony.' She waits until her father grunts assent then slips from the room.

Binding will shred the file, but reluctantly. And there is something else he hasn't told Stella. To protect her . . . and maybe also because she would be furious and tell him the one-upmanship with Pansy has gone far enough.

'It's in the interest of medical science,' he mutters to himself, thinking of Pansy's decision to film the six-day processing, purely to prove to Binding that he can do it. 'Stella just wouldn't understand.'

And anyway, disclosure doesn't matter now as the experiment is already underway. He and Pansy had selected the candidates together. They had the most outrageous luck too. Pansy had been trawling the local juvenile detention centre for subjects and had found a set of seventeen-year-old twins. Binding had checked them over and yes, they were perfect. In good health, apart from mild learning difficulties, probably the result of foetal alcohol spectrum disorder. The mother had died in one of Pansy's centres less than a year ago, of cirrhosis. She had been thirty-five. The twins ticked all the boxes: no living relatives, no economic viability, drain on the state, possible future crime risk and so forth.

One of the lads had been quite cocksure, joking with Binding that even a short stay in hospital would be better than a day in 'juvi'. He was a mere inch taller than his brother, almost handsome behind the acne and the chipped brown teeth. He said he was learning to read inside and fancied he would one day join the army and be able to look after a family. His brother had watched him joshing with the nurses, slack-jawed, uninterested.

'Whatever,' he had murmured when they had asked to take blood.

The cheeky one, Dan (or Twin One), would get the six-day process and his brother, Wayne (Twin Two), would be the control. Filming had already begun.

'My name's Dan and I'm your man!' Dan had grinned at the camera. He had an infectious cheeky laugh and the nurses couldn't help but join in.

You are indeed our man, The Good Doctor Binding had thought at the time.

There is a subtle knock on the library door and Binding looks up to see Gina is holding his dinner jacket. He sighs. 'Oh all right, I am coming . . . and Gina, make sure you lock this door behind me, all right?'

A Stupid Mistake

Gunter is about to step into the taxi outside the home he shares with Stella when he remembers he has left his copy of George Szirtes's *The Burning of the Books* in the library, and he needs it for his tutorial in the morning.

'*Kurde!* Damn!' he hisses. 'Hang on, please,' he asks the cabbie and dashes around the side of the house, waving at his wife's government security guard. 'Ben, it's just me. I left a book in the library.'

The guard nods. 'Righto, Mr Gorski, you're clear,' and carries on, leaving Gunter to scrabble in through the scullery. He dashes up the stairs, praying not to bump into anyone. He doesn't want to be caught in a conversation about where he is going or when he is coming back. He has a secret bolthole, the lobby of the run-down Bismarck Hotel in the West End, which he uses for private tutorials. There is a particularly beautiful Rhodes Scholar who wishes to discuss Rumi. In his experience, discussions of Rumi are often punctuated by the need to drink wine, which in turn might lead to the need to . . . anyway, he doesn't think Stella would approve of his teaching methods.

Does he feel guilt . . . yes. He loves . . . loved Stella. But she has become completely obsessed with her climb to the throne, and he is a man with a huge appetite for . . . 'Rumi'. A verse settles feather-like on his forehead.

> *Love has nothing to do with*
> *the five senses and the six directions:*
> *its goal is only to experience*
> *the attraction exerted by the Beloved.*
> *Afterwards, perhaps, permission*
> *will come from God . . .*

Yet he is not thinking about the Rhodes Scholar. He is thinking about that woman with the wonderful breasts and the eyes that were flaming and failing at the same time. Lovely eyes. Alex, wasn't it? Yes, his *ptaszek*, Alex. He remembers he jotted down her phone number, somewhere . . . He pauses.

The hall is dark. He can hear the muted tinkle of glass and conversation coming from upstairs and remembers the charity event. He breathes, relieved, and shoulders into the library, hitting the lights nearest the door and crossing the room quickly. He knows exactly where the poetry collections are and in seconds has his hands on the text. Turning back, he notices the central desk is covered in papers. He glances at it as he walks past, sees figures and pencilled scrawls. Not interesting. But wait. There is a photo. A terrible, frightening photo of an emaciated body on a bed. Not one, but two, three . . . *My God. What is this?*

Then Gunter makes a very bad mistake. He stops and looks more closely at the papers laid out on the desk. But his are not the only eyes glistening in the gloom. Gina almost comes into the library, pauses – and, touching her lips, retreats.

Chris and the Storm Crow

The ground has been baked dry by the sun. Sharp, miserable lumps of faded grass poke up from between Chris's paw pads. Even so, the intense joy he feels, a giddying rush in his pelvis, stomach, head is lessened not a jot. Free! Free!

A crow watches him from the fence, its head cocked to one side. Chris gets a waft of its wormy black cynicism but chooses to ignore it. Crows are such utter snobs. Freedom isn't just about being able to fly, you know.

Chris is sprinting to the horizon, puffs of dust rising up behind him. Faster and further. He has almost made it! Now he wheels around and gallops back again, head a whirl of happy speed and sensation, muscles stretching, heart pumping. Oh joy!

Alex is coming along. She is slow and talking into her phone, as usual. Chris pelts past her, heading towards the far field; the rush of wind lifts his ears, his tail whips in circles. And then, like a lasso, he is caught by a stink and must follow it. It leads him to another one, stronger. He squats and pees (guide dogs don't raise their legs . . . most indelicate). Another lasso of stench. Golden trails of piss and pungent territory-marking. And that one . . . that could be a rabbit. That one, a dead insect. That one, an old mouse nest.

'Storm coming,' says the crow. Chris pauses and raises his wonderful nose, breathes the sunlight. There is not a cloud in the sky and almost no breeze, but crows can't lie and yes, there it is, far, far away, a smell like the tinkle of distant Christmas bells, a glittering smell.

'It's days away,' says Chris.

'Going to be a doozy.' The crow stretches its wings, looking down its sharp lacquered beak.

'Righto!' says Chris, spinning around and dashing off again, feeling the whoop of wolf in his belly. *Arroooo!* He dives past Alex again, as if on the trail of a deer. He can feel bloodlust. He can feel power. Then boom, he stumbles over an old tennis ball.

'Alex, Alex, Alex!' He brings the ball, dropping it at her feet. 'Alex, ball, ball, ball!' He tries to make eye contact. 'Alex, ball, Alex, ball!'

'Jesus, Chris, where did you find that old thing? Gross. It could have anything on it.'

Chris knows exactly what it has on it. The saliva of about ten other dogs including a German shepherd called Arnold and a collie bitch called Poppy. There is also river mud, rabbit poo, dead ants and a lot of anonymous dirt. It is a wonderful thing. It is a ball.

'Alex, Alex, ball, ball!'

She throws. He throws himself after it. Brings it back. 'Again, Alex, ball, ball!'

The crow jumps into the sky and pauses, managing a little show-off free fall over Chris's and Alex's heads.

'Storm a-coming!' it caws again. 'Find shelter!' It flaps away, leaving Alex and Chris in the park. Alex watches it.

'Ignore the freakin' crow.' Chris drops the ball at her feet so she almost falls over him. 'Ball, Alex. Concentrate. Ball, ball, ball!'

Alex groans, reaches down and picks it up between her fingers. 'Yuk! You know guide dogs are not even supposed to play with balls . . . Ach, what the hell.' She throws.

The Riggings of the Wheelchair

Alex is sitting at her desk at the *Cambright Sun* when her colleague Jimmy gets the call from the local police desk. 'Ah, this is a cracker!' he shouts, leaping up for his camera and phone.

'Whatcha got?' Alex is curious. The last few days have been hellishly quiet in the office. Even Dino has run out of blog material.

'Some local kids got blown up. Four of them are in Allenbrook Hospital with bits missing.'

'What did you say?'

'Cops say gang-related! But it's mine, Killer. Fuck off out of it!'

Alex sits very still when Jimmy has gone. Her lips feel a little numb, as if blood has drained from her face. She licks them. If her brain were a computer it would say 'system failure' on the monitor. *They wouldn't*, she thinks. But they would, she knows. The Once Only rule? Under her nose? Or maybe . . . Boudicca?

*

THE CAMBRIGHT SUN
Has Gang War exploded on our city streets? Are our children safe? by Jimmy Mathesson, Crime Reporter

Four teenagers from the Mandela Estate were rushed to hospital at 6:30 p.m. yesterday evening after falling victim to a cruel prank.

Danny Freidken (15), Taylor Bent (16), Melanie Giggs (14) and Brendon Kenny (13) are being treated for serious injuries and second-degree burns.

It is thought that the teenagers were taking rides in an abandoned wheelchair when a device rigged to the underside of the chair exploded. Danny Freidken, who was sitting in the chair at the time, is still in surgery. Melanie Giggs may lose her sight after shrapnel was embedded in her right eye.

According to George Dingle, first on scene, the teenagers had 'borrowed' a wheelchair from a neighbour and were pushing each other in it along the banks of the canal when the accident happened.

'I just heard an almighty bang, and then screaming. The whole thing was a terrible mess, blood and bits of metal and rubber from the chair all over the path. I trod on something soft and when I looked down it was one of the kids' fingers.'

The police have begun an investigation, and the owner of the wheelchair, a Mrs Dawn Coomb, has given a statement saying she was away at the time of the incident visiting her sister in Edinburgh. PC Frank Marley states that the crime could be gang-related as Danny Freidken was a known member of the notorious Smitters Gang.

*

That afternoon Alex rings up the Ladies' Defective Agency reception. 'I'm sick. Can't make it in,' she lies.

'Hey,' says Laverne. 'Did you hear the news?' She sounds excited, almost exuberant. And why not? Those kids got exactly what they deserved. A serious arse-kicking, and it sounds like one or two of them might be joining the crip fraternity too, when they get out of hospital. Well, good! Maybe they will learn from all this, become compassionate and empowered local citizens.

As if. When she thinks about it, Alex becomes more and more uncomfortable. They're just ignorant, hopeless kids after all. She thinks about Helen and Jules singing the refrain 'Alone we fall, together we appal!' and shouting *Boudicca!* to the ceiling.

Boudicca. *We 're back to Boudicca.* She taps it into the computer again to see if she has missed any news on the group, any clues to who they are, what they might want . . . *or be capable of doing.*

Boudicca . . . queen . . . yadda yadda. Not that, but ah ha! Here they come, a scree fall of articles about graffitied walls and letters to the council. *Boudicca! We are coming!* The last graffiti splashed in red across the motorway bridge was done in the night, sometime last week.

Boudicca. Are they here? Are they blowing up children? Are they my friends? Alex rubs her tired eyes. The computer screen blurs and whites out. She blinks hard to clear her vision, feeling stupid, as if she has found out a lover has been cheating on her. And, as her stronger eye focuses, she sees something that causes her to pause, something on one of the photographs of graffiti. She clicks, blows it up, magnifies it more and more until the one

163

corner is taking up her entire screen. The red 'Boudicca!' tag has been sprayed over a TOSA/Grassybanks extension notification billboard. Scrawled underneath in black paint are the words 'Homeless, crippled, old, take Action! They kill us for their sport!'

What the hell did that mean? Was it an oblique reference to the Homeless Action! initiative, thinks Alex. There is the connection to Grassybanks and Dr Binding again. How can she unravel this knot?

She sits back in her chair and it creaks. Chris shoots up, ears perked. He can read her vibrations, and she is in need of a walk.

'Walk?' he suggests.

'How about a walk then, Chrissy boy?' Alex stretches and her shoulders crack. 'Hellfire . . . I could really do with getting back to the gym.' And at the thought of the gym, Alex remembers where she has seen Robin, the nurse from Grassybanks, before. Yoga class. She went a couple of times, and now she has a vision of his lanky form in loose tracksuit pants, his privates dangling horribly free from constraints as he lurches forward into 'downward dog'.

Yoga class. Well, it could be worse.

And It Is

Alex isn't happy. She is twisted into a grotesque position, arms grabbing buttocks and legs bent at right angles. Sweat drips from her chin. She can see Chris's shape lying against the far wall on his dog towel. She just knows he is grinning at her.

'And breathe into the stretch,' says the sumptuous, lean and lovely Sandra, class teacher and winner of the most annoyingly beautiful and serene person competition.

Alex tries to breathe in, but the way she is twisted means that she ends up making a rather unpleasant rasping sound, almost a death rattle. Her left leg has gone numb and her neck just creaked. If she wasn't on this investigation she would be in a pub and not in this class. She has never got on with yoga. However, her focus is set on the skinny balding man on her left with the too-short shorts and the fish-white hairy thighs. Robin. She hasn't been able to get his attention yet. He does a lot of his yoga with his eyes shut and his mouth slightly open.

Sandra is correcting the woman in front of Alex, an unsmiling German with steel-grey hair and steel-grey glasses. She might be seventy years old but she is as supple as a whip.

Fuck, if I could bend like that I would be fucking smiling about it, thinks Alex as Sandra allows them to unwind from the one position and begins to encourage them into an even more complex one.

Alex, doing her best to follow, finds herself trying to look backwards over one shoulder while balancing on the opposite leg. She begins to topple over and desperately flails with her arms, managing to make contact with Robin's outstretched arm and unbalancing him too. They both have to clutch at each other to keep upright.

'Oopsie! So sorry,' says Alex. 'Thank goodness you caught me.' She pauses to pull up the strap of her low-cut stretch camisole, jiggling her boob to get it back in place. Robin has definitely opened his eyes now. He moves closer and Alex gets a strong waft of garlic and unwashed tracksuit.

'Hey, isn't it . . . ummm . . . didn't we meet before?'

'Oh yes! Wow, what a coincidence. On the Grassybanks tour. I'm Alex,' says Alex.

'Sshhhhhhh,' spits the German lady.

'Sorry,' says Robin. He rolls his eyes at Alex and she grins back. For the rest of the class, he keeps his eyes open and on her, or rather on her arse or her breasts, 'helping' her into one or two of the final positions and allowing his hands to stray just a little. Alex would normally have clobbered him, but in this instance she just grits her teeth and giggles stupidly. She will clobber him later.

'Fancy catching a bite to eat after class?' she asks.

Unfortunately, it turns out that Robin is a vegan and strictly teetotal.

'You are kidding?' Alex bats her eyelashes, but the gorge is rising as she thinks about pumping him for information without a tot of alcohol inside her first. She may not make it. Luckily, she remembers the Living Stone Café, organic vegan food and organic vegan wine. Expensive, though . . . perhaps a bit too expensive.

'Oh, that's OK,' says Robin. 'I like that place. Great. I'll see you there at seven.'

It is the end of the class and Alex, who is harnessing Chris, realises Robin has suddenly gone silent. She looks up.

'What's with the dog? A guide dog? Are you training him?' Robin asks. He sounds rather put out and upset, as if she has just pulled a skunk from a hat.

'No, he's mine. I thought you realised. I'm visually impaired.'

'You don't look it. And you didn't have one on the tour, did you? You seem to manage fine without him and you know . . . you look so normal.' He thinks about it. 'Hey! You can see me, can't you?' He waves his hand in her face. He thinks he is being funny.

What is it with blokes? It is always the first fucking question they ask, thinks Alex, *'Can you see me?' As if that is the only important thing they can think of in the face of someone's blindness. Can you see ME?*

'Yes, of course I can,' Alex coos. 'I have extreme tunnel vision, but what I see is pretty clean. I can see your face,' . . . *and your paunch, and your bald spot, and your brown front tooth.*

'Oh that's good. I'm a handsome devil, you know!' He titters. Alex feels Chris wince. 'But I'm afraid I am not very fond of dogs. Any chance you could leave him behind tonight?'

Oh, you are so not getting any, thinks Alex. 'Sadly, I need Chris to get to the café, but I promise you will barely notice he is there.' Alex practises her simpering to go with his tittering. What a pair.

That Living Stone Café Date

Robin arrives having changed, but not showered. He seems quite proud of the fact. 'I am one of the greenest people I know,' he says. 'It is the most important thing. I conserve water carefully and shower quickly, but only once every two days, no matter what. Water is the earth's lifeblood after all.'

He carries on in this vein for quite a while. He was a founder member of the local veggie box scheme, was one of the campaigners for the Cycle 2 Work scheme. He even put in a request that the Grassybanks' cleaning products be environmentally friendly.

'Grassybanks?' *At last a way in*, thinks Alex. 'Oh yes, of course. How's that going? Nurse Dyer . . . she seems quite a character.'

Robin's thin lips twist. 'She may be a half-decent nurse, but she really is a seriously frigid bitch.'

Frigid. Alex hates that word when applied to women. She smiles encouragingly. 'Must be difficult to work with someone like that?'

'Grassybanks is difficult to work in, anyway,' says Robin, spearing an olive. He hasn't ordered any himself but seems quite happy to pinch hers. 'There is so much red tape at the moment. You can't do this, can't go there. You know we have to sign a contract forbidding us from talking to the press! What's that about?'

Alex leans in. 'Really? That's very strange. Why do you think you can't talk to the press?'

Robin sticks his fingers into the olives and sucks on a green one. Oil dribbles from the corner of his mouth and glistens on his chin. 'I think it's to do with the ward extension. We are already oversubscribed, you know. "A cycle of hopeless terminals", as Dyer calls them. It's sad, really, although I understand the idea behind it all – you know, environmentally how important it is.'

Alex feels a cold sweat between her shoulder blades. 'What is environmentally important?'

'The aubergine cannelloni?' A waitress has materialised behind Alex.

'Mine!' says Robin. He tucks straight in.

'And this must be yours, dear.' The woman plonks down a plate of stuff. On the menu it was called Broccoli Tarka Dhal, but to Alex, whose vision is fluctuating in the gloom of the room, it looks just like green sludge.

'Oh, what a gorgeous dog!' The waitress bends down and tickles Chris, who is tucked between Alex's chair and the far wall.

'You need to wash your hands, Miss,' Robin calls after her. 'The dog is not hygienic. Alex, I really don't think it is right to bring an animal like that into a restaurant.'

Finding it hard not to poke him with her fork, Alex tries to get him back on subject.

'So, the ward extension? You were saying. Something about the environment?'

'You know, I am surprised I haven't seen you around before? I mean . . . well . . . you are really pretty. And so tall!' Robin doesn't seem to notice when his mouth is full. Alex is repulsed but carries on, knowing she is on the edge of something, some vital clue.

'Thanks, Robin. You were saying about the ward extension?'

'Blimey, dog with a bone. Ha! That's funny, isn't it? I mean, you are a dog with a bone and you have a dog. Ah. I am just too good tonight! Why are you so interested, anyway?' His close-set eyes suddenly narrow. 'Now I remember, you asked a load of questions on the tour too.'

Alex improvises. 'Err . . . I have . . . my old mum and . . . err . . . yeah, we are thinking that Grassybanks might be the right place for her.'

'Oh. Oh well. Depends, really. Is she on her last legs? If you are thinking in the long term, I wouldn't pop her into Grassybanks, but if you are looking for a quick resolution to her pain and discomfort then you couldn't go far wrong.'

'Resolution? Robin, are you saying they will speed her death?'

Robin chokes on a piece of aubergine and spits it messily onto his side plate. 'Of course not! What on earth . . . no, no! What do you take us for? No, I just mean that they are more a palliative care kind of setup, especially recently. Dr Binding is a leader in his field, after all.'

'Dr Binding? We didn't see him on the tour, did we?'

'Oh no. Dr Binding leaves those to us. Well, me, mostly. He and I are pretty close. He knows he can trust me.'

'Oh, right.'

'Yes. I think we kind of click. He is always saying that some people are naturally gifted when it comes to nursing, you know. By the way, that is your second glass of wine, Alex. You're drinking it like water!'

'Oh yes, sorry, the company is so good I lost track.'

Robin sniggers, not hearing the sarcasm. 'I agree, although I really don't like women drinking. I think it's an ugly trait. Usually means they are neurotic or got daddy issues or something. I went out with a girl once who drank.'

I bet she did, thinks Alex.

'She would have, like, two glasses *every* night. Made her weepy and whiny. In the end I just had to ditch her.'

Right . . . Alex buttons her lip.

'Dr Binding would understand. He is a specialist in liver disease, you know. He has seen the impact of alcohol in the community. Like me, he knows the perils of addiction. If it was up to me I would just ban alcohol, but of course that is impossible. The government makes too much money from it all. I asked Dr Binding about it once, and he said that chronic alcoholics and drug users were untreatable. They should just be allowed to self-destruct quietly with support and comfort. He felt it would be best for everyone, especially for the sake of these people's families.'

'Dr Binding said all that?'

'Yes, but he still carries on trying to improve the lives of these people. He says it is his duty as a physician. He was key in setting up the Homeless Action! programme, you know, him and a team of other eminent doctors. It's all very exciting. They're planning to put the programme in place at Grassybanks.'

'Would you like to see the dessert menu?' That waitress again.

'Oh, yes,' says Alex.

'Oh, I don't know,' says Robin. 'And I don't mean to be rude, but sugar and fat is really not a good choice for an evening.

171

Stimulants . . . like the wine. Also—' here he even winks at Alex '—none of us need the extra weight now, do we?'

Alex can't help the flush of anger creeping up her cheeks.

'Oh, I didn't mean to embarrass you. I like a woman with a bit of – well, not "meat" per se, on her. But you know . . . body on her body!' He reaches over and squeezes her hand. His is sweaty.

'Shall we get the bill?' Alex croaks.

It is a small fortune. Robin calculates. 'You had the olives and the two naughty, naughty glasses of wine, and I had just the cannelloni and tap water. Gosh, yours is expensive!'

'What about the tip?' asks Alex, stupidly.

'Oh thanks. That is good of you. I'll see you by the exit. Need to take a piss.'

Alex's purse is emptied. Totally. She harnesses a bored Chris and, banging her way between tables like a pinball, knocking a glass or two onto the floor, manages to wend her way to the exit, where Robin is attempting to chat up the waitress.

'Yes, I was just apologising for the dog on your behalf,' he stage whispers. 'I told them about your . . . "problem".' He rolls his eyes back in his head and mimes feeling around sightlessly.

'It's not a problem,' says Alex flatly. 'I like how I see.'

'Oh, I'm sorry.' Robin seems a bit taken aback. 'I don't think you should make light of blindness, though, Alex. As a nurse, I see it first-hand. I realise your condition isn't very serious, but I know other people who find it terribly distressing.'

'Jesus, Robin.' Alex is almost spluttering. 'You . . . you . . . you really are a bit of a prick.'

'What?' Robin's eyes widen. The waitress glides away. 'Where did that come from? I hope you don't talk to your children like that?'

'My children?' Alex is confused, but then the penny drops. 'Oh I see . . . you think I am a schoolteacher, right?'

'Well, aren't you? You were on the school tour.'

'Robin, I don't have kids, I don't have students. I am not a teacher. I work for the *Cambright Sun*. I am a journalist. I arranged this date so I could talk to you about Grassybanks.'

It may not be very fair, but it is very satisfying. Robin's jaw drops and he appears to be about to faint. 'Yes, that's how I felt when I saw the bill,' says Alex and, picking up Chris's harness, she bashes open the door with her elbow and heads out into the night.

Night of the Drunken Poet

The Poet, real name Gunter Gorski, is drunk. He is also sulking, and really, who could blame him? Yet another dinner party with his wife's tedious friends and her terrifying father. He wants to be writing, alone, somewhere cold and harsh and open to the skies. He has been working through an idea, a dream he had following that extraordinary encounter with the blind woman, Alex, whom he can't seem to get out of his head. He has been trying to weave a poem around illusion, blurring, obfuscation.

He knows in his heart that his writing is wilting beneath the weight of his marriage. His wife is very attractive, extremely intelligent – and as compassionless as a dry glass. And the sex is boring. Her ambition vaults high over his head and his hard-on. They had sex this morning. Or rather, she jerked him off with one hand while talking to her office on her mobile phone. He had playfully tried to pull the handset from her grasp, and she had scowled at him, then pushed him down flat on the bed and finished him off as if milking an upended goat, all without pausing in her conversation about Prime Minister's Questions. Then, still talking on the phone, she had walked with her sullied hand held out to one side across to the en suite bathroom. He had heard her flick his spunk into the toilet. Someone down the line said something funny, and she had laughed like a girl.

He sucks up another warm, kind throb of brandy, direct from the bottle, and closes his eyes. They have been married for nearly eight years, both on their second marriages. He has a teenage daughter in Australia, Mandy, whom he hasn't seen for nearly two years now. His current wife, Stella, can't have children, but the Poet thinks she has never been the broody type. Stella Binding MP, daughter of the internationally renowned Dr Barnabas Binding, is on the rise. It would, as a politician, have been an excellent PR coup to have children to parade around like the prime minister does, but Stella has instead opted for the 'triumph of spirit over adversity' media angle. *'Her blue eyes are perfectly complemented by her elegant aquamarine shirt dress,'* writes the interviewer from *Her!* magazine, *'but she won't be drawn when I ask about children. She merely takes a sip of coffee and gives me a courageous smile.'*

'Gunter?' Her shout comes from downstairs. There is an edge of irritation in it. 'Hurry up. Daddy will be here in a minute.'

Ahhh, thinks Gunter, *The Good Doctor Binding. An interesting case of endearing psychopathy.* Gunter's own father and grandfather had both been academics in the field of medicine. His father had worked as a consultant to the Jagiellonian University's neuroscience unit. For his grandfather, however, there had been another, darker story.

Gunter's grandfather had been based in Lwów University in the late 1930s. Very bad timing for an ambitious Jew. One dark June night in 1941, Gunter's grandfather and his then pregnant grandmother had been woken up by loud noises in the corridors of their halls of residence. His grandfather had just enough time to push his wife under a large pile of dirty laundry before men in SS uniforms battered the doors down and took him away. He, along with several other professors and their families, never reappeared, and were assumed to have been tortured and killed. Gunter's grandmother had survived, but not unscathed. During the day she had been the sweetest, funniest old thing, and Gunter had spent many happy hours with her cooking, reading, doing jigsaws, walking, even dancing to the radio. But not at night. At night she succumbed to terrible night terrors and would wander around the house reliving the arrest over and over again, and in particular, the face of the man she and the other wives had gone to begging for their husbands' lives. He had been a middle-aged soldier with a wide moustache, blue eyes and a bloody bayonet hanging casually from his hand.

'He smiles at me!' Gunter's grandmother would shriek, tearing out clumps of her hair in terror. 'He smiles at me and puts the point of the bayonet into my stomach! He says he will eat the baby . . .'

For some reason, Gunter would be reminded of the 'smiling man' whenever he was with Dr Binding. It was odd because Binding was a hugely affable, generous fellow and had been since they had first met. He had held nothing against Gunter for being artistic, foreign or even a bit of a cad to his precious daughter. In fact, in the first few years of this marriage, Gunter had been in awe of the man.

No longer. Not since stumbling across the horrors of the Clearance, Disinfection and Disposal file.

'Gunter, for heaven's sake!' Stella howls up the stairs. 'They are almost here!' He hears her telling Gina, the maid, to answer the doorbell.

Gunter takes another deep chug on the bottle of brandy and smiles at himself in the mirror. *Handsome dog*, he thinks, and for a second the blind woman's guide dog springs into his mind. *Damn, that was a lovely animal!* And that thought leads immediately to another . . . the dog's owner. Alex. She had said she was a journalist, he seems to remember. He wonders if he has read any of her work. In his mind's eye he reaches out and touches her neck, pulls her forward into his embrace. What breasts that woman had. And the things she could do with her . . . He sighs. 'Down, boy,' he tells the rising lump in his trousers. 'Down!'

It has been another blazing day, and the evening is uncomfortably humid. Inside, the dining room is elegantly decorated but a little too warm even with the wide sash windows open. The table flower display is wilting, odd petals curling, edged with brown. Muted traffic noise booms like distant thunder.

The Good Doctor Binding is sitting where he always does at the top of the large dark oak table. One would expect his daughter's husband to be head of the table, given this is his daughter's house, but no, Stella always puts Daddy there. In fact, Binding can't remember her ever asking Gunter where he'd like to sit. She always places people herself, thinking carefully about her table planning.

This evening she has seated the chubby MP, Amelia Baker, next to him. Binding finds the woman a ghastly bore, overtly racist and an uninhibited prig. Tonight, he decides he can put up with her inane, faintly fascist twittering because of her plunging cleavage. He looks up and catches Stella's raised eyebrows. His daughter knows how to keep him amused. Opposite Amelia – who is the Secretary of State for Culture, Media and

Sport, no less, and in addition (and how does she do it?) Minister for Women and Equality – is her husband, a small spidery person wearing a suit that entirely blends into the furniture. The Good Doctor can't quite remember his name, although he comes to supper at least twice a month. Gordon or Gerald or something.

'Darling . . . where's Gunter?' Binding's wife Gloria calls over to Stella, who is showing a short, dark-haired man to his seat. Gloria is a decent old thing, but Binding can't help but wince at her indiscretion.

'He's coming down, Mummy. He was immersed in his writing.'

In a bottle more like, thinks Binding.

'Mummy, I'd like you to meet Henri Rennes.'

'*Bonsoir, madame.*' The man's voice is liquid amber. 'I must apologise for being so late. Work . . . *c'est* . . . what's the word? "A bit bloody" as you English say?' He gives a Gallic shrug and gallantly reaches over to kiss Mrs Binding's knobbly, jewel-encrusted paw. '*Enchanté,*' he says.

Bloody hell, thinks Binding. *The old dear is blushing!* He, of course, already knows Henri, the CEO of TOSA, and his young wife Krystal. *They do 'business' together, oui.*

'Krystal, umm . . . I hope you don't mind, darling, but I am separating girls from their husbands tonight. You are over here.' Stella takes the limp hand of the six-foot blonde with the enhanced front and the remarkable behind. Krystal models for *Ms Frisky*, *Vague* and *Titlar*. Binding is a little sorry to see her sway her way down to the far end of the oak table. She may be almost half silicone by now, but she is still a gorgeous creature.

'Stella tells me that you are working on a new project, Dr Binding.' Amelia's eyes narrow slightly and she jigs forward in her seat. The silver pendant of her necklace falls into the grotto between her breasts, and Binding watches it disappear.

'Yes,' he says slowly. 'And please call me Barney, Amelia.' He is aware that many within the current government are acquainted with the work he is doing in drug and alcohol rehabilitation. However, almost no one but Henri and the rest of the working group know the full details of the Homeless Action! experiment and the progression of the CDD programme. Amelia, for all her chubby charm, is as ambitious as his daughter, more so perhaps. She has the twinkling eyes of a mongoose baiting a snake, a medicated mongoose but one with teeth, nonetheless. The Good Doctor hesitates and is rescued, as so often, by his daughter.

'Oh Daddy . . . could you start the wine?' Stella sings out. 'Gina is still in the kitchen.'

'Of course! Here, let me,' says The Good Doctor, picking up a bottle from the table and filling Amelia's glass with a delectable Pinot Grigio. His wife next, and then he is up and moving around the table to offer the others.

At which point, Gunter emerges from the hallway, handsome, dark hair tousled, shirt undone at the neck. He could be on the set of an aftershave advert.

'Evening, Doc,' he says and his breath is a brandy-and-self-pity cocktail.

'Jesus, Gunter,' hisses Stella coming up behind them. 'We are about to serve starters!'

'Sorry, darling,' Gunter growls and turns sharply, kissing her neck. It is almost a vampiric gesture, and Stella sways and can't help but throw back her head, exposing more of that long white throat. Dr Binding moves off with the bottle of wine, a little irked by the show. Stella is wearing a silver sleeveless shift dress and her hair is up in a carefully messy knot. She looks exquisite, and next to Gunter with his wolfish smile and lean physique, they make an almost Hollywood pairing. All faces around the table are turned to them. Binding catches the glint of envy, lust and more in the eyes of the guests. *Fascinating*, he thinks.

Gunter wishes he could smoke. He has been 'placed' by Stella at the bottom of the table with his back to the kitchen and next to a living Barbie doll. The starter is a blood-red borscht. Stella calls it 'botch', thinking she has the Polish pronunciation right. It makes Gunter flinch every time. The soup is clear and light with a delicate whirl of sour cream in the centre. Cold, of course. As a child, Gunter's borscht was full of lumps of potato and beetroot, thick and salted, hot and filling. He despises cold soup.

Luckily, Gina serves an icy shot of Bison Grass vodka with each portion. Gunter winks, and without a word she waits while he drinks and refills his shot glass. On top of the brandy and the wine, it is a little much. He wonders what his vomit will look like on the white tablecloth. He feels a poem in his gullet.

Red bile
The grass of the Steppes
Opens my throat and . . .

'OMG!' The Barbie doll is speaking. 'Did you see that show last night? *Scumbag Street*?' Krystal has fiddled with but not eaten her soup. Even soup is too calorific for her to trust. Now her eyes, framed with long black lashes (false), are wide. 'I just couldn't, you know, like, believe it.'

'*Scumbag Street*?' asks Amelia Baker's husband, Whatshisname. Krystal doesn't reply. *Maybe Whatshisname is invisible to her*, thinks Gunter.

'You mean the show on Fourth Dimension?' asks Gloria Binding.

'Oh yes,' Krystal nods. 'That actual street, yah, it's only near where my stepfather lives! I just couldn't believe it, you know, the people cheating and like, you know, skiving. And they were so skanky . . . That whole place looks like hell now.'

Amelia is nodding. 'Actually, one of the media companies we support is producing that series.' She winks at Stella. 'Stell even got to contribute to the scripts. A little friendly advice about being "on message", right, Stell?'

'Scripts . . . oh no. I don't think that's right.' Krystal seems a bit dazed. 'It's a documentary. Aren't documentaries, like, for real?'

'Yes, my dove.' The delicious low tenor timbre of Monsieur Rennes floats across the table. 'Documentaries are "for real", *mais* sometimes they like to give the people they are filming an idea of what to talk about.'

'Really? Like, why?'

'So that the people watching don't get bored.'

'If you could imagine,' Dr Binding interjects, 'that there was a film crew recording this dinner party—'

Krystal lights up, giggling and flings back her mane of hair as if mid-photo shoot. 'Aw, I'd love that, Dr Binding.'

'Barney, my dear, call me Barney. Well, think how bored people watching at home would be. They wouldn't want to watch old Gloria here drinking soup and talking about her cats for twenty minutes.'

'Well, actually, I was enjoying your wife's . . .' Amelia's spidery husband Whatshisname is leaping to Mrs Binding's defence, but no one notices, least of all Mrs Binding.

'No, I s'pose not,' Krystal pouts.

'So they would cut out all the bits of real life – the eating and drinking and small talk that are of no interest, and stick together all the bits where there is excitement, action.'

'*Oui*,' Monsieur Rennes again. 'And then they might ask us to debate some big issues, things that the people at home are also interested in.'

'Oh, right. So, you mean like when the scumbags were talking about how much money they can get off of benefits, yeah, for having children, and how it would cost them more to be in work than to be a scumbag . . . ?' Krystal bites her lip as if taking a test.

'Yes, exactly.' Amelia claps.

'There was also a man who was pretending to be sick, right, so he could get off work and we . . .' She pauses to get the phrase right. Amelia mouths it with her: '*The Hardworking British Tax-payer*.' Amelia nods. Krystal continues, '. . . would all be paying for his rent. He and his girlfriend, they didn't even care. They were proud of themselves. I mean, there wasn't one of them who wasn't cheating the system and loving it. They were hateful.' Krystal's brow would have wrinkled if it wasn't so full of cow jelly.

'Oh, *ma petite*, you were so upset,' Monsieur Rennes can't help but wink at Stella. Binding sees the wink fly through the air and Stella's little smile in response. Monsieur Rennes continues teasing Krystal. 'And yet you also know of people who live like this.'

'Are you getting at my stepdad, Henri? That's completely different, right. I've told you he can't work because of his back.'

'And how is that different?' pipes up Gunter, who is awake, it seems.

'It's totally different, right! Those people on your show, Stella, they were flaunting it. They loved being scumbags.' Krystal's voice is rising.

'Are you sure?' Gunter leans forward. 'Remember what Barney said about editing bits together? You sure they didn't just stick bits together to make the people on the show appear hateful?'

'Oh right. I get it. You wanted us to hate them, yeah? Err . . . is that right?' Krystal is asking Stella and Amelia.

'Now, why would Stella and her producers want you to hate the unemployed people on *Scumbag Street*?' Monsieur Rennes sounds as if he is talking to a child.

Krystal reddens ever so slightly. She wishes she had never spoken at all. 'I dunno . . . maybe . . .'

'Krystal.' Gunter has placed his warm, slightly sweaty hand over hers. He gives her an encouraging squeeze. 'Do you remember that show from a couple of years back, same channel? It was a big deal, and called *Immigration Infestation*?'

'Oh yeah!' Krystal lights up again. 'That was really bad . . . I mean . . .'

'Shut up, Gunter.' Stella's voice is low and as chilly as the soup.

He doesn't. 'It was another one produced by Stell's "friends". Can you remember how it made you feel?'

'Well, yeah. *Immigration Infestation!* Yeah, right . . . I was really scared! I didn't know that there were so many illegals and how nasty—'

'It's called "propaganda".'

'Shut up, Gunter!' Stella is frantically signalling Gina to clear the table.

'Proper what?'

'Do you remember what happened just after that show?'

'You mean in real life?'

'Yes, Krystal, in real life.'

'Ummm.' Krystal sees her husband's stern shake of *non*. 'No, I don't remember.'

'I do, however.' The voice of Whatshisname, Amelia's husband, comes from the other end of the table. He has pushed his chair back to allow Gina to take his plate and now stands and projects his voice loudly and clearly. Everyone sees him now. Amelia watches him, shocked, open-mouthed, as if he is the madman on a bus who has just taken off his trousers. 'I remember exactly,' he is saying, 'because Amelia was on the working group that used that very show to get the Immigration Bill through Parliament. Then it was the vans—'

'The vans?' Krystal looks flummoxed.

'"Got an Immigrant Infestation near you? Call 08090 and we will bring it under control,"' adds Gunter dryly. 'It wasn't enough, though—'

'No, it wasn't, was it, Amelia?' Whatshisname sits down again and straightens his side plate. His little rebellion is over.

There is a small silence, a clatter of cutlery from the kitchen and Gunter hears his own voice again. He just won't let this lie. 'A few months after that, the government opened the first asylum-holding platform on an old oil rig off Aberdeen. One of the first TOSA initiatives.'

'Oh wow . . . yeah! The Suicide Rigs, right? Where all those illegals died jumping into the sea?' Krystal looks as if she has just won *Mastermind*.

'That's right, Krystal! Well done.'

Gunter looks over to Whatshisname for validation, but Whatshisname just carries on wiping crumbs off the tablecloth and won't make eye contact with him. Stella is glaring at Gunter, though.

Gunter takes another glug of vodka. 'Yes, how many people died again? Let's ask Henri. He knows all the statistics about that, don't you, Henri?'

Henri is very still.

'Enough! Gunter, you will not bait my guests.' Stella's face is white and tiny red spots glow hot on her neck.

'Another drink perhaps, Gunter?' says Dr Binding. 'Or perhaps you have had enough?'

Stella nods to Gina and announces the main course.

Lamb.

Plates are replaced with bigger ones; glasses now glisten with red wine and mouths drip with jus. Apart from Krystal's, of course. She licks her fork and then panics slightly. The grease!

'OK,' says Amelia. She is still a little unsettled by her husband's outburst. She had no idea he knew so much about her involvement in the offshore asylum rig initiative, let alone cared. She wants to change the subject. 'Say Stella's producers were here. What would they want us to talk about?'

'Stella? Give us a subject.' Gloria thinks this will be fun.

Stella, feeling things are back under control, manages a terse smile. 'Well, in one of the latest polls it would seem that people are worrying about food banks again.'

'Too many or too few?' asks her mother.

'Both, funnily enough. On the one hand there are not enough food banks to deal with the need, and on the other hand it is possible that food banks are encouraging people to be lazy about finding work. It does seem possible that food banks have become a . . . how should we put it . . .'

'A free supermarket?' Amelia grins. 'Another show, Stell? How about the title *Free Food for Freeloaders?*'

'You are fucking kidding?' Gunter splutters, knocking his fork to the floor. 'You think by starving people – families with kids – you will encourage them to find work?'

No one seems rattled by Gunter any more. They are beginning to realise he is performing the role of drunken devil's advocate.

'*Oui.*' Henri takes a glug of the ruby-red Rioja and swirls it around his mouth, swallows. 'Such delicious food, Stella. However, your husband, he has a point. Surely they will just turn to crime?'

'You see, Krystal,' Dr Binding smiles benignly down the table. 'This is the kind of discussion people watching might find interesting.'

Krystal simpers. 'I don't think young people would be interested, though. Food banks are pretty boring, aren't they? I think we are more into music and that, you know, celebrities and fashion, and anyway, I mean really, what could we do about it all? It's not up to us to make these kinds of decisions.' That she includes herself with 'young people' is rather a stretch, thinks Gunter. Under all that foundation he suspects Krystal is almost as old as Stella.

The booze is beginning to short out his neurons. The faces around the table distort, bubble like boiling plastic, form again. Obfuscate. What would the Polish equivalent be? *Ukryć?* Cover-up?

'Why starve them when you can just put them to sleep?' *Did he really say that? Shit.* Gunter looks up through the blur. The

186

table is still lively, people are chatting, eating. Perhaps he just thought it.

But then, in a moment of upended clarity, he sees The Good Doctor Binding looking right at him. The doctor is smiling but, without a word, he moves his hand slowly, ever so slowly, up to his collar and makes a long, cutting, sweeping gesture across his throat.

Gunter pushes back his chair, excuses himself, or tries to, and barely makes it to the bathroom before he vomits up lamb and beetroot, wine and vodka. Minutes later, in the clear bright bathroom mirror, he washes his face and knows himself to be a dead man.

Static Clouds and Sore Hearts

There has been no rain for weeks, and the ground is iron-hard. Alex has taken off her trainers, and under her bare feet the dusty top layer of the path feels warm and chalky. She steps onto the cool of the grass tussocks by the sluggish riverbank and wiggles her toes while Chris flops down on his stomach, panting. They have just walked along the river path in an eight-mile loop, four miles to the weir, across the bridge and back down through the shadow of the woods, across the dry mud knuckles of the ploughed fields, through the village and back to the riverbank. They are both hot, sore-footed and happy.

Alex pulls Chris's plastic bowl from her backpack and fills it from a bottle of water. He doesn't bother to get up, just plonks his muzzle in and slurps. Alex drinks from the bottle, folding herself down into a cross-legged position beside him. There is no one else around, and the sound of the shooshing river, the panting dog and the gentle rustling, as the mildest breeze moves through the tall grass in the field alongside them, brings a deep peace. Alex sighs and lifts her face to the sky, rubbing the sweat from her forehead with the back of her hand. After a while she slips onto her back, takes off her sunglasses and closes her eyes, deliberately refusing to allow thoughts of the Ladies' Defective Agency, of Boudicca, of the traumatised and injured teenagers, of Binding, or any of it, filter into her sun-dazzled brain.

A crow caws loudly close by and startles her. Chris too sits up, ear cocked.

'What is it, boy?' she asks. Chris has tilted his head up to the left and then, through Alex's damaged retinas and the sun prisms, she sees it too. An Everest-sized thunderhead in the sky.

Wow! she is thinking, when her phone rings. Alex wouldn't usually answer while she is out on a walk, but for some reason the huge cloud sitting so menacing and still on the horizon has unsettled her, and she finds herself pressing the answer button.

The line is distorted, messy with static and something else, a background pounding noise.

'Hello?' comes a voice. 'Hello, is that Alexandra?'

Alex freezes. The hot sun doesn't stop the sweat on the back of her neck going clammy.

'Hey,' the voice continues. 'Do you remember me? From . . . you know . . . that night?'

'Yes,' Alex whispers.

'I'm sorry, I can't hear you. I'm in London and it's pouring with rain here. A storm. Alex. Can you hear me?'

'Yes,' says Alex more loudly. 'Hi Gunter. How's it hanging?'

Not so good, as it turns out. Alex can barely take in what the poet Gunter Gorski is saying, not just because his voice is hard to discern over the noise of static, pouring rain and occasional peals of thunder, but also because what he is saying is so unbelievable.

'Where are you calling from? You sound like you're in a tin hut.'

'Ha . . . yes! I am in a shed. In the garden. I don't want anyone else to hear me.'

Alex isn't surprised. Gunter has just told her that his father-in-law is a murderer.

'I saw the CDD file, Alex. At first I was disgusted but not so afraid . . . now it is different . . . something has changed . . . I am scared.'

'What? Slow down, Gunter . . .'

'That file – it stands for Clearance, Disinfection and Disposal. It was full of photos . . . I am telling you, it was like an execution room, not a hospital.'

'You should go to the police.'

'No! They wouldn't believe me.'

'But you thought I would?'

'Alex, I didn't know who else to tell. If I go to any other journalist this will come back to Stella, my wife. But you . . . you and me have . . . had something. And . . . I read up about you, looked at some of your articles. You are an honourable person. You will see to it that the doctor is stopped. That what he is doing is exposed . . . but my wife and I stay out of all the trouble.'

'Gunter, I don't know who you think I am, but I can't keep anyone out of trouble.'

'Please, Alex. I am afraid – I think they . . . the people with Binding, the people behind all this . . . they will hurt me and Stella if they find out I know. Maybe even my daughter. I took pictures on my phone and then I panicked. But . . . I think the doctor knows I saw the file.'

'Gunter, what did you do with the pictures?'

'I . . . I . . . I put them on a memory stick and deleted them from my phone. But now I have the memory stick. I must get rid of it . . . Can I give it to you?'

He sounds a little deranged, maybe drunk. Could he be telling the truth? Alex is furious, frightened and excited. She can't believe he is on the phone to her in the first place. She has secretly fantasised that he would ring her and tell her how he made a mistake, wanted to be with her. She is furious with herself, knowing that it would never happen and wanting it anyway. She is even angrier with him.

'Are you fucking crazy? You want me, the woman you picked up on a train, slept with, a woman you know nothing at all about, to leak a story that could expose state-sponsored euthanasia at the highest level? While telling no one who my source was? Are you insane?'

'I am sorry. I am sorry, Alex. Help me.'

Is he sobbing? There is crackling, and his voice distorts and disappears into the thunder on the phone.

'Gunter?'

His voice returns, tired, a mere croak. 'Please . . . Alex.'

For a short moment Alex listens to the rain in London. It is so hot here. She longs for that rain . . . and the man in that rain . . . and if she helps him, maybe they can spend some time together? 'OK, Gunter. Where? I need to see the pictures on the memory stick.'

They arrange to meet in the café at Petertown station.

'But not tomorrow,' says Alex. 'I have to finish an article for my paper first, or I'll be fired. Let's say Thursday morning. 10 a.m.?'

'OK. Thank you. Thank you, Alex. I think you will be saving my life.' There is another quiet, a lull in the static. 'You know I am so sorry about how things ended that night. I didn't ever want that, you must believe me. You and I . . . it was incredible.'

Please, pleads Alex's sore heart. *Please say it might work out . . . together,* but he doesn't.

'The pantie thing . . . on the doorknob . . . that was quite something.'

'Oh, oh . . . yes.' Alex reddens, she can't help it. 'Did you get in trouble with your wife?'

'I should have done. I deserved to, after how I treated you. I am just lucky that my wife prefers breakfast. She went straight into the hotel restaurant.'

'Yeah, well then . . . you got away with it.'

'I didn't get away with you, though. It was a good night, Alex.' She can hear him smile. 'I have kept them.'

Alex smiles too. 'You bloody poets are all the same.'

As Alex ends the call, the wind picks up, a short furious blast of hot air that knocks Chris's ears back. Alex shades her poor eyes and looks up. The sky to her left is now entirely blue again, not even a stray woolly puffball in range. The storm cloud, it seems, has scarpered. She pulls on her trainers and picks up the water bowl. She is disappointed with the disappearance of that magnificent, maleficent cloud.

'Ach,' she stretches. 'We could really do with a decent storm.' Her stomach growls, and Chris sits back on his rump and tries to dislodge a grass stalk from his ear with his hind leg. *Gunter.* Alex tries not to think about his lips, his hands. *He wants to protect his wife. Alex, you are a bloody fool.*

Andre Watches Alex in a Creepy Manner

His metal lattice in tray is piled high with files marked 'Urgent'. He has weighted them down with a banana, but when the phone cheeps, Andre has to push through the paperwork to find the buried handset and the banana doesn't hold. Files and paperwork crash floorwards. Kicking at the paper in irritation, Andre, all booted and suited, snatches up the phone.

'Yeah what? I'm busy.'

'Sorry, Mr Watson. It is just, you told me to let you know if that blind woman turned up again.'

At first Andre found it freaky having his own secretary. Well, sharing a secretary with his boss, that is. She wasn't fit or anything like the ones he saw on adverts. She was chunky and old, at least forty, and she wore 'mum' clothes but she wasn't mum-like. Not like Andre's mum anyway. Andre's mum had always been a tough old bird, fag in her gob at all times, even when breastfeeding. This secretary, Pat, she was timid as a rabbit. She would flinch and jump when the phone went, take ages to get the courage to knock on a door and never asked for any help whatsoever. Which was fine, as far as Andre was concerned, as he barely knew what he was doing and couldn't have advised her anyway.

She pretty much did all his administration and organised his calendar. He was still under probation, so he was trying his damnedest to keep up with all the training. His new title was assistant supervisor, but in reality he was more like . . . well . . . more like an overpaid security guard. He was in charge of organising the security shifts and ensuring that all the security and cleaning staff were in the right place at the right time, didn't blab about their work or cause any trouble. This was a big deal, which meant he was a big deal, even though the work was dead easy most of the time. He didn't mind getting in early and leaving late now that he had a stonking salary. He was earning more than his stuck-up brother with his car dealership in Royceston. Loads more. Andre had his own place now, even though his mum had begged him to stay on at home because she wouldn't be allowed to stay in the flat if they found out she had a spare bedroom. Andre had promised to pay the extra room tax for her, but there was no way he was hanging around that place. No way.

'Where is she?' Andre asks Pat. That blind bitch had been causing trouble over the last few weeks. There had been all the phone calls and questions and requests to look around the wards again and again. Eventually his supervisor had called TOSA head office, but not before the bitch had written an article in the local paper about Grassybanks' refusal to 'come clean about the underground extension and the connection to the Homeless Action! initiative'.

She had even hinted at irregular medical practices, and that had brought the TOSA bigwigs dashing over in their Jaguars to convene a meeting with the nursing staff, Dr Binding and some flash gits from the communications department. Andre had been told the press were 'being handled' and that if he was to see the pig-ugly-crip-journo sniffing around he was to take no action but report directly to TOSA head office. *No action? What's wrong with giving the bitch a bit of a slap? It's not like she's going to see anyone coming, is it?* Andre scratches at his shaving rash.

'Ronnie on security says she is heading across to Riverside. Looks like she's meeting someone.'

'OK, OK, I'll deal with it.'

Andre is about to dial through to TOSA security offices when he pauses. *So she is heading across the common? It may just be a footie field's worth of bog but that is Grassybanks land now.*

'Pat!' he yells through the door. 'Call Ronnie. Tell him to meet me downstairs with the dog.'

No reason why we can't sort out our own backyard. It's my fucking job after all, he is thinking as he picks up his radio.

Dog!

For her final 'Why Work Works' interview, Alex is meeting the Paralympian superstar Rory Mortensen. She rings first thing to check if he is still up to it, given his insane training schedule. 'That's cool,' he says. 'Had a track session at 5 a.m., so will have the rest of the morning off.'

Alex hasn't seen 5 a.m. for quite some time. Not in a good way, that is. She grimaces.

Rory and Alex discuss wheelchairs and guide dogs, and decide on the top end of the common, where there is one of the few accessible walks alongside the River Bright. The path there is only a little stony and in decent shape, smooth enough to allow Rory's wheelchair to keep a grip on the asphalt, and Alex can let Chris off safely for a run.

'It will be good to wander beneath the trees, given the heat,' says Alex. 'Chris, my dog, is already panting and we haven't left the flat yet.'

She hears Rory chuckle down the line. He says that he got stuck in some sun-melted road tar only a few days ago. A group of French exchange students had helped him out of the road, but only after they had taken several photos on their phones. 'Cheeky fuckers. Righto, Alex. See you shortly.'

Alex is a little nervous. Nervousness always releases her inner crap comedienne. If she had a schizophrenic personality it would be this one, a fat trout making cheap gags at the most inappropriate times. Like now, for instance. She keeps thinking that *this interview could be a bit of a minefield.*

It was a minefield that took Rory's legs. In just five years, though, the man has picked himself up from the dust, quite literally, and gone from poster-boy soldier to crip-on-the-edge, to Paralympian hand cyclist. Along the way he has plucked up every gold medal possible. He is a phenomenon of physicality, courage and, let's be honest here, he is incredibly handsome. 'Devastatingly' was the adverb used in *Geezer* magazine, and that had been written by a bloke. Rory now works as one of the most sought-after coaches at one of the most snotty university colleges. *In a way he was lucky his previous career bombed,* quips Alex's inner trout.

The sun is pouring down, and the dead grass crackles beneath Chris's paws as they crunch across to the river. Alex, in a vest top, can feel her shoulders burning. She has, as usual in the rush to get out the door, forgotten her sun cream. She shades her eyes and aligns herself with the distant line of waterside trees.

'Thataway, boy,' she says to Chris, who nods, jaws slightly open and tongue lolling. He isn't really at his best in the heat, but he doesn't have a choice. Work for supper. That is the talking monkey deal.

A grasshopper blings up in front of him, almost hitting him in the snout. 'Kazam! Almost got him!' it rasps to its mate. Immediately another grasshopper springs and whacks Chris above his eyebrow. 'Shazam! Contact!' He snaps at it but only half-heartedly. He can hear the insects tizzing with grasshopper giggles and still feels the vibration of the creatures through his whiskers. Their happy makes him happy. And at least he is outside of the concrete flat, and above him the wide good sky, and below him the ancient old earth. Like the insects, little smells skitter joyfully past in the dry wind. Coconut sun cream, earthworms, pee from a dog who thinks its name is 'Oi!', grass oil and dark soil minerals. Little puffs of delicious life essence. And one in particular . . . Chris lunges sideways.

'OhmygodAlex! Someone dropped ice cream here a couple of days ago. It's all kinds of mould and vanilla. I should just have a sniff.'

'Chris!' Alex gently yanks the harness. 'Straight on!'

She is reminding him of their work agreement. Not that he minds working at all, *at all*, oh no, not Chris! Chris is very good at 'the working'. Building lines, obstacles, roads and kerbs, bring 'em on. But these little stinks are so seductive and it would only take a minute or two . . .

'Chris!' Alex's tone is a little sharper.

Chris sighs and his tail deflates. It's just so hot.

A little later, and they pass another dog on a lead. It's a springer spaniel bitch called Poppy who is all legs and ears and eyes, coat muddy and soggy from the river. Her nose is plunging at the ground, jerking her lead, scrabbling at the smells. She looks up and sees Chris in his yellow harness.

'Whatyerdoing?' she asks, tail in a confused half-shake.

'I, young Poppy,' Chris replies gravely, 'is working.' He carries on past her without another glance, muzzle high and pointed along the track, tail a diligent height and pace purposeful, all solemn, with a slightly martyred superiority.

'Blimey, good boy,' says Alex, surprised at his turn of speed.

'Gosh.' Poppy is dumbstruck with horror and admiration. Her legs go all quivery. 'Working?' she calls after him. 'That means no sniffing? No chasing? No leaping?' Her talking monkey-man has to drag her away.

They are running late, so Alex decides on a shortcut, squeezing through the gates at the top of the common. Alex doesn't see the black-and-white sign hanging from the fence next to the gate, and Chris can't read, so he can't warn her that it glares 'Under New Management. Private. No Trespassing'.

In ignorance, they cut across the fields behind the large concrete outbuildings of the adjacent Grassybanks complex. It's a nice easy walk, and the grass is shorter and greener due to the high water table. The shortcut becomes slightly boggy about halfway along, but it's not as bad as usual because of the drought and, nursing her usual hangover, Alex has dressed sensibly in ankle wellies and jogging pants. Water still manages to get in over the top of her boots and her socks begin to make embarrassing squelching noises.

Up ahead in her blotchy tunnel of sight, Alex spies a man in a wheelchair and a slender woman with long black hair beside him. Alex waves. They both wave back. As she approaches, she scans around, thinking about the sound recording, but it will be fine. No traffic and almost no one about, apart from the now distant dog walker.

They are closer to the river, and Chris lifts his nose to the cooler flirtation of wind from the surface of the water. He can smell the fish in the river, the layers of mud, the weeds. How wonderful! He almost groans with pleasure. He can read in Alex's mind and body that she intends to let him off for a free run.

Already his muscles are bunching, his claws deep in the gooey soil. As Chris drags Alex forward, she manages to get her foot caught in a clump of grass and staggers forward, right onto Rory Mortensen's lap.

'Err . . . hello.' Alex isn't sure what bit of him she has grabbed on her way down, but it wasn't metal. She feels the blush puddle up her cheeks. 'Sorry about this.'

There is laughter, and a strong and gentle hand pushes her shoulder until she is balanced upright again.

'You must be Alex,' he grins, and he is as dashingly handsome as his photographs, all strong dimpled jaw and broad shoulders.

Alex nods, aware of her slightly matted hair and now thinking the tracksuit a silly idea. Her socks squelch . . . *Shhh*, she tells them.

'This is Kate. My fiancée.' Rory introduces the woman who is, inevitably, also quite lovely, with gleaming black hair and an oval face with the almond eyes of Asia. She is being very good about not mentioning the fact that Alex has just fallen into her fiancé's lap.

'What a lovely dog! How is he coping with the heat? We have a cat who insists on sitting in the sink,' Kate says, and Chris almost stops being grumpy as she tickles him behind his now slightly soggy ears. 'I'm going to leave you guys to talk,' she adds. 'I've got something to pick up from the shopping centre, but I'll be on the phone. Text me when you want picking up.'

Then she leans down, kisses Rory on the mouth and begins to walk up to the car park. Her jeans are very tight, and Rory and Alex both watch her perfect arse as she sways away up the hill.

'Right,' he coughs. 'Shall we begin?'

Alex can tell he would rather be with that arse. She doesn't blame him. They turn left on the river path and gently mooch along, Alex holding Chris's harness with one hand and the micro recorder pointed towards Rory's face in the other. The path is lined with willows, oaks and lime trees and the breeze is stronger.

They small-talk a little while Alex fiddles with her micro recorder. She presses Record and is just turning to Rory to quiz him about his experience of finding work again after his re-habilitation when they hear a shout. After that everything happens very quickly.

Alex barely catches sight of a large dark shape flinging itself over the wet grass towards them before Chris's harness is jerked from her hand, and she hears him scream.

'Dog! Fucking attack dog!' Rory is shouting. 'Help! Loose dog! Dog!'

Alex, without pausing to think, drops the sound recorder and drives her hand deep into her pocket, her ears bursting with the sound of the vicious growling from the alien dog and Chris's high-pitched, terrified screaming. She grabs her can of LDA pepper spray, pulls it from her pocket and rips the cap off with her teeth and aims at the blur of writhing, screaming, growling dogs.

It is happening too fast for Alex's damaged retinas to make sense of the squirming canine bundle. She knows that Chris is still in his harness, and this will mean he won't be able to twist away from the bigger dog. He will be helpless, unable to fight back. She has to assume the big dog will be on top. She aims at the top dog's head and prays that Chris will be slightly out of firing range, then pushes the plunger over and over.

'Get off him! Get off him!' she screams, pumping until the

tube is dry. Now the other dog is whining pitifully and has broken away from Chris to rub its burning eyes against the wet grass. Then it staggers into a lope and dashes, still whimpering, off in the direction it came.

Shaking so much she can barely stand, Alex scans, but her eyes don't find Chris.

'Chris! Chris!'

'I have him, Alex!' Rory is behind Alex with Chris in his arms. She runs to them, and Rory gently lowers Chris to the grass. Alex eases off the guide-dog harness and runs her hands over his poor shivering coat to check for breaks and open wounds, dashing hot tears from her eyes. He is bleeding and drooling, shocked and shaking. A tiny whine comes from his throat. She feels him all over and finds puncture marks at his throat and on his rump. She doesn't think anything is broken, though, and his breathing, though shallow, is regular. But he is really badly hurt, resting his head into her shoulder, eyes rolled back and half shut. She can smell he has shat himself. The shit and blood smell terrify her.

'I need to get him to the vet,' she says, and Rory, nodding, is already on the phone, but then the light darkens. Several people have come up behind them.

'Thank God!' Alex whirls around on her knees. 'Help us,' she pleads. 'We were attacked. There is a dog on the loose!'

'Yeah, that was our dog, Hobgoblin, and you fucking crips are trespassing.'

There are four of them, three men and a hard-faced woman. The man in front is young and blond with small, close-set eyes.

'What are you talking about? This is the river path. It's a public space . . . Look! My guide dog . . . I need to . . .' Alex can't process what they are saying.

'Are you deaf as well as blind? I said you are trespassing. This is private property.'

'Are you fucking mad? There were no signs. I am calling the police,' says Rory.

The man kicks the side of Rory's wheelchair, rocking it. The phone flies out of Rory's hand and into the river.

'Hey, what the hell are you doing?' Rory is as confused as Alex.

'Oh yes, Big Guy. You going to get up and get it?'

Another man kicks the other side of the chair, and Rory has to grab the wheels to steady it. Alex, kneeling with Chris, can see Rory go pale. Chris shivers, whines and Alex rocks him gently. Everything is happening too fast.

'We need to get my dog to a vet,' she repeats.

'What you need, crip bitch, is to be taught a lesson, is what. You been poking your nose into places you shouldn't, and you 'ave upset a few people including the man at Grassybanks what pays my wages . . .'

What . . . ? Alex can't get her thoughts together. Why are they talking about Grassybanks?

'You have to stop your sneaky ways, cunt, and we might let your dog live.'

'Hang on, Andre,' says one of the other men, a thick-set brute with a tattoo of a spider's web on his cheek. 'Was that a guide dog? I love guide dogs . . .'

'Oh shut up, Ronnie, you fucking moron.'

'You stay away from them!' Rory's voice is steady, but his knuckles are white on the wheel-grips of his motorised chair.

'Or you'll what?' Andre turns to him grinning. 'Kick me in the bum, posh boy?'

He aims another kick at Rory's wheelchair, and Rory's hand shoots out and just manages to grab the hem of the man called Andre's trousers. Alex sees the muscles in Rory's arm swell and flex as he yanks the trouser cuffs, and the security man flies through the air, landing hard on his back.

The woman in their little mob actually cackles, a sound Alex hasn't heard outside pantomime.

'Andre, you been floored by a crip! Wait till I tell the boss.'

The others join in the laughter, but Rory and Alex are quiet as they can be. They cannot run. They must just wait. Alex is slowly levering her hand behind Chris's shivering body, reaching for her handbag.

The man, Andre, is slowly getting to his feet. He is taking his time, allowing his rage to build, and it floods his face, turning the skin from white to pink and back to white again. His cohorts slowly go quiet. A snicker from one of them disappears into the sound of the river water gurgling along the banks. For a moment there is a kind of stillness.

Then Andre grabs the woman's face and pulls her into him as if he is going to kiss her. Only he doesn't. He spits instead, and then pushes her away. She staggers backwards, yellow saliva dripping from her nose and chin.

'You fancy the posh boy, do you, Lou? The posh boy with no legs? Do you? Fancy a ride on his chair?'

The other men begin to warm to the theme. 'Yeah, Lou wants crip cock!' sings one, and kicks the back of Rory's chair, sending it forward into the woman's knees. She staggers, and Rory tries to catch her to stop her from falling, but she shrieks and slaps at his hands.

'Gerroff me, you fucking retard!'

Andre has a plan. 'You can have a ride in his chair, Lou . . . you just need to get him out of it.'

Alex's eyes are wide, horrified. She makes eye contact with Rory, and he gives her just the tiniest shake of the head. *No, don't even try and protect me. It will be worse for you.* Such a sad expression in Rory's beautiful eyes.

'What did you say, retard? You gonna stand up for the lady?'

Now all of them including the woman circle the wheelchair. One kicks and as Rory moves to deflect him, the second kicks and then the third. It is like a grotesque game. The chair begins to rock and it is too close to the water.

'Stop it!' Alex screams, she cannot help herself. 'Help, help!'

'Someone shut her up,' says Andre.

One of the men turns from taunting Rory and leans down to where Alex is crouching protectively over Chris.

'She's not bad looking for a crip,' he says, and coming behind her he reaches under her armpits and squeezes her breast hard.

At that moment, the others manage to kick Rory's chair over and he tumbles face forward onto the grass bank with his face in the water. He begins slipping forward.

Enough.

Alex has been around. She knows a thing or two about a thing or two. She takes a breath and relaxes, feeling the muscles in her thighs and back. 'Hold on, Chris,' she whispers, letting him gently down to the ground. 'Hold on.'

Then she pistons upwards, smacking her head backwards as hard as she can into the face of the man behind. She hears, as well as feels, his nose crack and senses the man tumble to the mud. At the same moment, she drags out her folded white cane from her handbag and, taking a giant step forward for balance, brings it two-handed across Andre's jaw.

Another pleasing crack. Both men have dropped out of Alex's vision, and the other man and woman are howling but have moved back, away from her. Alex desperately scans around just in time to see Rory slipping further into the water, head first. Diving forward, she manages to grab the back of his jeans with one hand, but he is too heavy and he is flailing, trying to raise his head from the river, and by doing so he is tearing away from her grasp.

'Help!' she screams, praying for a dog walker, a jogger, anyone. 'Someone help me!' She twists her head around and sees the woman, Lou, bending over Andre where he lies in a foetal position, moaning and clutching his face. Blood pours through his fingers.

'Lou, please,' Alex begs, 'help me! He's sliding into the water.'

'Fuck you, crip bitch and your fucking dog,' Lou snarls, and turns back to Andre, managing to hoist him to his knees.

'Get up, Andre, you fucking tosser! Someone's coming.'

The man with the now broken nose is staggering around in circles clutching his face, eyes shut. Blood and saliva drip through his fingers and down to his wrists, droplets spraying in all directions. Ronnie, with the spider tattoo, grabs him by the shoulders and pushes him into a staggering run.

'You can't leave us!' Alex screams furiously at their retreating backs. She is frantic now. She makes another gargantuan effort to pull Rory backwards. For a brief moment, Rory manages to get his head above the water, but without legs for leverage he cannot get traction on the bank. He gags and chokes and slides further. Alex's fingers have gone numb. She isn't strong enough to swing him back onto the bank. Her fingers begin to slip.

'Rory!' she is yelling, and another voice joins her, and there is the sound of thudding feet. People descend. Many people. Hands reach out, and suddenly Rory is flopped on his back on the path next to Alex, but he is very still, his lips are blue. She is pushed to one side as a dark shape drops to its knees next to Rory and begins resuscitation.

'Rory!' Kate has come back. She runs past, black hair flying, arms outstretched. Alex gets up into a semi-crouch and staggers to Chris where he lies, still bleeding, and gathers him into her arms. Her tunnel of sight is blurred now, the adrenalin is ebbing, and she is shaking so hard she thinks she might come apart.

A huge black man with a grey uniform and with a shining bald head is asking her if she is hurt, but she can only shake her head and point to Chris. She doesn't seem able to speak.

'Yes, I know, love.' The man has a baritone to rival Paul Robeson. 'We'll get him to the vet right away, don't you worry.'

There is an upheaval behind her, and she hears Rory vomiting and gagging. Kate is sobbing with relief. Alex can hear them being taken to one of the waiting ambulances.

At some point someone takes Alex's elbow and tells her to let go of Chris. She won't, so they are put on a stretcher together and placed in the ambulance with Community Transport Ltd on the side. Inside it's dark and Chris's muzzle is on her lap, and there is blood in his mouth. Another gap in Alex's memory, and then bright lights and the sharp biting smell of disinfectant. She realises they are not at the hospital but at the vet's.

Thank God we are here. Thank God, thinks Alex. Yes, she must have convinced the paramedic to bring her. There is more kerfuffle and to-ing and fro-ing as Chris is gently separated from Alex by the bald paramedic and Kelly, Chris's vet.

'We have to take him now, Alex honey,' says Kelly. 'Take a seat and someone will get you a tea. As soon as we have Chris settled I'll come back.'

A little later and Alex is sitting on a hard orange plastic chair in the vet's reception, waiting.

'How are you holding up?' comes the deep voice of the paramedic who brought Alex and Chris. Alex remembers now that this paramedic is with the Community Transport Unit and told her he had just gone off-duty after doing a final patient transfer into Grassybanks. He had heard the shouting for help and raised the alarm. *Off duty.* That's why Alex had been able to convince him to get Chris to the vet before taking her to any hospital. He squeezes his enormous bulk into a bucket seat next to her and taps a plastic cup of water against her stiff fingers. Alex doesn't unclamp her mouth quite yet. She is scared of bursting into tears. Her lips quiver and she stretches them against her teeth to stop it.

'Breathe,' says the paramedic.

Oh yeah. I forgot, Alex thinks. And does.

'I need to take another look at your head,' says the big man with the kind face.

Alex gives him a wobbly grin. 'I fear you may find teeth marks in it.' She allows him to inspect the back of her head again, where it has made contact with one of the attacker's faces.

'I am going to disinfect it. It will sting, but you'll live.' The medic's hands are large and warm. She shuts her eyes and leans her skull into them.

'What news on Rory?' she remembers to ask now.

'He's in Allenbrook Hospital but just for observation. He had inhaled water, but he is not in any danger. He'll be fine. It would have been a different story if you hadn't been there.'

The medic shifts in his seat to pull out some swabs from his bag. Opposite them sit a curious couple with a cat box. They don't hide their stares, and although Alex can barely make out the white ovals of their faces, she can feel their gaze. She wants to push them away.

She looks down at the floor, and water slops over the top of the plastic cup. 'This is really kind of you,' she says. 'What's your name?'

Shit. Her hands shake too much and water is dripping.

The medic gently takes the cup out of her fingers. 'I'll hang on to it for you,' he says. He smells of shoe polish and Imperial Leather soap and something slightly goat-milky. 'My name's Mosh.'

The door that leads to the surgery opens, and Kelly the vet comes out into reception, bringing with her the smell of antiseptic and faint dog shit. Kelly's glasses flash as they catch the light, and Alex leaps up and for a moment is too light, might keep rising up to the ceiling. The arm of the medic is back, a gentle firm pressure across her shoulder.

'Breathe out . . . again, slowly,' he says.

She does, comes back to earth.

Kelly takes Alex's hands, rubs them, looks into her face.

'Chris is going to be fine.'

Breathing, keep breathing.

'He's been badly bitten and lost a lot of blood, but he is a tough old thing. Nothing is broken, and there is no internal bleeding. We are going to clean out the bites and keep him here for a couple of days. He is shocked, and that, with the blood loss, is what we need to monitor. But he is going to survive this. I am going to go back in, and I'll call you in a couple of hours when we have him settled, OK?'

Alex nods and the nod becomes a slight sway.

He is going to be all right. Chris will be all right. 'I should never have exposed him to danger, Kelly. What happens if they take him away from me . . . maybe they should . . . I mean . . . maybe I bring trouble . . .' Alex can't stop this stuff coming out of her mouth. For a moment she remembers his bleeding muzzle in the crook of her arm, and she has to sit down.

'Sorry.'

Kelly leans down. 'You are having a reaction to the shock. Is there anyone you can be with this evening?'

'I'll be OK.' Alex's teeth begin to chatter.

'Don't worry,' Mosh says to Kelly. 'I'm going to run her to A and E in a minute for a full check. I would have taken her first, but she threatened to kill me if I didn't bring the dog to you.'

'Blimey, that is some service you are running,' Kelly smiles.

'I don't want to be any trouble,' mumbles Alex.

'Ha ha!' Mosh's bark of laughter makes the cat in the box mewl. 'Bit late for that, Alexandra.'

Kelly squeezes Alex's shoulder. 'I hear you were a fucking ninja,' she says. 'I hope you broke that guy's jaw.' She looks guardedly at Mosh, who makes a placating grunt, and she turns sharply and goes back into the surgery.

Alex knows better than to ask to see Chris. He will need sedation and rest, and if he sees her he'll want to come with her.

She would be more than happy to camp in the reception, but Mosh shakes his head.

'A and E. Now,' he says. 'Upsidaisy.'

Her head is thumping, and she has twisted a muscle in her stomach from trying to yank Rory out from the river, but apart from that there is no serious physical damage. Inside her soul, however, Alex bleeds rage and fear. Mosh insists she calls someone to be with her for the night.

'I haven't got any room,' she says irritated.

'Make some,' he says.

Alex wearily takes out her phone. She runs down the list of numbers: friends, exes, family. She can't think of anyone she wants to speak to right now. She couldn't face the questions. The 'I told you sos' and the 'omygodthat'sawfuls'. She is about to make a fake call for Mosh's benefit when she spies a more recent entry in her phone listings. *Hmmm . . . maybe this is the one . . . ?*

She rings. The person she calls is very shocked, sweet and gentle as Alex mutters and chokes her way through the situation and a request for a couple of hours of support. 'I really don't want to impose but perhaps just for an hour, even?' Alex says. 'The bloody Community Transport guy won't let me be home alone.'

'Really?' says the woman Alex has called. 'Put him on, would you?'

'Oh no, I don't mean – he is really nice, really,' says Alex, reddening, realising she might get the lovely Mosh into trouble.

'Don't worry,' says Jenny Jameson, for it is her that Alex has called. 'If your nice paramedic is called Mosh, then he is, in fact, my husband.'

The Lull

Jenny, together with baby Serena in her pushchair and a large bag of groceries, is already standing outside Alex's flat when the ambulance arrives. Mosh jumps down to help Alex out before going over and kissing his wife and daughter. 'She insisted on stopping at the bottle shop,' he whispers to Jenny. 'I don't blame her, but it's not going to help her any with the shock.'

Jenny nods and follows him and Alex into the flat.

'Gosh, it's chilly in here,' says Mosh, surprised. *Smells of breeze blocks too.*

'Sorry about the mess,' Alex says, lamely. She is so sore and tired she can't think of how to make conversation.

'I don't care,' lies Jenny, kindly. 'Don't worry about me, and Serena is already asleep. Mosh will come back to collect me in a couple of hours, and in the meantime I am going to cook you something to eat.'

Alex stands in the middle of her living room. She can't remember what comes next.

Jenny squeezes Alex's shoulder. 'Are you going to have a shower?'

'Yeah, thanks . . . yes . . . shower. Good idea. And thank you, Mosh. I . . . you got him to the vet . . .'

'It's no bother, Alexandra. You get some rest, now.'

And Mosh is gone, and Jenny doesn't say anything when Alex picks up the freshly bought bottle of vodka and takes it with her to the bathroom.

In the bathroom, Alex chugs straight from the bottle. She knows that it won't help anything, but she can't think of what to do to stop her brainstorm of fury and fear. She unpeels her clothes, wincing as she pulls her T-shirt over her head. There is dry blood in her hair and Chris's blood under her fingernails. She showers, and when the water goes cold she stands and sobs under it, scrubbing her skin with a loofah until it is raw.

She eventually emerges in a vaguely clean pair of tracksuit bottoms and a vest top she has found on the bedroom floor. Her hair is still wet, but her eyes are dry. The vodka bottle is half empty.

'OK?' asks Jenny, pretending not to notice the bottle. She is at the kitchen counter chopping onions for one of her vegetarian specials. They are all mostly cheese, lentils and onions, in various quantities. The smell of cooking is soothing, and the hiss and crackle of the onions frying is better music than the memory of Chris's screaming. Alex is glad Mosh insisted she call someone. The vodka has numbed her. She is in a neutral place where no one can get to her. She sits on the little sofa and folds herself into the cushions, just letting herself drift.

When Jenny's phone goes, Alex is asleep.

It's Mosh. 'Apparently the Grassybanks security told the police that one of their security dogs got out and attacked Alex's dog by mistake. They say they didn't come on the scene until after the attack. They also say that Alex attacked them.'

'Oh no! And the man in the wheelchair?'

'He wants to press charges, but his girlfriend says he can't. She says his international sponsor will drop him if there is bad publicity. I don't know . . . he doesn't seem like the type to be intimidated. Don't tell Alex. It's going to be really hard for her.'

'She's asleep, Mosh. I think I'll let her rest. She can deal with this in the morning.'

Jenny stands watching her baby and her new friend sleeping. She thinks about the men who attacked Alex, and a tingle of anxiety for her own daughter makes her skin goosebump in the dim flat.

Why? she wonders. *Why the weak?*

Chris Comes Back

When Chris comes back into his poor bruised body, he is a different dog. It isn't the attack so much as the anaesthetic and surgery that have caused the crucial change. Dogs' lives are short, so they live fiercely, every hour and every minute, close to the earth, caught in the residue of stenches from yesterday and the wafts of the stinks yet to come. Even asleep a dog is *alive*, dreams full of spice and fight and light. Chris may appear to be conked out on his dog bed for hours at a time, but he is vibrating in every part of his doggy brain and body, the sensations of pillow and carpet, of cotton, wool and wood under his body and the myriad scents in every cubic inch of air feeding him. So then, take a dog and anaesthetise him, even for an hour or two, and the dog falls from his own body into a fearful darkness, and on returning finds himself 'other' and, worse, older. It is as if a human had been in a coma for a week or longer. There is a terrible gap and much to relearn.

Lying on his side feeling the breath pushing in and out of his lungs, Chris can smell every other animal in the recovery room. Some, like him, are still waiting for sensation, pain and memory to return. Some weep. Some sleep. The cats, who travel in and out of their physical bodies all the time, have a better return from any surgery. They are gifted self-healers, and once they get over the dizziness, a purr can mesh bones and bodies back into shape in half the time. From a cage up over his head Chris can hear an old tom cat, now ex-tom, screaming in rage. 'Who took my fucking bollocks?! Come on, you freakin' cowardly monkeys! Come on! I'll fucking 'ave you! Which one of you was it?'

Across from him lies an Alsatian bitch. She has been cut into and rendered sterile. He feels the waves of deep sadness and confusion pulse through her and wash away into the antiseptic-coated air. 'Something's gone,' she says to him.

Chris can't respond yet.

In another cage is a snuffling hedgehog, a road-crossing survivor. She has smelt concrete and tar before but never Formica and plastic. 'What is this shiny place?' she is whispering. 'It is like winter, but warm. Where is the proper air? Has anyone seen my husband?'

A door bangs open and a human comes in. Chris doesn't move, although he recognises the smell, a sea-green cool smell with light lavender thrumming through the green. He is frightened. She was the one who sent him into the black, but still he doesn't move, and now she is on her knees at his cage door and her hands are on his fur and they are gentle.

'Hey there, Chris. You are going to feel rotten for a little while as the anaesthetic wears off, but you will heal up fine, I promise. Alex was here.'

Alex. The word makes Chris try to lift his head. Yes, he must have Alex. They need each other. Now.

'Sorry, boy.' The vet responds to his attempt to sit up. 'She isn't allowed back here yet. But you sleep, and maybe the day after tomorrow she can take you home, OK?'

She lays a cool hand on his head and he drops it back down and closes his eyes. Pain has begun to return like a smouldering fire. 'Alex,' he whimpers. 'I need my Alex.' His whole soul is stricken with loss. *Alex.*

'Yo, bitch!' yells the tom cat. 'It was you, weren't it? You took my nuts. Bet you needed both hands, right? Bet they were so big and heavy you almost fainted, right? You are going down, monkey tits. Going down!'

The vet stands and stretches. 'Aww hey, Hector, puss puss puss,' she says to the cat. 'You poor old sod. No more illegitimate kits for you, my man.'

'I can still spray, dumbass,' Hector screeches at her as she checks the Alsatian, hedgehog and other cages. 'I can still spray the piss out of that old bag's house, and you know I will. I am going to spray the walls, man. Spray the ceilings! Teach her to knobble my knackers!'

The vet heads for the door.

'My nuts, for Isis's sake! How could you?' Hector hisses at the door as it shuts. 'Fuck this for a lark.' He twists himself in two and begins lapping at the stitches. 'Gonna spray your house down, momma,' he is singing under his breath as Chris falls into a troubled sleep.

Alex Plays Pinball

Without Chris, Alex is incomplete, both in her head and in her body. The gaps in her vision seem bigger and whiter. The white billows and stretches like mosquito netting, obscuring the pavement, the car park, as well as the milling crowds around the entrance to the station. She manages to cross the taxi rank without getting killed, but only just. Heads appear like dark balloons bobbing ahead of her.

Alex has done this journey so many times, but without Chris pootling along by her left knee she feels as discombobulated as a moth in daylight. She is a pinball bouncing from one obstacle to another. Of course, she is used to her sight impairment. Her sight has deteriorated slowly over twenty years, giving her time to adjust. In fact, like the proverbial frog in a pan of water that doesn't realise the heat has been turned on, Alex barely pays attention to how much sight she has lost. Is still losing.

So, it is a rare thing for Alex to feel so out of her depth with it. It is just that she and Chris have been partners for over seven years. They have grown into each other in a way that two humans could never do. In the morning they yawn together, stretch together, and move in synchronicity through their worlds.

Sometimes Alex is sure she is dreaming of chasing bright yellow tennis balls across an endless stench-ridden beach. She wonders if Chris ever dreams of turning up at a party completely naked. Probably not, given his constant state of furry undress. He has snuffled into her nightmares on a couple of occasions, and she has been relieved, followed him out, waking with the sweat cooling on her face.

He knows when she is sad, when she is premenstrual, when she wants to dance. She knows silly things about him too. He doesn't like to be watched when peeing. He has a problem with whippets. He likes sheep and rabbits' droppings but declines horse poo. He worries about her drinking, does double sighs when she staggers to the fridge.

She knows when he isn't feeling well by the way his ears smell.

'What the hell is wrong with you, lady?'

Oh damn. She has been standing in front of the ticket machine for too long, but scanning and scanning, she can't see where the ticket has popped out. It's a new machine. Usually the ticket slides out of the side with a peep. Obviously not on this model.

'Oh . . . velly solly.' She is not sure what accent she is pretending to do . . . a Spike Milligan *Goon Show* Chinaman classic, possibly. 'Me no know this machine . . .'

'Jeez . . . fucking tourists. It's right there!' The man behind her reaches past and down, and Alex hears a flapping crack sound. *Oh, one of those machines with the slot right at the bottom.* She lets the man push the ticket rudely into her hand.

'Sank ooo velly much,' she says and quickly moves out of the man's way.

She isn't carrying a cane. In the current climate being a crip alone isn't altogether wise. She has a long purple umbrella instead, tightly bound up and with a long curved handle. She now uses this in the same way she would use a cane, to fend her way through the station doors, up the stairs and over to the platform.

The train storms into the station. Alex finds the bright red door easily and jumps up into the train carriage. She manages to get an aisle seat and pretends to read a book, waiting for the train to lurch out along the platform. She couldn't cope with anyone trying to interact with her. She checks the book cover is the right way up. Yes. She has chosen the one book that does not encourage curiosity, intrigue or collusion. Any fellow passenger will glance at the jacket and remain stolidly mute. *Self-Help for Substance Misuse and Addiction*. It's the best thing for a quiet journey.

She goes over the instructions Gunter had texted her. *Petertown station concourse. Café Coffee on the mezzanine floor. Third table back from the counter on the right.*

Easy enough, thinks Alex, feeling sweat in her palms and unable to keep her foot from tapping a manic rhythm on the train floor. *Oh God . . . what if I miss him? What if this is all hokum and there is no CDD file? And worse . . . so much worse . . . what happens if Chris can't work any more and Guide Dogs take him away?*

Petertown is the third stop, and she lets everyone else off first before carefully stepping down from the train and merging into the crowd of commuters as they stream through the barriers and out onto the bright central plaza. She almost stabs a toddler with her umbrella, but somehow, even with the bouncing sunlight adding to the messy reception at each retina, Alex finds the right café and heads to the counter. She moves slowly, umbrella-cane subtly sweeping the ground in front of her leading foot. There is a queue, and she has to pause for a little while to figure out which end she should join. She checks her phone for the time. Another ten minutes. She rolls her shoulders and instinctively lowers her hand to pat Chris's head, wincing when she hits air.

'Large cappuccino,' she says and then waits, refusing to let the stroppy woman behind her pass. Alex needs to be able to see exactly where the barista places her cup down, and standing right at the centre of the counter means she can get a full scan of the bar top.

'Some people,' she hears the woman hiss to her friend, 'are so rude.'

Alex has a momentary urge to throw the coffee into the woman's face. It's nerves. She recognises the feeling of irritation, near violence. She could be a cocked gun. She breathes slowly and, a little shocked by how much her hands are trembling, picks up the cup and saucer and carefully turns to the tables. *Third back on the right.* Is that the right facing or turned from the counter?

And she finds a table and a chair, and she sits and tries not to put her head into her hands. *Breathe, Alex.* She has thought about Gunter a lot over the last few weeks. In that one night he had nearly got her believing in the possibility of a relationship again, and that's quite a feat considering Alex's track record with commitment. She likes sex as much as the next person, but she is loath to share a bed for long.

She suspected 'love' wasn't going to happen for her, just as kids weren't going to happen. She reckoned she was just too selfish. She had seen a shrink once . . . OK, more than once . . . who had told her that she had abandonment issues. She had slept with the shrink to prove that wasn't the case. And then abandoned him to drive the message home.

Her father had been right. She wasn't a very nice girl.

She drops her hand again, and again flinches when there is no Chris. He will be coming home tomorrow, thank goodness. She has organised with Jenny, Mosh and that lovely man Euan Parnell a timetable for the next week. Chris will never be on his own when she goes to work or to Job Central or just the shops, not even for a second.

'Is this seat taken?'

Alex's heart leaps, and she looks up to see only a silhouette against the light. Even without the detail of the face she can tell it's not Gunter.

'Yes,' she says. 'I am just waiting for someone.'

'Oh well, all right . . .' The man hovers.

'What?'

'It's just that there are four places and—'

'Yes, he has children,' snaps Alex. 'Lots of them. And a dog. And a parrot in a cage.'

A parrot in a cage, Alex? Holy Monty Python, woman, get a grip.

The man sighs, shuffles off among the busy tables. Alex slurps her coffee noisily and gets the book out again. She isn't sure how long she and the book can hold the hordes off. It is lunchtime, after all.

'Alex Lyon?'

And there is another man, and yet another man who is definitely not Gunter. No, this man is Gunter's father-in-law. This man is Dr Binding. She recognises first his voice and then his moustache, and then his eyes.

Alex actually feels her jaw drop. Slams it shut and nearly bites her tongue.

'Ummm . . .' Her mind is not able to deal with the various

222

computations it has to go through to come up with a logical reason as to why Binding is standing . . . no – he has casually pulled out the chair and sits down . . . sitting across from her.

'Alex, isn't it? I am right? How nice to see you again.'

'Hello, Dr Binding. Gosh . . . err . . . what a surprise.'

'Is it a surprise, Alex? I suppose it must be.' He doesn't take off his jacket but just sits there, a large briefcase on his lap, staring over his moustache at her. 'Are you waiting for someone?'

'Well yes, actually, Doctor, I am.' Alex scans around the café frantically. Gunter can't bump into Binding! How will she warn him?

Binding doesn't move from his seat. He reaches into his briefcase and pulls out a newspaper.

'I'm sorry, Dr Binding . . . but I said yes. Yes, I am meeting someone so . . .'

He still doesn't move. His eyes are light blue and a little watery as he watches her. 'I take it you haven't seen today's paper?'

She shakes her head, and he pushes the paper across the table to her. She looks down but the print is just a blur. She shrugs at him with a forced smile.

'Oh my dear . . . of course . . . sorry. How stupid of me. You just look so "normal".' He blinks at her. 'You need me to read it?' His voice is gentle but there is something underneath . . . surely not a hint of mirth?

'That's OK. I have magnification glasses in my bag. You can just leave it.'

'I would rather you read it now.'

Alex is distracted, hardly listening. She scans the café quickly again. No Gunter. She hopes he has clocked the Doc and is standing somewhere out of sight. Should she tell the man to just get lost? That she is really busy? But it is rather obvious she is not. Her cappuccino is still half full.

'Oh for heaven's sake,' she sighs and begins the handbag grapple. Alex always puts her keys and glasses in the same pocket, and they always find a way to fall out and hide themselves in the crevices of her large handbag. She has tried buying smaller bags but it made no difference.

As she fumbles, the doctor reads the title of her book. 'Really, Alex? Addiction? You know I am a specialist? You should call me. I am sure I could help, especially by finding you a programme.'

'I am reading it for a friend,' she says hastily. Her voice is muffled because she is holding her sunglasses between her teeth. She has just found an old dog whistle she thought she had lost. Oh . . . and here is a cherry flavoured condom . . . what a bag of treasure!

'And no dog, I see? Did something happen?'

'No . . . just . . . no dog.' Alex has found her magnification glasses and drops everything else into the dark recesses of the bag. She raises her eyes back to the doctor's, slowly now, because Alex has finally twigged. Gunter is not here. Gunter is not coming. The Good Doctor has come instead.

'My dear . . . you look a little pale. Shall I get you some water?'

Alex ignores him and snatches the newspaper, pushes on her glasses and blinks rapidly as the print swims into schools of sentences. It's not the headline. It is further down the page. It's in its own little block of writing . . . the third one from the top. The column on the right. Ironic? Or did someone else send the text about the table?

*

AWARD-WINNING POET
INJURED IN FALL

The poet and writer Gunter Gorski (49), husband of the Minister for Health, Stella Binding, has been taken to hospital with serious injuries after falling from the second storey window of a hotel. A police spokesman has stated that Mr Gorski was visiting a friend in the West End's Bismarck Hotel when he fell from the balcony. It is not known at this time how Mr Gorski managed to fall, but the police think it unlikely that it was a suicide attempt. Mr Gorski was evidently enjoying his evening, according to witnesses, said a police spokesman. He had withdrawn briefly for some air when he fell.

The Bismarck Hotel management insists that all appropriate health and safety notices are visible and that the balconies are inspected for safety issues each month. 'Access to the balconies is not recommended for anyone who has been imbibing alcohol. It is clearly stated that anyone accessing the balconies does so at their own risk.'

Mr Gorski's family have issued a statement saying: 'Gunter is in a very serious condition and in a medically induced coma. We thank everyone for their kind messages of support and ask that we be given privacy while he is being treated.'

Alex takes a very, very long time to read these few short paragraphs. This is because her eyes are filling with furious tears and her heart is filling with a thump-thump-thump of unease. She has to pounce on each word as it tries to slip out of her focus, reading the article once and then again. She can feel the doctor's eyes on her face. If she looks up now he will be smiling with mock kindness. She can sense it. The Good Doctor Binding must have found out that Gunter was meeting her with the CDD file. The Good Doctor Binding has played a blinder.

He reaches across the table as if to pat her hand and she snatches it away with a gasp. He pauses only for a second, then his hand carries on and drops, pulling the newspaper, dotted with Alex's teardrops, back to his side of the table.

'Ah Alex, I can see you are very upset, and it makes me feel glad that I made the effort to come to this meeting personally. You see, I checked dear Gunter's diary after he was taken into the hospital and saw that he had arranged this meeting. I didn't know it would be you, of course. There wasn't a name, but I thought as it was on my way . . . I presume you were expecting to talk to him about the new book launch? Or did you know him . . . personally? He was a very "friendly" man.'

His tone is neutral, but Alex feels as if he has picked her up by the scruff of her neck and thrown her against a wall. *A very 'friendly' man.*

'As I said, I am on my way to Cambright now,' he continues. She can't look up at him yet. She will not let him see her confusion. 'We could take the train back together if you like. I presume you will be going home? Sadly a bit of a wasted journey for you, Alex. What a pity.'

Alex pushes herself back in her chair. *He is just an old man,* she says to herself. *He can't do anything to you in public.* She makes herself smile and it fucking hurts. Must look pretty horrific too.

'That's OK, Doctor. You carry on. There are a couple of other people I wanted to interview in Petertown anyway. Terribly sad about Mr Gorski. Your daughter must be distraught.'

'Sad times,' says the doctor. His eyes have narrowed. He must have been expecting a different reaction. 'Well, I am sorry again to hear about your dog.'

I haven't told him about Chris, though, she remembers with a shiver.

'I suppose he won't be able to work again either. That will be hard for you, my dear.'

She keeps the smile plastered to her face although her lips are suddenly very dry and catch painfully on her teeth She tastes a tiny iron droplet of blood. 'Oh, my dog is fine,' she lies. 'He had a run in with another dog but luckily wasn't hurt. It's just I thought I'd give him a day off.'

She thinks The Good Doctor Binding looks flustered, but maybe she only imagines it. He is standing now, adjusting his jacket, has stuck out his hand. She pretends not to see it, keeps smiling and eventually he drops it. 'Well, goodbye, Alex. Best of luck with it all.'

Alex nods. 'Goodbye, Dr Binding, and I do hope Mr Gorski recovers soon.' She pretends to go back to her book.

'Oh, I doubt that he will,' he says as he turns away. 'I seriously doubt that.'

She waits, feeling the thumping in her chest, hearing the chatter of the café, seeing nothing but blurred lines on the page in front of her. She counts backwards from fifty. She will not bolt, even though her nausea is building. She will not bolt.

Gunter is in a medically induced coma. How lucky was the timing on that, Doctor? Alex has never done coincidence. She has, however, done conspiracy. She is on the last ten in her countdown nine . . . eight . . . seven . . . six . . . when yet another person taps her on the shoulder, making her jump almost completely out of her skin.

'Jesus!'

'Sorry, madam, but the gentleman left this for you at the counter.' The speaker is a small, mousey teenager in a Café Coffee uniform. She has an envelope in her hand.

'OK.' Alex takes the envelope gingerly, as if it might contain anthrax. The girl scurries away, back behind the bar.

The envelope is still open. He must have licked the glue, but the envelope is old and it has only stuck in one corner. Inside is a scribbled note and two £50 notes. Alex pulls out the glasses again. The note says: 'It's not what you came for, but you might need a stiff drink when you get home. For the shock. B Binding.'

Somehow Alex's legs are still working. She finds herself, bag and umbrella in hand, leaving . . . *one step and another step*. As she walks to the glass café door she passes a man going up to pay at the till. 'I didn't see no kids and where was the bloody parrot . . . ?' he mutters sulkily.

Alex is still laughing when she gets on her train. In fact, she guffaws and chuckles and weeps all the way to Cambright and on to her local pub.

Back from Black

When Alex comes round she is in a strange bed, and her head is pounding. She inhales a revolting mixture of sweated beer and the hint of vomit. *This is going to hurt*, she thinks and opens her eyes. It does. Light is like a sharp object poking her eyeballs. She must have made some sound because someone says: 'Here she is, awake at last . . . oh shit, her eyes – shut the curtain!'

Cooler dimness settles over Alex. She manages to open her eyes a little wider, though they water like a bitch.

'Can you sit up?' It's Jules.

'Jules!' Alex croaks and bursts into hot tears.

'I do seem to have that effect on pretty women,' says Jules. 'Helen is here too.'

'Waaaa!' sobs Alex harder.

'Holy Mother of God, I thought she would be too dehydrated to cry!'

Jules snorts. 'Crying is good. She is still traumatised. She needs water and painkillers and another sleep.'

Alex hears the whine of Helen's chair and feels a cool hand on her own. 'Here you go, Alex love. I am holding out a glass of water and one of my whopper pills. Under your nose. But you need to stop crying and sit up.'

Sobbing uncontrollably, Alex manages to push herself up on her elbows. 'They attacked Chris!' she sobs. 'And they pushed my poet out of a window!'

'Yes, love, we know. We know. Now here is the glass. Here you are. Careful.'

Alex spills a lot of the water but manages to swallow the large pink pill, and Helen and Jules coax her back down onto the bed again. Everything aches, and then it doesn't, and she is asleep.

When Alex comes round this time she is still in the bed, only it is not so strange any more. She recognises it as one of the three beds for night staff at the LDA offices. They are in a bedroom off the clubroom bar, which is also handy for anyone who feels they need to drink and not drive their wheelchairs after dark. She is still terribly achy but feels much more herself. The room is cool and dim, not because of the curtain now, but because it is evening. She sits up slowly. There is a wave of dizziness but then she is all right enough to swing her legs over the side of the bed. Her hands seem slightly numb. She holds them up close to her face. Palm side is fine but when she turns them around her knuckles are red and hugely swollen. *Uh oh* . . . She is also mostly naked. On her knees are bloodied grazes that sting. She can't see clearly, but when she touches them gently she thinks she can feel a bit of gravel. On her elbows too, apparently. One side of her face seems puffy and sore, and her left eye is even worse than usual, the eye socket tender.

Alex knows herself. 'I was in a fight, wasn't I?'

Helen is whirring quietly around Alex's bed in her electric chair. Alex can see her shape as she gets closer.

'Yes, but, honey . . . you should see the other guy!'

Alex tries a smile but her face is too swollen.

'How's the head? You need another pill?'

'No thanks, Helen . . . not right now, but I might take one for later. Later? . . . Helen, what time is it?'

'It's 9 p.m., Alex.'

That didn't make sense.

'It's 9 p.m. on Friday the fifth of July,' Helen adds.

'Friday . . . Friday! No!'

'Yes love, you have been out for nearly twenty-four hours.'

'But I have to get Chris!' Alex is on the verge of tears again. She wishes she could punch herself in the face and is glad someone already has.

'Shh, Alex. It's OK. Yes. You had to get Chris but you couldn't, so we got him for you. He is in the next room. He is in much better shape than you, actually, but I didn't know how he would feel about seeing you semi-conscious and still drunk, so we settled him in the bar room until you came round.'

'Chris?'

'He is currently lying right outside the bloody door actually. He won't budge, even with Jules trying to tempt him into the bar with a large chew, several toys and plenty of water . . . which is what you need. Here.' She holds out a glass, and this time Alex gets it all down her throat. And another.

There comes a muffled bark. *Grwooof!*

Alex is weak for many reasons, but one is with relief. *Chris.* If she inhales, she could probably smell him. *Chris! How wonderful!* She begins to get out of the bed to open the door but pauses. She is beginning to remember things. She cannot help but groan.

'Helen . . . things are coming back to me, but . . .'

Helen pauses next to the bed and looks at Alex, head cocked to one side like a little brown bird. 'In a nutshell, you took a train to Petertown and instead of your poet arriving with a top-secret file about state-sponsored euthanasia, you were met by the remarkably creepy Dr Barnabas Binding. He showed you a newspaper article about your poet's fall from a window. For some reason he gave you £100, which you, very foolishly in my opinion, decided to drink your way through when you got back to town. You were probably about £80 in when a man called . . . now let me see if I can remember what you said his name was . . . a man called . . . oh yep . . . a man called "Complete Twat" tried to pick you up. When you refused, he said he knew you from Job Central, and you were a crip fake scrounger. I believe you "took it out into the car park". It appears you are quite the Muhammad Ali when in your cups. Luckily, when you were just £75 into the booze, you had called us.'

'I called Ladies' Defective . . . ?'

'Oh yes, you did, sweetie. And thank goodness! Laverne was on reception and managed to get Jules and a security team to come and find you. Took a while as you were seriously slurring. They got to you just in time to stop you killing "Complete Twat" but not in time to stop the pub landlord barring you for life and calling the police.'

'Wow!' Is Alex a little impressed with her bad behaviour? She shouldn't be. 'Shit. I love that pub.'

'I am sure they weren't serious, Alex. It would appear you are one of their best customers.'

Alex is too deeply humiliated and shamed to be any more embarrassed. 'The man had been a Complete Twat,' she says, as little flakes of memory return. But maybe he had not deserved the beating. Alex sees better with her fists. It is both a blessing and a curse. Worse, she had enjoyed the fight, the cathartic outpouring of rage, the complete loss of physical fear. 'I don't remember the cops, though?'

'No. Luckily you passed out as they arrived. We were allowed to take you away and get you cleaned up, but if "Complete Twat" or the pub landlord press charges, you will have to go in yourself.'

Alex's head is clearing and she suddenly sees herself as Helen must see her. A middle-aged drunk with scabs on her knees and a black eye. She drops her head into her hands as panic rises. She needs a drink. Her grief and shame is a disgusting gelatinous lump of unshed tears. It chokes her. If she had a knife to hand, she would cut her own throat just to find relief from her self-disgust.

'Alex.' Helen leans forward and takes Alex's head between her two cool hands. 'You are one of the bravest people I have ever met. You are a warrior. But you are reckless. You must get the drinking under control or you will kill someone. Or yourself.'

And Alex knows Helen is right and leans her head against the sharp twigs of Helen's clavicle and lets herself weep. After a while that mass in her throat has eased, and she feels almost refreshed.

Chris is now barking intermittently and scratching at the door. Alex plunges forward and pulls it open, kneeling so that the whirling frenzied furball that is her darling dog does not knock her over as he storms into the room, tail helicoptering and claws scrambling. Helen watches the bundle of bruised dog and battered woman, and dashes a little tear from her own eye.

DISPOSAL

Mrs Honey Cleans Early

7 a.m.

The wisps of the dead float with the dust motes up around the ceiling. Particles of ex-people, now part of the vibration of the whole room, moving through the cycle, ashes to ashes, dust to dust. They are a collective sigh, neither sad nor joyful but not empty either. They are the fingernail scrapings of dreams and desires, the sawdust of ambition and despair. Below them as they float up and around in lazy spirals, glittering briefly where they catch the sunlight beginning to stream into the windows, the cleaning crew make ready the reception. Today is a big day for the dead and the living. Today is the opening of Grassybanks new Ward C.

The Grassybanks administrator, Nurse Dyer and The Good Doctor Binding are expecting a good handful of Very Important People and a noisy entourage of press, PR, security and invited 'others' at midday. There will be cameras a-clickin' and tongues a-waggin', and all will gleam crisp and white and hygienic as disinfectant.

To ensure this whitewash, the cleaning crew has been doubled. Mrs Honey leads ten people in Grassybanks' overalls and dragging trollies of Grassybanks' colour-coded cleaning products cleverly crafted for complete cleaning. No fingerprints. No DNA. Not a stain shall remain. Mrs Honey hand-picked her team for this morning's shift, as she did for last night. She has a lot for them to do, some of it rather unusual. Some of it involving the secretion of pots of theatrical white stage make-up.

She puts a hand into the small of her back and stretches, feeling the muscles creaking and sore. She has done a double shift and every tendon tells her so. She glances at her watch. 7 a.m. The night-duty nurses are writing up handover notes and the night security officer is yawning his head off behind the reception desk.

'Your last fifteen minutes!' she calls to her team. 'Fifteen minutes!'

Haughty Couture

8:45 a.m.

Stella is excited, although she knows it is for the wrong reason. It is just that she gets to wear the most exquisite black Chanel shift dress – similar to the mourning dress, although without the ghastly jacket and veil, of Jackie Kennedy. Normally she would have to be careful about spending such a lot of money on designer clothes, but not even the most rapacious and predatory journalist would dare deny her black couture given her near-tragedy.

Poor Gunter in a coma. She checks her expression in the mirror. Yes, brave and beautiful. She will do. She had told Gunter his infidelity would be the death of him, and look, a tumble from the second floor of the Bismarck Hotel, hopelessly drunk, of course, and still warm from the clutches of that wild red-haired woman who was always at his gigs, a 'poetry student'. Yes, Gunter. There are many ways to teach poetry. Stella imagines his possible death and his books selling at last. She dabs her eye to stop her mascara marking her polished cheek. Maybe she does love him just a little.

She is meeting her father at Grassybanks with the other VIPs. There will be the usual tour, and then she will be expected to say a few words before Henri, darling Henri who has been such a rock, pulls the little curtain back from the plaque. She intends to look both brave and a little frail. She wants the press to see how she carries on in the face of tragedy. That she is still a winner.

Gina knocks to tell her the car has arrived. 'Is Mother all right?' Stella asks. Gloria had been devastated by Gunter's accident and, in a blaze of hysterics, moved into her daughter's house as support. Only she spends most of her time weeping in the bedroom.

'She took some tea today, madam. I am sure she will feel better before this evening.'

'Good.' Stella looks at Gina and Gina regards Stella. Something has changed. There is no deference, no modesty in Gina's gaze. Stella is unsettled. 'What is it?' she asks the maid.

'Oh . . . nothing, madam. I am just . . . sorry for your husband's . . . accident.' Gina doesn't quite wink but Stella feels the intention to wink pass through her like a thin blade. As she heads for the car she makes a mental note to fire the bitch.

Incoming!

'Incoming!' The crow lands at the top of the ancient oak, large claws splayed. She is old and fat, and the branch dips ever so slightly as her crow neighbours caw her name in welcome in their flat rasping voices.

The old crow has flown to the edge of the storm and back, and can report that it is currently travelling at a wind speed of forty-five knots. The winds are not quite strong enough yet to tear the storm apart, and the supercell is intact, so if her calculations are correct, and they always are, the storm will hit the tree in exactly five hours and fifty-one minutes. From the treetop the crow turns her shining eye to the west. From this height she can see a black knobbled line of cumulonimbus along the horizon. It is thickening slowly. 'Five hours and fifty minutes,' she caws then settles to rest and meditate while the others take off, like animated inky Rorschach blots, to pass the word.

'Storm coming!' they call. 'Hitting low and hard. Take cover. Take shelter. Check nest and burrow. Batten down hatches and hutches. Dig in deep!'

Some of the younger crows are surfing the pre-storm updraughts, already testing the bow waves of the thunderhead. It is dangerous; the wind can change quickly, snatching birds from their air space, but it is a rare young crow that won't take the challenge of a storm front.

'Five hours and forty-five minutes,' comes the cawing.

A human couple out walking in the bright blustery sunshine, their baby in a sling on her daddy's chest, glance up at the noisy birds as they erupt out of the oaks and flap off in every direction. The baby laughs and points at the crows, and the woman says something in the baby's ear and kisses her husband.

'Noisy stupid things,' says Daddy Mosh, looking up into the tree. 'Probably scared by a squirrel.'

Not a clue, thinks the old crow, shaking her beak and closing her eyes. *Humans. Not a freakin' clue.*

Tricky Technicians and Evaporating Staff

9 a.m.

Nurse Dyer is not a woman who takes well to having her routines disrupted. She can't help but feel a little sulky, even though she knows it is only for one day and is the wish of The Good Doctor Binding, for whom she has the ultimate respect. Already this morning she has overseen the smooth changeover of night to day nurses and felt pleased to notice there had been a great deal of care taken with the cleaning. This soothes her somewhat. Shiny surfaces are to Nurse Dyer what hugs are for little children.

It is now just after 9 a.m. and all is well in Grassybanks as far as the patients – privately, Nurse Dyer just can't bring herself to call them 'clients' – are concerned. Breakfast has been served, medication issued, drips changed, and at the far, dim end of Ward B a couple more beds have become available, with another two looking like they will be ready for emptying by the end of the day. Excellent. She is expecting The Good Doctor at 10 a.m. and so is thinking about a cup of tea when the technicians arrive. They come in through the main doors in a small noisy crowd, each one carrying various bits of kit and yards of electric cable and masking tape.

'Yo!' says the leader, a man with pockmarked cheeks and wearing a baseball cap.

Nurse Dyer doesn't answer to 'yo', so he has to drop the bags he is holding and come right up to the reception desk.

'Hey there! You Nurse Dyer?'

'Yes.' Her smile could freeze a polar bear. The man seems not to notice.

'We're the tech team from Shandy Productions. We are here for the opening ceremony.' The man moves gum around in his mouth as he consults his smartphone. 'Do you need the clearance papers? I have them here on my phone.'

'No. I have your clearances right here. I am just unsure why you would need so many people to set up a simple podium and film screen. This is hardly going to be international news.'

'Oh, right. So you want that I tell Rodney and the others to leave, and you and maybe a couple of your spare nurses could help me rig it all up. I am presuming you know what a sixteen-channel Allen & Heath desk is? Where to place the Mackie 400-watt speakers for best coverage and least feedback?'

His face is impassive and his tone calm, but Nurse Dyer knows when she is in a smackdown. Fuming, she takes her time signing the release sheet and makes each of the tech team sign in individually. 'You are not to go anywhere but the reception area and family room. You can use the family-room bathrooms.'

The man, who has signed his name as Nicholas Shandy, shakes his head. 'I am afraid we will need access to check your fuse boxes.'

Nurse Dyer scowls.

'Rather we fit splitters than your entire electrical system blows up.' The man glances behind him at the other techs. 'Isn't that right, girls and boys?'

One of the men snorts with laughter.

'Can just see that happening when the bigwigs arrive!' muses Shandy.

Again Nurse Dyer is forced to acquiesce. 'Well, I will call one of our nurses to show you around, then. But only one of your technicians need go with him.'

'Two,' says Shandy and cracks his gum.

'Two, then,' she hisses, and looks at her clipboard. 'I can let you have Robin for an hour.'

9:30 a.m.
'How many? You are fucking jesting me?'

'No, Andre. Honestly. Apparently, they're all off with winter vomiting virus.'

'It's fucking summer.'

'Yes, well, "summer" vomiting virus, then. And you know the regulations given all the elderly people we have here.'

Andre is furious. Today, of all days, he is going to have new security staff. He tongues the metal wire at the back of his mouth, the wire still holding his jaw together after the blind bitch cracked him with her stick, and stares at his secretary, Pat.

'Well, we need to get on to TOSA security. Maybe we should cancel?'

'I don't think you need to worry,' says Pat. 'I had a call already and they are sending a team. Should be here in . . .' She glances at her watch. 'Well, in five minutes.'

'Really? Guess Dyer must have called them.' Andre is both relieved and confused. 'They got clearance that quick?'

'Yes, well, today of all days, I suspect TOSA must have panicked a bit, what with the opening and all. Have you had the sniffer dogs through yet?'

Andre shakes his head. What with the security level for the Minister of Whatsit and the TOSA Frenchie, the H5 cops were to do a check of the whole building. With dogs. They don't have to say when, they can just turn up, but Andre has a Believe in Better contact in the dog team and knows they'll be coming at 10:30 a.m. *Those bloody new blokes from TOSA security better be up to speed by then.*

His phone rings and he makes a face at Pat. The face is the one he always makes to indicate Nurse Dyer, a horrible twisting of his lips. Only now, with the broken jaw, it makes him wince. Pat nods sympathetically.

'The TOSA security team are here,' says Andre. 'Let's go see what shit we are in.'

A Technical Hitch

10:47 a.m.

Robin is flustered – he seems to have lost both of the Shandy Productions technicians. It isn't his fault, though; after all, the police suddenly descended with their filthy sniffer dogs and he was called away from hunting down fuse boxes to ensuring the clients in Ward A were kept calm and relaxed as the dogs were led up and down the corridors. He doesn't think Dyer should have made him do the fuse box thing anyway. He's a nurse, not her bloody lackey, plus he didn't really know where the fuse boxes were. Anyway, during the sniffer dog round, one of the kids had got a bit upset and that had set off several of the other patients who began to panic, and when finally everyone had settled down again, Robin realised he had lost the technicians.

He wonders if he should tell Dyer. She is stressed to hell anyway. The opening is set for midday and Dr Binding still hasn't made an appearance.

Robin walks with anxious speed towards the gymnasium but slows when he spies one of the cleaners finishing up in the access corridor with a mop: a black, wide-hipped older woman with glasses, called . . . no, he can't remember her name.

'Err, excuse me?'

'Yes, my dear?' She squeezes the mop into the bucket and stretches, turning slowly to face him.

Her gentle, calm response in the midst of all the turmoil makes Robin feel better. 'I was just wondering if you had seen two men walk past just now?'

'Oh . . . oh, why yes, dear. Him, with a workman's belt on and laptop, and his mate? Yes, they said they had finished up and were heading back to reception.'

'That's great, thanks.' Robin takes a deep, relieved yoga breath, in one nostril and out the other. The cleaner is watching him, and so he feels he can't just walk away. 'Are you coming to the opening, Mrs . . . ?' He isn't sure if the cleaners have been invited like the other staff, but the woman nods happily.

'Honey. Mrs Honey. Oh yes, dear. Wouldn't miss it for the world.'

Robin doesn't know how he feels about that, but he supposes the cleaners will be in the back and not mingling with the important people up front. Already he is a little bit heady thinking about the arrival of Stella Binding, having had a bit of a thing for her for years. Now he will finally be able to meet her. He gets a little shiver thinking that Stella is now alone, a poor tragic near-widow. *I wonder if she'll notice me*, he thinks, *my life force, my vibrant energy?* He even showered after cycling into work today, which, for him, is almost unheard of.

He dashes back up the gleaming corridor and turns into the noise of excited chatter and squeaking shoes in reception. Everyone looks very busy. The Shandy Productions team have rigged up a small stage next to the little curtained-off plaque on the far wall. On the stage is a mike stand and speakers, and behind them a large white screen and a couple of computers. It all looks very professional and high tech, not his kind of thing at all. Nurse Dyer waves to him from the centre of the room and signals 'get over here'. She is clutching her clipboard a little too tightly and looks as if she would like to swipe it across the face of the man she is talking to.

'Ah, Robin. This is Mr Shandy. He is in charge of the—' she gestures at the stage '—"setup". He will be here with two of his team to make sure everything works. The rest will be leaving shortly and will return at 2 p.m. to dismantle.'

'Right,' says Robin. Shandy chews gum and smiles, but not with his eyes. 'Am I still on to lead the tour?' Robin tries not to sound overexcited.

'Yes, yes,' snaps Dyer. 'You will lead, and Nurses Pepper and Ashley will follow along to make sure there are no stragglers. Have you done a time check?'

'Yes.' Robin is proud. 'The full tour takes twenty-five minutes, excluding questions.'

'OK, good. Questions can all be asked back here after the unveiling. Right then, go and have a cup of tea, and make sure you are back here with Pepper and Ashley for eleven thirty. And get that stain off your uniform.'

Robin drops his eyes and sees his biro has leaked into his pocket. *Shit.*

'Still no Dr Binding?' he asks by way of diversion.

One of the technicians drops a pole, and it clangs loudly, making everyone jump. Nurse Dyer actually flinches. 'No,' she says. 'But he wouldn't miss this. I am sure he will be along any minute.'

Dr Binding Gets Diverted

11:15 a.m.

The Good Doctor Binding isn't sure what happened. He remembers telling his driver to go ahead and park at the far end of the car park; that way they wouldn't get blocked in by the crowds at the end of the event. He had been sauntering across to the main Grassybanks entrance when his phone rang. He thinks he answered it but can't remember.

The next thing he does remember is a crushing pain in the back of his skull and a nauseating rush of tarry black.

He is still in total blackness, only now he can feel his body again. He becomes aware he is lying flat on something firm but warm, and reaches out his hands to feel for sheets and blankets, but there is something around his wrists stopping him moving his hands more than a few inches from his body. He blinks, and coloured spots bounce around in front of his eyes and flare and die away, leaving him back in total darkness. His head aches, not badly but dully, like the thudding one gets after running too fast.

Have I been hit by a car? he wonders. *Maybe something fell on me from above?* There had been no one at all around. He hadn't walked under scaffolding. That much he did know. Not a soul. Just the phone ringing.

A stroke?

But then, and slowly, very slowly, his mind begins to focus. *But then why would I have restraints around my wrists and be lying in the dark?*

Perhaps you lost your sight? Lost your mind? Strokes can do that. Is that his voice? He isn't sure. Possibly he is dreaming or still unconscious. He gently moves his head from side to side. Although it aches, there doesn't seem to be anything on it apart from hair. No bandage, no neck brace. He tries to slowly twist his body to one side. Yes, he can feel his arms are bare, and there is a thin sheet beneath him. He moves a leg but, like his arm, it gets only a few inches, and then is held by something around his ankle. *This is quite ridiculous!* He wets his lips with his tongue, swallows and opens his mouth.

'Hello,' he whispers. His voice is croaky but there. He tries again, a little louder. 'Hello! Is there anyone here?' His voice seems to bounce right back at him as if he is lying in a kind of container. The echo of it makes his head throb more painfully. Is he in an MRI machine? Could someone have put him in one and then forgotten him? *Absurd!*

'Ahoy!' Louder now and the returning echo is definitely metallic. And close. The doctor suspects that if he sat up he would hit his head on the top of the . . . the what? The pod? The container? He is suddenly desperately claustrophobic and very, very frightened. He begins to thrash about. 'Help me!' he screams. For the first time in over forty years, The Good Doctor Binding's eyes begin to leak.

'Are those actual tears, Dr Binding?' It is a distorted voice, an electronic tenor, but Binding can't tell where it is coming from.

Sudden brilliant white light blinds him. He blinks rapidly,

feeling the hot tears slide down his recently shaved cheeks and into his ears.

Then he sees there is something on his chest. It looks like a torch on a thin pole, and attached to the torch is a little camcorder. A tiny red light is blinking.

'Nearly time for your close-up, Doctor,' says the tinny voice. 'Shame you didn't trim your nostril hair.'

Arrival

11:45 a.m.

Robin and the other nurses – Nurse Ashley, a smaller, sourer version of Nurse Dyer, and Nurse Pepper, a soft, fish-white, trembling, fat girl from North Wales – are scrubbed and smart and ready to greet the VIPs, press and mayor's entourage. The two blokes from Shandy Productions who have been left to ensure technical support have faded into the background, and so too, it seems, has Nurse Dyer.

Robin is a bit affronted by her absence. He knows she hates her routines being scuppered and her wards being walked through by strangers, but even so, he expected her to be here for the 'meet and greet'. Dr Binding hasn't shown up either, which is even odder, as Robin had seen the Doc's chauffeur sitting in the Mercedes parked up in the front of the car park, head down, reading a paper.

Well, there is nothing to be done about that now, thinks Robin, mouth opening and shutting as he breathes into his diaphragm using the Bhastrika Pranayama technique.

'You sound like you're snoring,' hisses Nurse Ashley, fidgeting and scratching her eczema.

'Here they come,' whimpers Pepper, so pale in her white uniform she could be an enormous marshmallow. She tries to grab Robin's hand for a squeeze of reassurance, but he pulls away, disgusted.

Robin, Pepper and Ashley are standing with the other on-duty staff in front of the reception desk. Amid a clicking and flashing of cameras, about ten people are walking in through the automatic doors towards them. First in are the two H5 security staff, followed by the great man himself, John Thorpe-Sinclair MP, the stunning Stella Binding MP, and the surly, short Frenchman, Monsieur Rennes, CEO of TOSA. Behind them comes the mayor of Cambright, Bill Pearson, his consort Clarissa, and a flurry of PR and press people. Everyone is smiling and chortling as if they have all just shared the best pub joke ever.

Apart from Stella, thinks Robin. He can see she is trying to be brave and professional, in spite of the anxiety she must be feeling for her husband. *Poor, poor woman.* His heart goes out to her as she stands there, gleaming hair in a chignon, black sculpted dress. *What lovely lean legs she has.*

The Grassybanks manager, a lugubrious, grey-suited man called Donald Skinner, greets the VIPs with a huge fake smile plastered across his long face.

'Welcome to Grassybanks. Without you, our Right Honourable friends, this exceptional establishment would not be operational.' Robin notices Skinner's hangdog eyes slide around the room. He too must be looking for Nurse Dyer and the doctor. Oh dear, are they going to get it in the neck!

'We hope you are OK with the grand tour first?' Skinner shouts to the crowd. 'Robin, one of our most experienced nurses, will lead you on the tour. We will then meet back here in a few minutes for the speeches and the unveiling of the plaque.'

Everyone nods, hands are shaken, and Robin is called forward.

'Don't mess this up,' hisses Ashley to his back. She really is a mini-Dyer.

Andre in the Doghouse

What Andre is beginning to realise, as the fog in his brain clears, is that he is lying on his side on a floor smeared with what looks like, smells like and so probably is dog shit.

Oh my God, gross! Repulsed, he heaves himself up into a sitting position, feeling as if he has drunk a bottle of vodka with a lager beer-barrel chaser. He remembers, although only vaguely, getting instantly sleepy and then possibly falling asleep, just after glugging a cuppa during the new security staff briefing. He is unable to keep a clear thought in his head. How long has he been out for, and why the hell is he feeling so cold? He blinks, and in that second realises he is fucking cold because he is starkers. Fuck and crumble! What has happened to his clothes? Is he still dreaming? Naked and covered in dog shit? What the . . . ?

'Awww . . .' he whimpers, and there is a low rumbling response from behind him.

He tries to turn around and chokes. He can't move in that direction. He brings his hands up gingerly to his neck and finds that there is a thick leather collar around his throat, attached to a heavy chain that loops down his body, across the floor, fixed to a metal hoop. The metal hoop is on the floor of the . . . cage. No, wait . . . not a cage.

There is another low rumble as Andre yanks at the chain to try, without luck, to loosen it. No, not a cage but a . . . and now he is very scared. A kennel. Andre freezes. The rumbling behind him dies down. Slowly, slowly, inch by inch, the naked man with the collar around his neck twists around and sees that a few feet from him, also in a collar and chain, lies Hobgoblin, the Grassybanks attack dog, the one who nearly tore the throat out of that blind bitch's dog.

'Good boy,' whispers Andre, trying not to let out the sob he feels pushing against his throat.

Hobgoblin opens one eye, growls again in bored warning, *Shut the fuck up*, closes the eye and pretends to sleep. Andre is going nowhere.

A Circus of Clowns

Robin feels he has done a really excellent job on the tour. He hasn't lost his cool, his voice has been loud enough, and they have moved swiftly through the wards, only stopping briefly to look into the newly furbished Ward C, which still smells of wet paint and disinfectant. The photographers tried to stall a couple of times to get some 'serious' shots, and there had been an attempt at a question or two from the tall, brassy blonde reporter with the local news team, but Robin has been firm, moving them along and now back to the main reception. His heart is thumping loudly as, on this final leg, the gorgeous Stella Binding is walking right next to him. He can smell her perfume, a heady mix of vanilla and spice. As they turn the corner, she reaches out and grasps his forearm. Surprised, breathless, he turns to her, but she isn't looking at him. She is staring past him through the open doors.

It is a shocking sight. In front of them, blocking Robin and the small crowd of excited VIPs, is a line of three empty wheelchairs. Standing behind the wheelchairs and grinning and waving are three clowns in nurses' uniforms. Yes, clowns. Huge red mouths and red noses, white faces and curly yellow wigs. Robin is trying to remember where the clowns appeared in the programme of events Nurse Dyer had given him – but he is drawing a blank. He thought it was just speeches.

The clowns are gesturing theatrically to the chairs.

Behind Robin, John Thorpe-Sinclair, now without jacket and with sleeves rolled up (as directed by Deedee, his PR person – '*It worked for Blair and Bush*') is smiling affably and sucking in his gut for the clicking cameras. His wide face is a shiny moon with a slight sheen of sweat. He blinks at the clowns and takes stock of the possible press comeback. There is, luckily, minimal press today: three photographers from various papers, and a local news team with the tall woman in those silly spectacles and her smelly roadie-like camera bloke. They, this local team, are apparently feeding footage back to their central website, *Cambright Sun Online*.

The whirr of cameras and the flashes and clicks make Thorpe-Sinclair feel a little high, almost randy.

'What's this, man?' he asks brusquely of Robin, inclining his head towards the clowns and wheelchairs blocking their entrance to the reception.

'Errrmmm . . .' Robin is entirely flummoxed. He stretches his neck looking for the manager, Mr Skinner, who doesn't seem to be in reception at all.

'I believe they want you to sit in them.' The voice on Thorpe-Sinclair's left comes from the tall blonde. The woman pushes her tinted glasses up on her nose and peers very hard at the clowns. The clowns silently applaud her. One pulls out a piece of A4 paper with 'You are invited to sit!' printed on it.

Still, Robin baulks. He just can't imagine Nurse Dyer allowing clowns in reception. Deedee sidles to the front, holding out her PR person's clipboard. 'It is in our agenda, sir,' she whispers, loud enough for Robin to overhear. 'Tour of wards followed by open-ing ceremony performance. Then the speeches, and then the unveiling.'

Robin realises with relief what must be happening, and indeed he recognises the wheelchairs. They are some of the brand-new ones presented to Grassybanks by the Kitty Fox Foundation last week. Dyer must just have forgotten to hand him the agenda, silly cow. Well, all right then! 'These are the best wheelchairs on the market,' he says proudly to the tour group. 'Worth a test drive.' The clowns clap silently again and hold up the sign.

Thorpe-Sinclair smiles and smiles, but he isn't happy. He turns and hisses over his shoulder to Deedee, 'How will this look to the Equality and Diversity people? Is it going to cause a stink?'

Stella Binding winces. Wheelchairs and clowns? Could be a bad move. She looks over at Deedee, who shrugs. 'If it's in the pre-approved programme it must have been cleared,' she mouths.

Stella relaxes. *Yes, of course.* And anyway Henri Rennes is already waving to the chattering crowd of press and leaping into the first wheelchair like a gymnast. He flicks his dark fringe back from his forehead, winks at Stella and can't help patting his knee. She blushes very prettily.

Thorpe-Sinclair is not going to be outdone by a bloody Frenchman. He strides over to the second clown and plonks himself down heavily into the wheelchair, grasping the wheels to spin it in a circle. The brakes are on, so he can't move it, and the chair nearly topples with his thwarted effort. The clown does an oversized double take and curtsies, and everyone bursts out laughing. 'Very funny,' smiles Thorpe-Sinclair, feeling the growl of hatred in his gut. No one laughs at John Thorpe-Sinclair and gets away with it.

Stella Binding is next, helped into the last wheelchair by her own gallant clown, who offers her a hand as she sits and then, pretending his heart explodes with love, collapses at her feet. The small crowd roar with laughter again and then quieten, remembering that it is probably inappropriate, given Stella's recent near-tragedy. Stella smiles gamely, and the clowns push the chairs in a little circle and lead the procession of press and important people towards the stage and the large white screen.

'But what the hell is going on now?' asks one of the photographers as they all move to the centre of the spacious reception area, for it is not just clowns now. Lined up on either side of the screen are two dozen or so men and women. They are all wearing black clothes and standing or sitting; several are in wheelchairs or on crutches. Each sports the most disturbing full-head rubber mask.

'They must be . . . *les résidents, oui?*' Henri whispers to Stella. She nods, looking at the variously shaped bodies under the masks, the motorised chairs, the splints, the canes. The bodies may all be different, but the masks themselves are all the same, a young woman's face, attractive and serene, long straight dark wig. Her oversized, calm, almost Madonna-like head on all the different bodies – some twisted, some missing limbs, some in wheelchairs – is rather unpleasant to Stella, although she is resigned to this kind of thing. *Oh God,* she is groaning inwardly, *not another ghastly disabled dance project.*

She recently opened a new residential home for orphaned teenagers with severe learning impairments and had to endure an hour and a half of what the producer assured her was a 'vital and inspirational interpretation of *Macbeth*'. It was a pathetic performance. The ugliness, the clumsiness and the smells – one of the boys had actually pissed himself on stage – had repulsed her, but watching it, she had felt comforted by the thought that the home for teenagers was on her father's list for CDD. If all went to plan there would not be another production to endure there.

Her PR people had promised they would check that, in future, any 'entertainment' was under half an hour. She turns her head to try to catch Deedee's eye but can't see the woman over the back of the chair and the damn clown. And there's another thing: for some reason she can't move very easily. Her back and bottom seem to be . . . well, stuck to the chair. She is thinking how odd it is when she notices Henri beside her beginning to jerk a little in his chair, as if he is stuck too. Stella, perturbed, tries to raise her arm, but her jacket sleeves are stuck to the armrests.

'What the . . . ?'

'Hey . . . ?' she hears Thorpe-Sinclair say with equal confusion. 'Is this some kind of joke?'

And then the music starts. Circus music, of course. Stella knows it as 'Entrance of the Gladiators' by the Czech composer Julian Fučít. *'Fučít', damned appropriate.* Stella hates the circus, and was it a clown joke to have glue on the chairs? If they have ruined her Chanel shift she will fucking sue them. *Da da dalalala da da dala* . . .

This way, this way! More clowns appear from behind the lines of rubber-masked people, dancing and gesturing silently, squeaking their noses and flapping their outsize shoes. These clowns gather up and wave the bamboozled mayor and his entourage, guests and PR people towards the wide-open doors of the family room. The family room is slightly off to the left of the stage and screen, with large windows looking in on the reception like an aquarium, and as each person enters, a clown-nurse sweetly holds up a sign that requests they drop their phones and bleepers, pagers and *cameras . . . cameras? Yes, cameras please!* into a large plastic children's storage box.

Don't worry, don't worry, you will have them all back soon, soothe the terrible clowns, signing with their gloved hands and smiling with their great red mouths and shaking their silly yellow wigs.

And into the family room are also ushered the press photographers. *Just for a little while,* sign the nurse-clowns and blink their eyes and wave their hands.

Da da dalala dada dala!

'Oh look,' says the mayor, frankly delighted by the clown show. 'There is another screen in here, too.' And there is. In the bright, colourful, cushioned family room there is another large monitor placed high up on the wall so that everyone can see it. On the monitor they can see themselves being ushered into the family room. The mayor, a jovial ex-academic, now alcoholic, waves to himself. His little TV self waves back.

'Who is filming? Who has this live stream?' hisses one of the photojournalists who had to give up his camera. He points up at the monitor. His colleague gestures through the family-room glass. There are only two other people from the tour (apart from Thorpe-Sinclair, Binding and Rennes) left outside. It is they who are, in fact, filming the action – the tall blonde with the specs and the smelly roadie from *Cambright Sun Online.*

There is a minor kerfuffle in the doorway. Deedee and the other PR people are unsure about leaving their charges in a separate area. 'It's just,' they are saying to the clowns, 'that we feel we should be on hand to advise them, especially if you are going to actually use them as part of a performance piece.'

'I can't actually believe this was ever sanctioned,' says Deedee. She has a very bad feeling that she is going to get the sack for this screw-up. 'I think we'll just need to check with our security team.'

Only now, when Deedee turns to look for the H5 security backup, there are none to be found. How long have they all been without security?

Beginning to panic, Deedee reaches for her phone, and a clown plucks it from her fingers and drops it into the plastic box.

'Hey!' She tries to grab it back and the clown pushes her hard. She falls backwards into another clown who whirls her around in a frenetic waltz.

Da da dalalala da da dala, da da dalalala da da dala . . .

Too shocked and out of breath to say another word, Deedee and the other PR people find themselves danced backwards into the aquarium-like family room.

The clowns close the door, waving and smiling to the crowd now safely inside. Some of the crowd, pressed happily up against the glass to watch the show, wave back. A few others, Deedee included, are beginning to feel something is very wrong. They rush forward to open the door and the clowns mime shock and sadness. *No no*, they wag their fingers. The door is locked.

Luckily for the clowns, the family room is soundproofed.

The Box Speaks

Jenny is spooning organic strawberry yoghurt into Serena's mouth. As Serena is yelling between gulps, a lot of the yoghurt is finding its way onto the floor where Chris is lying. He is being as helpful as possible, and – although as An Excellently Trained Guide Dog, the whole hoovering-up-under-dining-room-tables is frowned on – in this instance he feels surreptitiously licking it up will stop Mosh from slipping over in it later. He is only doing this as a favour, he explains to himself happily, as the strawberry smell makes his nostrils sing.

There is a lot of noise in the house. Downstairs, the television is on in the living room, and upstairs Mosh is drilling holes in the bathroom, attempting to put up a new shelf. Jenny is beginning to wonder if it is too early to have a glass of wine.

'Mumma, nooooo!' Serena's beautiful face rumples and crumples as she screams. She is hungry for the yoghurt, demands immediate yoghurt, but when she gets it she hates the yoghurt, and it is torture. *Baby brains are confusing*, thinks Chris, licking another dollop from the leg of the high chair. He likes the baby very much, and she is still young enough to be mostly vibration and instinct, but he still can't talk to her directly. He is aware she is teething right now, and he has tried to comfort her, but she is absolutely sure it is the fault of the yoghurt. Her screams in translation say *I want it but it hurts my mouth.*

Chris is feeling much better, rested and pain-free . . . well, almost pain-free. It still hurts him to run, and he is missing Alex, and that is a whole other kind of soreness. Since he came back from the vet's they have not been apart for a single moment – until today, that is – and she has even allowed him to sleep on her bed, which he loves, loves, loves! He will start curled up on the dog blanket on the end and through the night gradually snore his way up until he is lying with his head almost on Alex's pillow, spreadeagled to get as close to her warm body as possible. Every now and then she will wake up and shove him over but without much success.

And yet today he has been dropped here, and she has left him. It is difficult for him to understand why she has gone, even though he knew she was trying to explain it before she went. He wished she could learn to use her vibration to speak. Like the baby. Maybe the baby could teach her . . . when she gets back. Is she coming back?

Another slow pustule of yoghurt runs down the table leg. Chris is edging combat-style on his belly towards it when he hears Alex's voice, quite distinctly, coming from the other room. Joy rushes up into his heart and his head, like soda bubbles. He leaps up and whirls around, dashing as quickly as his sore rump will let him, in the direction of his beloved's voice. But in the living room there is no Alex, no Alex energy, no Alex smell, no Alex. He runs to the voice and then, disoriented and a little anxious, he runs back into the kitchen. He can still hear her.

'Alex?' he barks.

'What is it, Chris?' Both Jenny and Serena are staring at him. He runs to them.

'Can't you hear her? It's Alex? But . . . ?' He dashes back to the living room again, and this time it occurs to him that Alex's voice is coming out of the picture box. Is she in the box? Chris isn't stupid, but the whole TV thing is beyond him..

Jenny and Serena sit shocked for a second. Jenny realises that she has never heard Chris bark before. She pulls a wet wipe from the stack and wipes some of the yoghurt from Serena's face and unclips her from the high chair. 'Come on, sweetheart,' she says, hefting her up and onto a hip. 'Let's go see what's upsetting the dog.'

In the living room, the first thing Jenny notices is that Chris is sitting about two feet from the television. His ears are pricked, head cocked and he has one paw raised. He is spellbound.

Then Jenny notices something else.

'Mosh!' She has to shout over the sound of his drilling. 'Mosh, get down here quick!'

There is a pause upstairs.

'What did you say, honey?'

'Mosh! Come here, now!'

She hears him coming down the stairs and feels him as he fills the doorway behind her.

'Is everything—?'

'Mosh, where did you say Alex was today?'

'Hospital appointment.'

'I don't think that was the whole truth.'

Jenny steps to one side so Mosh can see the TV screen. 'What?'

She points.

Mosh peers. Then he makes a funny noise and steps closer and, hands on his knees, really looks. He has, even though he has not been anywhere near his daughter, managed to get a splodge of yoghurt on the back of his trousers.

'Oh my God!' On the screen is a journalist talking into the camera. She is a tall, attractive blonde sporting a pair of oversized tinted glasses.

'Where did she get that wig?' he asks Jenny.

'I don't think that's the issue. Listen to what she's saying.'

It is Alex. Mosh just needs to look at Chris's frozen posture to verify the fact. She is standing in what looks like a hospital reception, which is full of gambolling clowns in nurses' uniforms and lines of people in rubber masks. Rubber masks that are all the same face, that of a serene young woman. There is circus music playing, but Alex looks deadly serious. Mosh reaches for the remote on top of the TV and cranks up the sound.

In Which Alex Hosts the Show

'. . . am speaking from the scene at Grassybanks where the Secretary of State for Health, Stella Binding, the Secretary of State for Work and Pensions, John Thorpe-Sinclair, and the CEO of TOSA, Henri Rennes, have become part of a bizarre sort of . . . protest. We are still unsure as to who is in charge of all this. Hold on, we are going to try and get a bit closer and see if we can talk to one of the protesters . . .'

Alex is sweating under her wig. In fact, she is sweating everywhere, although she blasted herself with so much deodorant this morning she almost set off a smoke alarm. She had come here, to the Grassybanks opening, all Bond-style in her silly disguise, intending to confront Binding and Binding. She was blinded by anger. The doctor's last words to her, 'I'm sorry to hear about your dog. I don't suppose he will be able to work again either,' had clanged about her head for the entire week. The coldness masked by charm, the implied threat. And that terrible thought that kept her awake at night . . . had Binding pushed Gunter out of the window to stop him telling the truth about the CDD?

Alex refuses to be afraid, to be made afraid. It is enough that she has to spend her life peering at the world through a murky twilight, that she has already had to give up her ambitions of

TV anchorwoman, that she has already been humiliated over and over again at various Job Centrals, that life is hard and edgy and lonely. If Binding was in any way responsible for Chris's attack, for Gunter's fall . . . oh God . . . for the murder of these vulnerable people, then she will, she must, confront him. Alex, to put it simply, will no longer tolerate a bully.

It had been Kitty and Helen who had let slip about the 'official' opening of Ward C. Kitty had been invited as the Kitty Fox Foundation had gifted several brand-new, state-of-the-art wheelchairs, but she had no intention of going along herself. 'The entire place gives me the creeps,' Kitty had stated flatly. 'And anyway, it will be a fucking circus.'

Alex had seen a look pass between Helen and Kitty then, something both tender and terribly sad, but Kitty refused to discuss the opening any more and wheeled herself back to the studio.

Helen told Alex she should keep well clear. 'There will be hellish security.' She had peered closely at Alex, noting the tightness around her mouth. 'Alex, you will only get yourself in even more shit!' she had chided, urgently. 'Stop thinking about it.'

Alex couldn't stop, though. She had insisted on attending, told Gerald, her editor, that she was covering the ward opening no matter what, and his distress over Chris's attack had made him putty in her hands. 'I'll take Terry,' she had said. 'We'll feed back live to the website. No funny business,' she reassured him, lying. 'Straight-from-the-hip, professional journalism.'

But Alex being Alex, and therefore reckless, hasn't thought it through. She realises this now as she scans the mute rubber-masked faces and the gurning yellow-haired clowns. She had never thought that a louder voice than hers might take this opportunity to protest too. She had, in her own rage, forgotten that she was not the only person who would want Binding, and whatever is happening at Grassybanks, exposed. *Who the hell are these people?* Her mind races along with her heartbeat. *I wonder . . .* she thinks. *Could it be . . . ?*

Her friend, and now co-opted cameraman, Terry, is doing well, considering he has no idea what the hell is going on either. He isn't the official *Cambright Sun* cameraperson – he is more the IT guy – but he stepped in when Alex asked. Alex likes and trusts him, which is more important. 'These are the people who set their dogs on Chris,' she has already told him. 'They mustn't recognise me. Would you be OK if I go in disguise?'

Terry has never been the least rattled by Alex's visual impairment. He understands that in her disguise she *cannot be blind*, and he has taken on the role of surreptitious guiding arm without a second thought.

'Over here,' Terry whispers. He is guiding Alex via a Bluetooth earpiece. She starts moving off in the wrong direction and Terry reaches out and pulls her back. 'The screen is right in front of you. The wheelchairs are at one o'clock.'

Alex nods. She needs to calm down and, literally, focus. She blinks, stops, trying to catch all the action in her peripherals, and puts the large screen squarely in her constricted tunnel of vision. 'The circus music has stopped and the screen is flickering.' She turns, keeping one foot pointed at the screen as a marker, and speaks directly into the camera and then moves again so Terry can zoom the camera in on the action.

The clowns slow their insane jitterbugging and become still. They all turn to face the large screen. In the family room Alex can see everyone pressed up against the inner windows, gazing into the reception. *They must be aware now that it isn't just a show*, she thinks. *Surely someone will have called the police?*

There is a discordant shriek of feedback, and on the screen appears a huge, very luscious mouth, lips glistening with rose-pink lipgloss over perfectly even white teeth. The mouth smiles down at the world.

'Welcome,' it says. 'Welcome, John Thorpe-Sinclair. Welcome, Stella Binding, and welcome, Henri Rennes.'

'Wow,' whispers Terry. 'It's the *Rocky Horror Picture Show*.'

Alex doesn't recognise the mouth, but the voice . . . she swallows. She thinks she recognises the voice. 'Thorpe-Sinclair's trousers are tearing,' Terry tells Alex, adjusting the camera focus. 'It looks to me like they have actually been superglued into their seats.'

'Today is a very special day,' says the mellifluous voice of The Mouth, thrumming out through the speakers. 'Today we have three of the people who are at the very heart of the welfare reforms, and who are all in one way or another culpable for the results. We thought it was time to celebrate them in our own unique way! And who, you may ask, who are "we"?'

The clowns wave their gloved hands wildly, silently.

'We . . .' and the voice distorts, becomes louder and horrific, a tangle of electronics and noise.

'We are BOUDICCA!' it roars. The clowns screech and cavort and come back to their positions again.

'Boudicca,' says Alex to the camera. *Of course!* she thinks. *How could I have been so blind?* And she plunges into her commentary. 'The protest is being staged by a group calling themselves Boudicca. Up to now, this group has owned up to nothing more than graffiti and letters to the press.' *No one confessed to the booby-trapped wheelchair,* she thinks. *What could they want with Grassybanks?*

She can hear some people screaming faintly from the locked family room, so obviously they can hear everything from inside. *Must be playing through speakers.*

Alex turns and nods into the camera. 'And it would appear that Stella Binding, Thorpe-Sinclair and Rennes have actually been glued into their wheelchairs.'

The huge mouth on screen smiles and a wet red tongue slowly licks its milk-white teeth. When the voice comes again, it is back to its lovely melodic warmth.

'We thought a celebration would be appropriate, especially as we are about to give you each a whole new fresh perspective on life. After today you will be able to do your jobs so much better. You will be on the front line. You will be one of us. One of us!'

'This is outrageous,' Thorpe-Sinclair is spluttering, trying to wrench himself free. 'Someone call security!'

'Bring Thorpe-Sinclair! John Thorpe-Sinclair, the Minister for Work and Pensions,' The Mouth sings.

The clown pushing Thorpe-Sinclair's wheelchair swings him in a wide arc in front of the other clowns, who clap and cheer, and past the windows of the family room where the mayor, the crowd of press, PR and others watch fishlike, open-mouthed through the glass. Thorpe-Sinclair is struggling hard, and as the clown passes, Terry zooms the camera in on the politician's shirt and trousers stuck to the back of the chair. The seat of his trousers has ripped away at the top seam, allowing a little pink glow of buttock and white pant in the viewfinder. Thorpe-Sinclair is mouthing obscenities at the clown but can't twist around in his chair, so the clown pays absolutely no heed, just carries on pushing and smiling at the crowd.

'Definitely glue,' says Terry to Alex. 'That's gonna hurt coming off. Must have been on the seat backs, bottom and armrests.'

'We all know, John,' says The Mouth, 'because you tell us so often, that you do all that you do for the good of the nation. You are a man of honour and a patriot, and now, as the Minister for Work and Pensions, you have become wise. You have a plan for the people, especially for the broken of Britain. You know what is best for the depressed. Your nation salutes you! A million people back in work because of your changes? Well . . . OK, not a million exactly, right? Not people in full-time, permanent, contracted work, eh, but who's to knock a statistic as gorgeous as that one? In many ways the actual real numbers are inconsequential, given the moral war you are waging on the limp and the lazy, the scroungers and the work-shy. Surely, you say, any normal person would rather work for nothing than take from the hard-working British taxpayer. Any normal person would rather die than be seen at Job Central scrounging.'

Thorpe-Sinclair has gone quiet and is no longer trying to rip himself from the gluey seat. He is watching the screen, his head slightly cocked, trying to work out whether the voice is being sardonic.

The screen is now showing a montage of John Thorpe-Sinclair's most famous moments. There he is on the podium berating the malingerers, the work-shy, the parasites of Britain. 'The public think homelessness is about having no accommodation,' he is saying. 'Homelessness is just an attitude.' Here he is smiling as he unveils the plans for the shining new Care and Protect Act. 'Beveridge was a mug,' he says. 'Work is what makes people human. If we give them financial aid where is the incentive to work?' Here he is with the Queen, and now here he is at home, on his enormous estate with his little wife, Wilma, and here he is declaring, 'Anyone can live on the Basic Benefit. It just needs careful budgeting.' A whirl of news bites and radio clips, articles, photos, and then just his huge moon face smiling down on the assembled rubber-masked folk in the Grassybanks reception.

Silence.

John Thorpe-Sinclair still appears to have a small smile on his face. A cocky expression of 'that wasn't bad'. *Can he really be that stupid?* wonders Alex. *Can he really not see the danger he is in?* She steps forward, and a clown leaps in front of her, so close that even Alex can see the tired flecks of skin under the mottled white pancake make-up.

'Don't intervene, Alex,' says the clown very quietly and right into her ear. 'Not yet. You will get your chance to ask questions.'

The clown steps away before Alex can respond. Its arms swing strangely, the gloved hands hang down, the arms soft and jointless.

'Jesus . . . Jules . . .' Alex gasps.

'What is it, what did it say?' Terry is asking, but already Stella Binding is being wheeled forward to face The Mouth.

'Ahh, Stella. One hardly needs an introduction. Golden girl, daughter of a good doctor, childless wife to what is essentially now a crip in the making.' The voice is harsher, the poison dripping between every vowel. *Helen's voice*, thinks Alex with both awe and deep sadness. It may not be her mouth on screen but it is her voice. Her dear, birdlike, dark-haired friend, the very one who comforted her, saved her, after the attack on Chris and her stupid fight: Helen. *Helen is Boudicca.*

Stella's montage is similar to Thorpe-Sinclair's. Key moments from key speeches in her rise to Health Minister. Various podiums, speeches: 'The youth today must realise that work is not optional. Just because you went to university doesn't mean you are better than anyone else in this country. If the work is there, you damn well have to take it. But what about those unable to work, disabled or . . . ? We don't believe that people who are genuinely unable to work will be left behind. Our government has pumped millions into the Care and Protect Act. We are a government completely dedicated to ensuring the protection of the vulnerable.' There is another montage of her visiting hospitals, kissing children, with her husband. *Oh poor, poor Gunter.*

Alex and Terry move cautiously forward. Alex is breathing hard. She won't intervene, not right now. She realises now that she loves her LDA family, even if some of them may be brutal . . . may be Boudicca. Had she not also come today to shout and scream in public at Binding? To 'out' him? Does that make her Boudicca too? She understands now that she has been manipulated, led this way, pulled that. They needed her. They probably knew she would come today. Did Helen . . . Jules . . . did Kitty . . . did her friends set her up? She looks at the three wheelchairs with their prisoners.

Thorpe-Sinclair still doesn't get it. Stella isn't so slow. She has her face turned away from the images on the screen and is looking directly at Alex. Stella's face is tight with anger, her pale cheeks flushed with pink. When Henri Rennes is pushed beside her, he leans as if to offer her encouragement and she says something too quietly to be heard, but sharp enough to make him recoil.

The Mouth is back. Lips are licked, and glisten with fresh

gloss. 'But we are missing someone. Someone we need to play our Grassybanks Ward C opening games! Could it be?'

Now from down the corridor comes the sound of clattering and jangling. Two more clown-nurses appear from the wide double doors leading to the wards and they are pushing not a wheelchair but a full-sized bed, one of the adapted beds from Ward B. There is someone in it, someone struggling under the sheets.

'I believe some of you may have already met Nurse Dyer. She is here today to introduce us all to the original, specially designed Chiller Beds! These beds are only found here at Grassybanks. They have been adapted for one special purpose. But let's allow Nurse Dyer to show us, shall we?'

One of the clowns moves to the top of the bed and flings back the sheet covering the twisting body. Poor Nurse Dyer, hat now fallen over one eye, uniform rucked up to show her skinny knees and blue varicose veins, is furiously squirming. The clown leaps back, pretending to be afraid.

'Ah, don't worry,' says The Mouth to the clown. 'The fearsome nurse is in a Chiller Bed specially designed for people thrashing and twisting and desperate. Look, everyone. Bring the camera closer, please.'

Terry stumbles forward, pulling Alex with him. 'Not going in alone,' he apologises in a whisper.

Through the camera close-ups it is apparent that Nurse Dyer is restrained by straps around her ankles, wrists and waist. She has a white plastic gag in her mouth that drips with foam. Her furious eyes and foaming mouth make her look rabid.

Now the clowns line up in formation and point to each feature as The Mouth reads them out.

'Maximum adjustable working height – mattress support – ninety-seven centimetres. Minimum adjustable working height – mattress support – fifty-seven centimetres. Lateral tilt adjustable – two directions and angle gauges and emergency levelling – thirty degrees. Side-flap elevation adjustable – ninety degrees. Pressure-relief side-flaps lower – fifteen degrees. Back-lift profile adjustable – sixty degrees. Leg-lift profile adjustable and knee-brake – fifty degrees . . .'

The list goes on and on. The clowns feign yawns.

'Carrier rails for catheter bag and accessories at each side. Directional mains-power lead allows exit at either end of bed. IV drip stand – two sockets – at head end.

'But . . . !' the voice from The Mouth booms louder. 'In addition – and here is where it is totally unique and never before seen in any other residential home – the Chiller Bed does exactly that – it chills. At night the temperature of the bed can be reduced quickly and efficiently. It takes merely minutes and already, as you can see, Nurse Dyer is beginning to find things are getting a little cooler.'

On the bed Nurse Dyer is snuffling through her nostrils, and now a wisp of mist can be seen as her breath condenses. She is shivering. Even from a couple of feet away Alex and Terry can feel the deep chill coming from the bed. It is as if someone has opened a freezer door.

'The Chiller Beds,' says The Mouth, as if in a sales room, 'are perfect for reducing body temperature. Why, you might ask? Well, for the same reason that these beds are also fitted with sponge-like filler in the mattresses, so that in addition to chilling, the beds can be lightly sprayed with water. The combination of wet and cold is perfect for the Chiller Bed.'

One of the clowns has a little red watering can and is now watering Nurse Dyer. Her shivering becomes more pronounced, and she begins to gasp around her gag. It is horrible to watch.

'Please stop this!' Alex can't take this any more. She steps forward.

The Mouth tuts. 'But my dear, Nurse Dyer is fit and relatively healthy. If we stop this now, she will survive. Is that what you want?'

'Of course!' Alex is horrified by the implication, the realisation.

'It isn't what she would want for you, my dear, not if you were one of the elderly or disabled people who had come under her "care". Nurse Dyer has overseen several hundred people in these beds. She has not listened to their pleas for mercy, to their icy tears, to their confusion. Of course, Nurse Dyer keeps all her clients sedated in order to maintain the peace. She just lets the Chiller Beds do their job, as she has been instructed.'

Now Alex can hear several people shouting and banging on the glass of the family room. She turns, looking over her shoulder. Behind the windows the people are a blur to her. 'They look really shocked back there,' Terry whispers to her.

'Yes, you can ask them what they think,' The Mouth says calmly to Alex, as if reading her mind. 'They can hear us. Ask the mayor if he understands what has been going on in Grassybanks. Ask him if he understands the true nature of the Chiller Beds. Ask them all in the family room if they understand why Grassybanks always has room for more—' and here the voice on screen becomes a jangled electronic scream '—MORE FUCKING PATIENTS!'

The banging on the windows stops. Everyone, even the clowns, become quiet as the terrible roar echoes off the walls. The mayor and his entourage step back from the glass. There is a faint sound of sobbing.

'Take the bitch to Ward C,' says The Mouth. 'I think we have made our point.'

The nurse-clowns who brought Nurse Dyer in now wheel the bed out, heads down and sombre as a funeral procession.

'Where the hell is security?' Terry scans around. 'This is getting really serious.'

Robin Less Cock

Inside the family room Robin has his work cut out for him.

As soon as it became apparent that they had been locked into the room, a couple of the PR people had mild hysterics. He had sat them down on cushions and forced them to breathe into paper bags he had found in a drawer. Later, when the Chiller Bed with Nurse Dyer was wheeled in, he had become frightened himself. He knew about the Chiller Beds. Almost all the key nursing staff did. In fact, one of the tasks set for the night shift was 'watering the clients'. But because the wards were constantly monitored by CCTV, the watering cans came in the shape of hot-water bottles. It just looked as if the night staff were rooting around the clients to find the best place to put them. Instead, they were squeezing out ribbons of water to soak into the mattresses below the already icy, sedated bodies.

He wonders, staring out at the capering nurse-clowns, the stranger still rubber-masked army and the horrible huge mouth on the screen, if they are going to pull him out from the crowd in the family room and put him into one of the beds too. It isn't fair. They had been doing it all for the good of the clients. It was for the good of the environment. It was recycling, plain and simple. These people were used up, useless, a drain on society. It was the best thing for everyone, especially them, that they gave their lives to science. And . . . and . . . the deaths weren't so bad. They were allowed to use sedation . . . Dr Binding would explain. He would sort all this out.

All around Robin people are asking, 'Where are the police? Where are the police? What happened to the security?'

Oh hurry up, Dr Binding, thinks Robin. *We need you.*

The Storm

The storm is approaching the city exactly as predicted by the crows, although humans, with their limited senses, have yet to notice. The wind has dropped, and a headache of heat and stillness has descended like a sticky spider's web over Cambright. The immense thundercloud approaching is still out of sight, just over the horizon, but it's coming closer every second. It is breathing in, sucking up moisture and light and energy. In the hot, numbing pre-storm hush, many people become woozy, have to pause breathless and put a hand against a wall for balance. Like a mountain unchained from the earth, the cloud closes in. In air-conditioned shops and cafés they only notice the atmospheric change when the lights flicker and the cloud above blots out the sun. Across the city, people come to their windows, pointing at the darkness on one side of the sky. Anxious parents begin to move towards the doors to call their miserable, hot children inside.

And then the storm breathes out *WHHHHHHHAAAAAAA* and the dry, warm wind tsunami hits. Trees shake like dogs. All things not weighted down shift, skitter, flap and tumble ahead of the thunderhead. And then it brings the rain.

It is a monstrous thing, this storm, crackling with electricity, ravenous and with such ill humour. It seems to open great chunks of sky and pour the rain through without bothering to let it coalesce into droplets. Rivers of water sluice down from above, soaking the hot tarmac, the dry dusty ground, the sun-blasted tiles, and everything steams and splutters. In the streets, people are running for cover, newspapers and briefcases held hopelessly over their heads. Clothes turn transparent, water shines in the eyes of the young. Not even the bravest stands still beneath the oncoming weight of the weather. The smell is sensational, earthy, exotic, exciting, but no one pauses to breathe it in. The storm stomps on the city, and everyone must find shelter.

'My God! That's some downpour,' says Mosh as the rainwater hits their windows, rendering them momentarily opaque, as if someone has just dashed a huge bucket of water against the side of the house. Thunder growls, and Chris growls back, upset by the noise drowning out Alex's voice in the picture box. Serena is wide-eyed and her skin is goosebumped, but Jenny's eyes are narrowed, still completely focused on the television.

'This looks really serious, Mosh,' she says over her shoulder. 'Do you think we should call someone?'

At that moment Mosh's bleeper goes off.

'No point,' he says as he reads the text message and reaches for his car keys. 'The river's in potential flood. Police, fire, ambulance; everyone's been called out on general alert.'

The bow wave of wind hits the front entrance of Grassybanks hard, triggering the electric doors to slide open, and whooshes into the reception area where the clowns and rubber-faced army stand around the wheelchairs. Paper and pens, leaflets and wall-notices fly into the air, and the wind is strong enough to shove the clowns holding the wheelchairs, and knock Terry and the camera off balance.

'Get the door!' yells one of the clowns, its voice odd and discordant from under its silly wig, as the screen with The Mouth on it rocks precariously on its stand. Clowns dash around, but for the moment the wind is only messing with them. It has already withdrawn, sucking itself backwards through the doors, leaving those in reception staggering in the aftermath. The door slides shut with an apologetic ding, and to prevent it opening again, a clown turns its automated opening system off. As rain splatters with the noise of popping corn against the glass, the clowns near the door pause briefly, staring out, watching as men and women run hither and thither around the Grassybanks car park.

'There is something happening outside,' says Terry to Alex, 'but I can't see through the rain.'

'The police?'

'Not sure. Maybe. Flashing lights, far off . . . by the river. The clowns don't seem bothered. Looks like one has locked the door.'

'Focus, focus!' The Mouth is back on screen. 'Hellooo again!' It smiles. It looks different. The voice, however, is still Helen's.

Back at the Movies

And now there is another film screening at the Grassybanks cinema.

Two young men, maybe seventeen years old, are sitting in front of a camera in their pants and vests. They are twins, almost identical apart from the fact one is taller and looks chipper and alert, and the other seems half asleep. The chipper one seems to be enjoying all the attention. He has a charming, lopsided grin and a deep dimple that makes the angry-looking acne outbreak on his forehead seem inconsequential.

'Handsome kid,' Terry whispers to Alex as he films the film.

'My name's Dan and I'm your man!' says Dan, and off camera a couple of people join in his laughter. His crooked sweet grin is very endearing.

'Now Dan, what did we say?' A man in a white doctor's jacket moves into shot.

Alex blinks hard and gets confirmation from Terry. Yes, it's Dr Binding.

'Aww come on, Doc. I am just warming up the audience for you.'

'Quite so. Now, I need you just to say your name and your age. OK, Daniel?'

'Gonna be famous, me.' The lad makes a face and winks at someone, possibly a nurse. A clipped voice off-camera states: 'Day One of the Pansy–Binding trial. June twenty-first. Ten a.m. Daniel Warbray, now known as Twin One, and Wayne Warbray, now known as Twin Two. Both seventeen years, three months and two days old, one hundred and seventy and one hundred and seventy-two pounds. One is five feet, eight point five inches, the other five feet, nine point five inches.'

As Dr Binding continues to examine the twins, another man in a white coat moves forward, away from the lads, and quietly holds up two syringes to the camera. The clipped voice continues, 'The Pansy solution will be administered to Twin One for six days, and the control administered to Twin Two under similar conditions.'

The man holding up the syringes winks into the camera and whispers, 'I am telling you, Binding, only six days for a real result.'

The twins are moved into a twin-bedded ward and made comfortable. Dan is still chirruping to the nurses and pretending brazen confidence. His brother remains taciturn and unsmiling but gives no trouble. He watches Dan clamber into his bed and quietly gets into his own. There is a little hassle over the inserting of the cannula. The quiet twin, Wayne, refuses to let the nurse take his arm. Dan gets out of his bed and comes over to his brother's side of the room.

'He's frightened of needles,' he says solemnly to the nurse. 'I just need to hold his other hand.'

Dan punches his brother in the chest, gently, and uses the casual gesture to take his right hand. His brother almost smiles.

'When's supper, gorgeous?' asks Dan of the nurse as she bustles over Wayne's arm. He is trying to get his brother to think of something other than the hypodermic needle. 'I'm bloody starving.'

'Sorry, love. It's nil-by-mouth.' The nurse's response is a little cautious.

'Eh?'

'No food this evening.' She looks at his expression and wilts. 'Don't worry. You can have something tomorrow.'

'Promise?'

The nurse tuts, dropping her eyes to the bed sheets. She promises nothing.

The next eight minutes of footage covers the next five days. In the family room several people have to turn away, covering their mouths with horror. The mayor, however, refuses to even blink. He stares at the screen, face blotchy with shock and disgust. His fists are clenched and his nostrils widen as if he can smell sulphur.

Day two: the twins are still in bed, although the sun is streaming in through the windows. Dan is twitching and moaning. He seems to be in some discomfort. His twin, Wayne, sitting up in the next bed, is watching him.

In the night, Wayne pulls out his cannula and gets out of his bed. He crosses over and removes Dan's drip too, then gently removes Dan's sheets, pulls him up and carries him out of the room.

Day three: the little doctor in the white coat who goes by the name of Pansy speaks into the video camera. '. . . we have had to sedate and restrain the control as he caused a little trouble in the night, but I am still happy with the progression of Twin One.'

Day four: both twins lie side by side. They both look thin and frail. Dan looks terrible, cheeks sunken and sores around his mouth. His breath is intermittent and ragged. Wayne, although he seems to be sleeping, has tears sliding from under his closed eyelids. A nurse checks his pulse, dabs at his cheeks with a cloth.

Day five: Pansy is almost dancing. 'I think it might even happen today! Sod you, Binding. You said it couldn't be done, but look! You checked the patients yourself, healthy and strong, right? But only five days and seven hours and Twin One is going into heart failure.' He holds up a hypodermic. 'And it's all in this little baby! My "P Formula". "Natural" death as fast as you like! Just wait till that Frenchie Rennes gets a sniff of this. We'll be cleaning up society's slag heap for years to come!'

The footage freezes on Pansy's wink, his hand with the hypodermic high in the air in jubilation. Behind him the two tortured young men lie grey and still. A nurse is looking at her watch. The world stops.

'Where did you get this?' Rennes is screeching now, pointing at the screen, frantically twisting in his gluey wheelchair. 'This is all classified information! No video was made . . . *c'est* . . . *pour de faux* . . . it's a fake!'

'Shut up, Henri, shut up, Henri, shut up, Henri,' repeats Stella over and over. Her hair comes away in clumps, stuck to the back of the chair. She looks demented.

Alex and Terry are right there with the mike and the camera, but the clowns don't intervene. They move back, watching.

'What did you mean, "it's classified"?' Alex is trying not to shout too. She clutches the mike, stepping up to the writhing

Frenchman. Henri's face is a blur of white and black to her but she can just make out his open mouth. Now, maybe now, Alex realises why she has been brought along for the ride. What did Jules say? 'You can ask your questions later.' Yes.

She slows her breathing. Alex was one of the youngest journalists to be embedded with the troops in Iraq. Adrenalin doesn't make her lose focus. The opposite, in fact. She channels her inner inquisitor. 'Come on, Mr Rennes,' she cajoles. 'TOSA. Did you get in over your head with this lot? You can't possibly have realised that when they talked about "processing" the elderly, the vulnerable, that they meant killing them in cold blood and then disposing of their bodies?'

'Don't say a word!' yells John Thorpe-Sinclair at Rennes.

'We are not talking to you, sir.' Alex is polite, her fury cold and sharp as the claw of a snow leopard. 'Henri. Tell us, tell all of us, about what they made you sign up for. The Clearance, Disinfection and Disposal file. Was it yours or theirs?'

Henri's nose is running. But so too is his mouth. Into Alex's mike, down the camera, in English, in French, Henri Rennes talks. 'No, no, *non. Ce n'était pas moi* . . . it was them, always them . . .' He is unstoppable. In mere minutes, he has implicated at least four government ministers and several medical institutions. Alex and Terry just point their devices and film and record and breathe . . . in and out. In and out. What Henri is saying is so ugly and so clever that the questions are unnecessary.

Eventually, he pauses and John Thorpe-Sinclair puts his head back and yells 'Police! Police!' over and over again. Stella Binding looks over at him and joins in. 'Police! Security!'

The Good Doctor Takes His Own Medicine

'Be quiet!' The Mouth demands, and Thorpe-Sinclair and Stella Binding stutter into silence. 'So you can kill them, but how do you dispose of them?' asks The Mouth. 'Bring on the Resomator!'

The screen flickers, blurs and then there is a whole face, blinking in the glare of a bright light, snot bubbling from a nostril, eyes wet with tears.

'Daddy!' screams Stella from her wheelchair.

'Doctor!' screams Robin from the family room.

Alex grabs at Terry's sleeve. 'Is that an older man?' she asks quickly. 'Thick eyebrows . . . a moustache . . . ?'

'Yep,' says Terry. 'It is that doctor.'

'Dr Binding, I presume,' The Mouth's voice purrs from the speaker. '*The* Dr Barnabas Binding. We couldn't have a Grassybanks party without The Good Doctor Binding, now, could we? After all, it is him we have to thank for the unique design of the Chiller Beds. It is him we also have to thank for the swift disposal of the bodies who succumbed to the Chiller Beds! Hooray for Dr Binding, who did his research and found a scientific method for the eradication of the human detritus! Dr Binding, who designed the programme and brought Grassybanks the . . . *da da DAAA* . . . the Resomator. And here he is to demonstrate it.'

The camera, shining a light onto the doctor's face, moves swiftly backwards as if yanked on a thread and emerges to show a bunker-like room with no obvious windows. Now they can all see that the doctor is tied, hand and foot, lying in a container in the middle of the bunker, a coffin-shaped container that seems to be made from a thin, taut cloth. The transparent cloth is fitted to the inside of yet another larger metal barrel contraption, open at one end, the end the camera has just been pulled from.

'Now, who knows how a Resomator works?'

Clown-nurses jump up and down in front of The Mouth waving their gloved hands.

'No, no . . . you little eager beavers. I think we should ask The Good Doctor himself. Go ahead, Camera Two.'

Once again the camera in the bunker enters through the doorway at one end of the metal barrel and pushes up into the cloth container with the doctor's trapped body. Once again his face is full on screen.

'Can you hear me, Dr Binding?' The Mouth smiles.

The doctor is twisting his head to look down at the camera, mouth clenched shut.

'Speak to me, Doctor. It is your only option.'

'Daddy!' screams Stella again, and on screen Binding flinches.

'What do you want?' he manages to spit. 'You terrorists . . .'

'Ahh, there you are, Doctor. Now we have an audience for your work, which I know you will be very pleased about. According to your colleague, Professor Pansy – you remember, up in Manchester with the "P Formula"? Well, he assures us you have been longing to boast about this project, and now here is your chance. Tell us about the Resomator!'

'I will not engage with terrorists.' Binding furiously shakes his head and snot smacks the camera lens.

'Are you trying to play the hero, Doctor? Goodness . . . doesn't really suit a mass-murderer now, does it? A leetle beetle hypofuckingcritical. Anyway, it doesn't matter if you do or don't want to join in. We have a diagram.'

From behind the rubber-masked army, a clown pulls out a flip chart on a wheeled stand. There is a poster on it.

'The poster says "Resomator",' whispers Terry. '"Alkaline" . . . err . . . "hydrolysis" . . . "body liquefaction". What the fuck?'

'Bring the camera close, son,' says The Mouth, as if it has heard, and a clown tugs at Terry to move in to film the poster. 'That's right. Get a nice clean shot of the diagram. Now the family-room people can see it too. Look! You see where the doctor is? He is lying in a silk – how should we say? – "coffin", I guess. Yes, Doctor. You are lying right now in the Resomator in a silk coffin. Above you is a spray bar that will, when activated, combine the necessary levels of water and alkali. The whole thing will then be heated to a hundred and fifty degrees centigrade and you will become, in about three hours, a mere mess of liquid and soft calcium. Blackboard chalk, in fact. It is a wonderfully efficient method of disposal. And even more importantly, it is very green. No nasties into the environment. No smoke up chimneys . . . such a dead giveaway. Ah ha ha. I am a riot,' chortles The Mouth.

'The thing is, we don't think the diagram does the Resomator justice. As we have The Good Doctor all ready and waiting, what say we play our game?' The clowns spin in circles of feigned delight, but a couple are staggering, looking exhausted. There is a crack of lightning and then almost immediately thunder shakes the building. The lights and screen blink off and on again. One of the clowns faints. Really faints. A couple of the rubber-masked people break ranks and pull the clown away, into their midst.

'Yes,' says The Mouth, now sounding a little gravelly, a little tired. 'Let's play! Time is a tick-tick-ticking . . . You can answer "true" or you can answer "false". Only one is right. If you get the answer wrong, then we shall begin – now what do they call it here? – "processing" The Good Doctor. If you get it right, Dr Binding will not end up as chalk dust. It's that simple.' The Mouth grins. There is a tiny spot of lipstick on its brilliant-white incisor.

The three clowns push the wheelchairs closer and then, with a magician's flourish, one of them pulls out from under its over-sized nurse's bib what looks like a huge, ancient machine gun.

'Holy shit!' Terry spits, shocked, clapping a hand over his mouth. The camera wobbles.

'Stop this!' shouts Alex furiously, pulling off her stupid tinted specs and glaring around, scanning the room desperately, trying to source the person with the voice of The Mouth. *Where is the fucking Wizard of Oz, eh? Where are you, Helen?* Everything has changed now. With Dr Binding's appearance on screen it has become absolutely up-in-your-face obvious to every last person in the two rooms that this is not going to end well. And now guns?

The penny has dropped even for the denser of the trio in their wheelchairs. John Thorpe-Sinclair's face has drained of all colour and is almost translucent, his cheeks shuddering with tension. Stella's eyes are wide, glistening, her mascara smudged. Only

Henri Rennes hasn't yet seen the gun. He has just managed to yank one arm free and is bent over trying to pull his trousers from the glue and shouting something foul and French, spittle dashing like Braille across his shiny shoes. A clown prods him with the oversized semi-automatic and shakes a finger. *Oh, no no no, naughty Frenchie.*

Henri straightens slowly in the chair and sees the gun barrel pointed at his chest. His jaw drops and, apart from a short sharp fart, he becomes quiet and still.

'Come on! Question time for our celebrity welfare reform panel!' says The Mouth. 'Monsieur Rennes has now told us a great deal about Grassybanks. Let's hear it from the other horse's mouth, shall we? Thorpe-Sinclair, true or false? Is Grassybanks actually a front for government-sponsored euthanasia?'

'Wow,' whispers Terry. 'I have never seen anyone literally "quake" before.'

John Thorpe-Sinclair looks like he might vomit. Rennes can't keep his eyes off the gun; Thorpe-Sinclair can't bear to look at them. 'I don't know what . . .' he mumbles, his eyes flicking back and forth.

'A simple yes or no, sir. A man's life is at risk here. You know what euthanasia is. Killing off people deemed to be of no value. You know what the government is. You are part of it. You know what sponsorship is. You did the fun run for Children in Need last November. Now answer the fucking question. Are you and Grassybanks a front for state-sponsored euthanasia?'

'No!' Thorpe-Sinclair's voice is too fast and too high. 'I know nothing about this!'

'Ding, wrong answer! Poor old Dr Binding.'

A horrible klaxon noise goes off somewhere outside. 'That is a flood alarm,' Terry hisses to Alex. 'The river must be rising.' There is another peal of thunder and the rain *rat-tat-tats* at the windows, reminding everyone, as if they needed reminding, of the semi-automatic weapon being brandished by one smiling, red-nosed clown.

A sudden high-pitched whistling comes from the sound system. It isn't feedback.

'That noise is the noise of the Resomator,' shares The Mouth. 'The Resomator has now been activated! Water is being sucked into the pipes. Fun, fun, fun! Looks like we are going to be able to write on a blackboard with Dr Binding after all.'

Another whine adds to the whistling noise. 'Ahh . . . I believe that is the sound of the alkali flooding into the pipe to mix with the water. The Resomator is so efficient.'

A choking screech from Dr Binding.

'You better pull out of there, Camera Two,' says The Mouth. 'The alkali will sting like a bitch.'

The camera pulls back again and emerges in the bunker. The doctor's feet can be seen vainly kicking up and down on the silk coffin floor. A hand reaches in front of the camera and swings the metal tube door shut. It makes a terrible clanging sound, and the doctor's voice is silenced. On the screen now the Resomator hulks alone. It is beginning to shudder slightly.

The voice of The Mouth continues from the speakers. 'Stella Binding, dear lady and proud daughter of the poor doctor. You have the last word. True or false: Homeless Action!, the CDD, Chiller Beds, Resomators, disappearing human detritus? Is this all about state-sponsored euthanasia?'

Stella's eyes slide desperately from side to side. She wriggles and jiggles, trying to get unstuck. Her hair has come loose and hangs down, a thick blonde curl now also glued to the back of the chair. She sees Terry, sees the camera and has a flash of what it will mean if she, Minister for Health, admits to any of this. It may save her father, but she will be thrown to the dogs. She'll end up in . . . *my God* . . . in prison.

'I have no idea what you are talking about,' she spits. 'If you do this, then YOU are the murderers!'

'You would let your father be Resomated alive? Goodness. What a nasty child. Well, OK then.' The Mouth smiles. 'You said "false" and that was the . . . wrong answer!'

Now a deep glottal groaning sound mixes in with the whine and the whistle.

'And that is the Resomator doing what it does best. Cooking your old man to soft calcium.'

'You are insane!' screams Stella. 'You are sick! Murderers!'

Murderers! Stella's scream makes Alex wince. Her own eyes prickle with tears, not of fear, but of sadness. *This isn't the way . . . no, please . . . this will just get us all killed . . . they will hate us more. They will hate us forever.*

The screen flickers, goes blank, flickers again. Outside, the thunder booms, a mammoth boot slamming down on the earth, several miles away. The storm is moving off. The klaxon goes again. The wind howls.

And then, there is a small dark-haired woman in the room. She has appeared right next to Alex, in fact brushes past her, with a light pat on her arm. The woman is in a motorised wheelchair, unmasked. There are several Mouths on the screen, but there is only one Helen.

'You call us murderers,' she says, placing her wheelchair directly in front of the swooning Stella. She is still wearing a microphone clipped to the collar of her black jumper, and her words, although delivered quietly, can be heard everywhere. She moves closer to Stella, and now they are wheel-hub to wheel-hub, eye to eye.

'You call *us* murderers?' she repeats, and Stella sobs, cannot keep her gaze and drops her head as far as she can, given her hair is glued into the back of her chair. Helen raises her working arm slowly and points back up to the white screen.

The Wheels on the Bus

Chris is the first to hear the pounding, but he is loath to leave his vigil by the TV, and this tears at him deeply given that he can already smell the person on the other side of the door. He turns his head to the hallway, and his ears flare as he tries to source where Jenny is. Upstairs with strawberry yoghurt baby. The pounding comes again. A muffled yell and another waft of man at door. *Damn it!* thinks Chris. He has caught the scent of tobacco and dog, burnt buttered toast and leather. He turns on his stiff haunches, dashes to the front door and barks for Jenny.

'Jenny!! Get your arse down here and let in Mr Parnell!'

As soon as he sees her appear at the top of the stairs, he dashes back to the TV to check his beloved is still there. Thunder, like a bomb blast, rocks the house, and Chris whines and flinches as the lights flicker. There is crackling and static coming from the picture box but no picture. *Noooooo!* Has he lost her?

He is about to howl in distress when the sound and picture fizz on again, and he can hear Alex once more. Her voice is tempered, sounds calm, but Chris can hear the stress in her body, without having to be close enough to smell her.

He dashes back to the front door just as Jenny opens it, and Parnell, rain crackling off his umbrella, steps into the hallway.

His stench of dog and pipe-smoke, deep warm browns and clear blues, is immediately reassuring to Chris. He holds his snout gently over the sodden shoelaces, takes a long toke. Parnell's hand rubs Chris's ears.

'Hey there, boy? How are we doing?'

'Thanks for coming, Euan. Have you seen it?' Jenny's voice is high and anxious. 'It's insane, and Alex is bang in the middle of it.'

'Caught it on the website, and now it's on local TV. And been listening on the radio in the bus. It's on national RBR now and rolling news.' Parnell takes off his coat, apologising at the amount of water now pooling on the floor. 'Where's Mosh?'

'The river's flooded. All the emergency services have been called out.'

Chris can't stay politely still while they chat. He tries to herd them both into the living room. Gives up and zaps back to his seat in front of the TV. Barks sharply at them to be quiet.

Jenny and Parnell are behind him.

'I don't know what the hell to do. Chris is going nuts listening to Alex's voice on the TV, but I daren't turn it off.' Jenny is finding it hard not to be a teeny bit afraid of Chris. He is completely focused. Although sitting so still, he looks tense, poised, as if he might jump, snarl, whirl around at any second.

'I've been thinking, Jenny,' says Parnell, his voice low and urgent, 'when we did the tour I saw the place they had stocked the stuff for that godawful thing . . . what did they call it . . . the body liquefier?'

'The Resomator.'

'Yes. That. There was a separate entrance and access to Grassy-banks way around the back. Along the ridge.'

'What are you thinking?'

'I am thinking that it is all going to kick off in there, and some people – Alex, maybe some of Alex's friends – would appreciate a pickup.'

It takes a mere second for the penny to drop. 'You can't take the school bus into that place! What happens if you get arrested? What about the flooding?' Jenny feels hysteria rising.

'Storm's moving off . . . and the flooding is never as bad as they think. The water's already draining away. I don't reckon I'll have any trouble, and if I do I'll just say I got lost, is all . . . in the storm. They don't look like terrorists to me. They look exhausted and scared and . . . well, we can get at least six wheelchairs in the back of the bus at a push. I just think . . .' He trails off.

There is a short, breathy silence.

'I can't leave them there, Jenny. Did you know my wife was put on the list for Grassybanks when they diagnosed her MS? Just in case, they said.'

Chris senses Parnell's intention, the vibration of action and of 'collecting', 'hunting'. He comes to Parnell's feet, looks up at him, places a paw on his knee.

'We'll be very careful, won't we, boy,' says Parnell, resting a large hand on Chris's head. Chris gives an abrupt, encouraging bark.

Jenny sighs. 'That's decided, then,' she says, hefting Serena up to her shoulder. 'Drop me at the school, and I will open up the back classrooms and the first-aid room. They are going to need somewhere to hide out until the storm passes.'

In Which Mayor Pearson
Stands Tall

The sirens are faint but becoming louder, although it is hard to tell how far off, given the way the storm wind plucks the sounds of traffic and klaxon, shouts and thunder, and whirls them around and around.

'We ask for your patience.' Helen uses her stronger hand to manipulate the wheelchair's control and moves to the windows of the family room. 'We are going to ask everyone to come out and join us. But please, the police are coming. There is no need for hysterics. Our clown is weary and angry, and that makes it trigger-happy. Do you understand?'

The mayor pushes himself to the front of the sweating mass of people behind the glass. He seems a little taller, a little straighter. He holds up his arms and says something to the frightened people behind him. He nods at Helen.

'Thank you, Mayor Pearson,' says Helen. In Helen's voice Alex can hear the scissor of pain snipping at her muscles and watches Helen take a long drag on her oxygen. The clown, with the gun hanging at its side, opens the family-room doors, and the rubber-masked people move at last in formation, carefully, slowly, some limping, some wheeling, some clicking with canes and crutches. As the mayor leads his entourage, the guests and press out of the family room and into reception, they are each handed a rubber mask by a couple of clowns. Eventually everyone is clustered uneasily around Helen, Terry, Alex and the three dishevelled VIPs. Those not yet wearing masks hold them in sweating hands waiting to hear what comes next.

'We want to show you something,' says Helen. Her voice cracks, and her face contorts. A spasm. Just the one. She swallows. *Shit, she is brave*, thinks Alex. She is so fragile it would take just one of these big clumsy people to knock her down, kick the wheelchair over, break her in pieces, take control, but no one does. The onlookers are like pigeons watching a cat, eyes bright, ready to flap away on unoiled squeaky wings off to the rafters.

'OK, Boudicca.' The mayor, Bill Pearson, is pale but his hands, no longer clenched, are not shaking. 'You have already made your protest. You have frightened these—' he isn't sure what to call them, but gestures with his head to the three glued into their seats '—*people*. You have killed a man. Surely, enough now.'

'Yes, Mayor Pearson. We are so nearly there. Please understand, we will never have another opportunity like this. I hope we won't need it. I ask you to watch this one crucial last compilation of footage. All of you. I am asking for a final five minutes, in honour of the dead.'

'Don't you let her, Bill,' screams Stella. 'Don't you dare! Don't you bloody well dare! Not after what she did to my father.'

'What *you* did,' says Helen without rancour. 'We did not touch him.'

As if on cue, the double doors to the wards swing open and

two men, one wearing a Shandy Productions baseball cap, come in, panting, water dripping from their sodden trousers. Hanging between them, with an arm slung over each of their necks, is one Good Doctor Binding, gasping and shivering like a bream on a sandy bank. Apart from being soaking wet and obviously rather upset, he seems completely unharmed.

Robin, clutching the rubber mask he has been given, jolts. *They are the two technicians he had lost! What the hell . . . ?*

The man in the 'Shandy' hat discards Binding as if his touch burns him. His colleague, equally revolted, lets Binding slide to the floor.

'Daddy,' whimpers Stella. She wonders how much of the 'true or false' game he heard. She hopes not all. *Not all.*

'Shandy' man has dashed over to Helen and leans down to speak into her ear. His hand is ever so gentle on Helen's shoulder and before he stands, he kisses her on the cheek. She smiles, seems to find strength.

'OK. OK, calm down.' She turns to Alex and the others. 'The river is flooding,' she announces. 'A little water has already come into the basement. Help is on the way, but in the meantime we would ask all you nurses to return to your posts. Your patients will need you.'

Robin is dumbstruck.

'Sweet Mary, Mother of God, that's us,' says Nurse Ashley, raising her hand, as if she is in school.

'Yes, that's you, darling,' says Helen. 'Off you go, quickly. The flood defences here are good, but best to untie the people in Ward B, right? Try the fuck not to kill anyone else. EVER AGAIN.'

For the briefest moment the clowns and the rubber-faced

people move a step in around the nurses. They all make one gesture, fingers to eyes, fingers point forward. *WE see YOU.*

Robin actually squeaks, no longer able to make a coherent sentence, and continues to squawk in terror and relief as he and the other nurses dash away and down the corridor.

'Don't worry,' says Helen. 'Grassybanks has excellent flood defences.' She takes a deep, slow breath and pushes the pain back down. 'Please, Mayor Pearson,' she turns her chair to the mayor and his entourage, 'listen to your people.'

The Crow at the Crossroads

The old crow is warm and cosy, high up in her twiggy nest. She has one amber eye open wide, calmly watching the wild weather. The storm seems less irritated by the small creatures huddled up in the trees and the grasses, holed up under the earth and rolled up in the bushes. It stomps and pounds at the human things, their concrete and tar, their glass and their brick. Water pours onto the hot earth, but the earthworms rise and don't drown. Frogs gloat. Fish watch happily from the dark of the river basin as their kingdoms widen exponentially.

A drainage culvert by the river cracks open and more water gushes, dark and frothy, into the road. The storm seems to pause to contemplate what to batter next. Perhaps it is beginning to flag . . . but the wind winds up again and the crow's branch dips, as far below a large grey bus drives slowly along the watery track towards a crossroads. One road goes left to the front of the Grassybanks building where the field meets the river. Several other vehicles are sloshing to a standstill with water now over their axles. Men wearing bright reflective jackets are emerging from the trucks and cars, shouting and signalling to each other.

The other road swings right in a wide arc, away from the river and the car park, and wends up a slight ridge circling around to the back of Grassybanks.

The grey bus takes this right road, passing almost directly underneath the crow's nest. The crow can hear the *eeek-frum, eeek-frum* of the windscreen wipers squelching across the windscreen. The bus slides backwards, leaving a deep imprint in the grass to the side of the road as it slips on the bank, then gains traction again. Mud splatters softly, and gears are crunched within. And then the bus is over the ridge and disappearing behind the wide bank.

The crow closes her eye.

Chris, however, has both his open. He sits, sore rump perched on the front seat of the bus, his eyes fixed on the figure of Mr Parnell, who parks the bus and tells Chris to 'stay', before cautiously sliding his way down the sodden grass ridge towards the back entrance of Grassybanks.

The windscreen is fogging up with each hot doggy breath, and there is condensation on Chris's whiskers and droplets forming on the long hair in his pricked ears, but he remains stock still, absolutely focused. Parnell has made the bottom of the grassy knoll, and in several long strides through ankle-deep water he arrives at the back garage entrance, the very one he and Chris had stumbled upon previously. There are no piled-up barrels for Chris to lose a ball under now, just the rain, grass, the tar and a garage entrance, shut.

Parnell kicks at the slats on the garage door and feels for a handle, finding one near the ground just above pooling rainwater. He leans down, heaves and gives a loud yelp, clutching at his back.

Chris, shocked into action by the sound, twists clumsily around on the seat. His body is still aching and stiff from the dog attack, but he is getting impatient. His whole purpose is finding Alex, and he can sense that she is near. It isn't a smell yet and he can't hear her voice, but there is that vibration they have together. His whiskers quiver. Yes, Alex is definitely ahead. He can't wait any longer. He sticks his head and chest out of the open door on the driver's side of the bus, and his eyes narrow against the prickling rain. *Alexalexalex? Where? What direction?* And now his trembling, flared nostrils get a tiny hit. Fried onions, mushroomy underarms and mouldy trousers. Even in the homeo-pathic quantities of stench atoms to clean air, Chris's marvellous nose can capture the smell of . . . Terry! And yes! Terry will know where Alex is!

A few feet away, Parnell reaches down again, one hand on his creaking knee, and pulls again at the heavy door. This time it shifts upwards a few inches and water pours from inside in a gush, and then a lessening stream, and then a trickle. Parnell puts a hand on his lower back and leans again to the handle. Jerks harder. It comes up with a groan but just another few inches before sticking. Parnell yanks a couple more times but to no avail and begins to straighten up, shaking his head to clear the rain that is dribbling from his grizzled eyebrows.

A dark furry shape dives past him, under the gap of the door and into the darkness beyond.

'Chris! Come back, you daft bugger!' yells Parnell, shocked, but the dog has disappeared. 'Ah shit!' Parnell stands for a moment listening to the sound of barking echoing from inside the building, becoming fainter as Chris moves further away. *Well, I guess he'll fetch 'em quicker than me, all right*, he thinks and turns with renewed purpose back to the bus. He will need the jack to crank open the garage door. *No turning back now, old man.*

Behind the Masks

The storm clouds have blotted out the sun, and so Alex doesn't see the rubber-masked figure step forward at first. Terry does, and swings the camera.

'Alex, turn around,' he says, and Alex does. Some of the performers are unmasking. It is disconcerting in the extreme to see the rubber masks being pulled off people's heads. That soft, empty rubber mask of the girl pulled away to reveal many faces that Alex recognises from the LDA and many more she doesn't. Mayor Pearson is looking unsure, still protective of the little crowd of anxious people at his side.

'Oh, come on! Where is your sense of humour?' Helen whirls her chair in a tight circle and points at the miserable VIPs stuck in theirs. 'Think what we *could* have done! Maimed you, for instance. We considered it, darlings. Thought about gifting you a physical disability: a blinding, say, or an amputation or two, a quick lobotomy? But you all have so much bloody money and access to private healthcare – it probably wouldn't change a thing. It might happen to you anyway, life's odd like that. An accident, a genetic fuck-up, old age. One moment you are human, the next you are detritus. It isn't the physical, the mental malfunction in the end. It is unnecessary cruelty, shown and shown again. Surely that, after a time, becomes evil?'

The unmasking performers and some of the clowns gather and kneel, crouch or stand in front of Mayor Pearson and his entourage. There is a strange calm now, an expectation in the collected faces. Helen twirls again but when she speaks her voice is hoarse.

'So instead we thought we would show you what it feels like to be the butt of a joke. To be treated like a joke. To be stuck, afraid, always bloody afraid and to have your life in the hands of a bunch of clowns. You've gotta laugh, right?'

The performers raise and lower their hands but none are laughing.

'Here you go, Mayor . . . perhaps you can all laugh at this?'

Two people now, one taller, one shorter, stand, having pulled off masks to reveal a child of about seven and a stick-thin Asian woman. It is the kid who says to the mayor, 'My dad worked really hard, but he had a heart attack and then they told him he had to find work even though he was all panting an' he was breaving like a dragon breaves and . . . and couldn't really walk far, and then he fell down and he died, and my mum . . . she is always crying . . .' He tugs at his mother's hand and she curves her lips at him, but it isn't really a smile.

'Someone told us about Boudicca,' says his mother. 'They help us now. We join with them. We are Boudicca.' Alex recognises the woman now. She occasionally works behind the bar at the Ladies' Defective Agency. Alex scans, sees more, recognises more.

One by one the figures in the masks walk forward, removing their masks and relinquishing their stories. There is Mrs Honey talking about Joanna, and now Dawn wheels herself forward and shows her scars.

A woman pipes up, 'My cousin Leo was a meth addict. He had lost touch with everyone but me. He disappeared three weeks ago after being picked up by a group called Homeless Action! Later they said he had died of "natural causes" during the treatment.'

Another. 'Colin had uncontrollable epilepsy, but they told him he was fit for work. They laughed when they said that, "fit for work". They thought it was funny. He was a really sweet kid, but the stress was too much, and he had a massive seizure and died.'

More voices, more faces emerging from the masks. People clustering around the mayor.

'I am Boudicca! My husband killed himself when his appeal was rejected. He had severe depression, but they wouldn't listen.'

'We had faeces thrown at us because we took our wheelchairs to a cinema and blocked the aisle by mistake.'

'My mum has Alzheimer's. Her care assistant punched her in the face because she wet herself. We are Boudicca!'

The mayor is trying to listen, but what with so many people eagerly and angrily explaining why they had joined Boudicca, and the stories being so tragic and terrible and frightening and ridiculous, he cannot help recoiling, taking a couple of steps backwards.

Behind him, on the white screen, appear even more faces, each person in a little box, talking about themselves or someone they love, had loved, had respected, had cared for, being discarded or stomped on by the city. There are so many voices. One talks over another and another and another until, with the people gathered around the mayor and the faces on the screen, a hundred people and more are all talking at once, and the voices become a roaring thunderous sea of noise that drowns out the storm outside.

The lights die and so too, the noise. Now all is quiet, and in the sudden lull come just three countdown blips and then the screen lights up again. Now there is one small clear voice and one pale face on the large screen next to the plaque. A young woman with wide brown eyes, porcelain skin and long, dark brown hair. A young woman wearing a sky-blue cardigan and jeans. A young woman in a wheelchair. She is filming herself, and in the background there is a messy bedroom, clothes scattered on the bed and a large soft toy badger. On the wall a poster of the periodic table next to a female pop star in a ruby bikini.

'Hi Mum . . .' Her voice trembles. She starts again. 'Mum and Dad.' Stronger now. 'I know how much you love me. I love you so much too.' She pauses. Steadies herself. Her eyes glitter, but she won't cry. 'I know that you said we could get through this, but we all know that my condition is going to get worse. I am getting tired of the names, of having my chair kicked, of being spat at. I am not like you, Mum. I can't always find the funny side. I don't think I can be strong like that. The disabled loo wasn't working again today and Mrs Cleaver told me to use the girls' loo but I had to crawl and . . . and . . . and . . . a girl called me a mutant. We . . . people like me . . . like you and me, Mum, I don't want to grow up with this . . . I am so sorry, I know how badly this is going to make you feel, but I think it is the only way for all of us. They won't let you and Dad stay home and look after me when things get worse. I will have to go to some place, some centre and, I tell you, I *know* what they do

there! I wish you and Dad would believe me. If I have to be . . .
eradicated . . . I would rather do it myself.'

Now her tears fall, making dark blue patches on her pretty
cardigan. 'I love you so much. Please don't hate me. Please understand. If I do this . . . maybe people will listen . . . I dunno . . .
maybe this will help.'

The girl reaches up to the camera and the screen goes dead.

Laura Shandy . . . of course. Alex remembers now. The young
woman who had killed herself three years ago. Alex doesn't need
to be able to see clearly to realise that the young woman's face
is everywhere. The rubber masks worn by the Boudicca Army
are terrible empty-eyed replicas of her luminous loveliness.

'Her name was Laura,' says Helen. And then Alex sees it at
last. The resemblance. The man behind Helen, wearing a baseball
cap with 'Shandy Productions' on it, takes it off, leans down and
kisses his wife on the cheek.

Helen smiles at him, continues. 'She was my daughter. Nicholas, my husband, nicknamed her Boudicca because she was so
vibrant and beautiful and went everywhere in a carriage. She was
a straight-A student and really funny and friendly. I'm not just
saying that because she was my daughter. Ask anyone.' Helen
stops speaking for a moment, her breath is ragged. She raises her
head and looks directly at the three sat in the gluey wheelchairs.
'Laura – "Boudi" – rolled herself off the top of the central car
park in town. Three storeys. When we got to the hospital, they
told us she hadn't been killed instantly. Apparently, she took a
good hour to bleed out. No one was interested in finding out
how we could have stopped her. No one anywhere seemed to
care. In fact, one of the doctors turned to me and said I of all
people should know that she had done herself a favour. The

doctor said to us that it might be better for everyone this way. Later, someone graffitied "Test Your Wheelchair Here" at the top of the car park with an arrow pointing over the edge. We checked. It's still there and someone has freshened the paint. You got to laugh, right?'

The siren noise is outside now, and there is faint shouting, but inside no one says a word. Everyone is looking at Helen, and Helen in her wheelchair looks at the silent clowns, at Alex and at the others. Her face is twisted and her hands are spasming. She shrugs, unable to say another word.

Alex doesn't think there is anything more to be said, anyway. *It's time we end this and get the fuck out of here, before it's too late*, she thinks – but something inside her has opened to the possibility that it is already too late. She is so glad Chris is safe, is far away from all this. She hopes he is chewing something tasty. She wishes she could bury her face in his earth-and-honey-smelling coat, and she wishes . . . she wishes . . . what does she wish for?

Compassion? Revenge? *To just be left the hell alone . . . maybe . . . yeah, that would be nice.* Just thinking about Chris seems to cause her an audio hallucination. She imagines she can hear Chris barking, his low woof followed by two high yips. Impossible, surely. But Terry has also paused and now pulls off his head-phones, head cocked, ears pricked. Alex watches him, listens. The rain clatters, and the wind booms but there again . . . a woof and two yips. Alex is very alert now, her whole body an auditory receiver. Chris? It can't be!

Mayor Pearson hasn't heard the dog. He steps forward. His eyes are red-rimmed, as if bleeding. As Terry films him, the mayor takes the rubber mask that one of the clowns has given him and stares at the empty eye sockets. He shakes his head and then turns to Helen. 'I had no idea,' he says, 'but that is no excuse. I am culpable for letting this disgusting practice continue in our city. These . . . Nazis, here—' he gestures with his large hands at Binding, still kneeling on the floor, and at Thorpe-Sinclair, Rennes and Binding in their sticky traps '—must be condemned, but I too . . . I mean . . . this is inconceivable. How did I not know about this? I should be stripped of my office.' He sighs loudly and rakes fingers through his thinning hair. 'Boudicca, all of you . . . I am, on behalf of the people of Cambright, of England, truly sorry.'

Alex is moving slowly sideways, arcing around the mayor and edging backwards, instinctively drawn towards the back-corridor exit and Chris's 'Woof! Yip, yip!' A couple of the clowns catch the sound of barking too. They glance over shoulders, eyes flicker. They look battered now, these clowns, paint curdled on their faces, wigs limp, faint scowls showing through the huge red smiles. Alex recognises one.

'I think it's Chris, my dog,' she hisses to Jules. 'He must have run off to find me. I think . . .' She shrugs, feeling stupid and saying it anyway, 'I think he must have got in through the back. Maybe we should think about an exit strategy too?'

Jules stares at Alex impassively. Then she gives her head a little shake, as if waking up, blinks at Alex and nods. 'Your lovely dog, eh? OK, why not. I've heard stranger things. And,' she whispers, glancing behind her, 'you are right. It's time some of us got out anyway. Some of this lot are fragile. They don't all need to be here when the police arrive. You lead the way out, and I'll get them organised.' She hisses to one of the protesters, and he leans in to her painted face to listen to her instructions as Alex signals Terry and takes another step towards the sound of her dog's excited barking.

Andre Is Unleashed

Hobgoblin has stopped snoring and is standing alert, sniffing the air. From somewhere in the building comes the sound of another dog, barking its head off. Hobgoblin growls and Andre watches him, trying not to breathe too loudly. There is a loud clang at the far end of the kennels, footsteps and Hobgoblin barks, but joyfully, his stump of a tail flexing in a semblance of a wag.

'Hey there, Hobby . . .' A man with a spider's web tattoo on his long ugly maw is unlocking the cage front.

'Ronnie!' squeaks Andre, for it is indeed Ronnie, Hobgoblin's trainer. 'Help me! Get me out of here!'

Ronnie's face is a picture. He has come through the thunder and rain to check on Hobgoblin, worried about the possible flooding down the road. He realises there is something bad happening here but is finding it very hard to follow Andre's furious spluttering and is still unsure as to why his boss has lost his trousers. It becomes even more confusing to Ronnie when he opens up the store cupboard to get Andre a clean boiler suit and finds the Grassybanks manager, Mr Skinner, and two semi-conscious, fully armed H5 security men propped up against the far wall.

The Good Doctor
Saves the Day

Meanwhile, on the shining tiled floor upstairs, Dr Binding is crawling forward, keeping low. He is in his vest, pants and socks and soaked from the floodwater in the basement and his own once hot, now chilly, piss; he is humiliated and boiling with a kind of rage that makes him itch all over.

He is, in fact, unharmed. They never actually turned the Resomator on. At the time, he had thought they were really going to go through with it, though. All he could hear was the fake noise of pipes, the cacophony of screams and yells through the camera, and then the terrible silence, when the door at his feet slammed shut and he had thought . . . oh yes . . . that his goddamn goose was being calcified.

In those minutes in the dark and the clanging silence, he had thought about Stella and Gloria, about his practice, his love of medicine, his wish for his work to be celebrated. He had never thought of dying before, but now he realised he desperately didn't want to be rendered into chalk dust. He surprised himself by calling for his old mum. He had screwed up his eyes and waited for the terrible sensation of being cooked alive . . . part of his scientist's brain asking . . . *Hmmm, what will this feel like?* . . . and then, with a fizzing bang, the light had come shining in on his face again, and he had been yanked from the tube, emerging feet first, like a baby in breech from a womb. And like a birth, there had been water. Lots of water, but the people handling him had not been kindly doulas, calming and gentle. His midwives hadn't been speaking at all, just grunting. They handled him as if he were a sack of grain. A sack of shit.

And now there are clowns with guns, and other lunatics in rubber face masks, and no one seems to care a jot about what he has just been through. In fact – and here The Good Doctor feels that ice-cold fury squeeze at his lungs – someone has just intoned that he and his daughter were 'Nazis'!

Nazis! How dare they! How fucking dare they? Dr Binding is more hurt by this than by anything that has previously occurred. Every decision he has ever made has been in the interest of his patients. When they suffered, he could offer comfort. My God, surely if a loved one was on life support and in agony, who would want to prolong the pain? It had been that way with his end-stage alcoholics, his addicts, his no-hopers. He had given them comfort. An easeful exit from an unkind world that could not support them. How could anyone say anything else but that he was a good man and a damn good doctor? No, this was insane. *Where are the police?*

And what have they done to Stella? His darling girl looks terrified, and she seems unable to get out of her seat. But wait . . . *a wheelchair? They have glued her into a wheelchair? The god-damn thugs!* He almost calls out to Stella to say, as he always used to when she was little, 'Daddy's coming!' but he doesn't want to draw attention to himself. He has his eyes on the clown to his left, the one with the gun hanging from its arm. He slithers forward.

When the crippled girl had come on the white screen, he had used the distraction to slide closer to the gun-toting clown. And now, when almost everyone has their eyes on that wet arse of a mayor, his final assault is underway. He is almost directly underneath the clown holding his daughter hostage in that wheelchair. Looking up, he can see the white paint streaking into the red paint of the clown's mouth as it weeps. *Pathetic.*

It is only Helen who notices that Dr Binding is no longer where her husband had discarded him, but the pain in her bones is winning. She sees him crawling across the floor with his stained white pants and his muscular hairy calves as if from a great distance. She wants to warn the others but her chest muscles have gone into a spasm, knocking the breath from her. *Look out!* she is trying to say. *Jules!* But there is no air in her lungs any more.

It is Terry with his heavy HD camera on his shoulder who glances down and twists the camera just as The Good Doctor Binding pushes himself to his knees, reaches up and grabs the gun from the weeping clown.

And now they all see. And some jump forward and some jump back, but it is too late. The clown topples backwards, pushed in the chest, landing hard on its arse with a *whooomph*, but this time there is no laughter because he has fallen without his gun. The Good Doctor Binding has the clown's gun now. The Good Doctor Binding is King of the Hill, armed and ready.

'Put down your weapon!' His voice sounds funny to himself. Too high and warbling, like an old man.

Surprised by its lightness, Dr Binding swings the gun but points it not at Helen, with her crumbling bones. That would just be doing her a favour. No. He is in control now. He is going to . . .

'Doctor, no! You don't understand!' Another clown has run up and put themselves between the doctor and the rest of the crowd. The clown stands too close, blocking the doctor's view, its ridiculous red nose and its stupid wig completely infuriating.

'Put your fucking hands up!' the doctor screams.

But the clown does not.

'Don't shoot! Put your weapons down!

And that is the H5 police. *At last! At last, the police!* They are finally inside, although they seem to be confused, uncoordinated as if a little drunk. A short, nasty-looking, fair-haired man, stinking of dog shit and sporting a boiler suit, is pushing the security men roughly forward, and people are yelling and shouting and the doctor is still screaming at the clown. 'Get your goddamn hands up or I will shoot! I will shoot!'

And Helen finds her voice, and together with her husband and a couple of others they cry out frantically, 'She can't, Doctor! She has no arms! Jules! Jules!'

And yes, it is Jules, and of course she can't raise her hands, but the doctor couldn't know this and, enraged, his shaking finger hits the trigger. Shiny gold flakes shoot out across the reception in a twinkling spray that coats Jules, Alex, Helen and John Thorpe-Sinclair, Stella Binding and Henri Rennes. The gun is a glitter machine.

Only the H5 security men don't know this. And the H5 security men have real guns clutched in their clammy hands. In that same split second, half blinded by glitter, deafened by screaming and confused by Andre's shouts of 'Kill the fuckers!', the H5 security men panic and let rip.

24-HOUR BREAKING NEWS
RBR NEWS
Freak storm causes massive damage in Eastern Southern region

Gusts of over 100 mph were recorded as Met Office 'red warnings' are issued. Sixteen severe flood warnings remain in place.

Power and transport networks have been badly hit in what has been called an 'almost unparalleled natural crisis'.

The storm has left thousands of households without power, trees have been brought down, and there has been flooding and structural damage.

More than a thousand 999 calls were made to the police and fire services over a 24-hour period – a 'significantly' higher number than normal.

Residents in many parts of the UK have been warned not to go out.

In an unrelated incident three people are feared dead and several more have been injured in a shooting incident at the Grassybanks Residential Home in Cambright. Rescue services were called to the scene when the opening ceremony of a new ward was allegedly hijacked by protesters during the storm. Due to flooding, Grassybanks has been evacuated and police are currently investigating.

THE TONIGHT SHOW:
TV TWENTY-TWENTY

It has been confirmed that internationally renowned voice coach Helen Shandy, her husband Nicholas Shandy and her colleague Julia 'Jules' Kirkpatrick have died from gunshot wounds following an H5 security intervention into an alleged hostage situation at the Grassybanks Residential Home in Cambright earlier today.

Two government ministers, John Thorpe-Sinclair and Stella Binding, plus several other onlookers, were treated for minor injuries at the scene and later released.

Helen Shandy was the mother of Laura Shandy, a young disabled student who killed herself three years ago. Shandy founded the activist disability rights movement, Boudicca, in honour of her daughter.

RBR WORLD NEWS ROUND-UP
with Hugh Jericho

Last week's film footage of the protest that turned into a tragedy at Grassybanks Residential Home has gone viral, eliciting a massive national and international response both for and against the activist group Boudicca. Over 70 charities in the UK have demanded an investigation into the accusations of state-sponsored euthanasia and the use of the so-called 'Chiller Beds'.

The two H5 security men involved in the shootings have

been suspended from duty, pending further investigation into charges of disproportionate aggression.

The authorities are still trying to track down several Boudicca supporters and a local news team who may have been present at the event, and they would like any information on possible sightings of a large vehicle, possibly a grey van or bus, that was seen in the area at the time of the incident.

THE STATE OF PLAY INTERNATIONAL

In a response to the allegations of state-sponsored euthanasia put forward by the welfare reform protest group Boudicca, Lord Justice Gallagher has been appointed to head an inquiry into the Grassybanks Residential Home.

The inquiry has been widened to include several other similarly co-funded residential homes and hospitals across the country, including St Mark's in Manchester.

SHOCK BOUDICCA ACQUITTAL

The Boudicca hearing was brought to a close today after Judge Margaret Gee ruled that there was no case for imprisonment. Judge Gee stated: 'The Grassybanks opening ceremony had included the performance and film screening in its pre-approved schedule, and there had been no intent to cause bodily harm, merely to entertain.' The judge therefore had no choice but to acquit the performers of all charges.

As to the allegations of torture and restraint brought by Thorpe-Sinclair, Dyer, Rennes and Binding, Judge Gee concluded: 'There was insufficient evidence and reason to pursue Boudicca, and the performers were not to be made scapegoats, given the subsequent exposure of the horrific practices perpetrated by the staff and management at Grassybanks.'

The Judge went on to thank Mayor Bill Pearson for his invaluable input and support during this time.

In Memoriam: Helen and Nicholas Shandy. Family, friends and colleagues are invited to attend a memorial service at St Dunstan's Chapel, Cambright. No flowers, please. All donations to the Kitty Fox Foundation. No press allowed.

TRANSCRIPTION: RBR RADIO 4 TODAY IN PARLIAMENT

John Thorpe-Sinclair, the Minister for Work and Pensions, received a standing ovation in Parliament today as he returned to the front benches one month on from the Grassybanks protest incident. He thanked his colleagues for their support, saying that although being at the front line of the welfare crisis had made him a target for terrorists and bullies, he remained resolute in his stance on benefit reform.

THORPE-SINCLAIR: 'Our reforms are making sense. The results of our actions speak for themselves.'

Thorpe-Sinclair revealed, in a direct response to the Grassybanks incident, plans for an immediate co-ordinated review into benefit fraud. Measures to be implemented will include enforced access to homes and bank accounts of any person claiming Incapable Benefit. Officials will from today be given the right to enter homes without warning, to interview the claimants and seize bank accounts in order to confirm that the person in receipt of the benefit is not cheating the system.

THORPE-SINCLAIR: 'If some of these so-called "disabled" people are able to protest, as seen recently at Grassybanks, they are clearly well enough to work. We can no longer idly stand aside while the hardworking British taxpayer is being cheated. If people are truly sick or crippled and in need of our assistance, the government will not let them down. In fact, this new initiative will protect the truly needy among us by exposing the fraudsters and bringing them to justice.'

Thorpe-Sinclair has been accused of vengeful and ruthless tactics by the Shadow Home Secretary, Eve Barrellman, following these new welfare reform initiatives.

5,000 Miles as the Crow Flies

In Mozambique, in the heart of the raucous city of Maputo, sunlight pings off the pane of window glass as it is carefully carried across the newly painted office building by two workmen. The light briefly blinds Alex. Blinking, she looks away to allow her retinas to recover. White dots shimmy and skate away and she has a momentary flashback to the pandemonium of eighteen months previously.

Grassybanks . . . she shivers in spite of the tropical heat. Alex had been chivvying the evacuees along the corridor with one arm and hugging a soggy, deliriously happy Chris with the other when the shots had rung out and the screaming back in reception had begun. Everyone still in the corridor froze, Chris flattening himself down to the floor, tail tucked under his belly. And like that, the combat training Alex had received when embedded with the troops all those years ago had switched on.

'Go, go, go!' she had screamed at the last few terrified Boudicca witnesses, pushing them forward towards the exit and the waiting bus.

'What the hell was that?' Mr Parnell was shouting from the garage door.

'Get out of here!' Alex had screamed again, waving at him. 'Something's gone wrong. Get this lot out and take Chris!'

Bending low, she had taken Chris's snout and kissed it hard three times, looked him in those golden eyes and ordered him to go with Parnell. He had hesitated a mere second, then whirled and sped back out of the building.

Leaving Parnell hoisting the last wheelchair up into the bus, Alex had turned round and quickly felt her way back down the corridor towards the high-pitched sounds of panic in the main reception. Terry was still in there, filming, and she must join him. She was the reporter, after all. She had gone back into the fray, back into the noise, the harsh lights, back to where the blood was pooling on the antiseptic, white-tiled floor, and she had done her job.

Later, there had been the Boudicca hearings, the shock acquittal and the opening of the Gallagher Inquiry, all of which Alex remembered only vaguely, even though she had been allowed to remain as the leading local journalist. Gerald had offered her a full-time position at the paper, a good salary. Instead, she had consulted, in her own way, with Chris and Chris's vet and, after those heartbreaking funerals of Helen, Nicholas and Jules, she had gone to see Kitty Fox.

'This,' she had said, and handed Kitty a project file she had put together, marked 'Kitty Fox Foundation: Sub-Saharan African Outreach Programme'. 'You need to let me do this for you.'

And now . . . Alex stretches, feeling the sunburnt skin on her shoulders prickle a little under her blouse, then reaches down to feel Chris's cool wet nose nuzzling her palm. Nearly eighteen months and three sub-Saharan countries on, and Alex is almost herself again. Here, in the fearsome African heat, she is overseeing the setting-up of the third 'Women United' project; each project funded by the Kitty Fox Foundation and a mishmash of other charities to bring together local disabled people's organisations and provide advice on microfinance, basic human rights and sexual health. She, as the silent partner, has already earned Kitty Fox two UNESCO awards for humanitarian entrepreneurship.

Chris has taken to Africa with aplomb. It is more dangerous for dogs, of course – poisonous bugs, ticks, snakes, rabies, and more to watch out for – but his joy is in the layer upon layer of wonderful stenches that coat every moment of his day. There is such space. The mammoth sky canoodles luxuriously with endless sweet red earth, chock-full of curious, exciting new pongs. He gets more time off work now too, free just to run and run around gardens, especially here. The city is often too dangerous for him to guide Alex, traffic is crazy, pavements are haphazard and people don't know about assistance dogs, only guard dogs and farm dogs, pet dogs and feral ones. They are frightened by dogs, even ones as handsome and charming as Chris, so often Chris gets to stay on the beautiful chilli farm where Alex is renting a little cottage. He has been friended by the farm dogs, Pavlov and Eusebio, who are teaching him to guard chickens.

Alex's strong hand ruffles his ears and he gives a contented groan before dipping down to scratch a flea bite. He is always itchy here. Alex's phone beeps and she glances at it then grins, pulling out her magnifying glasses to look at the photo that has appeared on the screen. An adorable toddler sits, eyes wide, huge smile, in front of a cake with 'Happy Birthday Serena!' written in green icing on the top. Mosh, Jenny and the Parnells beam in the background.

'*Bom-dia*, Alex!' calls a young woman from the doorway,

expertly swinging her unresponsive legs forward between two red wooden crutches. Alex pockets her phone and steps forward to greet Hyancinta, the local solicitor. It's time to get to work.

WONDERWEB
The Free Encyclopaedia: Conclusion of the Gallagher Inquiry into the Grassybanks Residential Home

The Gallagher Inquiry sat for a total of 31 days and published a final report that outlined general recommendations on residential-care practice. This became known as the Gallagher Report.

Lord Justice Gallagher concluded that there was no evidence of systemic abuse at Grassybanks Residential Home and that the so-called 'Chiller Beds' designed by Dr Binding were 'practical and highly effective palliative care apparatus'. General care of patients was deemed satisfactory, and the Resomator would soon be in common usage in the USA and several countries across Europe, and therefore not something to be feared or prohibited.

See: Dr Barnabas Binding
Resomator
Chiller Beds
Euthanasia
Palliative Care

The National Deaf and Disabled Unity Movement claimed the Gallagher Report was a whitewash and called for direct action. Over 50,000 people gathered to protest the report outside the Houses of Parliament. The police used water cannons to disperse the crowds. One person was fatally injured, and over 200 other protesters suffered a range of injuries, some severe, including irreversible eye and ear trauma and broken bones.

See: National Deaf and Disabled Unity Movement
Houses of Parliament
Water Cannon

An independent panel was set up to investigate further allegations against Doctors Binding and Pansy but was declared invalid when several documents were discovered to have gone missing from the original file.

THE GRAPH BUSINESS REVIEW
End of recession

According to a new report from the National Institute of Economic and Social Research (NIESR), Britain's growth will exceed its 2008 high in the coming months.

Tamil Doors, director of NIESR, said: 'The end of the Great Recession is an important moment. The British economy is very close to exceeding forecast expectations.'

Mr Doors also expressed gratitude to the government. 'We would suggest that benefit cuts are pushing more people into self-employment and helping to create a new generation of entrepreneurs.'

The Bank of England said the trend was partly down to government welfare reforms, such as the benefit caps, pushing people back into work. John Thorpe-Sinclair, the Minister for Work and Pensions, told *The Graph*: 'Every one of our welfare reforms has been about getting Britain working, so it's encouraging to see the Bank of England explicitly linking our reforms with the strength of the UK labour market.'

The prime minister agreed that although mistakes had been made in the past, it was time to look forward and think positively. 'You cannot make an omelette without cracking a few eggs,' he declared.

THE SUNDAY MAGAZINE FEATURE
They call me Dr Death: Britain's top columnist Roman Telling meets Dr Barnabas Binding and, in a candid interview, discusses the notorious 'Chiller Beds' and the doctor's design for 'a better way to die'

I am meeting with Dr Barnabas Binding at a small café on the corner of his street. He is running late, and so I am already perched nervously inside the café when he arrives, accompanied by his companion, a good-looking, dark-haired young woman he introduces as Gina.

'This is my favourite café,' the doctor tells me. 'When I got the wheelchair they raised money for the outside ramp saying I had probably paid for it with espressos by now.' He has agreed to the interview on one condition; that he gets to put across his side of the story about those infamous Chiller Beds.

Binding is greeted warmly by the café owner and takes

time to pass on his regards to the man's wife, before he settles himself opposite me and reaches across to shake my hand. He is wearing a pale blue shirt, open at the neck, and an elegant cravat in darker navy, and looks relaxed and tanned from a recent trip to Sardinia. He is in his indoor chair, he says, 'pushable', and more slender than his favourite motorised beast. 'Both my wheelchairs are prototypes designed by the Kitty Fox Foundation,' he adds, while Gina is up at the counter, 'which is indeed ironic given that it was a Kitty Fox wheelchair that my own daughter was held captive in during the Grassybanks incident last year.'

It was this same incident that outed the doctor as the brains behind the Chiller Bed concept and ended in the shooting of two women, Julia Kirkpatrick and the Boudicca founder, Helen Shandy, as well as Shandy's husband. Binding himself was hit in the spine by an H5 policeman's stray bullet.

'They weren't sure what to aim at,' muses the doctor. 'There was glitter everywhere. They just sprayed the room with bullets.' His face contorts at the memory. 'Bunch of idiots,' he adds.

We chit-chat until Gina returns with his coffee, which she places in front of him quietly and takes a seat, protectively close. He smiles at her and shakes his head. 'Gina worries too much.' He is not in any pain, he says. 'At least not currently.'

'The bullet got me in the lumbar region and left me a stage-three paraplegic.' He assures me without irony that it's been a very interesting experience. His patients are adjusting to it too.

I ask him how he had felt when he had been struck off by the Medical Council. The doctor is rightly affronted.

'You should have done your research, young man. I was reinstated. After the Gallagher Inquiry I was completely exonerated.' He smiles at me but his teeth are clenched. His eyes are hard to read, and he has downed his coffee. I suspect that if I am not careful, he will end the interview. Gina says nothing, but she is staring at me quite intently. Her eyes are dark brown, her hair immaculate, her stare openly hostile.

A little disconcerted, I apologise and try another tack. 'You say you feel misunderstood, yet, you were the man,' I venture, 'who designed Chiller Beds to despatch people with your very condition.'

The doctor leans forward, his face suffused with blood. I fear I may have seriously upset him now. Gina puts a soothing hand on his arm and pats, as if the doctor is a recalcitrant child.

'Not true at all.' The doctor's colour has not improved. 'Let's get this straight. I was commissioned to help find ways to assist those who were already in the process of dying. Initially the Chiller Beds were designed to ensure that my late-stage alcoholic patients, the ones who were already in kidney and liver failure and with no hope of successful transplant surgery, would be given a pain-free end. Chiller Beds were a mercy to many. They prevented weeks, possibly months, of terrible pain, of agony.'

I have to interject. 'But, to be cynical, they also prevented excess money being spent on the patients' care.'

The doctor blinks and sits back. Then he smiles. He seems easier with this truth. 'Yes. I admit that they saved money as well. I am proud of that fact. Look at the economy now . . . it is a vindication of our experiment.'

Gina points at his coffee cup, now empty, and he nods without taking his eyes from me. She gets up to buy another round, taking his wallet from the table. The doctor's gaze is intense, but he offers nothing. I feel compelled to fill the silence.

'You have stated on record that you were aware that the beds were being installed in several different institutions and were to be used to speed the deaths of people who were deemed unfit to live.'

'People in desperate situations . . . for them, those beds were . . . are a blessing.' The sun comes out at last and the café floods with light, giving the doctor's face an almost beatific quality. In that moment, stern and yet serene in the golden light, I can almost imagine him healing the sick with a single gesture. *(Interview continues on page three.)*

*

Advert: Bath Literary Festival. We are honoured to announce that the Minister for Health, Stella Binding, will be introducing and reading selections of poetry by her late husband, the renowned Gunter Gorski, from his newly edited anthology, *The Choking*, posthumous winner of the W. H. Auden award. To book places please ring the box office.

THE DAILY SPUN

The People Speak: Don Poppet on Tuesdays
Ram raids and reality checks for crip fraudsters!

The cheating scumbags who pocket the nation's wealth are in for a good old-fashioned shakedown! Our mate, John Thorpe-Sinclair, MP, has got it in for the phoney crips! From this week on, and at any time of day or night, government officials will be allowed to storm the homes and bank accounts of anyone claiming any type of 'crip' benefit and cheats will be immediately cut off. They could even get put in the slammer!

Eve Barrellman has said this will 'infringe on basic human rights', but we say what about the human rights of the majority of hard-working British people? These so-called 'crips' are extracting the urine, Ms Barrellman. They say they need extra care and more money to get through each day when, in fact, we know from previous investigations and revelations from this very paper that they lie around doing bugger all or head for the golf course or a swimming pool in Majorca.

At last we will uncover what really goes on behind the doors of these fraudsters! We the people salute you, John Thorpe-Sinclair.

The Dog's Epilogue

The darkness all around the veranda creaks and squeaks with living things. High above Chris's head, the security light is a disco of shiny, hard-shelled insects and soft furry moths, popping, tapping and whacking against the glass. Below him, the wood under his paws is leaking the heat it soaked up from the sun. He can smell the wood oil, sharp and fresh, a hissy wisp of glue. In the surrounding bush, night-scented flowers open maws to the moon and the dusty moths. Wild things abound and everything is moving, growing, sinking, shifting. *Alive, alive oh!* Something small and hungry skitters through the grass at the bottom of the steps, followed by something bigger and hungrier. Chris hears and smells all these things, but what he is meditating on is a whole other stink, the incredible, ever-changing stench of iron and salt, blood and ancient rock. The sea.

He is lying on his belly, his snout raised into the little breeze blowing in from the bay. Alex, cold beer in hand, sits beside him in a creaky canvas chair reeking of the lemon eucalyptus oil she uses to keep off the mosquitoes. She swigs and sighs happily, her hand dropping to ruffle Chris's ears.

The sun has disappeared into the sea, and from their hillside hut they gaze out on a star-studded night sky with shed snakeskin filaments of cloud passing in front of a rising moon. Soon, the night guard will light his fire in the driveway, and Alex and Chris will head inside to the cool of the bedroom and the thrumming fan, but not yet. Chris can smell tomorrow coming in the hot sea wind. He wishes he could tell Alex about it. It's going to be exciting.

Ah well, he thinks, sighing and settling his muzzle on her bare foot, *we'll find out together . . .*

Afterword

In November 2016, the United Nations published a report citing 'grave and systematic violations of the rights of disabled people in the UK'.

In addition to two reports produced by the Equality and Human Rights Commission (EHRC) for the UN's Committee on the Rights of Persons with Disabilities (CRPD) periodic review, the EHRC followed up in April 2017 with a report titled *Being Disabled in Britain: A Journey Less Equal*, in which it presented research showing how, in every sector, from education and employment to basic care, independent living and human rights, disabled people in Britain were being denied equality and parity.

In August 2017, the UN once again reiterated the findings of its report. Cuts to social services have 'totally neglected' the needs of disabled people and created a 'human catastrophe', the chairwoman of a UN human rights committee has said.

Theresia Degener, who leads the UN CRPD, accused British politicians of failing vulnerable members of society.

UK officials have also faced allegations of misrepresenting the impact of policies through unanswered questions, misused statistics and statements on policies and legislation.

As cited in the *Independent*, 24 August 2017, Ms Degener said evidence seen by the committee and a review it carried out last year made clear the impact of austerity policies on the disabled.

She said the controversial 'fit to work' tests were based on a correct assumption that disabled people could find employment. 'However, evidence before us now and in our inquiry procedure as published in our 2016 report reveals that social cut policies have led to a human catastrophe in your country, totally neglecting the vulnerable situation people with disabilities find themselves in.'

A Note on the Author

Dr Tanvir Bush is a novelist, film-maker and photographer. Born in London, she lived and worked in Lusaka, Zambia, setting up the Willie Mwale Film Foundation, working with minority communities and people affected by the HIV/AIDS pandemic. Her feature documentary *Choka! – Get Lost!* was nominated for the Pare Lorenz Award for social activism in film in 2001. She returned to the UK to study and write her first novel, *Witch Girl*, published by Modjaji Books, Cape Town in 2015. She is the designer and facilitator of the Corsham Creative Writing Laboratory initiative and an associate lecturer in creative writing at Bath Spa University. She is based in Wiltshire with her guide dog and research assistant, Grace.

To have your say and let Tanvir know what you thought of *Cull*, visit https://www.surveymonkey.com/r/2PRZP8S

Acknowledgements

I give heartfelt thanks to Irving, Joan and Suzie Shapiro, without whose incredible generosity, kindness and continuous support this novel would not have happened at all. The same goes to Ruth Hartley and John Corley for all their generous support and encouragement.

My thanks to my sister Rachma and her husband Steven for feeding me up, propping me up and cheering me onwards, and to lovely Jennie Brunton, my support and comma-checker. Also to Polly Loxton, for being, always, the port in the storm.

My thanks to Tim Middleton, who kept me on track and on course, and Maggie Gee, an outstanding mentor, supporter and friend.

To the Cleeve Book Club and all who took part in the Book Club Experiment – thank you so much!

Thanks to my agent Karolina, and to the wonderful team at Unbound, and to everyone, too many to mention here, who supported and encouraged me all the way down this long road.

And lastly, thanks forever to Grace, my furry muse and friend.

Unbound
Liberating ideas

Unbound is the world's first crowdfunding publisher, established in 2011.

We believe that wonderful things can happen when you clear a path for people who share a passion. That's why we've built a platform that brings together readers and authors to crowdfund books they believe in – and give fresh ideas that don't fit the traditional mould the chance they deserve.

This book is in your hands because readers made it possible. Everyone who pledged their support is listed below. Join them by visiting unbound.com and supporting a book today.

Rachma Abbott
Lyn Adams
Mary Allan
Mark Annand
Paul Ashley
Becky Atkins
David Baillie
Janine Barber
Julian & Debbie Barefoot
Miranda Barnes
JJ Bees

Sarah Bell
Sandra Benardout Bush
Lel Bevan
Agnes Bezzina
Linda Blair
Laura Bolton
Kyra Borre
Annie Bowen
Gordon Bowen
Tracy Brain
Danielle Brice

Sarah Brock
Lucinda Bromfield
Colin Brown
Shelagh Brownlow
Jack Brunton
Jennie Brunton
Kate Brunton Broughton
Emily Buchanan
Kate Bulpitt
Rachael Burgess
Andrew Burnett
Benjamin Bush
Tanvir Bush
Anthony Butcher
Cortina Butler
Elen Caldecott
Simone Chalkley
Matt Chandler
Amrita Chandra
Becky Chantry
Vete Chapman-Moyle
Cynthia Cobban
Susanna Coleman
Alison Collier
Anita Collins
Martha Constable
John Corley
Tamsen Courtenay
Katie Cowan
Heather Crawford
Hilary Curwen

Penny Dale
Susan Daniels
Paulo de Sousa
Jackie Deas
Jennifer Debley
Paul Dodgson
Jenny Doughty
Suzie Drake
Sarah Dugdale
Dave Eagle
Penney Ellis
Simone Elmes
Jenny Elvin
Bernardine Evaristo
Tiffany Fairey
Richard Ferguson
Kylie Fitzpatrick
Camila Fuentes Diaz
Lisa Gee
Maggie Gee
Emma Geen
Sarah Gent
Jennifer Georgeson
Emma Giffard
Anne Gill
Jemima Gladwell
Ewa Gorska
Catherine Gosby
Terra Grandmason
Rebecca Greer
Murwani Groot

Chloe Guest
Tessa Hadley
Mike Hakata
Cleo Hanaway-Oakley
Emma Harris
Adam Hart
Ruth Hartley
Maryanne Harvey
Tania Hershman
Alice Herve
Viki Hess
Paul Holbrook
Julie Holmes
Alison Horman
Diana Hulin
Julia Hyde
Sarah Ingleby
Hannah Isaacson
Julie Jackson
Barbara James
Kate James
John Jones
Mel Jones
Tum Kazunga
Phoebe Kemp
Richard Kerridge
Dan Kieran
Thalia Kirkman-Koumblis
Kayt Lackie
Serena Langley
Warren Lapworth

Alison Lee
Trisha Lee
Nigel Legg
Emily LeQuesne
Lesley Loach
Ben Long
Lindsay Loxton
Anna Lyaruu
David MacArthur
Russell Mackintosh
Helena MacLellan
Colleen MacMahon
Islay Mactaggart
Lynn Mccartan
Deb McCormick
John A C McGowan
Moy McGowan
Chris Meade
Alice Meadows
Bob and Sally Middleton
Tim Middleton
John Mitchinson
Carol Moles
Bill Moody
Richard Morris
Sue Mullett
Edwina Mullins
Lauren Mulville
Jayne Mungai
Keith Munyama
Carlo Navato

John New

Diana Newport-Peace

Hilary Nugara

Lindsey O'Sullivan

Kevin Offer

Colin Ogg

Sally Ogg

Grace Palmer

Richard Palmer-Romero

Jenny Phillips

Joe Piper

Justin Pollard

Jim Potter

Anthea Prince

Liz Purling

Nicky Quint

Tej Rae

Nicholas Rankin

Rosa Rankin-Gee

Helen Rayner

Rachel Redwood

Kate Rigby

Jacqueline & John Rogger

Sara Rogger

Christine Russell

Janet Rutter

Vikki Ryan

Michelle Sandall

Sc Az

Susana Scott

Geraldine Sealey

Lindsay J Sedgwick

Shreeta Shah

Irving Shapiro

Susan Shapiro

Heather Sharfeddin

Rob Sherman

Jane Shevtsov

Zoe Shimanska

Rachel Shorer

Morag Shuaib

Elena Silaeva

Karen Silk

Helen Simmons

Judy Simmons

Malcolm Sinclair

Susan Slusser

Katharine Small

Emma Smith

Janet Smith

Maggie Smith

Michelle Smith

Karin Snape

Andrea Speed

Kate Stoop-Booth

John Strachan

Euan Stuart

Allison Swales

Lucy Sweetman

Hannah Taieb

Jeff Tate

Jane Teed

Hannah Thompson
Jamie Thunder
Lorraine Valenzuela
Damon L. Wakes
Eleanor Walsh
Beth Warriner
Nancy Weatherley
Rachel Whittaker
Harry Whomersley

Sarah Wilson
Catharine Withenay
Jack Wolf
Rupert Wood
Ellen Woolf
Ian Wright
Jemma Wright
Sue Wright